## An Honorable Thief

"She's turned out another wonderful story!"
—*All About Romance*

"A true find and definitely a keeper." —*A Romance Review*

"A thoroughly marvelous heroine." —*The Best Reviews*

"Dazzling characterizations . . . provocative, tantalizing, and wonderfully witty romantic fiction . . . Unexpected plot twists, tongue-in-cheek humor, and a sensually fraught battle of wits between hero and heroine . . . embraces the romance genre's truest heart." —*Heartstrings*

## How the Sheriff Was Won

"Anne Gracie provide[s] pleasant diversions."
—*Midwest Book Review*

"An excellent story with an engaging plot and well-rounded characters." —*Romantic Times*

*continued . . .*

## Tallie's Knight

## Gallant Waif

## A Virtuous Widow

# THE
# Perfect
# Waltz

Anne Gracie

BERKLEY SENSATION, NEW YORK

**THE BERKLEY PUBLISHING GROUP**
**Published by the Penguin Group**
**Penguin Group (USA) Inc.**
**375 Hudson Street, New York, New York 10014, USA**
Penguin Group (Canada), 90 Eglinton Avenue East, Suite 700, Toronto, Ontario M4P 2Y3, Canada
(a division of Pearson Penguin Canada Inc.)
Penguin Books Ltd., 80 Strand, London WC2R 0RL, England
Penguin Group Ireland, 25 St. Stephen's Green, Dublin 2, Ireland (a division of Penguin Books Ltd.)
Penguin Group (Australia), 250 Camberwell Road, Camberwell, Victoria 3124, Australia
(a division of Pearson Australia Group Pty. Ltd.)
Penguin Books India Pvt. Ltd., 11 Community Centre, Panchsheel Park, New Delhi—110 017, India
Penguin Group (NZ), Cnr. Airborne and Rosedale Roads, Albany, Auckland 1310, New Zealand
(a division of Pearson New Zealand Ltd.)
Penguin Books (South Africa) (Pty.) Ltd., 24 Sturdee Avenue, Rosebank, Johannesburg 2196,
South Africa

Penguin Books Ltd., Registered Offices: 80 Strand, London WC2R 0RL, England

This is a work of fiction. Names, characters, places, and incidents either are the product of the author's imagination or are used fictitiously, and any resemblance to actual persons, living or dead, business establishments, events, or locales is entirely coincidental. The publisher does not have any control over and does not assume any responsibility for author or third-party websites or their content.

THE PERFECT WALTZ

A Berkley Sensation Book / published by arrangement with the author

PRINTING HISTORY
Berkley Sensation edition / November 2005

Copyright © 2005 by Anne Gracie.
Cover art by Voth-Barrall Design.
Cover design by George Long.
Interior text design by Kristin del Rosario.

ISBN: 0-425-20680-7

BERKLEY® SENSATION
Berkley Sensation Books are published by The Berkley Publishing Group,
a division of Penguin Group (USA) Inc.,
375 Hudson Street, New York, New York 10014.
BERKLEY SENSATION and the "B" design are trademarks belonging to Penguin Group (USA) Inc.

PRINTED IN THE UNITED STATES OF AMERICA

10  9  8  7  6  5  4

*With thanks to all my writing friends
in whom I feel immensely blessed.
And to Linda B., Barbara H., and Bron J.,
who talked me over the bumps.*

*Berkley Sensation titles by Anne Gracie*

THE PERFECT RAKE
THE PERFECT WALTZ
THE PERFECT STRANGER
THE PERFECT KISS

# *Prologue*

⁓

*If one scheme of happiness fails, human nature turns to another;
if the first calculation is wrong, we make a second better.*

JANE AUSTEN

MANCHESTER, ENGLAND. MARCH 1818

HIS LITTLE SISTER WAS ABOUT TO PLUMMET TO HER DEATH ON the cold, gray cobblestones at his feet!

"Stop, Cassie! Don't move!" Sebastian Reyne kept his voice calm as he dismounted and passed the reins to the groom. What the devil was she doing on the roof? "Just keep still, and I will come up and rescue you."

"I don't need rescuin'!" Cassie yelled scornfully and to prove her point moved farther along the steep ridge of his tall, stone house.

"Then go back inside, immediately."

"I won't. Not while that bloody old cow is in there!" She inched a little farther, and he winced as her foot slipped. A slate smashed to pieces in front of him.

Sebastian followed the jerk of Cassie's chin to where Miss Thringstone, their newest governess, leaned out of the window. When she saw him, she began in shrill fury, "She struck me! Actually struck me! These girls are completely ungovernable—"

He cut her off. "Downstairs in my office, Miss Thringstone! Now! I'll speak to you after Cassie is safe inside the house."

She hesitated, then with dignity withdrew.

After a moment Cassie said, "Is she gone?"

"She'd better be," Sebastian responded grimly. "And if you know what's good for you, you'll get yourself inside, now!"

"I'm not comin' in if you're goin' to hit me, too!"

*Too?* "I won't hit you, Cassie. But you will explain your behavior to me, and if warranted, you will be punished."

He watched, heart in his mouth, as Cassie considered his words for a moment, then slowly climbed back along the spine of the roof. Another slate smashed to smithereens on the cobbles. She clambered in the nursery window, and Sebastian began to breathe again. He'd have all the girls' windows nailed shut within the hour.


"Now, miss, explain why you took such an insane risk."

"S'not a risk. I didn't fall, did I?"

"Did you strike Miss Thringstone?"

Cassie tossed her head mutinously. "Yes, I did! I know it was wrong, but I don't care. I hate her!" She put her arm around her younger sister. "We both do."

At least she'd admitted it was wrong. That was something. Sebastian glanced at eleven-year-old Dorie. Her head was down, and she cringed, peeping at him through a tangle of dark hair. He gentled his voice. "Miss Thringstone's job is to teach you both to become young ladies, Cassie. I know it must be difficult. But you have a new life now, and Miss Thringstone is here to help you prepare for it."

Cassie pulled Dorie tighter and set her jaw. "We hate that bloody old horse-faced bitch, and we won't learn nothin' from her!"

Sebastian ignored the deliberate bad language. Cassie was hot-tempered and difficult, but one thing he'd learned in the last four months was that if he was patient enough, there was usually a reason for her outrageous actions. Not necessarily a good reason, but a reason, nevertheless.

"Why do you hate her this time? And why did you hit her?"

"Coz she hit Dorie!"

Sebastian stiffened. When they'd arrived at his house four months ago, two skinny little urchins, Dorie silent and shivering and Cassie hostile and feigning indifference, he recognized the signs. He swore then and there they would never suffer a beating again. He'd instructed the governess that no matter what the provocation, she was not to hit the girls. Not ever. She would refer all serious misbehavior to him.

But he had to be sure. Cassie was clever and cunning and not above manipulating the situation for her own advantage.

"She hit Dorie?" he repeated. "How? And for what reason?"

"She slapped her across the face. Hard." Cassie gave him a flat look and added, "For *dumb* insolence!"

Air hissed in through Sebastian's teeth. Dorie looked up. Her hair swung back from her face, and Sebastian could quite clearly see the red imprint of a palm on her pale little face. *For dumb insolence!*

He reached out his hand to touch her hair, but both girls recoiled from the gesture. He swallowed and said quietly, "Go and wash your faces, girls. Cassie, you did right to protect your sister. You will not be punished."


"A good whipping on a regular basis would do both those girls a power of good!" declared Miss Thringstone, facing him across his desk. "They lack discipline, respect, and all sense of proper behavior!"

"I believe I made my views on corporal punishment clear." His fury firmly leashed, Sebastian selected a paper from the pile on his desk, the reference that had described her as "the finest governess in the county." He returned to writing her letter of dismissal.

Miss Thringstone tugged her jacket straight and stared

down her long nose. "Without whipping, those girls will never be fit for any respectable society, let alone to fulfill your ludicrous aspirations!"

"Those girls will, in due course, make their entry into the finest London society." It was a statement of fact.

Miss Thringstone refused to be intimidated. Of good birth and superior education herself, she had worked in some of the finest houses in the country. She said in a tone designed to depress the pretensions of a nouveau riche cit, "Mr. Reyné, I hardly think your own background allows you to appreciate the qualities required of young ladies of the upper levels of society. Birth and breeding is simply something that money alone cannot achieve."

His brow arched sardonically. "Indeed?"

The governess stamped her foot. "I can teach any young girl to be a perfect lady if the basic good material is there, but in this case, it is not. Cassandra is wild to a fault. She is rude, disobedient, argumentative, and uses language more fitted to the gutters." She shuddered. "We have already discussed that item she wears on her person, so I shan't mention it again, except to say that only a barbarian would carry such a thing!"

He inclined his head. "I am sure she has her reasons. Eventually she will feel secure enough to discard the habit."

Miss Thringstone gave a ladylike snort. "To allow an undisciplined child of mercurial temper to carry such an item—well, sir, it borders on insanity!"

He shrugged. "Perhaps. Yet when she attacked you just now, she used her fists."

The governess pursed her lips.

"Quite. Now, you said both girls needed a good whipping. I hope you do not expect me to believe that Dorie has been argumentative."

The governess reddened.

" 'Dumb insolence' was the crime, I believe." He let his words hang in the air.

She shifted her feet uncomfortably and would not meet his eyes.

Sebastian said with silky menace, "It could hardly be any other kind."

Defiantly, the governess burst out, "In her own way, Eudora is quite as stubborn as her sister and just as disobedient. And she simply refuses to be broken of the habit of stealing!"

He made a dismissive gesture. "Taking food from your own home is hardly stealing."

Miss Thringstone's lips compressed into a thin line. "Sneaking food from your own table, perhaps not. But she creeps downstairs in the middle of the night and filches food from the kitchen."

"We have plenty of food. It, too, is a habit that will pass when Dorie feels more secure."

Miss Thringstone persisted. "The butler says that mice are becoming a problem."

"Yes, he informed me also. I advised him to get a cat, but since cats make him sneeze . . ." He shrugged.

Miss Thringstone stamped her foot. "And will you shrug when Eudora, having seen these thefts go unpunished, takes to stealing other, more valuable items?"

He shook his head. "It won't happen."

Miss Thringstone flung up her hands. "That is the essence of the problem, Mr. Reyne! *You* are the reason those girls will never be fit to enter society! You simply don't care about their atrocious behavior and criminal tendencies!"

His voice was steely soft. "Oh, I care, Miss Thringstone. If I didn't, I might let you whip them into submission." He gave her a level look from cold gray eyes and said, "The task may seem impossible to you, but I am in the habit of achieving what I set out to do." He clenched his fist. "When the time comes, the girls *will* be presented at court, they *will* make their entry into society, and they will stand *equal* to every other young lady there."

Miss Thringstone snorted again, much less ladylike this

time. "Face facts, Mr. Reyne. All the money in the world is not going to make acceptable to the haute ton a foul-mouthed wildcat who carries a knife strapped to her thigh and a girl, however sweet-faced, who is mentally deficient and cannot speak."

She recoiled involuntarily at the look he gave her, stepping back as if she thought he might strike her, but his voice remained cold and unemotional as he said, "Your employment in this house is at an end, Miss Thringstone. You will leave within the hour."

As the governess stalked from the room, Sebastian sat back in his chair and sighed. The seventh governess in four months. Hiring another one would bring about the same results; he had no doubt of it.

He needed a different solution, dammit. He stretched and pulled the bell cord.

"Send for Morton Black," Sebastian ordered as soon as a servant arrived. He pulled out a fresh sheet of paper and began to write.

Forty minutes later, Sebastian's agent, Morton Black, walked in, his gait uneven from the wooden leg that replaced the one he'd lost at Waterloo.

Sebastian nodded a greeting. "Another confidential assignment, Black. It will involve a journey to London."

Black looked faintly surprised. "Very good, sir. What's the assignment this time?"

"I need a wife, a special kind of wife. She will not be easy to find. I have noted down the main particulars." He handed Black the list he'd just written.

With all expression wiped from his face, Black took the sheet of paper and eyed it cautiously. "I see. And what do you want me to do with this, sir?"

Sebastian frowned, impatient of his agent's uncharacteristic slowness. "Find me a female—a society lady— who fits those particulars, of course. It will not be easy, but I have confidence in you. Let me know her name, and I'll do the rest."

Black swallowed and said woodenly. "Very good, sir." He glanced at the list. "There is nothing here about looks, sir."

Sebastian shrugged. "They don't matter. Character is what counts. Looks fade, character strengthens."

Black looked doubtful. "But you're a young man, sir," he began.

Sebastian looked up. "Are the instructions not clear, Black?"

Morton Black stiffened and almost saluted. "Yes, sir, quite clear. I'll start on it at once, sir."

After Black had left, Sebastian penned another letter to his oldest friend, Giles Bemerton. This would involve courtship, something in which he had no experience. He would need Giles's knowledge of the world, his savoir faire, to get him through it.

He wasn't looking forward to the task at all. He'd not intended ever to marry again. But Sebastian Reyne was not a man who shirked his duty.

# Chapter One

∞

*If a man will begin with certainties, he shall end in doubts; but if he will
be content to begin with doubts, he shall end in certainties.*

Francis Bacon

London, England. April 1818

"But she's got no bosoms! You can't marry a woman with
no bosoms!"

Sebastian Reyne shrugged. "She is by far the most appropriate for my requirements, according to Morton
Black's report. Besides, of course Lady Elinore Whitelaw
has bosoms. She's a woman, isn't she?"

"She might not be," his friend, Giles Bemerton, declared darkly. "Swathed as she invariably is, in seventeen
acres of gray cloth, who could possibly be sure?"

"You are talking nonsense," Sebastian said firmly. The
two men were seated in a small, snug room that was part of
Giles's bachelor lodgings in London. It was late at night,
and a fire was burning merrily in the grate.

"And she is older than you by ten years at least."

"Only six." Sebastian sipped his brandy. "In any case, a
man looks for maturity in a bride."

Giles gave him a look of disbelief. "She has eschewed
marriage all this time, and yet she must have had offers—
despite her lack of looks—for her father would have left

her well provided for, even though he was estranged from the mother. Why would she change her mind now?"

"She has no choice. Her mother died last year, leaving her little to live on. Her father's fortune comes to her only after she has been married for three years."

Giles pursed his lips. "I see. But you don't need a fortune, so why shackle yourself to a cold little fish like Lady Elinore? D'you know, I danced with her once. She made it abundantly clear she found me repugnant! *Me!*" Giles glanced indignantly down at his well-formed person.

Sebastian suppressed a grin. With Giles's golden good looks, few women would find him repugnant. He said with dry amusement, "Another point in her favor. She shows great discrimination."

"Bah! She is a complete eccentric! Her only passion is for good works—museums and destitute brats and charitable causes." Giles shuddered eloquently. "It is madness, I tell you. Why would anyone choose to take a repressed little stick like Lady Elinore Whitelaw to wife, when there are plenty of prettier and more cheerful girls available on the marriage mart?"

Sebastian had engineered a meeting with Lady Elinore the previous week and found her small, quiet, and unremarkable. They'd discussed her charitable works, and Lady Elinore's responses had confirmed his choice. She had devoted much of her life to working with orphan girls. She would do nicely. "Stubble it, Giles. My mind is made up. Prettier, more cheerful girls do not have the . . . the fortitude and experience a woman will need to deal with my sisters."

Giles made one last effort. "But you'll have nothing in common with her, Bastian. She's plain as a pikestaff! One of those earnest, bespectacled bluestockings."

"I don't care. I'm not looking for beauty in a wife. My sisters need stability and a sense of family. I cannot give it to them because they cannot trust me; therefore I must take a wife, and Lady Elinore is the kind of—"

"What do you mean, they cannot trust you? You're the most trustworthy fellow I've ever—"

Sebastian cut him off quietly. "Thank you, but trust is not a reasoned emotion. Their . . . experiences have made them unable to trust me."

"I'm sorry, Bastian. I know how much you care about those girls."

Sebastian shrugged awkwardly. Nobody would ever know how much his little sisters' lack of trust hurt him. It did no good to repine. "The damage was done before I recovered them. But I won't give up on them. Lady Elinore is a woman of sense who places a high value on duty, and her experience with destitute children means that she will be less easily shocked than most." He sighed. "I have it on the authority of no fewer than seven governesses that Cassie is particularly shocking."

"Sense and duty!" Giles snorted. "What about love?"

"Love is a lie told to children."

"No, it's a game, a delightful game."

Sebastian snorted cynically.

"And you used to be such a romantic." Giles clenched his fist. "I wish to God you'd never met the damned Iretons. That witch and her father—"

Sebastian cut him off, saying mildly but with a thread of steel, "When speaking of my late father-in-law and my late wife, do so with respect, if you please. If not for them, I would still be living in poverty, my sisters would be lost forever, and none of this would be possible. One must take the rough with the smooth."

"I know, but still, what they did to you—"

"Yes, and I am such a delicate flower. Now drop it, Giles."

Giles gave him a frustrated look. "Lord, but you're stubborn."

Sebastian smiled. "I know. And you are very good to put up with me. Now, may I rely on you to assist me through the shoals of the ton?"

Giles laughed. "I wouldn't miss it for the world!"

"Thank you. I wonder why that doesn't fill me with confidence." Sebastian set down the empty glass and stretched.

"I must go. I have an early engagement in the morning."
He pulled a wry face. "Dancing lessons. Some finicky old
French fellow. Wears rouge!"

Giles gave a shout of laughter. "I've a good mind to
come around and watch!"

Sebastian gave him a dry look. "Do so at your peril,
Bemerton."

"All the world is here," Giles assured him as they entered the Frampton House ballroom some ten days later. He
immediately began to point out well-known people. Sebastian had no interest in them. He was here for one reason only.

"And Lady Elinore?" He'd calculated that it would take
six, possibly eight significant meetings before it would be
acceptable for him to propose marriage.

"Yes, yes, she's over there," said Giles impatiently.
"Though I don't know why she bothers, the way she
dresses."

"Good, then let us waste no more time." He made a bee-
line across the room in the direction of Lady Elinore.

"Subtlety, my dear Bastian. A little subtlety, I beg of
you," Giles complained in an undervoice as Sebastian
towed him through the crowd. "I have a reputation as a person of some finesse, I'll have you know! Slow down!"

Sebastian grinned, but his pace didn't slacken. He
wanted to get this courtship over as quickly as possible and
get back to what he knew best—work.

"Lady Elinore." He bowed. From the corner of his eye,
he saw Giles give him a look that recalled their earlier conversation and, without thought, Sebastian's gaze dropped.
Giles was right; she did not appear to have bosoms. He
said hurriedly, "You look charming tonight, Lady Elinore."

Both she and Giles gave him a doubtful look. She was a
small woman, very pale and thin, with mouse-colored hair
scraped back in a tight knot and a kind of cap thing pinned
to it. Tonight she was dressed in a plain gown of dark gray
bombazine. The gray fabric leached all the color from her

skin, and the severe, high cut of the gown did nothing to soften her scrawny frame. She wore no jewelry.

Sebastian shrugged mentally. It didn't matter whether the dress suited her or not. Women preferred compliments to truth. At least Thea had. Besides, he hated this sort of gathering, was absolutely out of his depth with the sort of light banter that Giles was so good at. A compliment or two could stretch a long way, he'd found.

"How do you do, Mr. Reyne," Lady Elinore murmured. "I wondered if you'd be here tonight." She glanced to his left with a faint look of inquiry.

"Ah, yes, my friend Mr. Giles Bemerton. Bemerton, I believe you have met Lady Elinore before."

Lady Elinore inclined her head regally toward Giles and said in a cool voice, "I don't believe so, although I suspect our families are connected in some fashion. You are one of the Staffordshire Bemertons, are you not?"

Clearly Lady Elinore had no recollection of the dance that rankled so in Giles's memory. Sebastian watched his friend master his chagrin and bow gracefully. "Quite so. Delighted to meet you, Lady Elinore."

Fearing further conversational fencing, Sebastian engaged Lady Elinore for the next available country dance and the supper dance also. Giles, prompted, he said later, because he didn't want his friend to be seen to be courting a complete wallflower, engaged her for a cotillion and a waltz. Sebastian thanked him gravely.


Sebastian paced with repressed impatience around the edge of the dance floor. Courtship was a tiresome business. He'd danced the first of his dances with Lady Elinore and was now awaiting the supper dance. Unfortunately, that was some time away. He was fed up with the sight of the beau monde enjoying itself.

The beau monde—the beautiful people. People who had nothing better to do than spend their time enhancing their looks with cosmetics and jewels. For them, clothes were adornments, designed to flatter their shape, not garments to protect a body from the cold and rain.

He watched them dancing, circling, laughing, and drinking, and his mood darkened. Beautiful. Frivolous. Not a care in the world. Lives of froth and bubble. They had no idea of the struggle for existence that most of their fellow humans experienced. Their bodies were well-nourished and well-formed, not starved and crippled by long hours of debilitating, repetitive factory work. Or crippled fighting for king and country, like Morton Black.

Sebastian didn't belong here. He wasn't one of the beau monde. He hadn't lived a charmed life, as most of them had. He glanced at his scarred hands, at the two misshapen fingers on his left hand. Giles had advised him to wear gloves at all times, but Sebastian hadn't. He wouldn't disguise what he was.

The sooner he got this courtship out of the way and returned to the life he understood, the better. His gaze wandered idly over the colorful throng. And halted, riveted.

He grabbed Giles's arm. "Who is *that*?" He breathed the question, staring across the ballroom floor, transfixed.

Giles heaved a sigh of relief. "Finally! Er, I mean, excellent. I knew the Frampton ball would yield up some entertainment. There's dozens of prett—er, dutiful girls of sense here. Not that you're interested in anyone other than Lady Elinore, I understand that. But it doesn't hurt to look. Which one has caught your eye?"

*Which one?* Sebastian thought dazedly. There was only one. Giles might think there were dozens of pretty girls in the room, and he was right. But this girl was not merely pretty; she was purely dazzling. She stood out from the others like a star fallen into a set of candles.

She swung around on her partner's arm, smiling, and for an instant she looked directly into Sebastian's eyes. His breath caught in his chest. Of medium height, she was slender and lissome and perfectly shaped. Her hair was gold—not yellow or flaxen, but gold, spun fine and clustering around her head in soft curls. Her skin glowed. He could not see the precise color of her eyes from this distance, but they were large and, he thought, blue. As for her face, he had no words to describe it; it was simply the most beautiful face he had ever seen.

An angel's face, only without the smugness and artificial calm of the painted angels he'd seen. This angel glowed with life, with delight and mischief, with the joy of living. And of dancing.

A blind man could tell that she lived to dance. This was but a simple country reel, its movements so familiar as to become rote to most people, but she—grace personified—brought a fresh delight to the dance that was infectious.

Sebastian watched, fascinated. He'd thought dancing a waste of time up till now. But this was not the rigid performance of steps and movements he thought of as dancing. This was something . . . magical.

She laughed up at her partner with unaffected gaiety, and he beamed back at her. Proprietorially. She twirled on to the next partner in the dance, and her smile took on a fresh warmth. Sebastian swallowed. To be the recipient of such a smile . . .

Her new partner was a spry, elegant old gentleman well past his sixtieth year. What had he done to deserve such . . . such warm intimacy from this glorious creature?

Sebastian tugged absently on his neckcloth, crumpling one of its severe, perfect folds.

The old fellow said something, and the girl laughed again. Sebastian was certain he could hear it, even though the room was filled with noise. Her laugh would stand out, he knew, like water in a fountain, like raindrops on diamonds . . .

It called to him. He stamped on the thought.

She was a belle of the beau monde, pampered and indulged and sheltered from all the evil of the world. She was created for pleasure and joy. He could tell just by looking at her that she expected to dance her way through life. And so she would.

Sebastian had spent most of his life in noise and smoke

and filth and hardship. Even if he was rich now, his life was still in that place, not this. The only reason he had entered this bright, tinsel world was to get the sort of wife his sisters needed. Not to lose himself in foolish, impossible dreams.

He needed a woman of fortitude, one with experience of the seamier side of life, a woman whose strong sense of duty would carry her over the rough patches of life with him.

This joyous, perfect little sprite was not for the likes of him.

One did not purchase a spirited Thoroughbred and hitch it to a coal truck. If he took her into his grim world, the joy and vivacity would be crushed out of her. He'd watched his mother die of slow disillusionment. No man could live through that twice. Certainly not Sebastian. He had enough guilt to live with.

Still, it did no harm just to watch her dancing. If a cat could look at a queen, Sebastian Reyne could look at an angel.

She skipped through the movements of the dance, so light on her toes the old gentleman beamed and huffed to keep up with her. She seemed to notice it, too, and suddenly feinted sideways in a teasing movement filled with charm and mischief. The old man chuckled. Sebastian couldn't help but chuckle, too.

The sound jolted him to awareness. He was standing on the steps leading down to the ballroom, blocking the entrance. A huge room filled with aristocratic strangers, and here he was, standing stock-still, grinning like a fool across a room crammed with England's finest, at a girl he'd never met and couldn't know.

Grinning like a *fool*.

Sebastian coughed, straightened his cravat, and hurriedly moved down the steps.

Giles led him to a raised alcove adjoining the dance floor. "We can see just as much here." He snapped his fingers at a passing waiter and ordered drinks, then returned to the question at hand. "Now, which filly caught your eye?" He raised his quizzing glass and peered. "Ah, of course, one of the Virtue Twins no doubt. You couldn't miss them. Lovely gals. Like peas in a pod, almost. Mirror images of each other, they are, in every respect."

Sebastian shook his head brusquely. His—the girl he'd noticed—was unique. "It doesn't matter," he said. "It was a moment of curiosity only. You know I'm only here for Lady Elinore."

Giles took no notice. "The curious thing is, one of 'em's left-handed while the other one's right-handed—though I can never remember which is which. The left-handed one don't like it known. But it's personality rather than looks that's the key to their difference, I'm told. Miss Faith is the quiet one, and Miss Hope is the merry one. Not that I'm particularly closely acquainted, mind. Respectable gals on the search for a husband—not my style, you know."

"Yes, I know. Look, it doesn't matter, Giles. I'm not here to play the field. I've made my choice," Sebastian's voice was firm.

Giles continued. "Is it the twin dancing beside the long meg in yellow, or the one next to Lady Augusta—the little round dumpling in purple silk? A charmin' old lady, Lady Augusta. Sir Oswald Merridew, the old chap in the set, is smitten with her, but she's led him a merry dance these last two years."

Sebastian grunted in what he hoped was a semblance of polite interest as Giles rattled on. He couldn't care less about the little fat lady in purple or whoever might or might not be smitten by her. He wanted to know the name of the glorious creature in blue. He could have said, "The one in blue," of course, but somehow he just couldn't say it aloud. It would . . . mean something. A declaration of some sort. Which was ridiculous. He didn't want it to *mean* anything. He wasn't interested. He was just . . . looking. Filling in time until the supper dance. He tugged on his neckcloth again, and the words just came out. "In blue."

"A Virtue Twin then—they're both in blue. I can't fault your taste, Bas. Glorious creatures, both of them. Gloriously sensible, serious, and dutiful, I mean!" Giles amended hastily. "So, which twin is it?"

Sebastian frowned. She was a twin? He examined the others in the set and realized there was another girl who looked a lot like his joyous sprite. But she didn't glow with beauty.

Giles nudged him impatiently in the ribs. "Azure blue dress or celestial blue?"

Sebastian gave his friend a look. "What the devil do I know what sort of blue it is? Blue is blue!" It was a lie. He could probably name the ingredients of the dye vat the fabric came from, but he wasn't going to say so. Giles wouldn't understand, and anyway, it wasn't important. All he knew or cared was that the delicate azure silk gown swirled and clung to her lithe young body in a way that made his throat dry and his heart pound. He swallowed thickly.

Giles shook his head and said severely. "If you're going to enter the ton, my dear Bastian, you will need to learn these things."

"I'm courting a woman, not setting up as a milliner!" Sebastian growled. "And besides, I have no intention of entering the ton. Once I marry Lady Elinore, I'll be able to put all this nonsense behind me."

Giles shook his head in mock sorrow. "You poor, deluded fellow. To begin with, you don't know that Lady Elinore will accept you." He held up his hand to block Sebastian's retort. "And even if she does, you will still need to learn to make polite conversation with females, for Lady Elinore is a female, even if odd. And so are your sisters—female, I mean. And they will have friends. Take it from me, these little things are very important to ladies, bless their prett—er, eccentric, dutiful, and sensible heads. Now, which girl in blue was it?"

There was a long pause. Finally Sebastian made himself say it. "The one twirling just now with the old fellow."

Giles looked. "Aha! Azure blue. The old fellow is Sir Oswald Merridew, and his partner is his great-niece. Miss Hope, I think."

Sebastian frowned, ignoring Giles's nonsense. "Mishope?" What sort of a name was that? The ton was prone to bestowing nicknames on people, he knew, but mishope?

"Yes, or Miss Faith. I did tell you I get the twins mixed up."

"Oh. I see." Miss Hope. Her name was Hope. Or possibly Faith. With an effort, Sebastian dragged his gaze off the sprite in the blue silk gown and glanced at her twin. She was very pretty, but not a golden sprite.

Miss Hope—if that was who she was—seemed to glow from within. She so bubbled with life and joie de vivre, it was almost tangible.

He should not be staring at this girl. Not. Not. Not. There was no point, when Lady Elinore was his chosen intended. It was madness to look.

He could not stop himself.

The next question grated from his throat unwillingly. "Miss Hope who? Virtue?"

"No, their surname is Merridew. Of the Norfolk Merridews. They're called the Virtue Sisters because all the sisters are named after virtues, or near enough." He ticked them off on his fingers, "There's Prudence, now Lady Carradice, and Charity, who married the Duke of Dinstable. Faith and Hope are the twins, and I believe there's another one called Grace, also a beauty, only she's still in the schoolroom. At any rate, someone dubbed them the Virtue Sisters, and it stuck. But Merridew is their name. The twins live with Sir Oswald during the season. Otherwise they're with Lord and Lady Carradice or the Duke and Duchess of Dinstable."

The string of names flowed off Sebastian's consciousness like water off a duck's back. Only one thing lodged in his mind. Her name was Hope. Hope Merridew. Or possibly Faith. The weight wedged in his chest came unstuck, and he found he was breathing again, raggedly.

Giles rubbed his hands together. "Well, come along then, I'll arrange an introduction."

Sebastian placed a restraining hand on his arm. "No, I thank you. I was merely . . . curious."

His friend stared. "You mean you don't want to be introduced? Demmed fine gels, the Virtue Twins." He frowned at Sebastian's expression. "Not the usual sort of beauty, either. You won't find either of them blowing hot and cold, setting their suitors in a lather just for the fun of it. Miss Faith is sweet and quiet, and Miss Hope—I'm pretty certain that's her in the azure—she's a lively little filly, full of fun. Well you can see that for yourself."

"I can indeed." Sebastian's voice was harsh with the effort of sounding indifferent. "My attention was merely caught for a moment by the way she was dancing. A certain . . . exuberance."

"Ah yes, exuberance," said Giles, instantly earnest. "That's true. There was definite exuberance. But only of the Proper Sort. I thought it was very sensible exuberance. Extremely rational. Not at all frivolous. And quite dutiful in execution."

"Stubble it, Giles!" Sebastian growled.

His friend laughed. "No, really. I think you should meet them. These girls are different; they actually do enjoy things. They don't pretend to be bored and jaded and seen-it-all-before, like most of the others. When they like something, they show it!"

"So I see." Sebastian watched Miss Hope Merridew stripping the willow with enthusiasm, leaving each man in the set grinning like a loon as she twirled around them and danced on.

"Well, then. Demmed refreshing, that's what it is!"

Sebastian grimaced and said in a cold voice, "So you say. I see a girl who is very free with her smiles—bestowing them on any man in her orbit—be he old or young. I daresay that is what the ton admires." He turned away, unable to watch her anymore. He was aware that his friend was staring at him, jaw agape, but he had to get away. She was dangerous. He could see it at a glance. She was everything he did not want—did not need in a wife. Lady Elinore Whitelaw was perfect for his needs. The sensation of being rocked off his axis would pass. He had to move on, get his breath back, allow his pulse to return to its usual steady beat. Resist the temptation. Return to his purpose.

"I say, Bastian, no! You've got it wrong! I didn't mean that at all. Perfectly respectable, pretty-behaved girls. Not that sort at all—"

Sebastian held up his hand. "I meant no slur on their respectability, Giles. I am here to court Lady Elinore Whitelaw. I have no interest in spoiled beauties, accustomed to having their every whim granted. Lady Elinore is more mature and responsible than any Miss Merridew could ever be. Now, shall we move on? I gather you wish to observe the other ladies on display tonight." He didn't wait for his friend to respond but began to stroll around the room, breathing in slow, measured breaths, willing his racing pulse to calm.

Giles took the bait as intended. "On *display*?" He winced artistically and followed Sebastian, explaining in a pained voice, "I can accept your lack of subtlety—though I'm dammed certain you can be as subtle as you want when it suits you—but really Bastian—*on display*? It's almost vulgar! And while you might not care about presenting yourself to the world as a crushing clod, you might consider my position a little."

Sebastian raised a sardonic brow.

Giles continued, "I have a reputation for charm, subtlety, grace, finesse—"

"Modesty."

"That, too. And I value my reputation!"

"Ah, well, with such grace and virtue at your fingertips, your unaccountable friendship with a great unsubtle clod from the north will be held to be a sign of depth in your nature."

Giles chuckled, but he added in a more serious tone, "I mean it, Bas. You do need to watch that blunt tongue of yours. You will put people's backs up unnecessarily. There is already some . . . talk about you. About where you have sprung from, speculation about your background, you know the sort of thing."

Sebastian gave him an inscrutable look. "People will always . . . talk. The chatter of the easily bored means nothing to me." He cocked his head. "Isn't that the cotillion starting up? You're engaged to dance it with Lady Elinore, aren't you?"

Giles swore mildly and hurried across the dance floor to where Lady Elinore stood alone, a small, drab stick of a woman. Sebastian almost smiled, observing the pair joining a set; Giles all fluid grace and charm in his immaculate evening clothes, Lady Elinore all angles and frigid formality in her shapeless gray gown.

He strolled on, watching his friend try to coax conversation out of Lady Elinore as they danced. With scant success. Sebastian approved. A chattering woman was a tiresome thing.

Three more dances before the supper dance. His frown grew from the effort of preventing his gaze from returning again and again to the girl in the azure blue gown.

# Chapter Two

∞

*Twice or thrice had I loved thee, before I knew thy face or name.*
JOHN DONNE

"MRS. JENNER, WHO IS THAT MAN?" HOPE MERRIDEW NUDGED her chaperone, a modishly dressed, middle-aged woman.

Hope had become aware of him during the last part of the reel. She'd felt his gaze pass over her, like a physical touch, with an intensity that made her shiver.

Tall and brawny, he had the sort of hard, tough physique that made her shiver. She'd grown up under the harsh rule of her tall, powerful, insane grandfather; she would not lightly put herself in such a man's power again. She preferred elegance and gentle manners to raw physical power.

She shivered again. Not that she was frightened—she'd grown in experience and confidence since she and her sisters had escaped from their grandfather's violent custody, and she wasn't easily intimidated. But there was something so . . . so particular in the way he was staring at her.

Since arriving in London, Hope had grown accustomed to being looked at, even stared at. People found twins fascinating; they were always staring and comparing to discover the similarities and differences between them. She'd outgrown the initial embarrassment of it, though her twin, Faith, still found it unnerving at times.

But this felt somehow different. As if he wasn't looking at both of them, he was watching *her*.

He bent and said something to Giles Bemerton. The contrast between the two men was delicious; Mr. Bemerton, the quintessential ton beau, was all slender elegance and golden good looks. His friend, the big, enigmatic stranger, was all hawkish angles and brooding, dark intensity.

Beauty . . . and the beast. Not that he was beastly, but life had left its marks on his face; even from this distance you could see that his nose had been broken at least once. But it wasn't his severe, dark looks that intrigued her so much, it was the way he carried himself with the bold indifference of a warrior prince in civilized climes. Not with strutting arrogance but with quiet certainty.

She shivered again. Mr. Bemerton was much more in Hope's style, lighthearted, charming, and funny, with all the latest on-dits.

The two men strolled on, and Hope saw she was not the only one whose eye was drawn to the tall dark man. She watched as they parted to skirt around a group of chattering girls, all in their first season. Their chatter died, and each one of the beautifully coiffed heads turned to watch him—the tall one—pass.

She'd read an account once of a tiger passing through a jungle—the jungle had fallen silent as it passed. Not a monkey, not a bird had made a sound.

She watched as he prowled on, oblivious of their interest, while behind him the girls formed an excited, whispering huddle. Hope smiled. Who was the prey here, she wondered, the chattering monkeys . . . or the tiger?

"Do you know who he is?" she asked her chaperone again.

"Hmm? Which one, my dear?" Mrs. Jenner peered vaguely around.

"The tall one over there. Dressed for a funeral instead of a ball and prowling the room with a hungry-looking scowl on his face. I don't think I've seen him before." She hadn't. Who could forget a man like that?

"Which gentleman?" Mrs. Jenner raised her quizzing glass. "Funeral, you say? Hmph! Half the young men these days dress for funerals instead of balls. In my day they dressed as young peacocks, in satin breeches and gorgeously embroidered—oh good heavens, that man!" Mrs. Jenner started slightly as she followed the direction of her charge's gaze. "That wretched boy, Giles Bemerton, has been introducing the fellow into all the best circles and cannot—positively will not!—be hinted out of it."

"Why should Mr. Bemerton not introduce him?" Hope asked, intrigued.

"Shoulders like a common stevedore!" Mrs. Jenner sniffed. "No surprise there, given his background!"

As if he was aware of being the subject under discussion, the dark man turned his head slightly and looked directly at them. Directly at Hope. Not at her and her twin sister. Not around the room. Just at Hope. There was no subtlety about the look he gave her. It was a direct expression of desire. Desire for Hope.

Unable to break the power of his gaze, Hope felt a long frisson of sensation pass through her whole body.

Mrs. Jenner snapped, "Avert your gaze, if you please, my dears. That fellow is unsuited for a lady's ballroom, let alone for a pair of beautiful unmarried girls." She turned and bustled the girls away.

Faith winked at her twin as they were shepherded to a small alcove with tall French windows leading out to the terrace, but Hope was in no state to wink back.

That brief wordless exchange had shaken her like nothing else. He'd prowled the room like a man very certain of himself, of his place in the world, indifferent to those who surrounded him. But when he looked at Hope, she saw a kind of hunger in his eyes. A fierceness, a wanting. Directed solely at her.

It touched a part of her she never knew existed. She wanted to walk back into the ballroom, to walk right up to him, to touch his hand. She wanted to look into his eyes again and hear his voice.

Was this the thunderbolt she'd dreamed of? It couldn't be. Fate would not be so cruel. She did not want a big, strong, tough looking man, one who reminded her of her grandfather!

They found seats. Hope was grateful to sit down. Her knees were shaking. Mrs. Jenner sent several of the hovering young men off to fetch them glasses of ratafia, then sent them to the right-about after they had fulfilled their mission. "Leave us be for a few moments, will you, gentlemen?" she ordered. "The girls and I need to catch our breath." She flapped her hands at the young men who'd pressed forward to talk to them and shooed them away like a flock of inquisitive geese.

From her seat in the alcove Hope watched. His height made his progress easy to follow. Mr. Bemerton greeted acquaintances here and there, introducing his friend, who uttered what appeared to be a scant greeting and then waited with an air of leashed impatience that was tangible, even from this distance.

She'd seen a tiger in a cage once, newly arrived at The Royal Exchange, pacing back and forth with just that expression, lashing his tail impatiently, indifferent to the onlookers on the outside.

Frowning, he made some comment to Mr. Bemerton, who flung back his head and laughed. The tigerish look faded, leaving an expression of ironic humor on his face. He was younger than she'd thought at first. About the same age as Giles Bemerton, she decided; not yet thirty. Odd how he'd seemed older at first, as if weighed down by something.

An interesting friendship, thought Hope. She didn't know Mr. Bemerton very well, but he'd always seemed a lighthearted type, an entertaining rattle, as Mrs. Jenner would put it, and somewhat of a rake. She hadn't imagined he could be on terms of friendship with someone so grim and intense-looking.

As they sipped their drinks, Hope remarked in a casual tone, "Mrs. Jenner, you must explain. Who is he? I confess I'm curious. He looks out of place in this company, but does he care? Not he!"

Mrs. Jenner sniffed, hesitated, then pronounced with genteel scorn, "He is a Mushroom."

Hope giggled at the image of a mushroom dressed in evening clothes. "A rather large mushroom, don't you think? He must be six feet tall."

"Pshaw! You know what I mean—he is a parvenu, an interloper, a thrusting social climber! More, he is a Person Not Fit for a lady's drawing room. Giles Bemerton needs a good whipping—poor boy! That devil must have a hold over him. There is no other explanation. Giles's mother is everything that is good ton."

"Really?" breathed Faith, entranced. "You cannot mean he has blackmailed Mr. Bemerton into taking him around and introducing him?"

Mrs. Jenner shrugged pettishly. "As to that, how should I know the sordid details? But it will be something—payment of a gambling debt or some such thing—mark my words."

"I wouldn't be so sure." Hope regarded the two men thoughtfully. There was genuine friendship there, she felt certain. And while the tall man looked as if he would not care the snap of his fingers about flouting the law, he looked too . . . too *big,* somehow, to stoop to blackmail. Blackmail was a weak person's weapon. This man didn't appear to have a weak bone in his body.

And for a man who had supposedly pushed himself into society, he made no attempt to ingratiate himself. Mushrooms and parvenus made every effort to charm. This man made no effort Hope could see to please or charm anyone. Unless he thought scowling fiercely and looking bored and impatient was charming, she thought with an inner giggle.

"What did you say his name was?"

"I didn't." Mrs. Jenner took a long, pointed sip of her ratafia. "Are not the decorations elegant tonight?"

"Yes, very elegant," Hope agreed. "And his name is . . . ?" She found her chaperone's determination to shelter them irritating in the extreme. Hope was very well aware of Great Uncle Oswald's ambition for her and Faith to make a splendid match—preferably to a duke or a marquess—but this was their second season, and they weren't schoolroom misses, to be sheltered from unpleasant truths.

Mrs. Jenner took out her fan and fanned herself with a faint air of desperation. "Of course it is most agreeable for the Framptons to host such a squeeze, but really, I do find this room overly warm."

"Yes, quite warm," Hope said affably, "but that breeze from these windows is very refreshing, is it not? I can always discover his name from someone else, you know. I am certain a dozen people would be only too happy to inform me. The ton has such a sad predilection for gossip, does it not?"

"Most reprehensible," responded Mrs. Jenner limply. "Oh very well, his name is Reyne, Mr. Sebastian Reyne."

Sebastian Reyne. It suited him. Big and dark and somehow . . . mysterious. "And—?" Hope prompted.

Mrs. Jenner rolled her eyes. "He has sprung from nowhere, has plenty of money—though the source of his wealth is . . . muddy."

"He has no family, then?"

Mrs. Jenner pursed her lips. "As to that, the Reyne family is well-known, but they don't recognize this fellow."

Hope frowned. "You mean he is illegitimate? If that's true, it's unfortunate, but I don't see that he can be blamed for it. It is no reason why he should be shunned, for there are any number of people we know who are not their father's true child—it is an open secret."

Mrs. Jenner was scandalized. "Hush! Do not think to compare genteel people of the ton with such as he! All I said was that the Reynes do not know him. Anyone can use a name. Whether they have a right to it is another matter."

"Well, why is he so undesirable, then?" her twin sister

asked. "He does look rather sinister. That black frown is quite intimidating. Is that what you mean?"

Sinister was putting it a bit strongly, Hope thought. Intimidating was right. He looked at her as if he could just stride over, pick her up, and carry her off.

She wondered briefly what it would be like to be picked up and carried off by such a man. She wouldn't like it, she decided.

Mrs. Jenner shook her head. "I'm not basing my opinion on just his looks—though I do agree, my dear, he is quite ugly."

"Ugly!" Hope exclaimed involuntarily. "I don't think he's ugly at all. Rather severe-looking, to be sure, but there is a certain . . . masculine strength about him that some might find appealing." She caught the surprised looks of both her sister and her chaperone and broke off, flushing self-consciously. "Not me! You know perfectly well, Faith, he is not my type. But you cannot deny he is interesting."

Interesting was an understatement. It was riveting the way he'd watched her, indirectly, but with force. And when he looked her full in the face, the expression in his eyes took her breath away.

Hunger such as she'd never seen in a man before.

She took a sip of her drink, hoping the slight tremble in her fingers didn't show. It was very confusing.

Her twin spoke reassuringly. "Mrs. Jenner, you needn't worry. Hope could never be interested in a man like that."

Hope looked at her twin in surprise. Mrs. Jenner asked, "Why do you say so, Faith?"

Faith smiled. "It's obvious. Change his face a little and give him another fifty years or so, and who will you be looking at? Grandpapa!"

Hope blinked. "He doesn't look the least bit like Grandpapa."

"He does, a bit. And physically he's the very sort you and I most dislike."

Hope had no answer for that. It was true. Or had been . . .

However, despite Faith's words, Mrs. Jenner continued to watch Hope like a suspicious hawk. From the other side of the room the man kept glancing across; a bigger, much fiercer hawk. The provocation was irresistible.

She waited for the next time he glanced her way, and the moment he did, she fluttered her fan in a mildly flirtatious way, not enough to be an open invitation, but in a way that discreetly signaled she was not unaware of him.

He stiffened and abruptly turned away, his frown blacker than ever. Hope smiled to herself. So, Mr. Tiger did not approve of flirtation. For some reason that pleased her.

Mrs. Jenner laid an urgent hand on her arm. "Don't you go playing with fire, missy, for that man is dangerous. Rumor has it he's on the search for a wife, and I pity the poor woman who gets him."

"Why?" Hope asked, a little disturbed by her chaperone's vehemence. "Why would you pity her?"

But just as Mrs. Jenner opened her mouth to explain, two young men came up to the twins to fetch them for the cotillion, and the moment was lost.

As Hope moved through the familiar steps of the cotillion, she felt him watching her again. It was a tingle at the back of her neck, a heightened awareness that lasted through most of the dance, as if someone were breathing on the nape of her neck.

Why would Mrs. Jenner warn her off him?

He did look dangerous. But then a number of men here tonight were held to be dangerous company for a young, unmarried lady; gazetted rakes, fortune hunters, gamblers, drunkards, and other shady characters. Hope and Faith knew all about them.

After their sisters, Prudence and Charity, had married, Great Uncle Oswald had decided he needed someone to take the twins about while he concentrated on his courtship of Lady Augusta Montigua del Fuego. He'd employed Mrs. Jenner, some sort of distant widowed cousin. She was a silly woman in many ways, but she had a fund of worldly knowledge. Between them, Great Uncle Oswald, Lady

Gussie, and Mrs. Jenner had educated the twins about the pitfalls and shoals of London society. But there were many things they thought were unfit for a young woman's ear. Perhaps this was one of them. Hope frowned. It was irritating to be treated like a child.

The supper dance was about to commence. She glanced across the room. His attention was fixed on something or someone else. She craned her neck to see, and he moved. Like a dark scimitar, he began to cut a swathe through the colorful throng.

Straight toward Lady Elinore Whitelaw.

She blinked in surprise. Lady Elinore? Who'd have thought such a big, virile-looking man would be interested in a confirmed spinster like Lady Elinore? Hope shrugged and allowed her partner to lead her onto the floor.

He danced the supper dance with Lady Elinore. They made an odd contrast, he so big and dark and menacing, she so small and pale and helpless. And not a splash of color between them.

He danced the supper dance, then led Lady Elinore in to supper. They sat with Mr. Bemerton and his partner, a voluptuous-looking lady in a green silk dress. Surrounded by family and friends, Hope watched them surreptitiously as she ate. Mr. Bemerton and the lady in green did most of the talking.

Why would Mrs. Jenner pity his wife? She longed to ask, but the table was crowded, and there was no opportunity for any but the most general conversation.

After supper, she danced several more dances, performing her part gracefully enough, and if she was rather quieter than usual, her partners had no fault to find with that and were happy to regale her with tales of their adventures. Hope listened with half an ear, scanned the room for a tall, dark man, and hoped her responses made sense.

As the evening wore on, she became cross with herself. It was foolish to allow her evening to be dominated by a man who, after those initial piercing looks, had not even bothered to seek her out. She was here to enjoy herself, and so she would. She wouldn't give the wretched man another thought. There were plenty of other men at the ball, many of whom she hadn't yet met, and the last waltz was about to begin.

The last waltz was Hope's special dance. One night, years earlier, when they were young and in the blackest despair, Hope and her twin had both dreamed a powerful, magical dream, a dream of love and destiny, sent to them, they were certain, by their mother. They'd woken up at the same moment in the middle of the night, and when they compared dreams, it was uncanny: the similarity and the small, significant differences . . .

In Hope's dream she stood in clear, cold moonlight, surrounded by threatening shadows. She waited, alone and desperately lonely. Then from out of the dark shadows came a man. She didn't see his face, but he took her in his arms and suddenly they were waltzing. And the shadows were banished, and Hope was never alone or unhappy again.

Faith's dream was much the same, except in her dream, her man didn't dance. He'd made music . . .

Such was the power of the dream, neither twin had ever forgotten. It had nourished their hopes throughout the grim years with Grandpapa, and it directed their actions throughout their first London season and again in their second. They'd received many offers, but none had been accepted. Their dream men had not yet appeared.

From the very beginning of her first season, Hope had refused to fill the last waltz on her dance card, leaving her choice open until the very last moment. She didn't know who he might be or what he might look like, but the dark and dashing figure of her imagination wouldn't tamely sign her dance card and wait his turn. So she kept the last waltz of the evening free, because one day he would come, and in the waltzing, she would know him. It would be the perfect waltz.

The practice was widely known—if not the reason—with the result that a small crowd of gentlemen approached her at the end of each evening and hovered, waiting to be chosen. She never chose the same man twice.

A light, pleasant voice at her elbow said, "Miss Merridew, may I present a friend of mine as a desirable partner for the waltz?"

"Perhaps—" she began flirtatiously, then broke off in surprise. It was Giles Bemerton with his big, fierce-looking friend looming silently at his elbow. A hollow pit opened up in her stomach, and for a moment she could not breathe. His gaze devoured her. She stared back, mesmerized.

"Giles, how very delightful to see you." Mrs. Jenner bustled up, her wide smile belied by the militant chaperonial gleam in her eye. "How is your dear mother? And you wish to dance with Miss Merridew. Of course, dear boy." She grabbed Hope's hand and thrust it into Mr. Bemerton's with genteel force.

But Giles Bemerton, well brought up though he may have been, was more than a match for any chaperone. He instantly transferred Hope's hand to the black-clad arm of the big, silent man standing beside him. "It is my friend, Mr. Reyne, who wishes to dance with Miss Merridew, but it is so delightful to see you again, Mrs. Jenner. Let us catch up on old times while we dance, shall we?" And without waiting for her response, he swept the baffled chaperone out onto the dance floor, leaving Hope standing alone with the dark and somber Sebastian Reyne.

Up close he looked bigger and more intimidating than ever. His eyes were gray, dark-lashed and intense. Hope drew back.

"So, Miss Merridew." His voice was soft and deep and seemed to resonate through to her very bones. "Will you grant me the honor of this waltz?" He held out his hand to her.

Hope hesitated, eyeing his big, scarred hand and powerful frame doubtfully. His potent physical presence was disconcerting, yet something about him intrigued and drew her. The gentlemen surrounding them saw her hesitation and pressed forward to make their own claims for the coveted last waltz, and in that instant Hope decided. "Yes, Mr. Reyne, I will."


Someone should have warned him, Sebastian thought. Someone—the French caper merchant or Giles—should have warned him that twirling around an empty room with a small elderly Frenchman in his arms was totally different to dancing with Miss Merridew.

Unspeakably, impossibly different.

Once he touched her, all notion of rhythm flew from his head. She'd extended her right hand, and it was simply the most beautiful arm in the world. He'd stared at it, entranced, for several seconds before he recalled himself. He took it in a firm grasp and felt her small, soft hand swallowed up in his great, ugly fist. He felt like an ogre crushing a fairy. And then he'd placed his other hand on the curve of her waist, feeling the warm resilience of her flesh beneath the delicate silken fabric of her gown. And was lost. The music swelled all around them. Sebastian stood like a rock, holding her, trying to master himself.

How could he possibly dance? He was supposed to take her in his grasp and yet not allowed to hold her in his arms. He was supposed to twirl her lightly around the room, making witty conversation, when all he wanted was to draw her close and wrap her hard against him.

Fearing he would forget himself, he held her rigidly at the correct distance and stepped out, as if stepping off a cliff. Not looking down. Sweat trickled down his brow.

He was intensely aware of her. Her touch, even lightly, even through her gloves, set off a reaction deep within him, rippling from the point of contact to the deepest recesses of his being, arousing his most primitive instincts. Instincts he had kept at bay his whole life.

Sebastian Reyne did not act on instinct. Logic and common sense were what he had always depended on.

He wanted her.

Wants were temporary, he told himself. They passed, as this dance would pass.

They twirled, and she bent and flowed gracefully in his arms, following the unspoken commands of his body.

"It is the usual custom to chat as we dance," a soft voice said from somewhere below his chin.

*Chat?* Sebastian blinked. *Chat?* He could not think of a single thing to say. Even if he had the words, he wasn't sure his voice would produce them. His mouth was dry, his tongue was thick, and every part of his body was reacting to her. He fought to conceal it.

"Ah. Indeed. Quite. Go ahead, then," he managed. Brilliant.

A soft chuckle floated upward, and it was just like water in a fountain, like raindrops on diamonds.

His whole body tightened in response, demanding he act now. Hold her. Claim her. Crush her to him and kiss her until they were both senseless.

He was in the middle of a ballroom. *One, two-three. One, two-three.*

"I haven't seen you at these events before. Are you new in London, sir?" Her voice was soft and musical.

"I am. Yes," he managed. Her skin was like rose petals. Her skirt swished and rustled with every move, its delicate fabric brushing against his legs. Every one of his instincts clamored to draw her closer, to pull her close against him, to tuck her softness against his hardness—even now, he could feel his body pulling her insidiously closer. His grip on her tightened as he locked his right elbow, forcing his traitorous body to keep her stiffly at a proper distance.

"And do you intend to make a long visit?"

"Not long." As long as it took to marry Lady Elinore.

"Oh, what a shame. There is much to enjoy here in London."

There was much to enjoy in his arms right now. Sebastian tried to concentrate. *One, two-three. One, two-three.* Her delicate scent wafted to him in drifts, the scent of woman with a hint of . . . roses? Vanilla? The ballroom was crammed with people, thick with overheated bodies and a hundred different perfumes. How then could he possibly smell her? But he could. He could smell her hair, the delicate fragrance of rich, golden curls. He longed to bury his face in them. He twirled her around in a reverse instead.

She leaned back into the support of his hand, giving herself wholly to his leadership, responding to his every movement with feather-soft delicacy. Her lips were parted and her eyes half-closed. She sighed rapturously. "The waltz is such a divine dance. Don't you just love to waltz, Mr. Reyne?"

"No. I do not," Sebastian grated, unable to take his eyes off her parted lips. So close . . . and yet so far. The punishment of Tantalus.

Her eyes opened wide in surprise and then warmed with amusement. She laughed. "You intrigue me, sir. If you do not enjoy waltzing, then why did you invite me to dance?"

A couple twirled dangerously close, romping rather than dancing. The man, a heavyset fellow dressed in purple knee breeches and a spangled coat, was clearly drunk, and even as Sebastian warned him off with a cold stare, the fellow overbalanced. His partner, a raddled woman shrieking with laughter, tried to straighten him, but his reeling weight was too much for her, so she stepped back and left him to his own devices. Collision was inevitable.

Sebastian pulled Miss Merridew against his chest and turned in a protective half circle, keeping her safe within the embrace of one arm as he took the full brunt of the man's toppling weight against the other.

The man lurched and clung precariously. With his free arm, Sebastian dragged him upright by the scruff of his coat, then thrust him firmly away. The man was noisily apologetic. "So sorry, dear fellow. Slipped, y'know. Demmed housemaids too free with the wax, y'see."

"Demmed guest too free with the brandy, more like," growled Sebastian and danced on, Miss Merridew still clamped to his side. He regained her other hand and frowned at her in concern. "Are you all right, Miss Merridew? That clumsy cod's head didn't bump you, did he?"

"No, not at all, thank you." She was flushed but made no move to put a proper distance between them. She looked up at him with wide, blue eyes. "You sheltered me from any danger of being bumped. Are you hurt at all? Lord Streatfield crashed into your arm quite heavily, and he isn't exactly a small man."

He stared at her in astonishment. "Me? Of course not. 'Twould take more than a drunken bump to hurt me." He twirled her around in a small circle.

She frowned, as if unconvinced, and her concern warmed him. Wishing to reassure her, Sebastian flexed his arm a couple of times. "See, no damage at all." She just stared at him, a small, thoughtful smile on her face, her body warm against his chest as she danced on.

His body clamored awareness. *Hold her closer,* it demanded. Sebastian fought the urge.

Perhaps she was shaken more than she wanted to admit. Highborn ladies were supposed to be extremely delicate. Miss Merridew was slender and dainty and looked fragile enough to break. No doubt she'd been wrapped in cotton wool all her life. The encounter with the drunken lord had probably overset her. That was why she was leaning against him, unaware of the impropriety. It could be the only reason. A girl like her would never encourage the advances of a man like him.

The primitive, dishonorable part of him wanted to take advantage of her distress, to keep her there, nestled against him as long as possible—preferably forever. The sensible part of him knew it was a foolish fantasy and reminded him that his duty was to protect her reputation, as well as her body. He eased back, saying gently, "You must be shaken. Shall I fetch you something—a drink perhaps? Or do you wish to sit the rest of the dance out?"

She laughed. "Oh, heavens no! I'm not such a feeble creature. And I wouldn't dream of wasting a single moment of our first waltz." She gave him a dazzling smile and said, "I'm enjoying myself immensely, aren't you?"

He stumbled and cursed silently. *One, two-three. One, two-three.*

She was enjoying it. Immensely. *"Our first waltz."*

Not simply "our waltz." Our *first* one. As if she envisaged a long line of future waltzes with him. As if this first dance meant something to her, the way it did to him. His first-ever waltz. Perhaps his last. He had already resolved never to dance the waltz with another woman.

It took Sebastian several minutes to catch his rhythm again —her smile and her words quite robbed him of his concentration—but he prided himself on his self-control, and soon he had them twirling efficiently around the ball-room. He darted a glance at her to see if he could somehow divine whether or not she had meant it about the first waltz, or whether it was just a meaningless politeness.

To his surprise, she was watching him, an expression in her eyes he could not identify. She dimpled. He glanced around the dance floor but could not see what had so amused her. He looked back at her and frowned an inquiry.

Her eyes were brim-full of merriment. "It's all right. I don't mind that you've gone all silent again. It is difficult to dance and talk at the same time. I perfectly understand, and I promise I won't bother you. When I danced at my first ball, I was terrified I would tread on my partner's toes."

Her voice was warmly sympathetic, but her words annoyed Sebastian. He was dancing quite efficiently. "It is not my first ball."

"Your second, perhaps?" Her eyes twinkled at him, an impossible, glorious blue. His primitive instincts responded wildly. He grimly suppressed them.

It was true, of course, but he wasn't going to admit it. She dimpled again, and as he twirled her onward in a precise, textbook manner, she added chattily, "I only recently learned to dance, too, you know. Monsieur Lefarge almost despaired of me at first, I was so inept. I could not get the rhythm right. I am so clumsy."

Clumsy? It was ludicrous to imagine this dainty, thistle-down sprite as clumsy. Then her other words sank in, and he frowned. *Lefarge*. That was the name of his Frenchman.

Unaware, she continued, "For the longest time I had to count under my breath like this: one, two-three, one, two-three." Her blue, blue eyes were almost dreamy as she added, "It was such an irony, to find myself such a dread-fully clumsy dancer. I so desperately wanted to learn to waltz, you see. To come to London and dance it in the arms of a handsome man was the summit of all my dreams." She glanced at him, then looked away and blushed rosily.

The effect on him was instantaneous. Arousal. Sebastian was horrified. He'd never had it happen in public like this—not since he was a young boy. He half closed his eyes to will it away.

To cover his confusion, he blurted out, "Are you Miss Faith or Miss Hope?" And then cursed himself silently for sounding—and feeling—like a gauche boy.

# Chapter Three

∞

*Lady you bereft me of all words,*
*Only my blood speaks to you in my veins,*
*And there is such confusion in my powers.*
WILLIAM SHAKESPEARE

HOPE SMILED, LIKING HIS DIRECTNESS. PEOPLE OFTEN PRE-
tended they could tell the twins apart, but very few could.
"I am Hope. Faith is wearing sky blue tonight."

He nodded. "Hope," he said, and on his lips her name
sounded special.

His accent was unself-conscious: cultured but with a
faint, abrasive undertone of the north. It was different. She
liked it. In her limited experience, people not born to the
ton either were almost belligerently regional in accent or
adopted painfully refined speech.

He was turning out to be altogether different from her
initial imaginings. She was no longer so daunted by his
tough-looking physique and the leashed power in his body.
How could she, when he'd used it so effectively to protect
her just now? But though it was too soon to tell what sort of
man he was, the dance itself was proving very revealing,
even if his conversation wasn't.

"You did not say what brings you to London, Mr.
Reyne."

He twirled her in a rigid circle. "Various matters."

"Oh, well, variety is nice. And where is your home?"

"I live in the north."

He would never be accused of garrulity, Hope thought. "So, just a short stay in London?"

"Yes. A few weeks. Perhaps longer. It depends."

Hope gave him a look of bright inquiry. "On what?"

He didn't respond. She hadn't really expected him to. Mrs. Jenner had said he was looking for a wife. He would hardly blurt that sort of information out on the dance floor. But he was busy retreating back into formality and distance, and Hope wanted to put a stop to that. The suspicion dawned that it was stubbornness that made him so closemouthed.

Hope had her own share of stubbornness. "And what are your impressions of the city?" she asked.

He shrugged. "I've been too busy to sightsee."

"Oh, but that's so dismal!" she exclaimed. "You cannot possibly visit London and not see all the famous sights. Why, when you return home, people will be quite cross with you if you cannot regale them with tales of your derring-do in the capital."

He said in a quelling manner. "Most people know better than to expect me to regale them with tales of derring-do."

Hope made a sympathetic moue. "How sad. But think how nice it will be to surprise them."

"Most people prefer not to be surprised," he said seriously.

Hope raised her brows. "Prefer not to be surprised? How strange. I adore surprises. I can see that you aren't the loquacious sort, but it does not do to keep your light wholly under a bushel, you know. Though why anyone would keep a light under a bushel is beyond me, for a bushel is a measure of weight, is it not? I know my grandfather used to measure the wheat crop in bushels. It's a strange expression, isn't it?"

He made a neutral noise. Hope smiled to herself. She

knew she was rattling on, but she was determined to provoke some sort of response out of him.

It was as if having petted the tiger and found him gentle, she was no longer as wary, and now was determined to provoke him to action.

She said chattily, "So who are your people at home? Would I like them?"

He gave her a forbidding look. Hope smiled artlessly up at him. She adored that stern face he put on. Tiger to lamb: "Stay away, or I'll eat you." Hope loved a challenge. The lamb skipped closer. One part of her wondered what on earth she was doing. The other part relished it.

She said, "It would be such a shame if you went back to wherever you live without a single tale of derring-do. Or a visit to a famous monument. Have you seen Lord Elgin's marbles? He brought them back from Greece, you know, and they're thousands of years old."

"I have no interest in antiquities, Greek or otherwise."

"Well of course you haven't!" she said, pretending to be shocked. "Nobody is interested in antiquities! But the marbles are all the rage, so you must see them. One must be à la mode, you know. My young sister is fascinated by such things, so I have become quite familiar with them. If you would like a guide, then perhaps . . ." She allowed her voice to trail off suggestively. No gentleman of her acquaintance would be able to refuse such an opening.

He gave her a quick glance, and she felt his hand tighten around her waist, but she soon realized it was to hold her at a more rigid distance, and all he said was, "I have no interest in Lord Elgin's marbles. Or anyone else's."

Drat the man! He was not a gentleman; she'd forgotten that.

The waltz drew to a close, and he bowed, thanked her, and escorted her off the floor. Mrs. Jenner came bustling up, Mr. Bemerton at her heels. She nodded coolly to Mr. Reyne and drew Hope's arm through hers. "Let us withdraw a moment, my dear. Good-bye, Mr. Reyne, Giles," she said in a less-than-subtle move.

Mr. Reyne bowed again, gave Hope a long, intense look that burned, and turned resolutely away, taking his friend, Giles Bemerton, with him.

Hope watched him stride away from her. She shivered, feeling cold now that she was no longer touching him. What a contradiction the man was. Having sought her out, he had determinedly kept her at a distance in more ways than one. Why?

And as for her own reactions . . . If he was a mass of contradictions, her own behavior was even less understandable. She was repelled by his strength yet drawn to his gentleness. He'd treated her with an unsmiling lack of charm, and it had charmed her. He'd made no attempt to ensnare her in any way, and yet when he looked at her in that intense, hungry way, she trembled deep inside.

She used to tremble when Grandpapa was in a rage. But it was not fear that made her tremble when Sebastian Reyne looked at her.

And when, in averting that accident, he'd held her hard against his big, tough body, she hadn't felt alarmed in any way. In fact, she'd felt protected in a way that took away her breath.

Faith hurried up to join them. "We have been invited to a special concert at Lady Thorn's next Thursday. Apparently there is a marvelous new violinist arrived in London—a Hungarian count, and by all accounts as dashing as he is skilled—and Lady Thorn has managed to secure him for a private soiree. I'm told ladies on the Continent have been known to faint, so overcome have they been by his divine music. May we go, please, Mrs. Jenner? May we?"

"Of course, my dear," Mrs. Jenner assured her. "We had nothing in particular planned for that evening, and though I must say all violinists sound the same to me, I know how much you love your music, and at least if this Hungarian is handsome, Hope and I will have something to look at."

Faith laughed. "Thank you. It will be wonderful, I'm sure. I am told he can make his instrument sing, and the vibrato he achieves—"

Mrs. Jenner patted her hand. "Yes, yes, my dear. Now, there is Sir Oswald and Lady Augusta. The poor man looks positively puce after that long waltz. It can't be good for him at his age, but will he admit it? Why don't you girls ask him to escort you into the garden to cool off, and while you do that, I will . . . catch up with a few acquaintances."

She glanced at Hope as she said it. She was going to collect gossip about Mr. Reyne.

Hope was torn. Part of her wanted to know every little thing about him. Another part of her wanted to ignore the gossip and unravel his mysteries slowly for herself. Gossip never spoke kindly about anyone. But Mrs. Jenner would not be stopped, she realized. It was a chaperone's job to check such things.

Faith interrupted her thoughts. "Poor Uncle Oswald, he looks so hot, and Lady Gussie looks as cool as a cucumber. Come on Hope, let us rescue the poor dear from his masculine pride." Her sister linked arms with Hope, and they walked up to where their red-faced guardian was standing, trying not to puff.

Lady Augusta Montigua del Fuego fanned herself delicately with an ebony fan. As the girls came up, she said, "A gorgeous big brute you had there for the waltz, Hope, my dear. I do like those big, dark, dangerous-looking fellows. Those shoulders . . ." She sighed appreciatively. "If I were half my age, I'd cut you out for him, you know. Did he live up to expectations?"

Great Uncle Oswald huffed disapprovingly. Lady Gussie winked at Hope.

Hope grinned back. "He was . . . most intriguing."

Faith looked at her in surprise.

Lady Gussie's eyebrows waggled suggestively. "Intriguing—I like the sound of that. He reminds me of my second husband—the Argentinean. He was the big, dark, brooding type, too . . ." She sighed reminiscently. "And a devil in b—" She caught her cicisbeo's eye and amended it. "—when roused to passion."

Great Uncle Oswald spluttered, "Gussie!"

Lady Augusta said with an innocence that deceived no one, "Well, he did have a very bad temper!" She gave their great-uncle a look from beneath her lashes and added in a dulcet tone, "You have the same . . . fierce temper, too, Oswald." She batted her eyelashes rapidly.

Hope and Faith giggled. Great Uncle Oswald tried to frown, but he was so delighted by the improper compliment that his eyebrows just waved about indecisively. He was blushing so hard, Hope thought he would explode.

"It's very hot in here," she said hastily. "Let us go outside for some cool air."

Lady Gussie chuckled. Hope linked arms with Great Uncle Oswald, and her twin took Lady Gussie's. For an old lady well on the shady side of fifty, Lady Gussie was not the slightest bit proper. It was an open society secret that Great Uncle Oswald had been trying to get her to marry him for the last two years, but she was in no mood to be tied down just yet. She'd been widowed twice already, she said, and if that didn't tell him something, it should. For the first time in her life she was enjoying being a widow and an exceedingly merry one, too.

Hope had even heard her say once that Oswald could make merry with her to his heart's content, but marry him she would not! In the past, she and Faith had speculated for hours as to whether that meant Lady Gussie was Great Uncle Oswald's mistress.

Now Hope doubted no more, and from the look on Faith's face, she agreed. It was quite shocking—at their age, too!—but all the same, rather sweet.

It would be lovely to still be in love when one was old, thought Hope wistfully. She so longed to be in love. There were some days when the hollow, aching, emptiness inside her was almost too painful to bear.

It wasn't as if she hadn't tried to fall in love. She'd tried so hard. In the last two seasons she'd danced with hundreds of men, given them smiles and encouragement and listened to their tales and their woes. They'd paid her compliments and brought her flowers and small gifts. Several had asked her to marry them. They'd kissed her hand, and even her lips once or twice, but none of them, not one, had moved her in the slightest.

She glanced across the room to where Mr. Reyne was bowing correctly over Lady Elinore's hand and frowned. Lady Elinore, again?

Sebastian felt her watching him and tried not to notice. He was here to court Lady Elinore. Of all the ladies on Morton Black's list, Lady Elinore stood out, as if tailor-made for the job. She was quiet and grave and earnest—all qualities he admired. He found her quite easy to talk to; she didn't mind silence, and she didn't expect to be charmed with compliments and whimsical fripperies. He was not the charming type.

And she was rational. All his conversations with Lady Elinore so far had been on wholly rational matters, which was a great relief. He didn't understand women. Any females, really. A woman who was rational would be a relief to deal with.

Best of all, there was no danger of him becoming vulnerable to her. She was not the kind of woman men fell helplessly in love with, and that, for Sebastian, put the seal on the deal. She would be a satisfactory wife, and he would take good care of her.

She was the only rational choice, and he'd considered his options thoroughly. He was not a man known for abandoning his plans. He saw them through to the end. And if unforeseen problems arose, he dealt with them and moved on.

He glanced across the room. His unforeseen problem was frowning: an adorable wrinkling of her brow, a jut of her perfect chin, and red lips pouting thoughtfully in a way that made him long to kiss her, just once. And then move on.

She stood with her family and friends on the other side of the ballroom, now laughing suddenly with them all at some joke. It could as easily be an impassible chasm as a polished parquet floor.

He nudged Giles and signaled his intention of leaving. Within minutes they were bowing over the hand of their hostess, taking their leave.

"What's the matter?" Giles asked as they waited for their coats and hats to be brought. "I thought you were enjoying yourself."

"The waltz was a mistake." Sebastian shrugged into his greatcoat. "I need to expedite this courtship in as short a time as possible." *Avoiding as much contact with Miss Hope Merridew as possible.* He took his hat from a liveried footman and crammed it on his head.

"Why do you say the waltz was a mistake?" Giles placed his silk-covered hat at a rakish angle and tucked his sword stick under his arm. "She did you a signal honor in selecting you for that last waltz, you know; the ballroom was knee-deep in men who'd kill for the chance."

Sebastian made a noncommittal sound. He knew it. And tried not to read anything into it. His heart pounded with the memory of it. That was why the waltz was a mistake— that damned pounding!

Giles went on, "I thought you and Miss Merridew looked charming together. And I'm certain with practice, you'll loosen up." They descended the steps into the chill, damp air.

Sebastian scowled but decided not to explain to Giles that the problem lay not with his knowledge of the steps but with the effect of the lady on his wits. And body.

"Charming looks do not come into it."

Giles stared at him. "Why ever not, my dear fellow? You don't have to make do with Lady Elinore. Just because

Miss Merridew looks like an angel doesn't mean she is lacking in all the qualities you seek."

"I'd be obliged if you ceased harping on this theme," Sebastian muttered. "Miss Merridew is not the sort of woman I need, and that's that." Their footsteps echoed as they walked.

Giles said frankly, "I'd say from the way you were dancing, she's exactly what you need."

Sebastian frowned, but decided not to pursue that line of argument. He said with dignity, "I need a wife, not for myself, but for my sisters."

Giles chuckled. "I don't think that's legal in England."

"Don't be ridiculous. You know what I mean. My sisters need a mother figure. They could scarcely find her in a chit only half a dozen years older than they are, now could they?" He quickened his pace. Tendrils of mist hung in the air as they walked.

"Strictly speaking, your bride would be a sister-in-law, not a mother, and who is to say that an older sister not so very far removed from them in age would not be the very thing they need?"

Sebastian shook his head firmly. "I need a wife who has seen something of life, who understands that fairy tales are lies told to children, who has experienced hardship, and will not be easily shocked by my—"

Giles interrupted him. "Miss Merridew might surprise you. She is stronger than she seems and has firsthand experience of hardship—"

Sebastian cut him off with a sharp gesture. "Why do you continue this harping on about Miss Merridew?" Sebastian exploded. "We shared but one dance!"

Giles grinned. "Yes, one rather intense dance. And a thousand looks."

Sebastian made a scornful-sounding noise and strode along the pavement.

Giles chuckled. "You may snort all you like, but I saw your face when you looked at her. Every time you looked at her. If ever a man was smitten . . . And if you are determined to run your head into a matrimonial noose, it might as well be with a girl as sweet-natured and beautiful as Miss Merridew. You have needs and desires, too, you know."

Sebastian quickened his pace. "My needs and desires are not important. Miss Merridew may be all that you claim, but she is the wrong sort of person for the girls. I need someone who can deal with harsh reality, not a girl who has spent her life wrapped in cotton wool."

"Yes, but I told you, the Merridew girls have experienced—"

"Enough! The subject is no longer open for discussion," Sebastian snapped and lengthened his stride along the cobbled pavement. Giles, like other members of the upper classes, had no idea of what true hardship was. Despite his sympathetic nature, despite what he knew of Sebastian's life, he was essentially ignorant of how the rest of the world lived.

Miss Merridew may have experienced what she considered hardships, but he doubted if she had ever been starved or abused. The Merridew girls might be orphans, but they were rich orphans, and they had a loving family to shelter them. He had seen the way Sir Oswald doted on them.

Hope and her sister had grown up to be happy, laughing girls. His sisters were not happy, laughing girls. Dorie watched the world with wary suspicion and had not uttered a sound in the four months since he'd recovered them. And Cassie carried a knife strapped to her thigh. A child of fourteen. Those facts alone spoke volumes.

His sisters had experienced horrors of which a laughing sprite like Hope Merridew would know nothing.

And it was Sebastian's fault they had. Sebastian had to atone. And if marrying Lady Elinore was what it took, he would marry her gladly.

"I was right, Hope. You must stay away from him; he is not at all a suitable *parti* for you—or any other girl of our acquaintance."

Hope raised an eyebrow. She did not like to have the law laid down to her. Faith, aware of the irritation, put a comforting arm around her waist, and Hope relaxed a little. It wouldn't do for either her sister or her chaperone to see how drawn she was to Mr. Sebastian Reyne. And how much she resented being warned off him.

Mrs. Jenner continued. "He used to be the verlest pauper brat—a worker, no less, in one of those very mills he now owns—"

"There is no shame in poverty or hard work," interrupted Hope. "Our maternal grandfather was a butcher, I believe."

Mrs. Jenner rapped her on the arm with her fan. "Well, for heaven's sake, don't spread it around, for it does not at all add to your credit! However that's not the point. It wasn't through hard work that Mr. Reyne gained his fortune, it was low cunning!"

"What do you mean?"

"He charmed the mill owner's daughter and tricked her into wedding him!"

*Married!* Hope felt as if all the breath had been driven from her body. Married!

Mrs. Jenner continued, "Heaven knew what her father was about, to let such a thing happen. She had been on the shelf for years. No doubt he is a silver-tongued charmer."

Hope frowned. She could vouch for the fact that he was not.

The chaperone clicked her tongue. "The foolish creature! She was the sole heiress of all her father's wealth. What did she think he wanted her for? And he was years younger than she!"

Hope managed to say in what she hoped was a casual manner, "Since he is married, I don't see what possible danger he can be to Faith or me."

"He is a widower."

Hope's stomach returned to its rightful place.

"But he's looking for another wife! And the pity of it is, he'll have no trouble finding one. Riches will buy most things, including wives—no matter what the risk."

Hope tossed her head, annoyed by her chaperone's melodramatic manner and the way she was drawing out the tale for maximum effect. "What do you mean, risk? All marriage is to some extent a risk."

"Not like this one." Mrs. Jenner lowered her voice. "I spoke to a dozen people about him, and none of them had a good word to say." She counted them off on her fingers as she spoke. "Sir George Arthurton—who has several interests in Manchester where That Man comes from—told me straight out that the man is totally ruthless! Others confirmed that. Lord Etheridge said Sebastian Reyne was an extremely dangerous man; they were his very words, and he has interests in the cotton industry and would know! And Mrs. Beamshaft told me a great deal about his history. He just sprang from nowhere. And ended up with everything. His wife and father-in-law dead!" She sat back and allowed her words to sink in.

Mrs. Jenner's smug delight in the scurrilous tale annoyed Hope. "So what are you saying, ma'am? You cannot mean to suggest that Mr. Reyne murdered his father-in-law and wife?"

Mrs. Jenner lifted a bejeweled forefinger to the side of her nose and tapped it significantly.

"What sort of an answer is that!" Hope exclaimed crossly. Her scowl took in both her sister and their chaperone. How dare they sit there, comfortably thrilled by the horrid gossip about Mr. Sebastian Reyne. To them, it was no more than an exciting story. To Hope, it mattered. Why, she did not care to examine at this point. But she wanted to know the truth.

"He is capable of anything," insisted Mrs. Jenner. "You can tell by looking at him he has a violent history."

Hope snorted. "I don't believe a word of it. If he murdered his wife and her father, why was he not hanged or transported?"

Mrs. Jenner rubbed finger and thumb together. "A few guineas to grease a palm here and there, witnesses intimidated—or worse! Anything is possible if you are lord of all you survey and not bred to it as a proper gentleman is. And he is not."

Hope rolled her eyes at the melodramatic tone. Like many members of the ton, Mrs. Jenner was prone to taking a shred of plain fabric and embroidering it into something quite different. But Hope was curious and could not help asking, "Lord of all he surveys? What does he survey, then?"

Mrs. Jenner waved her hand extravagantly. "You name it, my dear. Mills and manufactories in the north. Mines, canals, ships—he is immensely rich, there is no doubt of it, but how he got that way is another matter. One only has to look at his face." She shuddered. "Those pitiless, cold, gray eyes."

Hope did not think his eyes were pitiless or cold. Lonely perhaps. Hungry, she was sure. But for what?

Never a good sleeper, Hope found herself wide awake after the ball, tucked up in bed but thinking about the enigmatic Mr. Reyne. In the other bed Faith slept peacefully, untroubled by thoughts or frustrated dreams.

Hope ached to be loved by someone other than a sister. By a man other than a great-uncle. To be loved by the man of her dreams.

Sebastian Reyne was close in some ways to the shadowy man she'd dreamed of: dark, mysterious, brooding. He'd prowled the room with assurance, indifferent to society's approval, secure in himself, watching her hungrily, as a dream man ought.

Hope sighed in disappointment. He was close, but not close enough. Dancing with him was nothing like dancing with anybody's dream man. And she knew it had to be perfect for the dream to come true.

He was a terrible dancer, poor man. The moment he'd touched her, he'd become stiff, abrupt, awkwardly precise, holding her at bay as if she were a wild beast of some sort and steering her around the dance floor as if she were a delicate, fragile . . . wheelbarrow.

For some reason that made her want to hug him.

For most of the dance he'd been counting under his breath and minding his steps. But when Lord Streatfield had crashed into them, Mr. Reyne hadn't missed a single beat. Without hesitation he'd curled one arm around Hope and made a shelter of his body for her. He'd hauled the drunken earl upright, set him on his feet, reprimanded him for drinking too much, not caring a hoot for the earl's good opinion, and danced on, all the time sheltering Hope in the curve of his arm as if she was the most precious thing alive.

Defending her, he'd lost all awkwardness and self-consciousness, and his power and strength had flowed around her in a protective shield.

It had quite taken her breath away. And for a few moments she'd forgotten where she was.

She'd never met anyone like him. He was such a collection of contradictions. Public self-possession and private shyness. Physical strength tempered with rigid gentleness. Why she felt so strongly drawn to him, she could not explain; it had something to do with the way he held her with such tender, rigid awkwardness.

It certainly wasn't his powers of address. He had no conversation skills. Graceful, pretty compliments had not flowed from his tongue. And he'd scowled terribly at her as he asked which twin she was. There was a brooding, intense air of distraction about him, as if his full attention wasn't on her.

And yet she hadn't felt ignored or slighted. Instead, she'd felt . . . almost cherished. Which was silly, really—it was just a dance, after all. And not a very good one, either.

It was a shame he wasn't her dream man. Because he did interest her. But the waltz they'd shared had been as far from perfect as possible.

She sighed again and snuggled the bedclothes around her. She really ought to get some sleep.

A chuckle escaped her as she recalled Mrs. Jenner's description of him as a silver-tongued charmer. Sebastian Reyne was so prickly and standoffish, he could give lessons to a thistle! And she'd had to pry words out of him like a clam.

In the hall below, the clock chimed three.

He'd shown interest only in Hope and Lady Elinore. The contrast in them was so great, it was a puzzle. Why Lady Elinore?

The unwelcome thought lingered. Lady Elinore was a bit of an ape-leader, a rich, dowdy spinster who had no family to protect her from the wiles of a fortune hunter.

She turned over in bed and hugged the bedclothes tighter around her. He wasn't what Mrs. Jenner said he was. He wasn't.

He wanted Hope; she knew it, could feel it. In two seasons the Merridew diamonds had learned to distinguish between a boy's crush and the desire of a man. She and Faith knew to take steps to let the boy or man down gently, before it got too serious. But this was out of her experience. His compelling hunger and raw, brutally reined-in desire was something she'd never felt before. It created an echoing resonance deep within her.

A sensual shudder ran through her at the thought.

None of the boys or men she'd known had touched off any chord inside her. But just one long, intense look from Sebastian Reyne . . .

She wished he wasn't so big and brawny. He was even taller and more powerful than Grandpapa. Which meant he could hurt her more . . .

He was everything she thought she didn't want, but she'd never responded to a man so quickly, so strongly.

Would Mr. Reyne hurt her? That was the question. She'd felt the hard power of his muscles and had trembled. But she also recalled the ease with which he'd defended her from the drunken Lord Streatfield. He'd protected her so beautifully. Leashed power.

"You can tell by looking at him he has a violent history," Mrs. Jenner had said.

Hope had a violent history, too.

She turned over and thumped her pillows into a more comfortable shape. It was all too much to think about. Was he this? Was he that? Her brain was whirling. Things never made sense in the middle of the night, she told herself crossly. Tomorrow was a new dawn.

# Chapter Four

oge

IT WAS ONE OF THOSE MORNINGS. NOT QUITE DAWN. A FEW
hardy London birds starting the predawn chatter. Hope was
wide awake, feeling as though she was about to burst out of
her skin. Tense. Wound up like a spring.

She glanced across at her sleeping twin in the next bed.
When Faith felt like this, she found her release in music. It
never worked for Hope. She needed something more active.

She slipped from her bed and peered out of the window.
Cool and dry. Perfect. From her wardrobe she quietly
pulled her old brown riding habit, boots, hat, and crop and
tiptoed into the next room to dress.

Carrying her boots in her hands, she padded out into the
corridor and ran up the stairs to the servant's quarters, under the attic. She knocked softly on one of the doors. At
her second knock, a low groan came from inside. "All right
Miss Hope. I'll be down in a moment."

Grinning, Hope ran lightly down the stairs and sat on
the bottom one to put on her boots. Their footman James
would grumble, but he always enjoyed their illicit morning

outings, and the guinea she gave him each time she deprived him of sleep was a useful addition to his savings. It was no secret in the Merridew household that James was saving to go to America.

In the kitchen, she cut two thick, ragged slices of bread and slathered them with butter and apricot jam. She devoured one in a moment and handed the other to James as he came in the door.

He eyed the slice, then gave her a baleful look. "Trying to turn me up sweet with that great, crooked doorstop, Miss Hope?"

Hope grinned. She never had been able to cut a straight slice of bread, but at least she wasn't stingy. "But of course, dear, grouchy James. I cut them like this because you're always so hungry. Now do hurry up. I want to get there as soon as possible."

Grumbling good-naturedly, he followed her out into the dim gray streets, munching on his bread. Having known all the Merridew girls since childhood, he was used to her ways.

By the time the sun was starting to gild the spires of the churches, they were trotting in at Grosvenor Gate. Hyde Park was deserted. Hope's bay gelding sidled and danced mischievously, shying skittishly at stray leaves and imaginary shadows. He was full of oats, chafing at the bit, longing for a good gallop. Hope knew exactly how he felt.

"Come on, sluggard, I'll race you," she called to James, and without waiting, she urged her mount to a gallop.

The gelding moved smoothly under her, its hooves pounding the turf; she would tip the stableboy extra again. He always gave her the best horse, and once she made her preference known, this one was almost always magically available. Over the past few weeks, horse and rider had grown accustomed to each other's ways, and Hope could now do almost anything she wanted with him. This morning he seemed to relish the speed as much as she did.

It was glorious, thundering through crisp morning air free and wild, without care or thought. Exhilarating. Almost as good as being in the country—better in some ways, for there was an illicit edge to galloping here.

Cool morning air whipped at her skin, filled her lungs, blasting her free of all the rules and restrictions she had to live by. Here she was filled with air and light and excitement. The wind streamed through her as if she were flying. How she relished these secret early morning excursions. Dawn was the only time she could ride as fast and as wildly as she liked.

Later that day she would probably ride in the park with Great Uncle Oswald and Faith and Grace. A decorous walk, or perhaps a trot, stopping every few moments to greet someone and exchange idle chitchat.

She allowed the horse to run himself out of his fidgets, taking him in a great circle so as to remain in sight of James. She glanced back and smiled. James had snapped at the stableboy and as a result had been given the slowest of the hacks, a veritable slug. He huffed along in the distance.

The park was still deserted. She could practice her moves. Gathering the horse, she began to put him through a series of actions. He jibbed a bit at first, but soon he was responding perfectly.

"Oi, miss, stop that!" called James.

She laughed. "Try to stop me, if you can on that slug! This is such fun. This horse is wonderful."

Sebastian woke early the next morning, as usual. He'd woken before dawn most of his life. Machines never stopped, and people had to fit their sleep around them.

He stretched, wishing he could go back to sleep, but once awoken, he never could sleep again. In any case, he didn't need much sleep. It had served him well in the factories, and now it served him well, enabling him to combine society hours with the needs of business.

He had a great deal of work to get through this morning, but the events of that blasted ball had unsettled him. He hadn't slept properly. He always slept properly. Though sometimes he did awake demon-ridden. He knew the solution to that. It was one reason why he'd hired a house with stables at the back. His only solution to demons was to ride them into oblivion before they rode him.

But last night it had taken him half the night even to get to sleep. And it was not his usual demons keeping him wakeful but thoughts of Hope Merridew. Holding her wrapped in his arms as close as he wanted, her body clinging to his, moving in slow, languorous twirls.

And in the morning he'd woken, aroused like a uncontrolled adolescent!

He needed to clear his head. And exhaust his body. A good, hard ride would do the trick!

He dressed and walked around the mews. The stable lad woke as he arrived, but Sebastian sent him back to bed, preferring to saddle his own horse.

The city was barely beginning to stir as he entered the main gate of Hyde Park. For nearly ten years of his life he hadn't so much as touched a horse. He'd been taught to ride as a child, but it was only after he'd married Thea that he'd had the opportunity to mount a horse again. He'd been worried about making a fool of himself, of falling off in front of his new in-laws and their friends. But the moment he was in the saddle it all came back to him in a rush, as if riding had always been a part of him.

It was more than part of him. It was his escape.

He started with a slow, controlled canter, then allowed the horse to go faster and faster, losing himself in the power and the speed and the rhythm.

His blood was singing, and he felt young and strong, demon-free and ready to conquer the world when he saw it: a bay horse, galloping full pelt, with what at first glance looked like a bundle of cloth attached to one side. Then he saw a hat bouncing inches from the hooves of the horse and a glimpse of gold curls. To his horror, Sebastian realized it was no bundle, but a woman. She clung to the back of the saddle with one hand. Her right knee was hooked around the pommel of her sidesaddle, but the rest of her hung down over the left side of the horse. Her left hand stretched down beside the powerful forelegs of the animal, snatching helplessly at the ground, as if in some bizarre attempt to slow the panicked horse. He couldn't see her face. She wasn't screaming. Probably half swooning with fear.

Praying that she would retain enough consciousness to maintain her tenuous balance for a few more seconds, Sebastian urged his horse into a gallop, arrowing it straight at the runaway.

A rider in the distance, a man, waved and shouted. Her husband or groom. Sebastian waved back. He would save her.

He thundered after her. Her horse was good, but his was stronger and faster. He gained rapidly on her. As he neared, he tried to work out exactly how she was attached. Should he try to snatch her from her saddle or grab the horse's reins and slow it that way? Either way was risky. If she was tangled in the saddle, he wouldn't be able to lift her cleanly to safety. But she was seconds away from falling under those flashing hooves.

He decided on the snatch. If her habit was tangled in the stirrups, he would still be able to hold her and force her mount to stop. His horse edged up behind hers. He took his reins into his left hand and reached out his right arm to gather her up when she suddenly straightened, and with a joyous peal of laughter, brandished a twig in his face.

"I did it!"

It was Miss Hope Merridew, flushed, exhilarated, and triumphant.

And in no danger whatsoever.

"Oh! Mr. Reyne, good morning. Did you see? I did it!" She held the twig out.

He could see at a glance she was a consummate horsewoman. She hadn't been falling from an out-of-control horse, her head dangling inches from the horse's hooves;

she'd been deliberately galloping at an outrageous speed, dangling her head inches from the horse's hooves *in order to pick up a twig from the ground*!

Suddenly Sebastian was furious.

"Are you mad?" he thundered at her, his horse keeping pace with hers. "Risking your neck in such a foolhardy endeavor!"

She grinned at him and slowed her horse to a canter. "It's the first time I've done it!" Her tone was self-congratulatory, not the slightest bit apologetic or mollifying.

"What the devil possessed you to attempt such an insane thing this morning, then?"

"Oh, I've *attempted* it dozens of times," she corrected him. "I've been practicing for ages. This is the first morning I've actually *succeeded* in picking up a twig." She waved it merrily.

Her blithe insouciance infuriated him. He was lost for words. The thought of her risking that beautiful neck morning after morning drove all the breath from his lungs. How could she?

Eventually he mastered himself enough to speak. "Well for God's sake don't do it again," he growled, his heart still thudding from the fright he'd received. "Why in Hades does your groom allow it?"

"Allow it? James?" She gave a gurgle of laughter. "He doesn't have any choice. He couldn't stop me if he tried."

Spoiled. A pampered, protected daughter of the aristocracy, indulged all her life, no doubt. Couldn't imagine anything bad happening to her. Whereas Sebastian could only too clearly conjure up a vision of her broken or battered body . . . The thought was too horrific for words. He wanted to snatch her off her horse and wrap her up safe. He ground out, "Sounds like a poor excuse for a groom."

"Strictly speaking, he's our footman, not a groom, but even so, he does a wonderful job. James has known us all our lives. He doesn't like me doing these tricks, but he knows I'd do them anyway, so he comes along to keep an eye on me."

Sebastian glanced around and said caustically. "Some eye. He's a good half mile away."

She laughed again, "Oh, that's my fault. I always encourage the stableboy to give James the slower horse. To day he has the worst slug you have ever seen."

She needed a much firmer hand on the reins, he thought. If she were his to protect, she wouldn't be up at dawn riding alone and unprotected, taking insane risks to pick up a twig! The thought occurred to him that if she was his, neither of them would be out at dawn. A vision came to him of her in his bed. He swallowed and forced it out of his mind. To cover up his moment of weakness, he said harshly, "A groom's job is to ensure your safety, not watch you risk your neck morning after morning."

"Nonsense! James is very protective of my safety," she argued. "Why, he was the one who came up with the design for this extra strap, and that's what made the whole endeavor workable." She pulled back her habit and showed him the strap.

Sebastian gave the strap a fleeting glance, trying not to notice how the fabric pulled tight against the graceful line of her thigh. He said nothing. He was still too angry at the idea of her being assisted to risk her neck for a pointless trick.

"I fell off so many times before he came up with this."

He was so horrified he must have jerked on the reins. His horse pulled sharply back, and she passed him. He swiftly caught up. "You. Fell. Off?" He was furious again. Why the devil was she so driven to risk her safety for such a stupid reason?

She laughed. "Just minor tumbles. I'm very careful, you know."

"Careful? If that's your idea of careful, you ought to be locked up," he growled half to himself.

Her face changed immediately. "I know all about being locked up, Mr. Reyne," she said. "It's one reason why I relish the freedom to do things like this!" And without warning, she galloped away, veering off in an unexpected direction.

He wrenched his horse around and sped after her, but she'd had the jump on him, and he couldn't reach her in time. Under his horrified gaze, she once more leaned down over the left side of her horse, stretched out her hand, and snatched another leafy twig from the ground.

"Ha-ha!" Again she brandished the twig in victory.

In fury at the deliberate provocation, Sebastian spurred his horse and thundered down on her. This time there was no question in his mind. As he came level with her, he reached out and snatched her forcefully off her horse. She gave a squeak of surprise, struggled a moment, then suddenly gave in and let him take her, kicking free of her stirrups and letting go of the extra strap.

He pulled her hard across his thighs, wrapping one arm tightly around her.

He expected a tirade, or a slap, or some other example of feminine outrage. She surprised him. Apparently quite unfazed by his unceremonious manhandling, she said nothing, just wriggled her bottom into a more comfortable position. The movement almost brought a groan to his lips. If he hadn't already been quite painfully aroused, that would have done it. Her warm curves settled into the cradle of his thighs. Sebastian felt himself break out in a sweat.

She slipped one arm around his torso and, supported by his left arm, leaned against his chest. "What the devil do you think you're doing?" she said in a conversational tone, adding in a mocking imitation of his earlier speech, "Are you mad, risking your neck in such a foolhardy endeavor?" She sounded amused! Silky, golden curls tickled his chin. He could smell her perfume and under it, the sultry tang of feminine heat. He tightened his grip and set his jaw. Quite possibly he was mad, he thought grimly. He'd never snatched a lady from her horse in his life. He had no idea what had come over him.

She shifted her bottom, and he stiffened. He'd never carried a lady across his thighs, either.

With her left hand she played with the buttons of his

waistcoat. "Kidnapping is an offense, you know." She sounded quite unworried. "What ransom do you plan to set?"

He snorted. Another example of how sheltered a life she'd led. He could easily have kidnapped her in truth. Anyone could have. London was a hotbed of crime. And she'd be worth a pretty penny.

Kidnapping had once been a quite respectable occupation of the aristocracy. An acceptable method of filling coffers. And arms . . . He savored the warm weight of her against him. He could see their point. If he were a medieval knight and she a kidnapped lady, he wouldn't ransom her, he thought. He'd marry her. His arm tightened. But life was not a story book. Especially not his life. "You know perfectly well I'm not kidnapping you. I'm saving you from the consequences of your own recklessness."

"Oh, I see. Is that what it was? An exercise in stuffiness. Forgive me for not immediately perceiving it." She wriggled her bottom again. The effect was about as far from stuffy as he could imagine.

"Will you keep still!" he growled and then remembered to add, "Please."

For answer she squirmed again. He made a sound under his breath, and she said in a breathy voice, "Sorry, but this mode of transport is new to me, and a little . . . unsettling. Before this the closest contact I'd had to a man's body was during a waltz . . ."

He couldn't think of a thing to say. He was remembering their waltz. Her innocent admission told him she was also aroused, but being so sheltered, did not realize it.

He rode slowly back with Hope Merridew in his arms, tucked against his chest. Her rose-vanilla-woman scent teased his nostrils, her curls tickled his chin, and her soft backside pressed against his rigidity.

He wanted her like he'd never wanted any woman in his life. If only they could just ride on like this, into the future, to some place far away, where his problems would disappear . . .

But problems never disappeared, he knew. They were either dealt with or they got worse. Sebastian knew how to deal with his problems. He'd already found the solution. And it didn't involve Miss Hope Merridew. She was just a beautiful dream.

And he wasn't a man who indulged in dreaming. He preferred plans to dreams.

He glanced around and saw her groom ride up to where her horse had stopped to graze, lean down, and capture the dangling reins. "I see your groom has finally done something to earn his keep."

"He isn't my groom, and I won't have you criticize him."

Sebastian snorted. "How do you think you'll stop me? His job is to protect you, and he failed."

She said nothing, but it was such a provocative silence he was forced to look at her. It was a mistake. Their eyes met. He hesitated for a few seconds. He was drowning in her eyes and fighting it all the way. He knew better than to complicate matters, and Hope Merridew was a complication if ever he'd met one. He swallowed. Just one kiss wouldn't hurt, surely . . . Just to taste her, to know . . .

She gazed deeply into his eyes, her baby-soft skin blushing deliciously. Her eyes were huge and as blue as a summer sky in the morning. This close he could see each individual golden lash, clustered thickly, curling at the ends. They fluttered, and her lips parted slightly. It was all the invitation he needed. Deliberately, he bent down, his eyes locked with hers, and captured her with his mouth.

The taste of her entered his blood like wine, going straight to his head. He tasted her again, deeper, warmer, more intimately. He told himself he should stop, that he shouldn't be doing this . . . but he couldn't help himself. His body strained to get closer to her, aching to taste more of her, fully, all over.

He felt her hands, soft, cool, gloveless, slide up his jaw, holding, exploring him. Her fingers tangled in his hair, and she pulled him closer, as if she was as absorbed in the kiss as he.

The horse sidestepped, breaking the kiss. He stared down at her, drowning in her blue, blue eyes, gazing hungrily at her damp red lips.

"I'm so glad we met again this morning," she whispered. "The waltz was very nice, of course, but this . . ." She sighed and smiled mistily up at him. "This is so much nicer."

At the sweetness of her smile, guilt flooded him. He should not be toying with an innocent so. And he was toying with her; it could be nothing else. He'd considered his situation from all angles weeks ago and charted his plan. He'd commenced his run, the die was cast, and all was in place.

This sweet young woman did not fit with his plans in any way. Her body curved perfectly into his, fitting as if she were made for him, but in no other way did she fit with his plans or his sisters' needs or his life. No. It was impossible to change direction now. She might be what he wanted, but his wants were not important. She was not what he needed in a wife. Lady Elinore was what he needed.

As the knowledge settled over him, he felt his face harden. Miss Merridew's groom trotted toward them, her hat in his hand, her horse in tow. With every pace, Sebastian's heart closed back in on itself.

"If he'd been any sort of decent groom, he would have protected you from this, too." He gave her one last hungry, driving kiss, then slipped her off his lap, lowering her to stand on the dewy grass of Hyde Park.

"Good-bye, Miss Merridew." She lifted her hand, and he caught it in one last, hard grip. "Don't take any more foolish risks. Not with sticks and horses' hooves. Nor with strange men." And he cantered away.


He rode like a god, Hope thought, a very controlled god just now, but earlier, when he'd thundered to her rescue, lifting her effortlessly out of her saddle, indifferent to the fact that he was astride a powerful beast galloping flat out, he'd been more centaur than cit. That was probably why she'd let him carry her off.

She narrowed her eyes, watching as he disappeared into the distance. How did a man who'd started life as a factory brat learn to ride as if he'd been born to the saddle?

"You all right, Miss Hope?" James arrived. "What happened?"

Hope sighed rapturously. "I met a man, James."

"Yeah, I saw. Sorry, Miss Hope, I should've stopped it. I'm going to throttle that Jasper!"

"Jasper?" She took the reins from James and groped in her pocket for a lump of sugar for her horse.

"At the stables. Giving me this . . . this creature!" He gestured in disgust at his mount. "I won't call it a horse. Clothes horse more like! Got as much get-up-and-go as one! Anything past a trot is beyond it!" He fixed her with a stern look. "But even if I wasn't there, Miss Hope, you know full well you didn't ought to be riding with a strange man like that."

Hope smiled dreamily. "I know. But he's not a stranger. I danced with him last night, in fact."

"You don't mean this was an assignation, Miss—cos if it was, I'm not having a bar of it, and I'll never take you out in the morning agai—"

"Calm yourself, James, dear. It wasn't an assignation, I promise you. I had no idea anyone else would be here. He just galloped up out of nowhere." She rubbed the velvet muzzle of her horse and said softly, "He thought he was rescuing me from certain death, and I didn't have the heart to stop him."

James snorted.

"He was furious when he realized I didn't need rescuing." She smiled to herself, recalling his protective anger and the careful way he'd tucked her body against him. "I suspect I've met a hero, James."

James snorted again.

She gave him a mischievous look. "Getting a cold, James?"

"If anyone saw you, miss, you'd be in the suds. And so would I."

"Oh, pooh! Nobody saw me, and you know perfectly well I wouldn't let anybody blame you for my misbehavior. Now stop being so stuffy and get down and help me to mount my horse, please. I'm hungry, and I want my breakfast."

"Lady Elinore mentioned she would attend the musical evening at Lady Thorn's tonight," Giles said casually. The two men were dining at Giles's club. "And as I happen to have an invitation, I wondered if you'd like to attend. Further the courtship and all that."

"A musical evening?" Sebastian pulled a face. "Bunch of tabbies sitting around listening to some dashed soprano!" He shook his head. "No, thank you. Not my sort of thing at all."

"And dancing is, I suppose," Giles said with an ironic look. He set his port glass aside and stretched. "It doesn't matter. I just thought you might like the opportunity to further your courtship of Lady Sensible. I believe she invariably attends these things. And it's not a soprano, it's some Hungarian violinist, fresh from the Continent. Has all the ladies swooning, apparently." He added mischievously, "Even the sensible, dutiful ones. Thought I'd look in on it, see what all the fuss was about. Sure you don't want to come?"

Sebastian shook his head. Apart from being uninterested in music, he didn't want to risk running into Miss Merridew again. "No, I am taking Lady Elinore for a drive in the park tomorrow. That is more my idea of an efficient courtship. I shall return to the house and write some letters." It wasn't just efficiency. The visit to the park had another purpose. He needed to erase a persistent image from his mind, the image of a slender, feminine body swinging from a horse, of golden curls tickling his jaw and chin, of a warm feminine body pressed against his.

Another visit to the park with a different lady would erase those images, he thought.

Giles nodded. "A much better notion, I'm sure. Lady Thorn is calling it a small private soiree, but half the females of the ton are said to be going. This fiddle player has 'em all in a twitter. 'Twill be a shocking squeeze, no doubt." Giles carefully picked a speck of lint from his jacket. "Alas, the Merridew girls are not going. I would have liked to further my acquaintance with them. Such delightful girls. But music is not at all an interest of theirs."

Sebastian frowned. If Miss Merridew wasn't going to be there, there was no reason why he should not attend. He'd resolved to avoid her if possible. He drained his port glass and stood to leave. As they waited in the hallway for a footman to bring them their coats and hats, Sebastian said thoughtfully, "Now I come to think of it, it's probably not a bad idea to attend the concert tonight. It will give Lady Elinore and me something to discuss when we drive out tomorrow."

It seemed Giles had discovered more fluff in the folds of his coat, for he mumbled something in response, but Sebastian could not hear it. When he eventually donned his coat and looked up, Giles's eyes were dancing. "Very sensible of you, Bas, I agree. It will make a most useful topic of rational conversation." He clapped his hat on his head at a rakish angle. "On to Lady Thorn's then for an evening of serious pursuit—I mean cultural pursuits. Of the dutiful sort. Any pleasure we might have out of it will be swiftly shown the door."

# *Chapter Five*

&

*All the world's a stage,*
*And all the men and women merely players*
*They have their exits and their entrances.*

WILLIAM SHAKESPEARE

LADY THORN POUNCED ON GILES AND SEBASTIAN. "TWO YOUNG
gentlemen! How delightful! So difficult to balance the
numbers, you know—I don't know why people should
imagine only females would enjoy the dear count's music!" She beamed at them in a proprietorial manner as she
steered them into the large salon. "I shall scatter you about.
Break up the clumps of females. Giles, dear boy, how does
your mother do these days? An age since I saw her last!
Such a shame she did not come to London this season! Sit
there, if you please." She thrust Giles into the center of a
group of ladies.

Lady Elinore Whitelaw was one of them, Sebastian saw,
dressed in unrelieved gray twill. "Lady Thorn, I would prefer to sit there with—"

"Nonsense! You can rejoin Giles after the concert. The
ladies will not eat you, and waste a man I will not! Besides,
every man in the room wishes to sit where I am going to
seat you. The poor dears will be furious. I do so enjoy putting the cat among the pigeons!" Lady Thorn towed Sebas-

tian deftly through the dense feminine throng. "Are you enjoying your visit to London, Mr. Reyne? Excellent! Ah,
here we are. Now you sit here and be good!" she exhorted
as if he were five years old, and she disappeared in search
of another hapless gentleman to be strategically seated.

Sebastian found himself seated in the middle of what
seemed to be a family party. Largely female and mostly
young—the girls had formed a tight, chattering circle. He
could not see their faces. He could not imagine why anyone else would envy him his seat. He glanced over to
where Giles was seated. Dashed bad luck, he thought. He
would have much preferred to sit next to Lady Elinore, and
Giles would be delighted to sit in the midst of this party of
bright young lasses.

On the other side of the girlish clump sat an elegantly
dressed old gentleman. Sebastian nodded to him over the
knot of female heads. Sir Oswald Merridew, Miss Merridew's great uncle. Why would he be here? He felt a cold
thread of apprehension slide down his spine.

"Mr. Reyne, how nice to see you again," a voice said at
his elbow. A soft voice. One that had visited him in
dreams. It was suddenly clear why every man in the room
would envy him his seat. His pulse suddenly pounding, Sebastian leaped to his feet.

Their eyes met, and he was in instant danger of drowning. He averted his gaze, trying to think of something polite and innocuous to say. All he could think of was the last
time they'd met, and the kiss. He could not refer to that incident. He was blocking it from his mind.

"I did not think you would be here tonight," he blurted.

She looked surprised. "Oh, but we never miss a concert.
My twin has a passion for all kinds of music. Mr. Bemerton could have told you that." She blushed.

He was going to kill Giles. He couldn't think of another thing to say. In desperation, he reverted to his usual
comment for ladies, "You look charming tonight, Miss
Merridew."

And then he looked at her dress. She wore a pale jonquil

dress, with a tiny row of soft, gauzy ruffles framing the very low neckline, caressing the gentle rise of her breasts. Standing above her, it seemed as if there was nowhere else he could look. Sebastian swallowed. He must not think of her breasts. He was courting Lady Elinore Whitelaw, a sensible lady who did not even seem to have breasts. That was the sort of lady he could cope with.

Recalling that he was the owner of several fabric mills, Sebastian attempted to view Miss Merridew with a professional eye, concentrating on the material of her gown rather than the enticing body within it. The fabric was imported, he noted disapprovingly: the finest oriental silk, so fine it clung lovingly to every curve of her slender young body.

His cravat was suddenly too tight. He persisted in the inventory of her clothing: her fine white-on-white embroidered shawl was from Kashmir and not Norwich, her reticule made from matching silk. He ought to speak to her about supporting local industry.

He fixed his eye on the tiny confection of silk and net and feathers she wore on her head but could think of nothing to say.

With a warm, glowing smile, she rose and stepped closer, so close that with the slightest movement, their bodies could touch. His mind blank, Sebastian stood as straight as a flagpole, hardly breathing. She swayed toward him. He abruptly stepped back and crashed into a chair in the row behind.

By the time he'd caught the chair and straightened it, with apologies to those around him, she was there again, so close he could smell the scent of her skin. He breathed in deeply.

"Mr. Reyne." She gave him her hand. He took it and stared down at her, completely unable to think of a thing to say.

"How do you do?" he croaked eventually.

She smiled again, an absolute dazzler, and said in a low, intimate voice. "I am very well, thank you."

A silence stretched between them. Her smile grew, and

all he could do was stare at her mouth and tell himself not to move, or he would disgrace himself. Her glance shifted with some amusement to the front of his shirt and as he followed it, he realized he'd imprisoned her hand against his chest. How had it got there? Sebastian wondered. He dropped it like a hot coal and stepped back again, managing not to kick over the chairs behind him.

"You remember Mrs. Jenner, don't you?"

Ah yes, the chaperone who'd glared at him the other night. With some relief, Sebastian turned away from that mesmerizing smile. He bowed and murmured something polite. The chaperone shook his hand with two limp fingers and pursed her lips in a forbidding manner. She seemed to have eaten something sour at dinner.

"And this is my twin sister, Miss Faith Merridew."

Seeing the twins side by side, Sebastian still could not understand why people had such trouble differentiating them. There were strong similarities, but Miss Faith didn't hold a candle to her sister in looks. Miss Hope had an inner fire, a glow that her sister lacked.

Not that beauty interested him in the least. Character was everything.

"And this is our beloved great-uncle, Sir Oswald Merridew."

"Sir Oswald."

"How d'ye do, my boy. Glad to see another man in the place. Fond of music, are you? Can't say I am, though the ladies apparently can't get enough of this Hungarian feller. And as for fiddle music—dashed caterwaulin' in my book. Still, my gels were mad to come—they adore music—and I can't deny the pretty creatures anything." He beamed fondly at his "gels," one of whom included an improbable redhead well past her middle years.

"Have you met my—our very dear friend, Lady Augusta Montigua del Fuego?"

Lady Augusta was the plump older lady with the coiffure of bright red curls who he'd seen at the ball the other evening. Tonight she was gowned in a stunning dress of purple and gold satin, cut very low across a magnificent bosom. "Mr. Reyne. We have not met before. I certainly would have remembered you." She eyed Sebastian up and down with brazen feminine approval and gave him such a mischievous look he was torn between being shocked by her forwardness and amused by her blatancy. He could not help but smile.

"My lords, ladies, and gentlemen . . ." Lady Thorn tinkled a small silver bell for their attention and swept her gaze around the room with beady imperative. Those still standing and chatting hurriedly found their seats.

There was a small scuffle as Mrs. Jenner tried to get Miss Hope to change places with her, but Lady Thorn glared at her with a such a sweetly fierce expression, she subsided. Sebastian glanced at the chaperone. She looked bilious.

She probably wanted to be seated closer to the door in case she felt worse and had to leave, he thought. Miss Hope was near the end of the row of chairs, and Sebastian was seated beside her. He ought to offer to exchange places with the chaperone, but Lady Thorn would be sure to object to any further delay.

A hush fell.

He should have changed places, Sebastian realized belatedly, and not for the sake of the chaperone. The chairs had been placed so closely that he could smell Miss Hope's perfume. And from the corner of his eye, he could see the gentle rise and fall of her chest as she breathed. He would not hear a note of the concert, he was sure. A good thing he didn't much care for music.

But he would not have much to discuss with Lady Elinore tomorrow. He glanced back to where Giles was seated, right beside Lady Elinore. A good fellow, Giles, looking out for his friend's interests.

"Count Felix Vladimir Rimavska."

A slenderly built man of medium height strode out onto the low stage as if he owned it, a violin tucked under his arm. Dressed in a magnificent Turkey red jacket of vaguely military style, with epaulets and gold frogging down the front, he wore tight white breeches and highly polished black boots. He was darkly good-looking, with a pale, tragic face and unreadable slavic eyes. His hair was black and overlong and windswept, and it fell over his broad, pale forehead in wild curls. He somehow managed to combine a military look with a flavor of gypsy. He swaggered to the front of the stage and stood there in silence, smoldering with silent passion.

Sebastian loathed him on sight.

The feminine section of the audience sighed and clapped excitedly. Count Felix Vladimir Rimavska flung them a sulky look. Instantly, a breathless silence fell. He raised the violin to his chin.

The wool of his jacket, Sebastian decided, was of inferior quality. Nor would that red dye last well. At the first good shower, the dye would probably run, staining those tight white breeches a streaky pink. The thought was immensely satisfying.

Count Felix Vladimir Rimavska threw his head back, closed his eyes, and played. His violin sobbed, soared, and wept with emotion. Sebastian might know little about music, but he didn't need to be told: the bastard was good, dammit! All around him, ladies sighed and almost swooned, their bodies moving slightly to the throbbing rise and fall of the music.

Sebastian could not bear to watch the popinjay onstage, tossing his wild pomaded curls about as angelic music soared from his violin. He averted his gaze and found himself staring, mesmerized, at the soft ruffles framing the delicate skin of Miss Hope's chest. The ruffles rose and fell. That gown was far too low in front. Her chaperone ought to do something about it, he thought, and then suddenly realizing where he was staring, he turned his gaze abruptly back to the stage.

The count moved about as he played, his narrow hips thrust forward in a way that made Sebastian long to punch him.

Sebastian closed his eyes, but then all he could do was smell Miss Hope's perfume. Vanilla, rose, and woman. Their shoulders almost touched. He fancied he could almost feel the warmth of her skin. She sighed deeply. And all he could think of was breasts framed in ruffles. Or framed in nothing at all. Or framed in his hands.

Which was a disgrace. He opened his eyes, stretched out his legs, crossed them at the ankles, and stared at his shoes. It was the safest thing to do.

Blasted Continental fiddle music. It did things to people's emotions. He glanced again at the count, hoping that irritation with the man would replace the inconvenient arousal of his baser self.

Resigned, Sebastian folded his arms, stared at his shoes, and set himself to endure an evening of hell. Or forbidden heaven.

Hope sighed as the piece finished. She hadn't really expected to enjoy herself tonight: music was Faith's passion, not hers. And since most of the people who wanted to see this dashing Hungarian were female, Hope hadn't at all expected to see Mr. Reyne. But not only had he come, he had been seated next to her.

His friend Mr. Bemerton sat on the far side of the room with Lady Elinore Whitelaw. Perhaps Mrs. Jenner was wrong; perhaps it was Mr. Bemerton who was pursuing Lady Elinore, not Mr. Reyne. Or perhaps it was a ruse to scotch some of the gossip.

Were both of them interested in Lady Elinore? Was that why Mr. Reyne was cross? Hope examined the lady in question from a distance. From outward appearances, she seemed hardly the kind to have two good-looking men vying for her favors. She had a reputation as an eccentric, and judging from tonight's outfit, she did look distinctly dowdy. Actually . . .

Hope frowned. She had met Lady Elinore once or twice before, but she hadn't made much of an impression at the time. She'd seemed very quiet and disapproving of Hope, so Hope had more or less dismissed her, but tonight, looking at Lady Elinore's severe gray dress, all-enveloping gray shawl, and her hair scraped back and mostly covered by a plain, unflattering cap, Hope was strongly reminded of the way Grandpapa had forced them to dress.

As if to be female was a crime . . .

The violinist stamped his foot, and Hope jumped guiltily, but it wasn't a device to recall her wandering attention; he was beginning a dramatic gypsy song with lots of flourishing and stamping. He strode about the small stage, his violin throbbing with life and drama. The man was certainly handsome, Hope thought. Those wild, boyish curls and that sulky, beautiful mouth would have half the ladies of London at his feet. He was a figure straight out of one of Lord Byron's more fanciful poems.

He didn't move her in the least.

The count stamped again, like a cossack, she supposed. She glanced around the room. Everyone seemed entranced. Ladies sat forward in their chairs, hands clutched rapturously to bosoms, sighing with delight as the count played and stamped and tossed his long black curls. There was something a little stagey about him, about the way he presented himself. And something more than a little vulgar about the tightness of those white breeches. She supposed that went with being a performer. Certainly he could play. Not that she was much of a judge of music; she left all that to her sister.

She glanced at Faith and smiled. Her shy sister sat bolt upright, gripping her reticule tightly, staring at the Hungarian with wide eyes, her mouth half open as if enchanted. Count Felix Vladimir Rimavska wasn't just good, she realized; he must be absolutely brilliant. Faith could be quite critical of inferior performers and had a tendency to admire anyone who played well, but she'd never seen her sister look at any musician with quite that degree of admiration, almost reverence.

Faith was welcome to him. For all his talent and dark good looks, Hope didn't find the count nearly as attractive as the big, glowering man at her side. She glanced sideways to see if Mr. Reyne was enjoying the music, but he was staring at his shoes, lost in thought. What was he so cross about? she wondered again. Was it Lady Elinore, or the music, or was it something else, some problem in his life? He seemed so tense and unhappy. She wanted to lean across and slip her arm though his and comfort him.

After a final crescendo, the count, exhausted by the energy he had expended, reeled elegantly and sank onto a nearby chair, declaring he needed refreshment before he could continue. Ladies and servants rushed to his aid.

There was a muffled snort from Mr. Reyne.

Hope smiled. She'd seen from his rigid attention to his shoes that Mr. Reyne was not fascinated with the count; now she suspected their opinions of the man might coincide.

"So, Mr. Reyne, what do you think of—" she began, but her sister grasped her arm urgently.

"Hope! Hope, I must meet him! Come on!" Faith was adamant. It was unusual for her twin to make such a compelling request, so with a small apologetic smile at Mr. Reyne, Hope allowed herself to be dragged off to join the throng of ministering females.

The count petulantly rejected the forms of refreshment first rushed to him. "Wine and cakes? Pah, food for ladies. I am a man!"

He waved away the champagne. "Is zere no vodka in the house? Very well, if zere is nozzing else, brandy will have to do. But in Paris, they give me the finest vodka." He took the glass of brandy offered, flung it down his throat with one dramatic movement, and shuddered extravagantly. He opened his eyes and regarded the waiting crowd through slitted eyes. He looked like a partially satiated pet panther. "Anyzing to eat?"

Hope watched, faintly amused by the man's pretensions and by the way his adoring feminine acolytes rushed about trying to please him.

"Ham? Bah! Would you poison me?" He regarded the offending plate with disgust. The lady who'd offered it shrank away apologetically. A moment ago, she'd snatched the plate of shaved ham from a footman and offered it to the count in triumph. A baronet's wife, fawning over a performer. As was half the extremely well-bred room. It was an extraordinary sight.

Could they not see that refusing to be pleased was part of his act? Hope turned to her sister to share the joke, but Faith was not there.

"Perhaps a morsel of smoked salmon on some lightly buttered bread, Count Rimavska?" In amazement, Hope heard her sister's soft voice make the offer. Had everyone gone mad?

The count paused for a tense moment, then gave an approving smile. "An angel of sustenance. From your fair hands, O divine one, I would even risk ham!"

Faith glowed as he drew her closer. Hope turned away, shocked. What was Faith doing? It was taking musical admiration to extremes.

She sought out Mrs. Jenner. "Do something!"

"What would you have me do?"

"Stop my sister making a fool of herself."

Mrs. Jenner looked incredulous. "But she is not making a fool of herself. I think it is charming."

"But he's—he's—" Hope could hardly speak. "She's waiting on him like a servant!"

"Nonsense, she's just being helpful." Mrs. Jenner raised a brow and gave Hope a smug look. "He's a count, of excellent lineage, I'm told. And fabulously wealthy. He's also a very good musician and extremely handsome. At least dear Faith hasn't had her head turned by an unsavory cit!"

Had her head turned? Stunned, Hope watched as her sister passed morsels to the count. It didn't seem right. The man was a poseur. She turned to older, wiser heads. "Great Uncle Oswald? Lady Gussie? What is Faith doing? I've never seen her act so bold."

Lady Gussie patted her hand. "It's just a bit of fun, dear.

Faith is enjoying herself. He's a very pretty man, and he plays like an angel. It's a pleasure to see shy little Faith flirting for a change. Too serious, that girl."

Hope frowned. *Flirting?* Faith never flirted. "Oh, my God," she whispered. "A *musician!*" Was this Faith's dream come true?

Great Uncle Oswald heard her. "Yes, but no harm in that. Titled, and the family is disgustin'ly rich. And since there's a shockin' shortage of dukes at the moment . . ." He shrugged. "So run along and let your sister be."

Sebastian watched as the count ate his way through the plate of smoked salmon and then picked over a plate of lobster patties, both held adoringly for him by Miss Faith Merridew. Several glasses of the despised brandy disappeared down his throat.

It wasn't refreshments the fellow needed—it was a good thrashing! The way the women crowded about the man made him grind his teeth. Miss Faith was feeding the man, and her sister was standing by, watching every movement tenderly. Unable to stomach the sight any longer, he crossed the room to join Giles and Lady Elinore. At least Lady Elinore hadn't rushed to join the throng of ladies, he noted with satisfaction. A rational woman!

"Well, what do you think of that?" He jerked his head across the room. "Ever seen anything like it?"

"No indeed. A most exhilarating performance," agreed Lady Elinore.

Sebastian snorted. "It's a performance, all right."

"I had heard him described as Byronesque," Lady Elinore said, "but I had not realized the degree to which it would be so apt. There is a tendency in society to exaggerate such things, but in this case it seems appropriate. Do you not find him so, Mr. Reyne?"

"Find him what? Appropriate?" Sebastian blinked. Miss Hope hadn't taken her eyes off the dratted fiddle player.

"Byronesque."

Sebastian frowned. "I thought he was Hungarian."

Both Giles and Lady Elinore laughed, as if he'd made a very good joke. Giles said, "Yes, as if he'd stepped right out of 'The Giaour.'"

Sebastian supposed that the *Jowr* was some place in Hungary. He didn't know about such things. He'd had only had a few years of schooling, as Giles very well knew, and poetry wasn't part of it.

"Oh no, 'The Corsair,' I think," Lady Elinore said. "'His forehead high and pale / The sable curls in wild profusion veil; . . .'"

"Apt indeed," Giles agreed. "'And oft perforce his rising lip reveals / The haughtier thought it curbs, but scarce conceals.' Though it does seem as if he's quite willing to share his haughtier thoughts aloud—about the inferiority of the refreshments offered, for instance."

Giles laughed at his own wit. Lady Elinore frowned. Sebastian, having not a clue what the devil they were talking about, frowned also. Miss Hope was paying far too much attention to the blasted fellow!

Lady Elinore said with cool severity, "Mr. Bemerton, I hope you are not mocking the count. I was in absolute earnest in my admiration. Count Felix Vladimir Rimavska is the finest violinist I have ever heard. The fact that he also resembles Lord Byron's most romantical hero is not, I believe, a reason for flippancy. On the contrary, it only adds to his attraction." She walked off, leaving Giles staring after her, his jaw agape.

"Did you see that?"

"I did indeed," murmured Sebastian, who hadn't taken his eyes off the scene next to the stage. "An absolute disgrace."

"She reprimanded me! Again!"

"Hmm? Who?"

"Lady Elinore! She reprimanded me for my flippancy and walked off in high dudgeon!" Giles was astounded. And from the light in his eyes, amused. "I've never had any woman talk to me that way, let alone a dowdy little quiz at her last prayers."

"Ahem!" Sebastian cleared his throat meaningfully, but Giles missed the hint, so he was forced to add, "Recall, if you please, that you are talking of my intended."

"Oh, right. Yes, of course. Sorry." Giles stared after Lady Elinore.

"What did you do to offend her, anyway?"

Giles jerked his chin in the direction of the stage. "Insulted the fiddler."

Sebastian snorted. "A man like that cannot be insulted enough! Blasted coxcomb!" He glared at the Merridew sisters, still apparently entranced by the count.

Giles nodded. "Fellow needs a punch in the nose, if you ask me."

"My thoughts exactly!"

In complete accord they watched the ladies thronging around the count. The Merridew girls were in the forefront, standing right beside him. Lady Elinore had quietly attached herself to the edge of the adoring circle. Sebastian said, "I'm not staying to watch any more of this."

Giles shook his head in disgust. "Me neither. I need a drink."

However, when they reached the house Sebastian had rented for the season, it was to find there was an urgent message waiting for him from his butler in Manchester. Cassie and Dorie were missing. They'd been missing for— he checked the date on the message—three days now. The butler had taken the liberty of calling in Mr. Morton Black.

*Missing.* A cold chill enveloped his body, and for a second he could not think at all. They could not be missing. He could not have lost them again!

Feeling sick and more worried than he'd been for years, Sebastian instantly ordered a fresh horse to be saddled. He explained briefly to Giles. "I must go, immediately."

"Yes, of course, my dear fellow. I shall look after things for you here, shall I?"

Sebastian, his only thought for his sisters, said distractedly, "What things?"

"You have an engagement to drive out with Lady Elinore tomorrow morning, do you not?"

"Oh yes. Damn! I should write—"

Giles laid a hand on his arm. "Don't give it another thought. I shall call on Lady Elinore in the morning, explain to her that you were called away on urgent family business. I'll even take her on that drive, if she wants. I've no other engagements."

"Thanks, Giles. You're a good friend. Now, I'll just get out of these evening clothes and be off."

In less than ten minutes, Sebastian, in boots, buckskins, and riding coat, was ready and set off northward, into the night.

# Chapter Six

∞

*I had a dream, which was not all a dream . . .*
*The dread of vanished shadows.*

LORD BYRON

HOPE TURNED AND TWISTED, TRYING TO ESCAPE. DARK. JUST A
chink of light. She reached for it, for the handle. Can't
move. Pain. She tried again. "The Devil's hand." The rope
burned into her wrist. "I forbid you to use it."

*She fought for breath. Her heart thudded in her ears.*
*She was dying. He'd locked her in here to die.*

*Faith, where was Faith? Where was her twin?*

*Dark. So dark.* Can't move hand. "I'll teach you to use
that hand."

*She fumbled with her other hand, groped at the chink*
*of light. Should be able to work the lock from the inside.*
Try, try!

Can't! Too clumsy! "Tainted." *Can't use her right hand*
*like everyone else. Can't get out. Can't breathe!*

*Coffin.* She tried to hammer on the lid. *Hand won't move.*
*Good hand. Bad hand. Rope bites into her flesh, tight. Tight*
*enough to cut off the flesh, the bad hand.* "Evil. Tainted."

*She tried to breathe.*

"Faith," she called again. "Faith! Twin!"

"Hope! Hope darling, I'm here. Wake up, my dear."

Light. Blessed light. Blinding her but oh, thank God! Sister. Twin. Faith, her other half. In a nightgown. She was saved. She gasped for breath.

"Breathe deeply now, Hope, dear. You're safe. It was just one of your dreams."

The words finally penetrated. A dream? She was not back at the Court? Thank God. Thank God.

"It was just a nightmare, love. You're safe now, safe in your own bed, far away from Grandpapa." Faith smoothed Hope's tangled hair off her damp forehead.

Hope blinked, dazed, still partly in the grip of her nightmare. Her twin reached down and took Hope's left hand and raised it in front of her. "See? No ropes. No marks. It's all behind us, now." She hugged her.

Hope gave several deep, shivery breaths and rubbed her left wrist as if the rope burns were still there. "I'm sorry, twin," she said gruffly.

"Don't be," said her gentle sister almost fiercely. "Do you think I don't know what these nightmares are about? How often you took punishments intended for me?" There were tears in her eyes. "I just wish I could suffer the nightmares for you."

Hope smiled shakily and hugged Faith. "Don't worry, twin. You have your own nightmares, I know. We all do. It is Grandpapa's legacy."

Her sister's words of the other night came back to her. *"Give him another fifty years or so, and who will you be looking at? Grandpapa!"*

Was that what had brought the nightmare on? Did he really, deep down, remind her of Grandpapa? Was the dream a warning?

She thought about it. Sebastian Reyne was not like Grandpapa, he was not. She was sure he was not.

Almost.

• • •

Wearily, Sebastian turned into the driveway of his home. Lights blazed from the house. He was drenched, filthy, and exhausted. He'd ridden almost nonstop for the last twenty-two hours. He'd lost track of the number of horses he'd exchanged on the way. He dismounted, staggering briefly, as his muscles cramped.

The front door was flung open before he had even reached the steps. The butler hurried to greet Sebastian. "It's all right, sir, the girls have been found!"

Sebastian stumbled on a step.

"Mr. Black, he found them, safe and well!"

Sebastian stared at the butler, almost unable to take in his words. He glanced up. Behind the butler, Morton Black stood at the open front door of Sebastian's house, and behind him stood Cassie, looking both belligerent and embarrassed, her hand clasping Dorie's. Dorie looked no different from usual: wide-eyed, wary, and silent.

Relief flooded him. "Thank God!" He raced up the steps and bent to embrace the girls. They flinched and stepped back. Sebastian froze. In his relief at seeing them safe, he'd forgotten.

Hurt, and angry with himself for overstepping the bounds the girls had early established, he ran a rueful hand over his unshaven chin. "Sorry. I forgot how wet and filthy I was. A right bear I must look."

They said nothing.

Stripping off his wet coat, hat, and gloves, he wiped his hands on a towel provided by his butler and held his hand out to Morton Black. "Thank you once again for coming to our rescue, Black. I am extremely grateful. Now, shall we all go into the drawing room? I would like to get to the bottom of this. And Treece," he turned to the butler. "I am famished, and I am certain Mr. Black and the girls will not be averse to some refreshments also."

He ushered the two girls before him into the drawing room and sat down on a hard, wooden chair. "So, Black, did you have to travel far to find them?"

Morton Black shook his head. "Not far at all, sir. Just as far as your own attics."

Sebastian frowned. "My *attics*?"

Black nodded. "I was all set to start scouring the streets, but when I discovered that they hadn't taken their coats and sturdy boots with them, it gave me pause. Not sensible, you see, and these girls are not . . . stupid. Foolish, perhaps, but not stupid." He gave them a mildly censorious look. Cassie jutted her chin at him in silent defiance. Dorie sat mute and still.

Black continued, "Then I overheard the cook accusing the scullery maid of pinching food from the kitchen, and I put two and two together. I ordered the house searched from top to bottom." He gave a satisfied nod. "Found 'em in the attics. Miss Dorie sound asleep in an old armchair and Miss Cassie sittin' on the roof, surveying her surrounds. Should have known."

Sebastian felt relief swamp him. They must have had no intention of running away from him.

But that didn't explain why the girls had hidden in the first place. They weren't the kind for idle mischief or practical jokes. In fact, he'd feel a lot happier about them if they did show such normal childish traits. He went straight to the heart of the problem. "Yes, but why hide in the first place? They are perfectly safe, now."

Black shrugged. "That I can't tell you, sir. The girls have said nothing to me."

"Cassie?" Sebastian turned to her. "Why did you and Dorie hide?"

There was a long silence.

"Was it a prank? Something you thought might be fun, to trick everyone?"

Cassie flung him a scornful look in response. Of course she wouldn't do such a thing for fun, the look said.

"Then why, Cassie?"

She shrugged, her face sullen and uncommunicative.

He clenched his fist in frustration but said in an even tone, "I will have an answer, Cassie. If you had good reason for what you did, no one shall punish you. If not, you will be punished."

Dorie's gaze flickered to Sebastian's fist, then to her sister. Her little face was white and pinched, and instead of her habitual blankness, she looked anxious.

It was like a hand squeezed around Sebastian's heart. His voice softened. "It's all right, Dorie, nobody will hurt either of you. Cassie, was it something to do with Dorie?"

Cassie glanced at her sister, then shrugged, as if indifferent. "And if it was?"

Sebastian sighed wearily. "Just tell me, Cassie. I am tired and angry and relieved all at once. I've been traveling nonstop day and night, worried sick that something terrible had happened to you."

Cassie's eyes narrowed skeptically, as if she didn't believe him.

Sebastian continued, "Yes, worried sick!" He shook his head, puzzled at her attitude. "Of course I was! You're my sisters! Why else do you think I dropped everything in London and came home to look for you?"

Cassie frowned.

He said, "I wasn't the only one. Treece and Mrs. Elliot and Mr. Black and Cook and everyone else in the house have been worried sick, too, searching for you high and low. I suspect none of us have slept properly for days."

She glanced at Black, who nodded confirmation.

Treece had just come in carrying a pot of tea, a bottle of brandy, and a plate of sandwiches. Cassie glanced at him, and he nodded, "He's right, Miss Cassie. We've all been that worried about you and the little one. Mrs. Treece hasn't slept a wink for fretting, neither."

Sebastian, seeing that Cassie was genuinely taken aback by their concern, explained, "We all imagined you dead in a ditch, or worse! So the least you can do is explain why you put us all through that."

After a moment's silent reflection, Cassie said slowly, "It wasn't a trick. I'm sorry we upset you all." She glanced at her little sister, and some silent communication passed between them. "Dorie was frightened. She thought she saw . . . someone."

"Who?"

"Cassie shook her head.

"Did she tell you? Can she speak?"

Cassie said impatiently. "You know Dorie doesn't speak."

"Then how did you—" He broke off. "Very well, I accept that Dorie was frightened and that I was not here to protect you from whatever she thought it was. But why did you not tell Treece or Mrs. Elliot? Why hide instead?"

She gave him a flat look, and he realized it hadn't occurred to her. She didn't expect to be protected. It was why she carried that knife strapped to her thigh.

He said gently, "While I am away, there are more than twenty people in this house, Cassie, and their only task is to see to your and Dorie's welfare. Their *only* task."

Cassie shrugged uncomfortably, unsettled but determined to feign indifference.

"Is there anything else you can tell me about who or what frightened Dorie?"

She got that stubborn look in her eyes again, and Sebastian realized he'd got all he was going to get out of her. "Very well, it's late. Mrs. Elliot can take you up to bed now. I shall consider what is to be done in the morning, when I've had some sleep and can think more clearly. Good night, Cassie. Good night, Dorie."

"G'night, sir," Cassie mumbled and took Dorie's hand. It was another cut. Cassie refused utterly to address him as Sebastian, as he had asked her. She addressed him as the servants did—*sir*—making it clear that he was nothing personal to her.

Sebastian watched them leave. As they reached the door, he said in a low voice, "Girls, I know I sound angry, but you have no idea how thankful I am that you are both safe and well."

The girls paused on the threshold, then glanced at each

other. Slowly, reluctantly, Cassie turned. "Sorry we worried you," she muttered, addressing the room in general, not Sebastian in particular. It was a victory, but a hollow one.

"Sleep well, little ones," he said, feeling unutterably weary. They would punish him forever for losing them in the first place.

"So I've brought them to London with me," Sebastian told Giles ten days later. He jerked his chin at the ceiling. "They're asleep now. The journey has worn them out, poor little things." He'd arrived in London in the late afternoon and sent a note around to Giles, informing him.

Giles raised a brow. "Having two young girls on hand is going to complicate your social life, you realize."

"I know, but what else can I do? It's obvious I can't leave them alone. More than ever, I need to take a wife, and the longer I delay it, the more the difficulties multiply."

"What difficulties? Are the girls getting harder to handle?"

Sebastian shook his head. "No, not really, though I must admit this last escapade threw me. But it is the mill, also. There are things needing my attention, and lately, there's been a lot of unrest in the area. I've managed to keep it from affecting my mills—my workers are better off than most and know it—but still, a few hotheads can . . ." He noticed the glazed look around Giles's eyes and said, "I see I'm boring you. Suffice it to say, I need to expedite this courtship in as short a period as possible and get back to normal. I sent a note around to Lady Elinore an hour ago."

"So you haven't changed your mind about courting Lady Elinore?"

"No. Why should I?" Sebastian firmly drove images of golden-haired Miss Merridew from of his mind. "This episode with the girls has confirmed more than ever that I need a wife who can understand their special circumstances."

"So it is fixed in your mind that your own desires do not matt—"

"We shall keep my desires—whatever you imagine them to be—out of this, Giles, thank you."

Giles smiled skeptically. "Very well. Your own desires do not matter, and only Lady Elinore could understand your sisters' situation, not . . . anyone else. Miss Merridew, for instance."

Sebastian frowned. His friend was like a cat, seemingly uninterested until he unsheathed a lazy claw. He explained forcefully, "Miss Merridew is a lovely girl, but she's led a sheltered and privileged life. Lady Elinore might come from the same privileged class, but she's spent most of her adult life working with poor and troubled orphan girls." From the look in his eye, Giles would not give up, so he turned the subject. "Thank you for smoothing things with her, by the way. Did she mind very much that I didn't turn up for our drive?"

"No, not much."

"Good. You explained, then."

"Yes, I explained."

"Good. In my note, I invited Lady Elinore to come out with the girls and me for a drive in the park tomorrow morning."

Giles arched an eyebrow. "I see. And has she accepted the invitation?"

Sebastian shook his head. "Not yet. I only sent the note around an hour ago. But she will, I'm certain."

Giles sipped his port meditatively and said nothing.


"This is Hyde Park," Sebastian explained, as the open carriage swept between the railed gates. "Everyone who is anyone promenades here in the afternoons—all the smart people. Glamorous ladies and important gentlemen."

"They don't look glamorous, they look stupid." Carrie sat hunched in the corner of the carriage, kicking her feet against the leather seats, scowling at the promenaders.

"This is not the hour for promenade. There are only a few people at the moment. In the afternoon, this place will be crowded with the most fashionable people in the world."

"I hate crowds." Cassie was determined not to be pleased by anything. She had not wanted to come to London. She did not want to come out in a carriage this morning. She had seen enough of London.

It was behavior Sebastian would not normally tolerate from anyone, but for the moment, he'd decided to ignore her rudeness. He was learning to understand her ways better. It was token rudeness. He suspected that under her hostility she was relieved to have him take control of them, relieved to share the burden of Dorie's silence and her nameless fears. It was nothing he could put a finger on, just a feeling.

However, Cassie still needed to assert some independence. A prideful little creature, she never missed the opportunity to remind him that she had managed all her life without him. The knife still strapped to the leg that kicked at the upholstery was a invisible symbol of it.

A high-perch phaeton swept past them at a smart trot, pulled by a pair of matched grays. Giles owned a very similar rig. Sebastian craned his neck, but from this angle he could not see who was driving, just a man in high-crowned beaver and a lady in a gray bonnet.

He shook his head. What was he thinking? Giles never rose before noon.

*Thud. Thud.*

"Stop kicking the seats, Cassie," said Sebastian firmly.

She tossed her head defiantly, but the kicking stopped. Her hostility was paper thin. Yesterday, as they'd entered the metropolis, Cassie had grumbled that she didn't want to live in London, even for a month, but she hadn't been able to help craning her neck to take in some of the sights, and her eyes were bright with excitement. And now in the park, she was taking in every detail of the costumes of the ladies she'd called stupid-looking.

She was a spirited little handful, and Sebastian was

thankful for it. He didn't mind the difficulties. Cassie was like him—a survivor. She hadn't been crushed by her experiences.

It was Dorie who worried him most. He hadn't a clue how to handle her. She seemed so fragile.

She sat on the seat of the carriage like a thin, neat little doll. Her skin was porcelain-pale and fine, her eyes wide and dark, too large for her pinched, too-small face. For someone who stole food constantly, her body showed no signs of it. He wished he could communicate with her in some way.

That governess was wrong. Dorie wasn't mentally deficient. She just didn't speak. She understood everything anyone said, and Sebastian believed she could read—at least she seemed to derive pleasure from the books he had provided. She utterly refused to write, however, except to copy a text. Apart from these instances, she was at all other times perfectly docile and obedient. Unnaturally so for a child just turned twelve.

Sebastian worried about her constantly. He'd tried to have her examined by a doctor once, to see if her silence was caused by some damage to her throat, but she'd resisted it strenuously, and the sight of the white-faced child silently fighting off the doctor with frantic little fists had cut straight to his heart. He'd sent the doctor away.

Her big, gray eyes had reproached him for weeks afterward.

She sat neatly on her seat now, obediently observing the sights of Hyde Park. He had no idea what was going on in her head. But he had to keep trying.

For the dozenth time he wished Lady Elinore was with them. She would know what to do, how to talk to them. But she'd sent her apologies, claiming to have another morning engagement already. Sebastian knew an excuse when he saw it. Lady Elinore must be offended by the way he'd rushed off to Manchester, leaving his friend to pass on his apologies. He should have taken a moment to pen her a note, at least. And made arrangements for his butler to send her flowers.

"We're coming up to the pond, now," he said. "Dorie, would you like to feed the ducks?"

She glanced at the pond but didn't respond. He signaled the driver to stop.

"Why are we stopping?" Cassie demanded.

"To feed the ducks."

"What with?"

Sebastian produced a large packet of stale bread. "Come on. Out you hop."

"I don't want to feed the stupid ducks," Cassie grumbled. "I hate ducks."

"I don't care. I want you to feed them, and the fresh air will do you good."

"There's no such a thing as fresh air in London!"

"Yes, you must miss the pure, sweet atmosphere of Manchester," Sebastian agreed ironically. He added pleasantly, "Get out of the carriage now, Cassie, or I'll feed you to the ducks as well. Although with that scowl, you'd probably give the poor creatures indigestion."

Sulkily, Cassie scrambled down. Sebastian stepped down and then turned to help Dorie out of the carriage. She instantly pulled back, and he cursed himself for forgetting. Cassie pushed past him and held out her hand. Dorie took it and carefully climbed down the steps. She looked as if a puff of wind would blow her away.

They crossed to the pond, and Sebastian broke up the bread and gave it to the girls to throw. The ducks came flocking, quacking in noisy exuberance. After a moment or two, Cassie forgot she hated ducks and threw them bits of bread, laughing as they fought for each piece and scolding them for stealing from each other.

Progress.

Dorie carefully broke her bread into tiny pieces and tossed them in one by one, seeking out the smaller ducks, the injured and the shy ones. She did it solemnly, with deliberation, as if engaged in some great endeavor.

She liked doing this, Sebastian decided. They would do it again. Each tiny positive moment was a step forward.

When he'd decided to bring them back to London with him, he had taken comfort from the notion that Dorie was somehow relieved to see him when he returned. Of course she hadn't shown it by word or deed, but it was his impression, confirmed by his housekeeper, Mrs. Elliot, that the child had relaxed in some slight fashion when he came home. And though she still kept a physical distance from him, she seemed somehow less anxious when he was there, like a person who was frightened of dogs nevertheless taking comfort in the presence of a large, fierce watchdog.

It was progress of a sort. As was feeding the ducks.

"Ah, I see the ducks have you well-trained also, Mr. Reyne," came a voice from behind him. "They are demanding creatures, are they not?"

It was Miss Merridew, looking ravishing in a green muslin walking gown and a green and white pelisse, frogged with Russian braid in a vaguely military style. On her it did not look the least bit military. Over her curls, she wore a jaunty little cap with gold braid trimming and a red feather. She smiled up at him with an unaffected warmth that took his breath away.

He stared dumbly at her, his throat suddenly thick with desire.

"How do you do, Mr. Reyne," another voice said coolly, jolting him out of his trance. He suddenly realized that both the Misses Merridew were standing in front of him, accompanied by a beautiful child with red gold hair, and that footman/groom carrying a rush basket.

He was torn by contradictory emotions. It was eleven days since he'd seen Miss Merridew at the concert. Eleven days of drama and anxiety, and yet, despite it all, he'd missed her.

But he hadn't planned to have his sisters meet people yet, particularly not society people, apart from Giles, who knew about them, and Lady Elinore, for obvious reasons. Cassie and Dorie weren't ready to meet people. They needed more time to feel secure, more time to learn how to behave in company.

Miss Hope put her arm around the beautiful child's shoulder and drew her forward. "Mr. Reyne, this is our sister, Grace. Grace, this is Mr. Reyne."

The little girl curtsied and gave him a shy "How do you do, sir?" She would be about eleven or twelve, he thought as he greeted her. She looked with pleased expectancy at his sisters.

Damn, damn, damn! He didn't even know if his sisters knew how to behave with other children. That's why he'd come to the park at such an unfashionable hour and gone to the most remote bank of the pond. Now, three society females were smiling at his sisters and crowding around, and there was no escape, for Miss Hope was saying, "And these two young ladies are—?"

Sebastian didn't know what to say. If he introduced them, Cassie would be rude, and Dorie would be exposed as a freak who could not talk. Within days the whole ton would know of it, and Sebastian would not allow that. His sisters were not fodder for any gossip mill! He wanted to protect them, to snatch them up and run with them back to the safety of the carriage, only if he grabbed Dorie, she would struggle, and then no doubt Cassie would pull her knife on him, and then all hell would break loose. He frowned at Miss Hope, wishing she and her retinue would just disappear.

But before he could utter a word, a small elbow thudded into his hip, and Cassie pushed past him. "The cat seems to have got my brother's tongue. I'm Cassandra, and this is my sister, Eudora, only we call her Dorie. She doesn't speak." She flung it out as a challenge, but Miss Hope Merridew only smiled.

"How do you do, Cassandra, and you, too, Dorie." She took the hand that Cassie proffered and, smiling kindly, held out a hand to Dorie.

Dorie regarded her impassively for a long moment, and Sebastian braced himself, but then the child reached forward and shook hands, and he sighed with relief.

Miss Hope went on, "We are so happy to meet you two—aren't we, Grace?—for Grace does not know anyone her own age in London and is bored to death with shopping and other pursuits that we older ladies enjoy so much."

Grace nodded her head and eyed Cassie solemnly. "Have you been to the Tower of London yet?"

Cassie shook her head.

"It's where they used to chop off people's heads—even kings," Grace informed her with relish. She turned to her sister. "We could go again, could we not? Take Cassandra and Dorie?"

Her sister nodded. "Of course, if Mr. Reyne allows it."

Cassie looked at him with a belligerent expression, daring him to refuse. "That would be very nice, thank you," Cassie said, "and you may call me Cassie."

Sebastian blinked and tried to keep the smile off his face. Who would have believed that his knife-carrying, contentious little sister could produce such gracious manners! Even her accent sounded more refined than usual.

She was a good mimic, he suddenly realized. She'd answered the ladies in their own pure accent. How interesting.

"Have you run out of bread?" the other twin, Faith, asked. She took the basket from the footman. "We've brought plenty. Cook saves it for us. Here." She handed several large chunks of bread to each girl, and they hurried back to the water's edge and flung bread about like three very ordinary little girls. Miss Faith went with them.

Sebastian realized he had been holding his breath. *Like three very ordinary little girls.* He sighed.

"My, that sounded very heartfelt," Hope said.

He made an indeterminate sound of acknowledgment, thought for a moment, and then produced a gruff, "Fine weather, is it not?"

Hope took the rebuff philosophically. He had looked simultaneously glad and horrified to see her when they first arrived, but once the children had run off, he relaxed. She supposed many men were awkward with children. Not all were as easy and natural as her brother-in-law, Gideon.

She slipped her hand though the crook of his arm and said, "It is fine indeed. Quite delightful. Shall we stroll for a moment or two while the ducks feast?" He froze at her touch, and she added, "Faith and James will keep an eye on them."

Staring ahead, he said stiffly, "Very well, we shall stroll." He marched forward at a rapid pace. She had to skip to keep up with him. It took him a moment to notice, then he slowed abruptly. Another silence fell.

He looked around the park with a faint air of desperation and said, "Are those elm trees over there? Very useful trees, elms. Shady. Particularly in sunny weather." He paused for a moment, apparently thinking, and then added, "And yes, it is fine. We have had a lot of sunny weather lately, have we not?"

Hope smiled at him. It was just like the other times she had touched him. On one level he seemed to freeze up and become socially stilted and awkward, addressing her with all the charm of a municipal speech, but at the same time his big, warm hand had instantly come up to cover hers, clamping it possessively to his arm. She was certain he was unaware he'd even done it. The contrasts within him were utterly compelling.

He glanced toward the girls, who were hurling chunks of bread at the noisy ducks. "I suppose the ducks would prefer more rain."

Hope perceived that unless she took control of the conversation, they would end up discussing vegetation in the park, ducks, and possibly the chance of showers.

With a little gentle pressure on his arm, she said, "Shall we investigate those willows?"

With faint reluctance, he headed toward the willows. He was an enigma, but he drew her like a lodestone. She was determined to get to know him better. "Are your sisters newly arrived in London?"

He gave her a wary look. "Yes."

"You're very brave."

He gave her an even warier look. "Why do you say that?"

She chuckled. "Most men of your age would hate having to take on a pair of young sisters, especially when you are making an entrance into society."

"No, I am very glad to have them with me."

It was not simply a polite phrase, Hope realized. He meant it. She looked at him thoughtfully. "But is it not a great bother, having to take them on outings and keep them entertained? Most people I know would leave that to a governess."

He gave her a dry look and said, "We have tried governesses, but they never seem to take. Cassie is something of a handful."

Her eyes twinkled at him. "You could always send them away to school," she said lightly.

"I would *never* send them away, never!" He spoke so vehemently it surprised them both. They strolled on for some moments, but his vehemence hung in the air between them.

He kept glancing back to check on his sisters.

She said with mild reproof, "My twin is very responsible, and we've known James all our lives. I know you don't approve of his skills as a groom, but I assure you he is both sturdy and protective."

At her words he jumped, as if pulled back from some unpleasant thought. "I'm sorry. I didn't mean to be uncivil." He said, then added awkwardly, "I lost them once, you see."

"Lost them?"

"Yes. I left them with a woman, paid her to take care of them. But she took them away, and so I lost them." His arm was stiff under her hand, and the hand covering hers gripped hard. She was sure he was unaware of it.

"How long did you lose them for?"

There was a long pause before two bitter words rasped out. "Too long."

She wondered how long was too long, but he'd said it with such bitter self-recrimination she didn't like to ask. Instead she said, "I'm sure you are too hard on yourself. Surely your parents should carry the main responsibility for your sisters' care."

He shook his head. "My parents were dead. It was my

fault." He stared out across the gray surface of the lake. He looked so desolate, she wanted to hug him.

She pressed his hand sympathetically. "I'm sure it was not your fault, entirely, Mr. Reyne. And you obviously found them again, safe and well, so is it not time to forgive yourself?"

He looked down at her hand resting on his and frowned as he realized how he'd been holding her. He pulled his hand away and said awkwardly. "I don't know why I told you that. I . . . I didn't mean to."

"I'm honored by your confidence," she assured him. "How did you hurt your hand?"

Instantly he thrust it in his pocket. "I'm sorry," he repeated. "I know it is hideous. I did not expect—"

"It isn't hideous in the least!" she interrupted fiercely. "It is merely a hand with two damaged fingers. And if you want to know the truth, I liked the way you covered my hand with yours. It felt . . . nice. Warm. Strong."

Knowing she had gone too far, she blushed and looked away. "I'm sorry, I shouldn't have said that. Please forget it." She tried to tug her hand out from his arm, but he kept it pressed tight to his side.

"Stay, lass." There was command, as well as a faint hint of brogue in the way he said it.

She stared up at him. He stared back, her arm pressed possessively against his side. She could feel his heart thudding. His eyes seemed to devour her. Slowly, slowly his hand rose until it touched her cheek, so lightly and tenderly that if it was not for the heat radiating from him, she would never have felt it. She could not help herself; of its own volition her cheek rubbed against him. His eyes blazed, and she lifted her face to his in mute invitation. He cupped her jaw, stared at her a long, long moment, and slowly lowered his mouth toward hers. Hope leaned forward and clutched him and—there was a splash and a scream.

"The girls!" He dropped her and ran back the way they'd walked.

Hope stood there, trembling, poised on the edge of . . .

nothing. He'd been about to kiss her, right there among the willow fronds. And disgraceful as she knew it to be, she would have let him. In fact, she would have kissed him right back. Shamelessly.

Gathering her scattered wits, she hurried after him. Rounding the bend in the path, she could see the whole scene. Cassie had fallen into the duck pond. She was floundering in the murky water, splashing and squealing, half with laughter and half with frustration as she tried to climb the slippery bank and fell back. The ducks had long since fled.

In seconds her brother reached her, and without hesitation he stepped into the water and picked her out of it. She immediately fell stiff and silent. All traces of laughter were wiped from her face.

He carried her to a bench and set her carefully down. "Are you all right, Cassie? How did it happen? Are you cold? Here, take this." He shrugged off his own coat and wrapped her in it.

Cassie endured it with a closed look on her face. She was embarrassed, Hope saw, as well as angry. Angry with herself, perhaps, Hope speculated, for attracting so much of her brother's attention.

"I'm all right," Cassie muttered ungraciously as he drew a handkerchief from his pocket and began to wipe her face. She snatched it from his hand and wiped her own face. She looked a sight with her hair hanging in sodden rat's tails and her blue muslin dress ruined by weeds and mud. It clung to her body like a second skin.

"The ducks had a wonderful feed at any rate," Grace said, breaking the awkward moment.

"I'm sure they have, greedy things," said Hope in a hearty voice. "Luckily they were probably too full to eat Cassie." She grinned at Cassie, and the girl's sullen mouth softened.

That's when Hope noticed it. Under the sopping blue fabric, what looked like the sheath of a knife was strapped to Cassie's thigh.

Hope glanced at Faith to see if she had noticed. She had. Her twin's eyes were troubled. Grace noticed, too. "Is that a kni—" she began, but Faith stopped her in time with a sisterly nip on the arm.

"We'd better get this girl home and into a bath," said Mr. Reyne, apparently unaware of the undercurrents. "Miss Hope, Miss Faith, Miss Grace, I bid you good-bye. Cassie, Dorie, let us go. The carriage is waiting."

Hope walked with them to the carriage, while Faith and Grace fed the last of the bread to the ducks. The girls hurried ahead, as if anxious that he should have nothing to do with them.

He hadn't looked at Hope since that almost-kiss. Why not? Cassie was perfectly all right, just wet and muddy and cross.

The girls scrambled into the carriage. Hope and Mr. Reyne were some yards away from it when Hope said, "Mr. Reyne?" She was surprised to hear her voice was steady. "I did enjoy our walk. And our talk." *And I wish you'd kissed me.* The words hung unspoken in the air between them.

He paused, then turned back. Faint ruddy color darkened his cheekbones. He began stiffly, "I must apologize, Miss Merridew. I had no right—" He broke off, cleared his throat, and said in a hard voice, "It was a mistake. I have come to London with the specific intention of courting Lady Elinore Whitelaw."

It was like a slap in the face.

He continued, "I am sorry if I misled—"

Mortified, Hope cut him off, saying in a falsely bright tone, "Apologize, Mr. Reyne? Whatever for? Nothing happened, after all. A stroll in a very public park with my sisters and yours close by. I am sure nobody could object to that."

She wished the earth could swallow her up. She wished she had never got up this morning, never come to the park. It was clear from his demeanor that he'd thought her forward, that she had been the one making the moves. He probably wouldn't have thought to kiss her except that she had encouraged him.

It occurred to her that her and her sister's status as beauties made them less fit to cope with normal life than most females. Hope had never been rejected by a young man before. It didn't matter that she had never offered herself, even the smallest part of herself, to a man before. She'd offered herself to this man—a kiss in a public park, no less— and he'd baldly rejected her. In favor of a notoriously eccentric and plain older woman.

She could feel her cheeks warming again and turned away, saying, "I think it is going to rain soon. We should hurry home. Good-bye, Mr. Reyne." She shook his hand briskly, trying not to recall that the same hand had cupped her cheek so tenderly only moments before. She waved to the girls. "Good-bye, Cassie, Dorie. I hope we shall meet again one day."

"Oh, we will," Cassie responded. "Miss Faith and Grace have invited us to go with you to Green Park tomorrow morning."

Hope blinked.

"If Mr. Reyne permits it, of course, Cassie," Faith reminded her gently as she came up behind Hope.

Cassie said nothing, just glowered at her brother.

Hope clenched her fingers, willing him to refuse the treat. He could take his sisters to Green Park himself. She didn't want to be thrown together with the Reyne family any more than could be helped. She watched him from the corner of her eye.

He hesitated, glanced at Dorie, whose eyes were fixed on his in silent entreaty, and nodded. "Of course. What time would you like the girls to be ready, Miss Merridew?"

Hope said nothing. Faith made the arrangements to collect the girls in the morning, and then they all went their separate ways.

# Chapter Seven

∞

*Doubts are more cruel than the worst of truths.*
MOLIERE

THEY WALKED HOME IN SILENCE, RATHER MORE QUIETLY THAN they had come.

"Are you all right, Hope? You look a little upset." Faith took her sister's arm as they walked back to Great Uncle Oswald's house in Providence Court. Grace walked ahead, talking to James.

"It's nothing, a touch of the headache, that's all." Hope lied, adding in what she hoped was a light tone, "That man is so difficult to talk to. It's like getting blood out of a stone."

Faith gave her a doubtful look. "It didn't look like you were having difficulty communicating. And you don't look as if you have the headache—you look upset."

It was almost impossible to deceive her twin, so Hope changed the subject. "Lady Thorn is arranging a masquerade ball, had you heard? The count is to be guest of honor. She's calling it a Hungarian gypsy ball, and we are to dress in costume!"

"I had heard," said Faith quietly. "I think it's a delightful notion."

They walked on a few steps. Her sister was blushing slightly. Hope said quietly, "You seem very interested in the count, twin."

"Count Rimavska is quite the finest musician I have ever heard." Faith's blush intensified. Hope sighed. She hoped he wasn't Faith's dream man, but with Faith blushing like this over nothing, she very much feared he was.

Faith darted her a look. "You find him flamboyant and showy, I know."

Hope said nothing. She couldn't deny it.

"His clothing and presentation is part of his expression as an artiste," explained Faith gently.

Hope nodded. "If you like him, Faith, then I am sure he is charming."

Her twin smiled shyly but did not say any more. Hope pondered the problem. She could not at all see why her sister would be so enraptured by the pretty count—apart from his music—but then, Faith didn't understand why she could be attracted to Mr. Reyne, either.

"Faith, do you have tender feelings for him?"

Faith blushed even harder, but she shook her head. "It is too early to say."

"Be careful, twin, will you?" Hope said. "You don't know him very well. You're very softhearted, you know. You need to keep your heart well-guarded until the right man comes along. And you must be sure he *is* the right man."

Faith gave her a wry look. "You don't know Mr. Reyne very well, and yet, what was it I saw just before, under the willow tree? You let him kiss you."

Mortified, Hope blustered, "No! I did not kiss anyone!"

"I could see you through the willow leaves, you were swaying toward him, face upturned! I've never seen you look so. Oh, Hope, what is it like, to have such strong feelings for a man?"

Hope said sadly, "I wouldn't know. He is not interested in me."

"I don't believe you."

"It's true. He told me to my face. He has come to London for the sole purpose of courting Lady Elinore Whitelaw."

Faith put her arm around Hope. "Then he is not the one," she said soothingly. "I didn't think he was."

Hope sighed. "No."

They came up to James and Grace, waiting on the steps of Great Uncle Oswald's house. Grace rapped the knocker. Niblett, Great Uncle Oswald's ancient butler, opened the door, and knowing his penchant for gossip, neither girl spoke until they were upstairs.

The moment they were alone, Faith continued, "Any man who treats his sisters like that could not be the man for you."

Hope was puzzled by the vehemence in Faith's normally gentle voice. "What do you mean? I didn't notice any ill-treatment of his sisters."

Faith replied, "Not when we were there, no. But you must have noticed how Cassie changed when he pulled her from the water."

"She was embarrassed."

"That wasn't all. She hated him touching her. It was obvious. And—you saw it, I know—she wears what looks to me like a knife strapped to her leg! What does that say about Mr. Reyne, eh?"

Hope frowned and said slowly. "I did wonder about the knife."

"And little Dorie is so silent and haunted-looking, poor child. Something must account for it. And do you know, several pieces of that stale old bread never reached the ducks."

Hope frowned.

Faith nodded. "Yes! I don't think Grace noticed, but I certainly did; Dorie surreptitiously pocketed stale bread. There's something wrong there, and those two poor little creatures are under the care of their brother, a man who Mrs. Jenner says has a terrible reputation. I am sorry you are sad, Hope darling, but I am glad to see you out of his clutches."

She laid her hand on Hope's shoulder and said earnestly, "If anyone needs to guard her heart it is you,

dearest! And if you must worry about someone else, don't
worry about me—worry about those two poor little girls."

Faith's words returned to haunt Hope that evening as she
lay in bed, trying to get to sleep. Sleep had never been her
friend. Either it brought nightmares stealing out of the dark
to swallow her whole, or it eluded her as she wrestled with
thoughts, as was the case tonight.

She tossed and turned, her night rail twisting about her
body. The gossip about him was rife. The accusations of
murder were, she was fairly certain, salacious inventions.
The ton was full of such horrid stories. There was no way
two rich people dying suspiciously and a third poor one
inheriting a fortune as a result would not be thoroughly
investigated.

Nor was he a fortune hunter. It didn't make sense. He
was rich himself. Besides, it was no secret that the Merridew girls would inherit their great uncle's reputedly enormous fortune. Sebastian Reyne would know she stood to
inherit as least as much as Lady Elinore. And without being vulgar or immodest, why choose the older, dowdy
heiress over the younger prettier one?

But there was definitely something wrong with his sisters. Hope had to agree. Having been subject to the cruelty
of their insane grandfather throughout their youth, the Merridew girls recognized certain symptoms in others.

In the park, he'd seemed protective of the girls. She'd
thought it rather sweet of him. But now, she wondered.

People used to think Grandpapa was protective, but he
wasn't. With Grandpapa it was all about power, control,
tyranny . . .

That story Mr. Reyne told her about losing his
sisters . . . Had the girls tried to run away from him? As
Hope and her sisters had escaped from Grandpapa?

*"If anyone needs to guard her heart it is you, dearest!
And if you must worry about someone else . . . worry about
those two little girls."*

That's what she would do, Hope decided with sleepy resolution. She would discover what she could about those young sisters of his. If those two children were in any danger whatsoever, she would save them. She knew what it was like to grow up in fear. Hope would not stand by and watch it happen to others, not without trying to do something to help.

It would mean seeing a great deal more of Mr. Sebastian Reyne. There was a risk in that; Faith was right. Hope would have to guard her heart. Even knowing he was courting Lady Elinore, even with her doubts about his sisters, she was still, reluctantly, drawn to him.

But then—she yawned, sleepy at last—she had ever been perverse.


Sebastian woke at his usual hour. He lay there for a few moments, stretched, and climbed out of bed. The city had not yet begun to hum.

He rose, washed, and dressed by candlelight. He walked softly down the hallway to the girls' room and opened the door. Since they'd gone missing, he always looked in on them, first thing in the morning, last thing at night. As he had when they were babies.

Dorie had climbed into Cassie's bed, as usual. Sebastian tiptoed over. The two children lay curled together, like kittens, their little sleeping faces washed free of care. He wished they always looked so. As he turned to leave, a floorboard creaked under his foot, and Cassie started. A blade flashed in the faint dawn light.

"It's all right, Cassie, it's only me," he said softly. "Go back to sleep. You're safe."

She grunted, the knife disappeared back under her pillow, and she snuggled back down in the blankets. Dorie hadn't moved, but he was certain she was awake. She was too still and tense to be anything else. "Sleep well, Dorie. You are safe, too," he murmured.

Sebastian closed the door carefully behind him. His

heart felt like a lump of lead. Would his failure to protect them forever haunt these little innocents?

He thought of going for a ride, but ever since he'd met Miss Merridew on horseback, his early morning rides hadn't granted him the oblivion they used to. He was always looking over his shoulder, searching for a slender feminine figure galloping *ventre à terre* on a bay horse.

He went to his office, lit the lantern at his desk, and began to work. There were letters to read and to write, accounts to check, instructions to send, shipping news, reports to read: a mountain of work in which to lose himself. Thank God for the demands of business.

Shortly after nine o'clock there was a knock at the front door. Since Sebastian happened to be walking past it at the time, he opened the door. Behind him, a footman skidded to a halt.

A sudden hush fell as his face became visible to the visitors. As if they'd been talking about him. Three pairs of glorious blue eyes regarded him coolly.

"Good day, Mr. Reyne," Miss Hope said. "We are calling for Cassie and Dorie, as arranged." She held out two fingers of a gloved hand and did not quite meet his eye. She looked . . . wary. Every other time she'd met him, she'd given him a warm, wonderful smile. Today there was no smile.

He'd intended just such a response when he'd brusquely informed her of his courtship of Lady Elinore, the day before. He hadn't realized how much he'd miss her smile. He felt it like an ache.

Absurdly hurt, he barely touched her fingers and stepped back. He said stiffly, "Please come in. The girls are not quite ready yet."

Miss Merridew and her sisters entered, followed by their footman bearing a large urn and a strapping young maidservant with a basket over her arm. The maidservant eyed him curiously.

"I'll send someone upstairs to fetch them." He snapped

his fingers to the tardy footman, who immediately ran upstairs.

Miss Faith arched her eyebrows at her sister, then saw he'd noticed the gesture. "An unfashionable hour to call, I admit," she said, "but since we were going to Green Park, we thought the girls might enjoy watching the cows being milked."

"Cows?" Sebastian frowned.

Seeing his puzzlement, Miss Hope explained, "There is a herd kept in Green Park to provide London residents with fresh milk."

Sebastian nodded brusquely. He had no interest in cows, particularly when she had not looked at him the entire time she was talking to him.

As soon as they came downstairs, he would wave the girls off and return to his accounts and reports. He was a busy man and had more important things to think about than whether or not her feelings had been hurt.

Morton Black was keeping an eye on local events in the mill, but it was a potential powder keg. And a cotton shipment was late. The mine production figures were showing several anomalies, and a report from the shipping company was annoyingly incomplete. Several blistering letters were in order.

He wished his courtship of Lady Elinore was completed. He was very good at accepting reality. It was knowing that things were not settled between them yet that was making his mind unsettled and his body rebellious.

If only Miss Merridew hadn't dressed in that soft muslin walking dress that caressed her curves with loving subtlety. And chosen a tight blue silk spencer that hugged her bosom. Her bonnet was in the same blue silk, and the effect of all this glorious blue was to make him feel he could drown in her eyes.

And if only her mouth wasn't solemn and doubtful instead of smiling cheerfully, he wouldn't now be battling with the need to take back those words he'd spoken, to make her smile and look up at him the way she had under that willow.

And he wouldn't have lost sleep wishing he'd kissed those tender pink lips just one more time.

"Good morning, everyone!" Cassie clattered down the stairs, followed by Dorie. "I'm sorry we're late. Nobody came to wake us, so we slept in." She darted an irritated look at Sebastian, who had given orders that they were to be allowed to sleep as late as they needed. He knew from his morning and evening checks on them that they were unusually light sleepers for children, and he had an idea that Dorie, in particular, suffered from sleeplessness. Something had to account for those shadows under her eyes.

Cassie pulled on her bonnet, and Sebastian was touched when young Grace Merridew went to help Dorie with hers. The two children were of an age, but Grace glowed with health and confidence, and Dorie was pinched and little and pale. Dorie gave Grace a shy smile, and Sebastian's mind was made up.

Dorie had just smiled.

He had to look away, to collect himself.

Miss Hope was watching him. He swallowed. A morass had opened up before him. He had to allow Dorie to see more of Grace Merridew. He would do anything for more of those shy little smiles, even if they weren't directed at him.

It would take some clever planning, since he intended to eschew Grace's sister's company, but not impossible. He was good at planning. He would plan to avoid Miss Hope.

Sebastian prided himself on his self-control. He had learned early to subdue his personal desires in order to do what needed to be done. All his life he'd had other people depending on him, and he was not about to forget that simply because of a beautiful, blue-eyed chit. With a luscious mouth.

The girls were ready. The footman-in-training hurried to open the door. Sebastian stepped forward, intending to see them off. The girls were in good hands, he told himself. The Merridew twins would look after them.

Miss Hope looked up at him with those glorious blue eyes and said softly, stiffly. "You don't need to worry, we'll take good care of them. And I'm sure they'll enjoy themselves."

Sebastian swallowed. He tried not to look at the slight curve of her soft mouth, tried not to recall the taste, the feel of her lips under his.

Staring at that mouth, it occurred to Sebastian suddenly that he had never been to Green Park himself. He ought to ensure that it was a safe place for his sisters. For all he knew, it could attract the worst sort of riffraff. The footman was a sturdy-looking fellow, but he hadn't impressed Sebastian when he'd acted groom. And there were five females to protect, six if you counted the maid.

He glanced at Miss Hope again and swallowed. It was extraordinary what that particular shade of blue silk did to her eyes. And her delicate complexion glowed.

He wondered whether the sprigged muslin was a foreign import or whether it was a local product. It would be useful to find out. As a textile manufacturer, he ought to know such things.

"I shall accompany you," he announced.

Cassie immediately glared at him; Doric's face remained unreadable. The three Misses Merridew exchanged glances. The temperature in the vestibule dropped significantly. What the devil was up, he wondered. Each Merridew sister was regarding him with varying degrees of cool disapproval.

Miss Faith Merridew opened her mouth, but before she could say anything, Miss Hope said, "That would be delightful, Mr. Reyne, would it not, Faith?"

Her twin murmured something polite, looking anything but delighted.

They must have noticed Cassie's knife, after all. He'd hoped that under the folds of sopping fabric yesterday the outline of the leather scabbard would not have been recognizable to ladies. Seemingly it had been. And the ladies blamed him.

Fair enough. Sebastian blamed himself, too.

The footman produced his coat, hat, and gloves, and Sebastian stepped out into the weak morning sunshine. To his surprise, no carriage awaited them, and he wondered if perhaps their great-uncle did not keep a carriage in town. He should call for his own, for it was a fair distance from Hill Street to Green Park, but before he could speak, the group was moving at a brisk pace down the street.

The footman and maid led the procession, next were Cassie and Grace, and then Miss Faith with Dorie's hand held in hers. Cassie and Grace walked, arms linked and heads together, chattering like old friends instead of acquaintances of one day. He glanced at Dorie, walking silently and demurely with Miss Faith. He would give anything to see her chattering girlish nonsense like the other two.

"Coming?" Miss Hope prompted him. She seemed to have put away her earlier stiffness, though she was still cool and reserved compared to before.

"Sorry. Woolgathering," he explained as they hurried down the street after the others.

"Your thoughts didn't seem happy ones."

"Not at all," Sebastian said shortly. He wasn't going to explain. The last time he'd confided in her, he'd almost kissed her—and in Hyde Park, of all public places! He'd already told her far too much. And somehow her arm had become tucked into the crook of his, which was a little unnerving, since he didn't remember doing it—had vowed in fact never to do it again.

"I was merely wondering whether to order my carriage. Green Park seems rather a long way for ladies and young girls to walk."

She laughed. "We don't need a carriage. It's such a pleasant morning, and whenever the weather is fine, we enjoy a brisk walk while we can. We were brought up in the country, you know, and are much addicted to walking. I hope you don't mind."

"I don't mind." He drew her aside to avoid a man hurrying along with a large tray of muffins on his head. "But at this time of day the streets are full of clumsy oafs like that." He nodded at the muffin man. "Tradespeople, butcher's boys, servants, and all sorts of riffraff."

"Yes, indeed. It's so interesting, isn't it?" she said, sniffing. "Don't those muffins smell delicious? I never saw half so many different sorts of people in my life before I came to London. We lived a very restricted life before then."

Sebastian grunted. It was not what he meant at all. He had meant that as a highborn lady, she ought to be sheltered from this sort of company. He was sure Lady Elinore would never walk such a distance to Green Park, relishing the crowded pavements and rubbing shoulders with the hoi polloi, despite her work with female orphans.


Apparently Green Park at this hour of the morning was the place for nurses to bring their charges out for air. It thronged with children. The Merridew girls seemed quite accustomed to the scene and happily ducked flying balls, bowling hoops, and pull-along carts as they made their way toward the herd of dairy cows. The air was filled with shrieks, laughter, piercing whistles, and one very persistent drum, where a squad of very short soldiers drilled with sticks. Sebastian had to wait at one point while Miss Hope stopped and fed an invisible apple to a wooden hobby horse and discussed its paces with its serious young rider.

By the time Miss Hope resumed the walk, Sebastian had slipped into a pensive mood. He'd never imagined children could live such carefree lives. If he ever had, he'd forgotten it.

The cows lowed and pushed as they waited to be milked. Dairymaids, under the supervision of the cowman, sat on low stools, milking busily. Creamy white milk spurted into pails. People lined up to purchase the fresh milk, bearing all sorts of containers with which to carry the milk home.

This was where the fresh milk for London ladies' morning chocolate came from, Miss Faith explained to Sebastian's sisters. They seemed fascinated by the cows. Sebastian was puzzled. He'd always believed Widow Morgan had taken them to live on her brother's farm, yet they appeared fascinated by a sight he'd assumed they would have grown up with.

"Do cows not have beautiful eyes?" remarked Miss Hope. "Liquid amber, fathoms deep. I would love to have lovely eyes like that."

Sebastian stared at her in amazement. "But your eyes are much loveli—" He broke off, recalling his resolution not to encourage any form of intimacy with her, and covered his lapse with a violent cough.

He was only here now to keep an eye on his sisters. And to investigate the source of the sprigged muslin Miss Hope was wearing. For business reasons. With determination, he turned away from Miss Hope and watched his sisters.

Cassie frowned as she watched the dairymaid's strong hands pull rhythmically on the cow's udders. Streams of creamy milk jetted into a bucket. "Does that not hurt the poor cow?" she asked.

The Merridews' buxom maidservant answered, "Not a bit of it, missy. It'd hurt 'em more if they weren't milked."

Cassie looked to the twins for confirmation. Hope explained, "Lily lived on a farm before coming to work in my grandfather's household."

Sebastian raised a brow. "I thought Sir Oswald was your great uncle, not your grandfather."

"He is. He is our grandfather's brother," Hope said.

Grace added fiercely, "Grandpapa is the biggest, horridest beast in the world, and we hate him!" She glanced at her sisters and added, "But we don't live with him now, and so everything is all right."

Sebastian waited for one of the twins to comment, but their footman arrived with a large jug of the fresh milk, and the moment was lost. Sebastian was disappointed. He would have liked to hear more about this grandfather. Young Grace was certainly very vehement.

"Now, girls, who would like a cup of milk?" Miss Faith asked. "I promise you, if you haven't tasted fresh milk still warm from the cow, there's a treat in store for you. Lily has the cups, and James will pour. Cassie? Dorie?"

Cassie and Grace nodded. Dorie hesitated, but to Sebastian's surprise, she stepped forward and held out her hand. She sipped the milk gingerly, and then her solemn little face cleared, and she drank the whole cup down. Lily, the maidservant, grinned. "Tastes good, don't it, missy? Want some more?"

Dorie cast her a fleeting smile and held out the cup again. Sebastian was stunned. He watched as the footman refilled the cup and passed it back to Dorie. She took it from him without hesitation and drained the cup.

Two cups of milk. It was the most Sebastian had seen her eat in one sitting. It was a start, he thought gratefully. He had done the right thing by bringing them to London. Thank God Miss Merridew had invited them to the park this morning. Thank God he'd gone with them. He might not otherwise have discovered Dorie would drink milk. Two cups of fresh milk each day might put some flesh on those frail little bones. It might put some roses in her cheeks . . .

What a morning; two smiles and two cups of milk.

Hope stood back, observing. The Reynes were an enigmatic little family. Cassie and Dorie seemed to want nothing to do with their big brother, and he almost never addressed them or engaged them in conversation.

Yet now he watched over them like a big, silent mastiff, and watching his face as the girls drank their milk, she could almost swear he was moved by the sight.

Though how she gained that impression, she couldn't say; his was not an expressive face. It was a strong face, hard and uncompromising in some ways. Stubborn. And his eyes were hard and gray and bleak. But when they softened . . . and Hope had seen them soften . . . then he was quite a different-looking man.

"Look. There's a crowd gathering. I wonder what it is?" Grace exclaimed, catching Cassie's hand in hers. Cassie glanced around, grabbed Dorie, and the three of them ran off. James handed Lily the jug, saying to Hope, "I'll go with them, miss," but Mr. Reyne was before him.

"I'll fetch them," he announced. "They ought to know better than to run off like that!" He strode grimly off.

Faith caught her eye. "It's as if he's afraid of letting them out from under his thumb."

Hope's heart sank, knowing there was a worrying degree of truth in the statement. The Merridew girls knew all about men who needed to keep little girls firmly under their thumb.

Faith said quietly, "Do you think he beats his sisters the way Grandpapa used to beat us?"

"Hush, Faith! We know nothing about him, and it is not right to speculate. Besides, I don't believe Mr. Reyne is at all like Grandpapa! In anything except physique." She couldn't imagine Grandpapa riding to save someone the way Mr. Reyne had tried to rescue her from her so-called runaway horse. That morning, Mr. Reyne had been gentle and protective. Such words were not even in Grandpapa's vocabulary.

"You cannot deny there is something wrong with those girls."

"Yes, but we cannot know he is the cause."

Her sister looked at her thoughtfully. Hope knew what she was thinking. She was defending him too forcefully for someone who did not care. She fought a rising blush and said mildly, "I said we would find out more about the girls, and we shall. On our way back, you talk to Cassie, and I will talk to Mr. Reyne."

"Wouldn't you rather *I* talked to Mr. Reyne?" Faith suggested gently.

Hope did blush then. "No, it's all right. I will."

• • •

Mr. Reyne returned, shepherding the girls in front of him. He looked angry and frustrated, Cassie and Grace looked mutinous, but Dorie's face was still and blank.

It was a terrible look: it reminded Hope of her twin in the days when they lived in Norfolk, when Grandpapa was in a rage. Faith used to go still and silent and shrink into herself, making herself as small and insignificant as possible in order not to attract Grandpapa's attention, Grandpapa's violence.

Dorie looked like that just now. And her brother was angry.

Hope couldn't bear it. She hurried forward and took each of the Reyne girls by the hand. "I have thought of something delightful! We shall all go to Gunter's for an ice! What do you think of that?" It was far too early to be thinking of an ice, but she was desperate to put a happy look back on that child's face.

He said curtly, "Thank you, no. I have just recalled I have an engagement in an less than half an hour. Business, Important business. My sisters and I need to return home directly. I'm sorry if it inconveniences you, but I had not planned to spend the whole morning in idle pleasure seeking."

Hope blinked. "Idle pleasure seeking? A walk in the park and a cup of fresh milk is hardly dissipation."

His stern visage softened. "No, you are right. That cup of milk . . . I am most grateful, Miss Hope, Miss Faith, Miss Grace." He bowed to each of them with stiff precision. "Nevertheless, we must return immediately. I intend to hire a hackney cab to convey us home. May I offer you a lift?"

Mindful of the plan to discover the reason for the girls' behavior, Hope was about to accept when Faith said instead, "Thank you, no. We prefer to walk."

"Very well then. Good-bye, ladies. Make your curtsy, girls."

The girls curtsied, and Cassie thanked them very prettily for the outing. As she watched the threesome walk briskly toward the nearest exit, it suddenly occurred to Hope that she'd never seen Sebastian Reyne touch his sisters in public. Except for that time he'd pulled Cassie from the water, he never held them by the hand or walked with their arm tucked into his. He didn't so much as pat them on the head.

Grandpapa had never touched his granddaughters, either. Except to beat them.

She watched them go, torn by conflicting feelings.

"Come on, Hope, let's go home," Faith said quietly.

"We don't know anything—not for certain," Hope said quickly. Faith had not voiced the accusation, but she knew what her twin was thinking.

"No, we have no proof."


Twenty minutes later, as they walked home in silence, an elegant green and black curricle passed them in the street. Mr. Reyne was driving. A liveried footman clung on behind. Beside Mr. Reyne sat Lady Elinore Whitelaw.

They watched the curricle turn the corner. "His important business engagement," Faith remarked. "I wonder, does she know he refers to her courtship as a business matter?"

# Chapter Eight

*I . . . chose my wife, as she did her wedding gown, not for a fine glossy surface,
but such qualities as would wear well.*

OLIVER GOLDSMITH

"I AM VERY GLAD YOU DECIDED TO ACCOMPANY ME THIS MORN-
ing, Lady Elinore." Sebastian slowed the horses to a trot as
they entered a narrow, cobbled street in the east end of the
city. It was not precisely a slum, but it was not the sort of
place where he would expect to see a lady of Lady Elinore's quality. No wonder she had brought her footman instead of a maid. He'd wondered at the time. She seemed
such a stickler for the proprieties. But a footman would offer the sort of protection a maid could not.

She was wearing gray again. Gray dress, gray pelisse,
and a gray bonnet. All plainly cut and unembellished.

Lady Elinore inclined her head graciously at his words,
swaying subtly away from him as they turned the corner.
She'd done it every time, avoiding even the slightest brush
against his shoulder, no matter how much the curricle
swayed. It might be propriety, but Sebastian suspected it
was more than that: she did not like to be touched. It made
courtship more difficult, but it was no real bar to the kind

of marriage he was set on. He was marrying for practical reasons, not for passion.

A vision of Hope Merridew sprang to mind. He forced it away. If he had no responsibilities, if he were a free agent, he would pursue Miss Hope Merridew with all his heart. But she was a . . . a . . . He groped for a suitable word. A silken elf, a fragile creature from a world he could never inhabit, full of laughter and high spirits.

If he took such a delicate creature into the mess he had made of three lives, it would crush the spirit out of her, and that he could never bear.

It was hard enough to bear her new cold looks. His own fault. His intention. He'd had to tell her about Lady Elinore. He needed that barrier between them to protect her. At the lakeside the day before, he'd all but disgraced her in a public park. He would have kissed her, which would have taken things further.

Sebastian Reyne, reaching for the moon again. When would he learn?

He forced his mind back to the matter at hand. And the woman. "I am sure your presence must lend weight to my cause, Lady Elinore. I am aware that my offer is a controversial one and that not all of your associates agree."

Lady Elinore's gray bonnet bobbed in agreement. "I must confess I opposed it when you first broached the matter, but now I understand your motives better, I have changed my mind. I am certain our charges will benefit from your involvement, and I know that several of our patronesses are under some financial strain: something to do with investments and the late war." She grimaced and shook her head. "Your purchase of the institution will relieve their difficulties."

"Happy to be of service."

She had no idea of his real motives. No one did. Sebastian was even uncertain himself. All he knew was that he had to buy this particular orphan asylum. No other one would do.

No other institution had housed his sisters, after all.

Lady Elinore had no idea of his relationship with the place. Morton Black's investigations had shown that Lady Elinore's mother had died just before Cassie and Dorie had been brought to the institution. Girls brought in were routinely renamed, though their original names were recorded in a book. Morton Black had been willing to destroy that page, but as it turned out, there was no need. There could be no traceable connection between Carrie and Doreen Morgan and Cassandra and Eudora Reyne.

Sebastian reined in his horses, and the curricle drew up outside a tall, narrow building of grim aspect.

He leaped down and held out a hand to assist Lady Elinore down. She barely touched him. Even her gloves were gray. "Forgive my ignorance, but are you in half mourning, Lady Elinore?"

She shook her head. "No. Not at all. It is not quite a year since my mother died, it is true, but mourning dictated by convention is not a belief I subscribe to. If it is the color of my clothing you are referring to, the choice is deliberate. I have worn gray all my life, as did my late mother. Colors inflame the masculine passions."

Sebastian raised a brow. "Do they?"

"Yes. My late mother, Lady Ennismore, made a close study of such things. If all females understood it and avoided colorful clothing, our lives would be much more peaceful and rational."

"Indeed," Sebastian murmured noncommittally. If everyone wore gray, it would make life a great deal drearier, in his opinion. Nor would it be profitable for the textile trade.

His doubt must have been inadequately disguised, for as they mounted the steps to the front entrance of the building, Lady Elinore explained earnestly, "It is quite true. My mother conducted a number of scientific investigations and published them in a book; you may have heard of it: *The Principles of Rationality for Enlightened Ladies*."

Sebastian confessed that he hadn't heard of it.

"I shall present you with a copy, then, for I am hoping to

get this entire institution run according to my mother's Principles. I have already made some innovations, but not all of the other ladies agree. But I digress, for we were discussing the hue of my attire. Mother found that gray was the color that most inspired neutrality in masculine breasts."

Sebastian could not argue with that. There was not a lot one could say about gray, he had to admit. And observing her in her gray ensemble, he also admitted to a strong feeling of neutrality.

She tugged the bellpull. A bell clanged in the far recesses of the house, and in an instant the door was opened by a large woman dressed in a black serge dress.

She conducted them in silence to a large room in which six ladies sat waiting for him. They ranged in age from a beefy matron of about fifty to a desiccated old stick who had to be well past eighty. Three were dressed in unrelieved, unadorned gray, one was dressed in black, and the remaining two were dressed in such brilliant colors, Sebastian almost blinked at the contrast.

As he entered, six pairs of eyes narrowed with varying degrees of approval and suspicion. Sebastian was accustomed to the scrutiny of strangers. He did not care, as long as he got what he wanted.

"Ladies," he said, after the introductions had been made. "You have known of my interest for some time, so I'll not beat about the bush. I would like to purchase this institution. You have my assurance in writing that I will continue its good work, and you have had Lady Elinore testify to my character. Furthermore, I am willing to allow three of you to remain on in an advisory capacity, so all that is left is for me to make the offer." He named a sum, and from the sounds of the stifled gasps, it was more than acceptable. He stood up. "Perhaps someone will show me around, while you are discussing my offer. As you know, I have never before ventured past the entrance." And he was curious to see the place that had taken in his sisters.

"I shall escort you," Lady Elinore said. "Everyone here knows my views about the sale."

She conducted Sebastian around the building, explaining the purpose of the establishment and answering all his questions. He was interested in the place, but not so much the theories behind it. He knew nothing about the upbringing of girls. As long as the inmates were clean and warm and well fed and cared for, he didn't mind how the place was run. He left that to others, who had knowledge and beliefs about how it should be done.

And Lady Elinore, he discovered, had very passionate beliefs. "The thing is, Mr. Reyne, these girls—through no fault of their own—have been exposed to the vilest aspects of human nature. We must redress that imbalance, so that they can recover from their ordeals and grow up to live useful, respectable lives."

She talked of how a quiet life, with routine, study, and work, would settle down the more extreme aspects of the girls' behavior. She explained how they would grow in dignity and independence as a result. It sounded good to Sebastian. It seemed to him that she would know exactly how to manage and care for his sisters. He had made the right decision, as personally painful as it was.

He couldn't see Miss Hope Merridew settling for quiet routine, study, and work. To be honest, he couldn't quite see Cassie settling to it, either, but what he saw convinced him it must be possible.

She conducted him to a room where girls sat in rows, sewing, while a lady read aloud to them from a book. "Improving tales," explained Lady Elinore in a whisper. "Each one is about a girl who has strayed from the correct path, and each contains a moral lesson. My mother wrote it. We alternate between my mother's writings and the Bible. Replacing their former lives of depravity with a sound moral foundation."

Sebastian nodded. What did he know about the education of young girls?

"The girls learn all the domestic skills, from cooking to cleaning and dressmaking, and then are apprenticed to a trade, according to their talents and abilities. They work throughout the day, of course. We do not allow time for idle hands, for idleness leads to depravity, as everybody knows. We allow breaks for meals and also for exercise—my mother was a great believer in exercise for females. She ascribes a host of female ills to the lack of it."

It was a sound principle, he thought. Exercise breaks were more than most little factory workers got, he knew. Some of the boys and girls he'd known as a child had become crippled from fourteen hours a day on the factory floor, with no time allowed to move about or stretch their aching muscles. The moment he'd taken over as manager of the mill, he'd instituted short exercise and meal breaks, and it had paid off. No more children were crippled in his mills.

He had a sudden vision of the children running about so happily in the park and asked, "So, you take them out for walks?"

She shook her head emphatically. "No, for there are too many temptations outside, and many of these girls will backslide at the smallest opportunity. We do not allow them out until we are certain they are morally strong and prepared to resist temptation. The world is full of unscrupulous people who will prey on unprotected and gullible young females."

Sebastian thought of his sisters and nodded in heartfelt agreement. Lady Elinore's passion to care for these girls touched him. He was certain that with a little encouragement, she would redirect that compassion toward his sisters. Lord knows they needed someone, and they would have nothing to do with him. And Lady Elinore was that impossible combination, a high-bred lady of the aristocracy who understood how harsh and terrible the world could be.

She was no fragile silken elf, created purely for joy.

Lady Elinore nodded briskly. "I'm glad you approve.

Now, shall we return to see if the board has made a decision about your offer?"

Sebastian agreed. The board had decided the moment he'd named a sum, he thought cynically. But the time he'd spent being shown around the institution had not been wasted. Apart from satisfying his curiosity, he fancied he was slowly winning Lady Elinore over. She had been quite willing to dance with him or go for a drive in the park whenever asked, but she'd remained coolly reserved and formal, until now. Explaining the program, she'd become almost friendly.

He still had no idea what she thought of him, but one thing was clear: she did not have a very high opinion of men.

Sebastian was not a man who gave up when he encountered an obstacle. He felt sure that if he tried hard enough, he would eventually win Lady Elinore's respect and esteem. That was as much as he wanted. He didn't want a wife who would smother him with emotional demands. He was marrying for practical reasons.

He didn't mind her eccentricity, as long as she kept it within bounds and remained an accepted part of the ton. He even rather liked it, liked the way she stuck to her beliefs. And if the care of poor orphan girls was her passion in life, it could also be the chink in her defenses.

She would not be able to resist his offer of marriage, when it came, knowing that as his wife, she would have total sway over the running of the orphan asylum and could institute Rational Principles to her heart's content.

He might even name it after her. It would make a nice unconventional wedding present: The Lady Elinore Reyne Institution for Indigent Girls.

Giles gave a crack of laughter. "The Lady Elinore Reyne Institution for Indigent Girls? You wild, romantic dog, you! What a wedding gift! After this, all the ladies of the ton will be clamoring for their own personal orphanage!"

Sebastian gave him an austere look. "It is the sort of gift Lady Elinore would appreciate."

Giles gave a rueful laugh. "You are no doubt correct. She is certainly an unusual creature."

Sebastian frowned. "I need to speed things up, get this courtship over and done with. Do you think I should send her flowers or something? As a thank-you for her company today? A sort of courtship gesture."

Giles shook his head. "No, she says flowers are not Rational."

Sebastian raised his brows. "How do you kn—"

"Has she met the girls yet?" Giles interrupted.

"No, not yet."

"Then what are you waiting for? They're the reason for all this."

Sebastian hesitated. "I'm not so sure the girls are ready for social interaction."

"From what you've told me, they're meeting the Merridews every second moment. If that's not social interaction, I don't know what is."

"You're right. I shall arrange something immediately." He thought for a moment. "I shall send Lady Elinore a note and invite her on an outing."

"To where?"

Sebastian shrugged. "You know London better than I. You suggest a place."

Giles shook his head, laughing. "Oh, no. You won't make me responsible. Why not tell Lady Elinore you'd like to take her and your sisters somewhere and ask her for a suggestion. She's a Londoner and presumably knows the sort of thing young girls would find amusing."

"Excellent idea, Giles. I shall send her a note at once."


"It was Sir Hans Sloane who we have to thank for this splendid opportunity," Lady Elinore explained. "He was a physician, naturalist, and collector, particularly of botanical specimens, and when he died, some sixty-five years ago, he bequeathed some seventy-one thousand objects, a library, and herbarium, to King George II—he was the grandfather of our regent—for the nation."

She looked at Cassie and Dorie expectantly. They said nothing. Cassie darted a long-suffering look at Sebastian.

"Very interesting," Sebastian supplied.

"Yes, it's fascinating," Lady Elinore enthused. "They appointed trustees to see that his will was carried out, and after a great deal of debate, an Act of Parliament established the British Museum." She gestured to the edifice. "The foremost monument to rational pursuits in the world."

"Hmm," Sebastian nodded. "Most impressive."

"To my mind the botanical exhibits are the most interesting, so we shall start with them," said Lady Elinore. "You study botany, I presume, girls?"

"No," Cassie said baldly.

Lady Elinore sniffed. "I suppose you do watercolors and embroidery and Italian and music. I have nothing against the last two—it is Rational to learn another language, and while my late mother did not approve of music, I must say I have a weakness for it, myself."

"No," Cassie said again.

Lady Elinore was nonplussed. "Oh. Well, let us begin our botanical studies here. Classification is the most exciting science. The founder of modern botanical study was, oddly enough, a Swede, Dr. Carolus Linnaeus, a medical physician who—"

"Why is it odd?" Cassie interrupted.

"Because, Cassandra, he was not English, and it is not polite for young ladies to interrupt their seniors," Lady Elinore explained kindly. "Dr. Linnaeus died forty years ago, after developing a system for examining and classifying the natural world. It was called the *Systema Naturae,* which is Latin. After his death, his papers came to England, and a number of his students also came to England. One traveled, for example, on one of the voyages of Captain James Cook—you will have heard of him, I hope."

"No," said Cassie. "Is he dead, too?"

"Yes," Lady Elinore responded, oblivious of irony. "He died not long after Dr. Linnaeus, I believe, nearly forty years ago."

"Is everyone in the British Museum dead?" Cassie asked.

Lady Elinore looked perplexed, but only for a moment. "Well, yes, of course. Except for the people who work here and the visitors, of course. Now, let us view the botanical exhibition. The most marvelous plants have been collected."

"Dead plants?"

"Yes, Cassandra, of course. Plants cannot be properly preserved if they are living, can they? And these plants come from all over the world."

"So they will be all brown, not green."

"Yes."

"My friend Grace said there are Egyptian mummies here and big marble statues that Lord Elgin brought from Greece. She said they were broken, but very interesting."

Lady Elinore compressed her lips, declared, "Such things are not proper for young girls to view," and marched with a firm tread toward the botanical section.

Cassie turned to Sebastian and gave him a long, silent look.

He gave her an equally silent response through narrowed eyes, and after a moment she shrugged her shoulders and stomped after Lady Elinore, towing Dorie with her. As a demonstration of martyred dumb insolence it was masterly, but Sebastian could not find it in himself to be annoyed with her. His contentious little sister was doing quite well, given the dreary nature of the outing.

Why on earth had Lady Elinore chosen this place for an outing?

The answer came at the end of another hour of viewing pressed, brown vegetation. "You may be wondering how I know so much about the museum and all its exhibits."

"No," muttered Cassie under her breath.

Luckily Lady Elinore didn't hear her. She continued, "My late mother used to bring me here once a month. It was the special thing we did together, as mother and daughter." She smiled at the girls. "My mother, Lady Ennismore, was a famous educator and writer, you see. She was always extremely busy, giving lectures or having meetings or working. I never saw much of her when I was your age. But she always made time for this." She glanced around the big, echoing building with a fond expression. "I used to look forward to the hour we spent here, every month, just Mother and me. This place is almost like home to me."

Cassie stared at her. "That's the only time you saw your mother alone?"

Lady Elinore gave a little shake of her head and said in gentle reproof, "When one's mother is famous and has A Calling, one must make sacrifices. I am proud to be Lady Ennismore's daughter. I was bred to carry on her work."

There was a short, uncomfortable silence.

"I can see how you could become fond of this place then," Sebastian said at last. "Thank you for bringing us here."

"Oh, but we haven't nearly finished."

Cassie directed a silent glower in his direction. She was running out of her small store of acceptable behavior, he realized. Her momentary sympathy for Lady Elinore wouldn't last. He needed to get her home before she did something outrageous.

"I think the girls have taken in as much botany as they can for one day. I think it is time to return home for some refreshments."

"Very well," Lady Elinore agreed. "Though there is a great deal more to see. But a cup of tea would be most welcome."

Sebastian ushered them quickly to the carriage. As Cassie climbed in to take her seat, he said quietly, "You have been very good today, Cassie. If it continues, I shall try to think of a treat for you and Dorie."

Unfortunately, Lady Elinore overheard. "A treat? I know the very thing. I shall give you both a copy of my mother's *Improving Tales for Young Girls*."

Sebastian could tell by the rolling eyes that Cassie had heard quite enough of Lady Ennismore's ideas for education. He held his breath and stared at Cassie, conveying a silent message that if she thanked Lady Elinore graciously, he would indeed think of a very special treat. And if not . . .

Cassie gave him a cool look and said with paralyzing politeness, "Thank you, Lady Elinore. I'm sure the tales will be as fascinating as your botanical lectures."

To Sebastian's gratitude, Lady Elinore missed the irony. His gratitude did not last long, though, for Lady Elinore was moved by the compliment to wax lyrical about the collection of botanical specimens once more.

Cassie stood it for five minutes, then announced in a clear voice, "Lady Elinore, did you know I wear a knife strapped to my thigh?" She began to lift her skirt to show it.

"That's enough, Cassie," Sebastian thundered. He itched to throttle her. It was the kind of statement that had caused several of their erstwhile governesses to faint, particularly when she proceeded to pull up her dress, shamelessly baring a naked thigh in the process, and demonstrated how sharp the knife was.

Cassie eyed him cautiously and left her skirt where it was, thankfully, still decent.

"I'm sorry, Lady Elinore," he began to apologize, but stopped when he saw she was in no danger of fainting. She peered interestedly at the lump outlined by the muslin under Cassie's hand. She seemed utterly unshocked by Cassie's statement.

This was why he was courting her, he recalled. If ever she proved that she would be able to cope with Cassie's outrageousness, it would be now.

She leaned forward and said to Cassie, "Isn't it inconvenient, having to reach down under all those petticoats to get it?" There was not a trace of irony or sarcasm in her voice.

Cassie frowned. It was not the reaction she'd hoped for. She glanced suspiciously at Sebastian, as if suspecting a plot. Sebastian kept his face as blank as he could. Lady Elinore looked as if she could handle things, and he judged it better to stay out of it.

Cassie decided to call Lady Elinore's bluff. "No, I can get it easily. See?" She reached under the skirt and pulled out the knife, brandishing it fiercely. The blade glinted in the afternoon light.

Lady Elinore nodded. "Yes, a little cumbersome, but a very adequate defense. It looks nice and sharp." She reached out and took it from Cassie's surprised hand, tested the blade in an expert manner, and handed it back. "Yes, very good. A knife is useless unless it's sharp." She turned to Dorie, smiling, and said, "And Dorie, do you also have a knife?"

"No!" Cassie and Sebastian exclaimed in horrified unison. Sebastian added, "Why the devil would she?"

Lady Elinore looked at their shocked faces in some surprise. "Oh, I'm sorry. I assumed yours was an enlightened family."

"What do you mean by that?" Sebastian asked.

"Oh, my mother was a very strong advocate for ladies to carry means of their own defense."

"Means of their own defense?"

She nodded and explained in a composed manner, "There is a great deal of violence in this world, and females must look to their own defense, for males are driven by passions that are easily inflamed—as a sex, they are prone to violence—and cannot always be relied upon to be benevolent."

Indignant at the slur on his gender, Sebastian said sarcastically, "So I suppose you also carry a knife strapped to your thigh."

"Oh, no. As I said, such a large knife would be too unwieldy for me. I carry this." And she drew from the seam down the front of her bodice a long, pointed hatpin. She smiled kindly at Cassie. "Just as sharp and much more convenient to hand. All of my gowns, day or evening wear, are constructed to carry one. If I am going farther abroad, traveling or venturing into less salubrious neighborhoods, I carry a small pistol as well."

The sight of Cassie's face banished all of Sebastian's annoyance. His little rebel didn't know what to think. She was staring at Lady Elinore, openmouthed. She looked quite shocked and more than a little disapproving. Having vanquished several governesses with the same tactics, she hadn't expected to be outgunned—or outknifed—by a small, prissy, titled lady. Morton Black was right: Lady Elinore was more than a match for Cassie's antics. Even her eccentricities could be beneficial.

But he was curious. "Have you ever had to resort to your own protection, Lady Elinore?"

"No. But my mother dinned it into me that one day I might, so I am prepared at all times."

"I see." Though it went entirely against his protective instincts to have females wander about armed, he could hardly disapprove. He had not always been able to protect the females in his care; it was prudent for them to be prepared for danger, even though it lacerated his masculine sensibilities.

A shout interrupted them. "Hey, Bastian, hold up!" It was Giles, waving down their barouche, which had slowed as it turned into Berkeley Street, heading for the house in Hill Street. Sebastian signaled to the driver to pull up.

Giles, mounted on a handsome black gelding, trotted up beside up the carriage. "Good afternoon, girls, Lady Elinore. Stunning dress, Lady Elinore. Of truly remarkable cut and hue."

Lady Elinore, who was wearing one of her usual shapeless gray dresses, sniffed, turned her head, and pointedly examined a spot on the far horizon.

"Cassie, Dorie, you look delightful, too." Giles gave

them both a wink. "Now, where is this barge of beauties headed for?"

Sebastian answered, "We've been visiting the British Museum and we're now going for some refreshment."

"I, too, am parched," Giles exclaimed. "So, where are you going? May I join you?"

Sebastian had planned to have tea and cakes at home, but at Giles's question, he suddenly remembered Miss Hope Merridew's suggestion of the day before. And they were, after all, almost at Berkeley Square. He glanced at the girls. "I thought we'd go and have an ice at Gunter's."

Cassie's and Dorie's heads came up in surprise. After her naughty behavior, Cassie certainly hadn't expected any treat, but since she'd been so soundly routed, Sebastian decided it didn't matter.

He said, "Lady Elinore, are you agreeable to the suggestion? I know Gunter's is somewhere around here."

Lady Elinore gave a small sound and a stiff little shrug, which he took to be assent. She was still sniffy with Giles, he could see. The two of them just didn't get on.

"It's just there, near the corner of the square." Giles pointed. "The place with the sign of the pineapple. You find a nice shady spot for the ladies, Bastian, and I'll send a waiter over to you."

"What? Don't we go into the shop?"

Giles shook his head. "You can, of course, but on a glorious day such as this, everyone eats their ices out of doors in the shade. Don't worry, the waiters will bring everything you need out to you." He trotted off.

They found a place to park the barouche under some cool, wide maple trees and soon saw that, as Giles said, many people were eating their ices and cakes out of doors. Ladies sat in their carriages, spooning up creamy concoctions with long-handled Italianate spoons. Elegant gentlemen idled by the park railings, chatting to the ladies as they ate their ices.

"Excellent spot," Giles declared as he strode up. His horse was hitched to a post a dozen yards away. A waiter hurried up behind him. "Now, what does everyone want? What flavor ice?"

Sebastian looked blank. So did the girls. Lady Elinore said nothing. Finally Cassie said, "I've never had an ice, so I don't know what flavor they are."

"Never had an ice?" Giles exclaimed in mock horror. "Bastian, they've been in London for—how many days?— and they still haven't eaten an ice!"

"I've never had one either," Sebastian admitted.

Giles turned to Lady Elinore, "Lady Elinore, come, it is our duty as Londoners to rectify this shocking situation. What flavors do you think the young ladies would like?"

Lady Elinore said coldly, "I have no idea, Mr. Bemerton. I have never eaten an ice either. Nor do I intend to. My mother did not approve of food that comes in the extremes of hot or cold. An ice is not Rational food."

"It certainly isn't," Giles agreed fervently. "It's food for the gods! So it's the first time for everyone, then— excellent! Waiter, what flavors do you have?"

The waiter rattled off a list. Sebastian didn't catch them all: there were water ices or cream ices in flavors that included strawberry, barberry, pistachio nut, bergamot, royal cream, chocolate cream, burnt filbert cream, parmesan cream, jasmine, white coffee, tea, pineapple, elder-flavored muscadine, and lemon water, as well as some in French that he couldn't catch.

There were so many to choose from, nobody could decide, so Giles took the initiative. "Very well, for the ladies, I recommend a strawberry ice—"

"I'd prefer a pistachio nut ice, please," Cassie said, ever contrary.

"Excellent! So, waiter, two strawberry ices, one pistachio nut ice, and how about frozen orange punch for us, Bastian—it's laced with rum."

Sebastian nodded. "Sounds good to me."

"If you are ordering that extra strawberry ice for me, I won't eat it," Lady Elinore declared. "As I said, an ice is not Rational food."

Giles looked at her thoughtfully. Under his scrutiny, Lady Elinore's nose raised another inch in the air.

"I'm sorry. Do you eat brown bread, Lady Elinore?" he said in a humble voice. "I can have the waiter bring you brown bread."

"I do," she admitted, reluctantly mollified.

Giles said something to the waiter, who nodded and ran off, dodging the traffic as he crossed the busy street to Gunter's.

"That's all sorted then," said Giles and climbed into the open-topped carriage. He squeezed between Dorie and Cassie, opposite Lady Elinore, who fastidiously tucked her knees as far away as possible to prevent them touching. He took no notice and began to question the girls about their excursion. Sebastian was touched to see that Giles addressed questions to Dorie as well as Cassie, phrasing them so she could nod or shake her head. A good fellow, Giles.

"Mr. Bemerton, do you know, Lady Elinore is armed, just like me?" Cassie blurted.

Giles blinked and looked at Lady Elinore.

She lifted her nose a little higher and said nothing, but a faint flush crept across her cheeks.

"You don't say, Cassie? Where does she keep her weapon? In the same place?" He peered provocatively at Lady Elinore's limbs.

She twitched her skirts defensively around her. "Certainly not! Cassandra, it is not polite to discuss such matters in company."

"A big hatpin. In her bodice," whispered Cassie.

Giles peered at the bodice in question. "I can't see anything there," he whispered back and winked at Sebastian.

Sebastian kicked his friend on the ankle and firmly changed the subject. They talked horses until the waiter arrived, his tray laden with glass dishes brimming with colorful, creamy confections. Giles distributed napkins, then handed the ices out; a creamy pink one for Dorie, a pale green one with flecks for Cassie, two pale orange mounds of shaved ice crystals for himself and Sebastian. And one creamy confection the color of toasted biscuits.

Lady Elinore looked down her nose at it. "For whom is that?"

Giles grinned. "You said you'd eat brown bread. This is brown bread ice cream." He dug the long-handled spoon into the confection, lifting a mouthful temptingly. "Doesn't it look delicious?"

Lady Elinore primmed up her small, plain face. "No! I agreed to eat bread, not—mmmphh!"

Sebastian should have been cross with his friend, but the expression on Lady Elinore's face surprised a chuckle out of him. The girls, too, giggled.

With dignity, Lady Elinore swallowed the spoonful of brown bread ice cream that Giles had so rudely popped into her mouth while she was talking. As she swallowed, an extraordinary expression passed over her face.

"Told you you'd like it," said Giles smugly.

"It is not Rational food," Lady Elinore said feebly, eyeing the bowl in Giles's hand. She licked her lips.

"Might as well eat it now," Giles said reasonably. "Only go to waste. A terrible sin, to waste good food." He leaned forward and placed the bowl in Lady Elinore's hands. "You can use that hatpin on me afterward if you like."

Turning immediately to the girls, he said, "So, girls, how do you like your first taste of ice cream?"

Lady Elinore eyed the bowl with equal parts of suspicion and desire. She darted a quick look at Giles to see if he was watching, but since he appeared wholly occupied with Sebastian's sisters and did not even glance her way, she picked up the long-handled spoon and ate another creamy mouthful. An expression of bliss appeared on her face, animating it surprisingly. She glanced again at Giles, but he was turned toward Cassie, so she took another mouthful, then another.

Cassie tasted hers and said, "Ohh. I thought it would taste like snow. But this . . . ummmm . . . This is the most utterly . . . ummmm . . . delicious thing I have ever . . .

ummmm . . . tasted!" She spooned up her pistachio ice vigorously, as if fearing it would disappear.

Sebastian watched Dorie. She took one small spoonful of the strawberry cream ice at a time, allowing it to melt slowly in her mouth and run down her throat. He smiled at the ecstatic look on her face.

"Come on, Bastian. Yours will melt if you don't eat it."

With a start, Sebastian remembered his own frozen orange punch, and dug in. It was sweet yet tangy, with a burst of rum on the tongue. Food of the gods, indeed.

Ironic to think he had Hope Merridew to thank for the eventual success of the girls' first outing with Lady Elinore.

The museum had been a dreadful failure—and yet he was sure it contained other exhibits the girls might have enjoyed. And he had misgivings about the way Lady Elinore treated the girls; long lectures and firm reproofs—very much the tactics of seven failed governesses. He thought about the way the Institution for Indigent Girls was run. Cassie was already poised on the brink of open rebellion.

Lady Elinore's only success was with the knife.

It was not a warming thought. Nor was the sound of her relationship with her mother. If that was what she thought being a mother was about . . .

If Miss Hope had been with them, it would have been quite a different outing, he was sure. There would have been fun. And laughter.

An image popped into his head of Giles's mischievous slipping of the spoonful of ice cream into Lady Elinore's mouth.

And it wouldn't be Giles feeding Hope Merridew with ice cream, it would be Sebastian.

He frowned. It wasn't like him to give up at the first hurdle. A plan needed to be tested thoroughly before he changed it. He would not give up on Lady Elinore yet.

# Chapter Nine

∞

*And every tongue brings in a several tale,*
*And every tale condemns me for a villain.*
WILLIAM SHAKESPEARE

"DO YOU KNOW WHAT THAT MAN HAS DONE NOW?" MRS. JENner came rushing up to the twins at the assembly the following night. "He has purchased an orphan asylum! For *female* orphans!"

Hope blinked. "Why would anyone purchase an orphan asylum?"

Mrs. Jenner flipped a hand dismissively. "Oh, that's common enough. Men of substance frequently own such charitable institutions. They put the inmates to work in their manufactories."

Hope frowned. "It doesn't sound very charitable to me. It sounds to me like the men get free labor."

"Nonsense! They feed, house, and clothe them! It is an excellent piece of charity all around, for what use, pray, are beggar children?" declared Mrs. Jenner. "Such schemes clear the streets of unwanted brats, cut the crime rate, and rid us of a nuisance."

"But the children would be little better than slaves!"

"Don't be silly, Hope, dearest. How else would they earn their supper?"

Hope could see Mrs. Jenner would never understand her point of view. "So why do you object when Mr. Reyne does it?"

"It's not the acquisition of orphans that is the scandal— it is that they are *female* orphans! What pray, could a *young* man like Mr. Reyne want with a collection of young, unprotected females? And I have it from an excellent source that he wanted the whole transaction kept quiet, which proves that it must be immoral!" Mrs. Jenner shook her head, making her clustered ringlets dance.

"Many philanthropists prefer their good deeds to be quietly done."

"You are too innocent to understand, but believe me, there can only be sinister reasons!" Mrs. Jenner shuddered dramatically. "You forget what we know of his past!"

"Nothing," Hope said.

"Nothing to his credit, you mean! It doesn't bear thinking of. Hope, my dear, he is not at all the sort of man you should associate with. If he comes up to ask you for any more waltzes, I shall send him about his business!"

"Please do not," snapped Hope. "I hope he does ask me to dance. I shall then ask him about the orphans! And I am very sure I will find that there is nothing sinister about it. He is not that sort of man!"


It was no use, thought Sebastian gloomily as he stepped through the paces of the country dance with Miss Hope Merridew. He was weak. He could have ignored her. But she'd come up to speak to Lady Elinore when he and Giles were there. And the music had started, and perfidious Giles had whisked Lady Elinore off to dance, leaving him alone with Miss Merridew. And it would have been too uncivil not to have asked her to dance when she was just standing there, looking at him with those big blue eyes.

It was a mistake. He should have been uncivil. Even holding her hand for a country dance was torture.

She cleared her throat. She'd done that several times, he realized. He looked at her. She looked back, frowning.

He realized they had been dancing for some time in silence and that he might very well have been frowning the entire time. He tended to do that when he was thinking. Frown. Giles had informed him once he looked extremely menacing while deep in thought. He performed another movement, then, as they came together again, he said abruptly, "I'm sorry. I didn't mean to be impolite. I was miles away."

"Yes, I have something on my mind, too," she said. "You recently purchased an orphan asylum."

He blinked. It was the last thing he expected her to say. "Yes."

"Why?"

He stiffened and said coldly, "My reasons are private." He should have expected this. People always wanted to know things. But he would explain to nobody, not even Miss Hope Merridew, his family connection with the Tothill Fields Institution for Indigent Girls.

"You are a mill owner, are you not?" She moved forward in a *chassez* step, spoke, then retreated.

He frowned at the faint note of accusation in her voice, and when they came together again, he said, "Yes. It is not a secret."

"You have never mentioned it before, however."

Her tone flicked him on the raw. "No. I did not think you would be interested. I am not ashamed of my mills."

"Apparently not!"

This annoyed him. A great many people in the ton owned such things as mills and mines and other manufactories but would not admit it openly. "In fact, I own several mills."

"Indeed?" She twirled around him, nose in the air.

"Woolen mills as well as cotton mills."

"Fascinating."

It took several movements of the dance before he was able to say to her, "And I am not the least bit ashamed of it."

"No, well why should you be? And I suppose you have children working in frightful conditions for long hours, as well, and are not ashamed of that, either." She met his gaze squarely, awaiting his response.

Sebastian was so angry he refused to answer.

The silence stretched. She stopped in midstep. "You *do.* You exploit little children under frightful conditions for your own profits."

He forced himself to say in a clipped voice, "I use child labor. There isn't a manufactory in England that could survive without it. But the conditions are not frightful—"

"I completely and utterly disapprove of the employment of children in manufactories."

"You know nothing about it." If mills did not employ children he, his brother, his mother, and baby sisters would have starved. Mind you, having experienced the conditions firsthand, he had made a number of changes since he became the owner.

"I have listened to several speakers on the subject, and their descriptions have moved me greatly. Children, little more than babies, imprisoned in fiendish mills, slaving twelve to fourteen hours a day for a crust of bread!"

"My workers are not babies—"

"How could you—how could any man who calls himself a gentleman—justify it! Getting fat off the misery of children!"

Fat! Nettled by her accusation, he snapped, "I am not getting fat off—!"

But Miss Merridew wasn't there to hear him hammer in the final nail. She had stalked off the dance floor, leaving him standing alone.

Sebastian watched her go, furious with himself and with her. He knew what she was asking—what people were whispering about what he wanted with a pack of female orphans. Girls of *that* sort. She might not know—few people did—that the Tothill Fields Institution for Indigent Girls made a specialty of rescuing girls from child brothels! Even so, he was furious that the suspicion had so much as crossed her mind that he would exploit any young girls! Or any children!

The children who worked for him were not exploited, dammit!

He wanted to storm after her and shake her till her teeth rattled! He wanted to kiss her senseless until they were both too weak to stand! He would then tell her the truth.

Instead, he decided to drown his sorrows. He stalked off the dance floor, indifferent to the stares he was receiving. So what if she had deserted him in the middle of a dance? What did he care for the opinions of a parcel of overfed aristocrats?

The thought reminded him of her final accusation. Why that should rankle worst of all was a mystery to him—but it did.

He found Giles sprawled loose-limbed on a bench beside Lady Elinore, a look of lazy amusement on his face. Lady Elinore sat bolt upright, her reticule clutched tightly in her hands. Her lips were pursed, her nose was in the air, and her small, pointed chin jutted pugnaciously. Their dance had apparently ended early, too.

Morosely he joined them. There was a long silence after he'd greeted them. Lady Elinore took the opportunity to stiffly excuse herself. She scuttled away.

Giles watched her go, grinning. "You've frightened her off, Bas, with that fearsome black scowl of yours. Whatever has put you in a temper?

"You didn't see?"

"No."

"You didn't miss much. Miss Merridew and I had a difference of opinion, that's all."

"I see. What about?"

Sebastian had no intention of going into details. But there was that one thing he could ask an old and trusted friend about. "She said I was getting fat," he said indignantly. "Am I fat, Giles?"

Giles's response was a loud crack of laughter. "Tell me all, Bas. Tell me all."

Hope spent the next hour alternatively fuming and feeling guilty. Great Uncle Oswald and Mrs. Jenner had hauled her over the coals for leaving a man standing in the middle of the dance floor in such an uncivil manner. And when she'd tried to explain, each of them had reprimanded her in no uncertain terms.

"Good God, missie, tellin' a man who he should and shouldn't employ! It's none of your business. A lady shouldn't even think of such matters!" Great Uncle Oswald snorted. "Besides, there's probably not a man in the room who don't benefit from child labor—as do the children, missie, so don't look at me like that!" He'd wagged a stern finger at her. "Would you rather they starve, eh? Besides, country's economy depends on it." He gestured. "D'ye think that elegant Persian rug over there was made by genteel ladies sippin' tea, or brawny men with rolled-up sleeves?" He shook his head. "Persian children. Their fingers are the only ones small enough for such fine work. Same goes for dozens of things. Children are cheap and have nimble fingers. And England must compete, keep the prices down, otherwise the country will go to the dogs. Besides, it keeps them usefully employed and out of mischief. Otherwise we'd have swarms of beggars and pickpockets on the streets! Bad enough as it is!"

Mrs. Jenner, too, was very severe. It was unforgivably rag-mannered of Hope. Yes, he was a cit, and Mrs. Jenner didn't intend to encourage the match, but it wasn't Mr. Reyne she cared about, it was Hope's own reputation. "Mark my word, my girl, no gentleman will ask a lady to dance if he fears that a chance word might prompt her to humiliate him in public!"

Hope glanced at her dance card to see who she was engaged to dance with next. Her heart sank. Mr. Bemerton. The very last man she wanted to dance with. Hopefully, good manners would prevent him from raising the subject, but even so, it would be a trial to dance with him, knowing he would probably wish to scold her as well. She wondered if she could plead the headache. She glanced at Mrs. Jenner and received an implacable fishy stare in response. No, she would not get away with leaving another man partnerless.

Mr. Bemerton walked toward her, his face serious for a change. He'd obviously heard what she'd done to his friend. Hope girded her loins, pasted a brittle smile on her face, and allowed him to lead her onto the floor. And when he questioned her—showing no manners at all—she was completely frank with him.

"You accused Sebastian Reyne of exploiting helpless little children?" Mr. Bemerton threw back his head and laughed. He laughed so much Hope grew quite cross. He was drawing unwanted attention to them.

"Hush!" She hissed. "I do not see what is so funny. He admitted it himself."

"He told me you said he was fat."

It took her a moment to recall the conversation. When she did, she was inclined to feel indignant. "I said nothing of the kind. I accused him of getting fat off the misery of the children who labor in his mills!"

"Do you think he's fat? Can't see it myself."

"Oh, don't be ridiculous! You know perfectly well Mr. Reyne is as lean as a lone and hungry wolf!"

His eyebrows rose at this, and Hope realized her choice of words might be misinterpreted. "You know what I mean," she muttered, trying not to flush and fearing from the heat in her cheeks she was not succeeding. "He's not fat."

"Yes, I know." Mr. Bemerton smiled quite kindly. "You may not know it, but he himself was once one of those miserable little child laborers in the very mill he now owns."

Hope's mouth dropped open. "I had heard. I forgot."

He nodded and continued. "The details are his to share or not, as he wills it, but no one in this room is more aware than he of what children endure, or of the dangerous conditions in which they labor." He glanced at her. "You will have noticed his damaged fingers?"

She nodded.

"Again, the details are private—he will tell you one day, I am sure—but they were injured in a mill accident when he was a child."

Hope bit her lip. She felt dreadful. After some time she asked him, "How do you know all this?"

Giles smiled. "I can tell you that, for the story is mine as well as his. I first met Sebastian Reyne at school, when we were boys of seven."

"School? But you said he was a factory—"

He nodded. "Bear with me, Miss Merridew. His family—and this is for your ears only—he'd kill me if he knew I'd told you—is as good as yours or mine, though why he doesn't want it known is beyond me. We became friends at school, and I'll tell you now, he was the best friend I ever had. I was a scrawny little fellow in those days." He grinned. "Not the fine figure of a man you see before you now."

Hope returned his smile. Slender, elegant, and of medium height, Mr. Bemerton would never be called a large man. She could easily imagine him as a small boy.

"Add to my lack of inches the crime of possessing long, golden locks, and you will perceive how I was most horribly bullied as a child." The light, merry tone dropped. He said quietly, "In fact, my life was a total misery."

He paused as the dance separated them, and Hope reflected that all children had their crosses to bear. To look at Mr. Bemerton, one would think his life had been all ease and pleasure and indulgence.

"Well, as I said, I was utterly miserable. Tried to run away from school, but always got dragged back." He grimaced. "To make a man of me, you know. Schools are the modern version of fostering that medieval sons of knights experienced, so I suppose I should be grateful that nobody was trying to chop bits off me with a sword as well."

He shook his head as if to clear it of memories. "Anyway, all the bullying stopped when Bastian Reyne arrived. He was a bit of an outsider, too, but he was big even then, and he knew how to use his fists. He used them on my behalf, and he showed me how to use mine. That sort of thing forges enduring friendships."

"Then how did he end up on a factory floor?"

Giles Bemerton pulled a rueful face. "To cut a long story short, his father committed a number of acts that made both society and his family disown him, and Sebastian disappeared from school one day under a cloud not of his making. I ran into him quite by chance years later when we were sixteen. I was driving though Manchester. He was a ragged factory laborer as tall and skinny as a lath, except for those shoulders of his. I wouldn't have recognized him, except that I saw his eyes as he looked away from me. He didn't want to know me, thought I'd disown him, too. But . . . as I said, our friendship was forged in a hot fire." He grinned at her. "And I've already told you more about Sebastian Reyne than anyone in the ton knows."

"I see." After a moment she asked, "Why would you choose to confide in me?"

He shrugged. "What are friends for? I knew you'd misjudged him. And I know that Sebastian would rather gnaw off his paw than to court anyone's pity, so he won't tell you. But to call him a vile exploiter of children's misery!" He chuckled. "If you ever wish to see a northern mill owner spit with fury, ask him about Sebastian Reyne's child laborers."

"Spit with fury? Why?"

Giles winked. "Reyne's letting the side down. Oh, he pays the same sort of wages, but he won't take the very young ones. And he feeds 'em, morning, noon, and night. Not fancy meals, but none of his little workers have the gnawing belly he had as a child. And one afternoon a week they attend school to learn reading, writing, and arithmetic. The clever ones do more. He says he'd never have risen above the factory floor if he hadn't had those first few years of schooling. Brilliant with numbers, he is. Anyway, all of this makes him grossly unpopular with other mill owners. They see him as a dangerous radical, one who needs to be stopped."

Hope suddenly recalled Mrs. Jenner's words. *"Lord Etheridge said Sebastian Reyne was an extremely dangerous man . . . he has interests in the cotton industry and would know!"* But what Lord Etheridge meant by dangerous was not what Mrs. Jenner imagined.

"Oh, I have so misjudged him," she said remorsefully. "And I didn't even give him a chance to explain."

"He wouldn't have anyway," interpolated Giles. "Too proud. Loathes being pitied."

"I am so mortified. He must despise me."

Giles regarded her thoughtfully. "You must discover his true feelings for yourself. All I ask is that you not reveal my confidences to others. He is a private man and would hate his story to become fodder for the gossips."

"Oh, never," she assured him. "I shan't tell a soul." Her mind was spinning with what she'd learned. And her heart was eased by the thought of how he'd protected Giles from bullies. A boy who'd fought bullies on another's behalf would never grow up to become a bully of little girls.

As soon as the dance was finished, Hope lost no time finding Mr. Reyne. He stood alone, near the window, gazing out, looking morose and bleak and alone. Her heart went out to him.

She took a deep breath, walked directly up to him, and touched him on the arm. As he turned she said, "Mr. Reyne, I am deeply sorry for what I said to you earlier and for abandoning you during the dance. I should never have let my temper get the better of me. I haven't changed my opinions about the exploitation of young children, but I sincerely regret causing you any embarrassment on the matter. It was most unfair of me, and I apologize unreservedly."

He said nothing, just stared at her in silence, looking black and grim and harsh.

Hope bit her lip. "I hope you will find it in your heart to forgive me," she said in a small voice.

He gave a sort of nod and made a sound in his throat that might have been assent. Or not.

Hope swallowed, feeling as if she could cry. "I shall save the last waltz especially for you." A stupid thing to say, she thought as soon as the words were out of her mouth. As if he would risk dancing with her again, risk being abandoned once more on the dance floor in front of everyone! But she didn't know what else to say.

He was so grim and silent she just wanted to shrivel up at his feet. She curtsied to him. "I'm so sorry." And fled before she disgraced herself further with tears.

She'd apologized. Apologized to him for misjudging him. And for embarrassing him on the dance floor. He could not believe it. The toast of society had humbled herself to apologize to a mere cit. He hadn't been able to say a word. He was so stunned at her generosity and honesty.

He'd had the stupid impulse to kneel at her feet and kiss her hem, like a knight of old before his lady.

Oh God, it was worse than ever, now.

He had to fight it. Forewarned was forearmed. A waltz with Miss Hope Merridew would be the end of him, the end of his plans, the final betrayal of his sisters. He would leave the assembly now, before he lost all his discipline.

He hadn't lost his discipline, Sebastian told himself some forty minutes later as he waltzed Miss Hope Merridew around the dance floor, he'd lost his mind.

No, he hadn't lost his mind. It was a matter of honor, he told himself. Miss Hope had more than made up for abandoning him in the middle of the dance; it would be churlish to refuse her now. To dance publicly with her—particularly her much-prized, special last waltz—would show the world there were no hard feelings on either side.

No, he told himself as they circled the room for the third time, it had nothing to do with reasons and everything to do with his inability to resist. It would, of course, be their last waltz. He was marrying another woman for an honorable purpose, one that had nothing to do with these unsettling, ephemeral desires.

And as for hard feelings, he had them in plenty, dammit, but of a different kind . . . a most unsettling and insistent desire.

He straightened his back. It was worse than last time they'd waltzed. Then he did not know her. Then he was simply dazzled. Now he knew how sweet-natured she was, how generous, how mischievous, and yet how kind she could be . . . And now he knew what it was like to hold her against him, body to body. He knew what her hair and her skin smelled like. He'd tasted her mouth.

Now to waltz with her was even more of an exercise in torture, to have her in his arms yet not hold her, to touch her, but only though layers of cloth, to circle endlessly and get no closer, to smell her, touch her, see her, and yet not kiss her.

"Are you still angry with me?" Her question startled him out of his reverie. He'd been miles away, lost in some fantasy.

"Angry? No, not at all."

"I'm so pleased you decided to dance with me. I half thought you'd leave."

"Well, as a matter of fact—" He stopped. He wasn't going to explain. He couldn't.

"In that case, thank you. If you hadn't, I probably would have tossed and turned all night, regretting my wretched words to you earlier."

His mouth dried at the image of her in her bed, tossing and turning, her slender, creamy limbs tangling in the white sheets. He closed his eyes a moment and, forcing his body to behave, drew her into a triple twirl. He was getting the hang of this dance. If he had someone else in his arms, someone who didn't have this drastic effect on him, he could probably even acquit himself with panache.

"So you forgive me, but you just won't talk to me, is that it?"

He started again. "No. Not at all. I'm sorry. It's just that I am . . . distracted."

"Anything you'd like to talk about?"

"No!" Aware it had come out a trifle explosively, he moderated his tone. "No, thank you. It is a private matter."

"Your sisters?"

He looked at her blankly a moment. "No, they are well." He thought of something. "I followed your suggestion."

"My suggestion?"

"I took them to Gunter's for an ice. It was their first-ever ice. It gave them much pleasure, so I thank you."

She gave him a thoughtful look. "You care a great deal about those girls, don't you?"

"Of course." Her look was unsettling, so he added, "Lady Elinore and I took them to the British Museum, and we went to Gunter's as a treat afterward. Lady Elinore and I enjoyed our first ice also." The mention of Lady Elinore was to remind himself as much as her who he was still officially courting.

The warmth in her eyes dimmed. "Of course, Lady Elinore. And I'm sure the girls enjoyed the British Museum. I know Grace loves it. She has a fascination for ancient worlds, you know."

Somehow she'd moved closer during the last twirl. His legs brushed against hers several times. Unable to think of a single thing to say, he produced a strangled sort of noise.

She said softly, "I suspect you'd prefer to dance the remainder of this waltz without the encumbrance of conversation, isn't that so, Mr. Reyne?"

He nodded brusquely and tried not to draw her even closer.

"Then let us simply lose ourselves in the music and the movement," Hope whispered. She closed her eyes and let him and the music take her.

Thus blinded, in his arms, she was totally his. It would be their last waltz. He had spoken of Lady Elinore again. But for just this one dance, she could pretend he was hers.

He danced with awkwardness and precision. She loved how he danced, holding her as if she were so precious and delicate, yet steering her around the floor like a wheelbarrow instead of a woman. And yet, somehow, she felt more fully a woman dancing with him than she'd ever felt with anyone.

She could get grace and elegance anywhere. She opened her eyes briefly and saw Giles Bemerton waltzing by with Lady Elinore. Even such an unlikely pair danced with harmony.

But nobody waltzed like her Mr. Reyne, with that unique mix of stiff, protective awkwardness amid waves of severely repressed passion.

Hope closed her eyes and wished the waltz would go on forever.

"Why did you choose him again, twin?" Faith asked as they were disrobing for bed. "Everyone knows you never choose the same partner twice for that dance. And after that quarrel."

Hope squirmed at her sister's gentle inquiry. She flung off her clothes.

"Will you mind the gossip? Because there will be gossip, love, you know."

Hope thought about it as she shrugged into her nightgown. "People will gossip about anything. I was in the wrong, and I wanted to make it up to him."

"It was a very public apology." Faith looked troubled. "I thought you had decided he isn't the one, Hope."

Hope slumped on the bed. "I just don't know, Faith. I do feel drawn to him, but if you'd ever waltzed with him, you'd know why I'm so uncertain! In the dream it was perfect, absolutely perfect!"

Faith tilted her head. "He's never asked me to waltz. You know, he can tell us apart."

Yes, Hope knew.

"I spoke to Lady Elinore this evening," Faith said. "She's invited us both to visit Mr. Reyne's orphans on Friday. I think it will be very interesting."

"I'm sure it will be."

Faith regarded her thoughtfully. "You're very certain he's a good and decent man, aren't you?"

Hope stared at her, frustrated. She'd promised Mr. Bemerton she wouldn't reveal the details of Mr. Reyne's life, and she meant to keep her promise. "I am. Mr. Bemerton told me some things about Mr. Reyne, but he told me in confidence, so I can't tell you."

Faith stared at her, dismayed. "What? Not even me?"

Hope shook her head unhappily.

"But we always tell each other everything."

Hope bit her lip. "I know, and I'm sorry, twin. But I promised."

Faith gave her a long, hurt look, then turned away, folding her petticoat slowly.

It pained Hope, too, not to share. All their lives she and her twin had been as close as two peas in a pod—closer. They'd shared everything: hopes, dreams, fears. All their lives they'd longed for love. They'd shared their visions of love, analyzed it, shared their dreams of shadowy heroes, shared the waiting and yearning for for nineteen impatient years. It had seemed so simple then.

Now everything was suddenly unclear. Hope was more than halfway in love with a man who did not fit her dream at all, and Faith . . . well, who knew what Faith felt? She was certainly dazzled by her violin-playing count. But was it love?

Then, as one, both girls turned to each other. They spoke simultaneously.

"It's so much—"

"It's not that—"

They stopped and laughed and then got a bit teary. "Oh Faithy, I'm sorry. It's so much harder than I thought it would be. I wish Prue were here." Prudence was their sister, but she was the closest thing they'd had to a mother for most of their lives.

"And Charity," her sister said, putting her arms around Hope. "Sometimes I really miss them so badly it hurts.

Think what it will be like when we are all married and in different places."

Hope hugged her sister hard. "I know." Below in the hall the clock struck two.

"It's late, we should sleep," Hope said.

"Shall I stay?"

Hope nodded. "Like we did when we were little. Who knows, it might be the last time we share a bed."

And so the sisters climbed into bed together, two halves of a greater whole, facing the future in the way they'd always faced things, side by side and hand in hand, but knowing now that the path before them branched.

# Chapter Ten

∞

*And listen why; for I will tell you now*
*What never yet was heard in tale or song.*
JOHN MILTON

RAIN PATTERED AT HIS BACK AS SEBASTIAN RANG THE DOORBELL
of Sir Oswald Merridew's house. The friendship that had
sprung up between Grace Merridew and his sisters was
proving an inconvenience for a man determined to avoid
Hope Merridew.

The logical thing would be to put a stop to it, to find
some other companion for his sisters. But Cassie and Dorie
always came home from an afternoon or morning at
Grace's home with such a light in their eyes, Sebastian
could not bring himself to do the logical thing.

He would not normally come to pick the girls up in person, but this morning Cassie had said that Miss Hope and
Miss Faith were attending a picnic at Richmond, so the
coast was clear. Besides, he was curious to see what his sisters enjoyed so much.

He rang the doorbell again. Lady Elinore would put his
sisters' needs before her own pleasures. The Merridew
twins were forever out at balls and routs, parties and picnics.

He was ushered to the nursery by an ancient butler. Sebastian knocked. He could hear music, and when no one answered him, he opened the door and looked in. It was a large, cozy room with worn, comfortable chairs and a square table in the middle. A fire crackled in the grate, and in the corner stood a pianoforte. Miss Faith played while the others sang. It was a lullaby Sebastian had not heard in years.

> *Sleep my child and peace attend thee,*
> *All through the night*
> *Guardian angels God will send thee,*
> *All through the night*
> *Soft the drowsy hours are creeping*
> *Hill and vale in slumber sleeping,*
> *I my loving vigil keeping*
> *All through the night.*

He stood in the doorway, unnoticed, remembering another room, small, cramped, and bitterly cold without a fire. His newly widowed mother, her ill-fitting clothes dyed a cheap black, stretched tight across the mound of her imminent pregnancy, rocking a fretful Cassie and singing the same song. As if music could soothe hunger pains. He and his little brother, Johnny, had come in from long hours of work and scavenging. His mother's question, the one that greeted him each time he arrived home: had he brought any food? Sebastian, feeling angry and helpless and guilty, producing only two bruised apples and a quarter loaf of stale, hard bread.

"Mr. Reyne?"

He looked up, suddenly aware that the music had stopped. Miss Hope walked across the room and asked in a soft voice, "Are you all right? You had such a strange look on your face."

With an effort, Sebastian banished the memories. "I am perfectly well, thank you." Aware that his response had been brusque, he retreated into politeness. "How do you do, Miss Hope, Miss Faith, girls. I . . . I thought you were on a picnic."

"The weather turned nasty, so it was postponed."

He nodded and ran a finger around his cravat to loosen it.

"I've come to collect my sisters. I hope it's been a pleasant visit."

Hope placed a hand on his arm. She had a way of smiling at him that made him feel warm clear to the bone. "It's been delightful. But you must stay a little longer. We are in need of an audience."

"I—I have an engagement this evening. I cannot tarry."

"Please, Mr. Reyne. We've been practicing so hard," Grace added her plea.

Cassie tossed her head as if she couldn't care in the slightest what he did, but there was enough tension in her indifference to alert him. And Dorie watched him with big eyes. In her hand she clutched a triangle.

He did not want to hear the song, did not want to be dragged back into those times. But his own wants were as nothing to the look in Dorie's eyes or Cassie's careless, heartbreaking feigned indifference.

"Very well," he agreed stiffly and was instantly rewarded by a glowing look from Miss Hope.

"Lovely." She took his arm and led him to the fireplace. "Stand here, where it's warm. And Lily will bring tea in a few minutes. The girls' reward for all their hard work."

He leaned against the mantelpiece, arms folded, heart braced, trying to look interested. He hoped they'd perform only one verse. Or two. He did not want to listen to the third verse, the one where his mother's voice used to get choked and husky. That verse she did not sing to the child in her arms, nor yet to the babe in her belly or the sons who watched. She sang to her dead lover, her husband, Sebastian's father.

Faith played the opening chords on the pianoforte, then the others joined in. Hope and Grace sang the melody. Faith, in a clear, pure voice, helped Cassie's wavering treble maintain a descant harmony while silent Dorie played a large silver triangle, her small face frowning with concentration, as each *ting!* came right on the beat. Sebastian bit his lip watching her, touched that the Merridew girls had included his mute little sister so naturally in their song.

The sight of the earnest little girl, proudly *ting*ing away on her triangle, combined with the emotions churned up in him by the old song was almost more than Sebastian could bear. He clenched his jaw, keeping his face as impassive as possible, but when they came to the third verse, he turned his back. He stared into the fire, overwhelmed by memory and grief and bitterness as they sang . . .

> *Love, to thee my thoughts are turning*
> *All through the night*
> *All for thee my heart is yearning,*
> *All through the night.*
> *Though sad fate our lives may sever*
> *Parting will not last forever,*
> *There's a hope that leaves me never,*
> *All through the night.*

The familiar words and melody tangled in his throat so he could hardly breathe. His mother's voice echoed with every note. She'd yearned for his father, even after his death. After all he had done to them, his mother had still loved the man—loved him more than life itself.

How could she have loved him? His father's weaknesses had brought his family to this place of desperation, and then he'd taken the easy way out—death—leaving Sebastian in charge. And he'd tried so hard, and failed them anyway . . .

No better than his father.

He closed his eyes, trying to force back the unwelcome memories. Nothing good came of dwelling in the past. Only pain and determination. He would *never* make the same mistakes as his father.

He suddenly realized the music had stopped.

"Didn't you like our song?" Cassie demanded in a hostile voice. "I thought it was lovely!"

He turned. "It was," he agreed. "Very lovely. The harmonies were beautiful. And the triangle added the perfect touch. It's just . . ." His voice cracked, and he rubbed his forehead awkwardly, as if somehow he could rub away the emotion.

He was about to claim he had a headache, but something in their expression told him they deserved the truth. Even if it did reveal his weakness. Even if Miss Hope was there to witness it.

"It took me back, you see. I haven't heard that song since our mother sang it to you, to help you sleep, when you were a toddler in the days just before Dorie was born. Mama used to sing it over and over, right up until the day Dorie came into the world."

There was a sudden silence. Cassie and Dorie stared at each other, their faces shocked. Cassie turned on him, furiously. "What do you mean, *our* mother! You didn't know us then!"

Sebastian frowned, surprised. "Of course I did. I was there when you were born." He glanced from one to the other. "I saw both of you come into the world."

There was another long silence. He was aware of the Merridew twins exchanging glances, but he was too surprised by Cassie's response to take much notice.

Cassie narrowed her eyes at him, still obviously suspicious. "You don't mean you're our real, *actual* brother?"

There was such intensity in her voice that Sebastian was confused. He nodded. "Yes, of course I do. But you knew that already."

"That's what you *told* us, but people are always telling us they're our uncles or fathers or our aunty." She almost spat the last out with scorn. "You're trying to tell us we had the very same mother?"

Sebastian was shocked, but suddenly a number of things fell into place. The girls' reluctance to tell him of their past, Cassie's hostility, Dorie's lack of trust. If they had been handed from "relative" to "relative," no wonder they hadn't taken him at his word. He glanced at Miss Hope. This was intimate family business. He should not embarrass the Merridews by dwelling on such private matters. He was about to tell Cassie they would discuss it later, in private, when Miss Hope squeezed his arm.

"They need absolute assurance on this, now," she whispered. "Don't worry about us. Tell them what they need to know, Mr. Reyne." She nodded and gave him a small, encouraging smile.

He glanced at her, then turned back to Cassie and said, "Yes, we all three of us had the very same mother. And the same father. You and Dorie are my true blood, legitimate, legal sisters. Dorie and I even have the same gray eyes—Papa's eyes."

Cassie's gaze flew from his face to Dorie's, comparing.

He continued, "And though Dorie has more of Mama's features—Mama was a beauty when she was young—you have Mama's beautiful blue eyes and her pretty singing voice. Alas, Cassie, you and I have Papa's nose, though yours is the smaller and prettier."

Cassie touched her straight little patrician nose, then examined his longer, equally patrician one, crooked from where a fist had broken it. She paused, screwed up her nose in thought and then asked, "Who was Mam, then? And how did you come to lose us?"

He hesitated. Miss Hope intervened, seeming to read his mind. "Why don't you three come and sit by the fire? If you prefer, Mr. Reyne, we can leave, and you can tell your sisters in private."

He looked at her in silent gratitude; he'd never told the whole story to the girls—mainly because they'd made it clear from the beginning they wanted nothing to do with him. And he did not want to explain the great failure of his life in front of everyone, especially her, but Cassie said, "No, stay. You're our friends, and I want you to hear it, too." She looked at Sebastian and said in a challenging voice, "I'll tell Grace anyway, you know, and she'll tell her sisters."

He looked at Miss Hope and said, "I must warn you, it isn't a pretty story."

Hope laid a hand on his arm and said, "Don't worry about us. We know how to keep a confidence, don't we, girls?" Her sisters nodded, and Sebastian felt a lump in his throat. She added, "Besides, our own story is hardly a tale for bedtime telling."

Sebastian gave in. "Very well, the whole story. Let us sit down." He sat down in a blue plush armchair, and his two sisters squashed into a matching one facing him across the fire. The Merridews quietly seated themselves on an over-stuffed sofa and waited.

Sebastian wasn't sure where to start. Then he remembered Cassie's question. "You asked who the woman you called "Mam" was. I knew her as Widow Morgan—"

Cassie nodded at the name.

"—and I paid her to take care of you after our mother died."

"How did she die?" Cassie asked. "And what about our father? Tell us the whole story."

"Our father was a wastrel," Sebastian said stiffly. "He was born a younger son of good family, but everything he wanted was given to him, without effort, and he never learned responsibility. He was also a gambler and . . . well, suffice it to say it was either feast or famine in our house. My early life was pampered and privileged, as was Johnny's, my younger brother."

The girls sat up at that. "You never mentioned Johnny before—"

"I'll get to him later. He was two years younger than I, two years less lucky. I went to a good school for nearly four years. It made all the difference to my life."

Hope watched his face as he spoke and recalled how Giles Bemerton said he'd known Sebastian at school.

"But Johnny was sickly, and in the end he never went to school, for by the time he was well enough to go, there was no money. Papa had disgraced himself." His face hardened. "He was disowned by his family and could no longer lead the life he was accustomed to. He sold everything we had of value, but that was soon gone. He tried to live by the cards, but nobody would accept his vowels and—" He shook his head. "Well, you don't need to know all the details. We slipped lower and lower down the social scale until by the time Cassie was born, we were living in rented rooms in the poorest part of town—in Manchester."

He stared into the fire and said in a low voice, "I was there when you were born, Cassie, because there was no other choice. There was no money for a midwife, and Papa had been gone for days, off trying to raise some money. Mama told me what to do, and I did it." He swallowed, fighting emotion. "I'll never forget the first sight of you, all red-faced and angry and squalling your displeasure to the world. And then Mama fed you, and you stopped crying." He glanced at Cassie and said thickly, "You were so beautiful."

"How old were you?" Hope asked softly. He must have been just a young boy. She wanted the girls to realize it.

He glanced at her. "Twelve."

She nodded. "The same age Dorie is now."

He stared at her as if wondering what possible relevance his age had. "Yes. I was older, of course, when Dorie was born. Papa had . . . died, by then." He paused. There was something he wasn't telling them, Hope realized, something about his father's death.

"Didn't you have any relatives to turn to?"

"No, Mama wrote, but . . ." He shook his head. He contemplated the fire again, brooding. "Dorie was born a few months after that." He jerked his chin at the pianoforte and added, "That song you were singing before, Mama used to sing it to Cassie over and over while she waited for Dorie to be born." He stared into the fire for a moment, watching the flames dance, listening to the hiss and crackle, lost in memories.

"If your father was dead, how did you live?" Hope prompted. She had a feeling that if she didn't ask, he would skip over the most important part—the role of Sebastian Reyne, hero. She wanted his sisters to understand what hardships he had faced and how very young he had been. If they did, they would surely stop repudiating his care, and perhaps some of that haunted look he carried would fade from his bleak, gray gaze.

He shrugged uncomfortably and muttered, "I'd always managed to do an odd job here and there, and help out at the market."

Hope had seen a ragged urchin at a market once, picking up bruised fruit and vegetables from the gutters. That was how Sebastian Reyne kept his family alive?

"But I got a job in one of the mills after Papa died—he wouldn't let me take a proper job before—'Not fitting for one of our class!'" His mouth twisted.

Hope suddenly understood the source of the vehemence with which he occasionally referred to the ton.

"I got Johnny a job soon afterward. Luckily, Dorie was born in the middle of the night, otherwise we'd have been at the mill, working, and Mama would have been alone."

Hope glanced at the Reyne girls and said for their benefit, "So you and your younger brother supported your mother and two babies."

He grimaced. "Supported was hardly the word. And we didn't do a good enough job. Mama died while Dorie was still a weanling." He swallowed and said in a voice that grated with emotion, "After that, I took you two babies to Widow Morgan and paid her to look after you for us."

"You were only, what, fourteen? And Johnny twelve?" Hope asked, her voice suddenly husky as she imagined a young boy, alone, desperately struggling to keep their family together. "How could you afford to pay her and keep yourselves?"

Judging by the discomfort he showed at the question, it was another area he'd been about to skim over, Hope thought.

He shrugged awkwardly, "Johnny and I slept at the mill so we didn't need to pay rent for a room anymore." He looked at his sisters and said, "But I looked in on you at Widow Morgan's every morning and every night, to check for myself that you were all right."

Cassie stared at him and whispered, "You still check on us now, morning and night."

He grimaced wryly and nodded. "I can't seem to break the habit."

"How did you come to lose us then?" Cassie asked.

His face contorted briefly, then he mastered himself and said baldly, "Johnny died. An accident at the mill."

Cassie and Dorie glanced at each other. They were clutching each other's hands tightly. Cassie said, "Johnny died? What happened?"

He shook his head as if unwilling to talk about it, but his sisters were staring up at him, and Hope could see he was trapped. He twisted his hands and spoke. "It was at the end of a shift. Most accidents happen then, for the children are tired."

"After working for twelve long hours," Miss Hope prompted.

He shook his head shortly, "The shift was fourteen hours in those days. Anyway, Johnny was tired, and it made him slow, clumsy. I tried to keep an eye on him, but they'd put me in the office by that time—I'm good with figures—and I didn't see how tired he was. I did come out to check, and I saw it happen . . ." He kneaded his big, scarred hands painfully as he told the story. Hope noticed Dorie watching them.

"I tried to help, but Johnny was . . . just . . . gone." He shuddered, and Hope knew at once that it had been a particularly ugly accident.

She'd read a description of such an accident once: in seconds the machines had ripped the body of a twelve-year-old girl apart, leaving it scattered about in bloody chunks. She'd felt sick just reading of it. And Sebastian Reyne watched it happen to his brother. She wanted to go and comfort him, but he sat there, a big, dark, lonely man, fiercely independent, determined to show no emotion, as if emotion was weakness. And she did not have the right to comfort him.

His sisters sat opposite, watching him with painful intensity.

"That's how you hurt your hand, isn't it?" Hope said.

Cassie and Dorie stared at his hand, and she could tell by the change in their faces that they understood more than he was telling them.

He immediately shoved his hand in his pocket and said in a hard voice, "After Johnny died, there was less money to pay Widow Morgan. It—it didn't seem to be a problem at first. She knew I'd pay her in the end, and she seemed fond of you girls . . ." His face twisted with remorse. "But one night, a few months after Johnny . . . when I went to do my usual check on the babies, I found Widow Morgan gone, along with you two. She'd never given so much as a hint she was leaving. She knew I'd never let her take you away . . . We'd worked so hard to keep you . . ." His voice broke.

Hope's eyes were swimming with tears. She blinked them back.

He compressed his lips fiercely and said after a moment, "I searched everywhere. One neighbor thought she'd gone to stay with her brother on a farm, another said the brother lived in London . . ." He shrugged, the movement carrying an echo of that long-ago despair. "Nobody could agree: some said a farm, either in Yorkshire or Leicestershire, some said London. Another said she'd gone back to her husband's people in Ireland. Wherever it was, I'd lost you. June sixteenth, 1807." He looked at them. "I'm sorry. I did my best . . . It wasn't good enough."

Cassie looked uncomfortable. She said, "But you found us in the end."

He nodded. "Morton Black did, nearly six months ago." He looked down at the girls and, with a soft look in his eye, put out a hand as if to touch them. It almost broke Hope's heart when he hesitated, then put his hand away.

Even after what he'd told them, he still blamed himself, still didn't expect to be forgiven.

She could see now why he was so tough, why he drove himself so hard. He'd done more than any young boy could have been expected to do, and yet he still believed he'd failed them, failed the girls, failed his brother, and probably his mother, too, and for all she knew, his late wife as well. No wonder the man looked so bleak and grim.

"Where did Widow Morgan take you girls?" he asked. "Now it's your turn to explain."

Hope looked at him in surprise. He'd found them, and yet he didn't know where they'd been?

He caught her look and said bitterly, "I know where they were found, but they can't have been there all their lives." He glanced at his sister and said gently, "Cassie, I only want to know where you spent your childhood. Not about—not about the later part."

Hope frowned. She was missing something here. There was something he wasn't talking about, something Cassie knew, too. Something he, at least, wanted kept secret. Something terrible.

The silence stretched. Cassie hunched her shoulders, uncomfortable with the sudden focus on her.

Suddenly Grace said, "Tell us about the knife, Cassie."

Every adult in the room gasped. "Grace, you should not—" Hope began.

"But we all know she's got it, and I for one think it's very clever of her. If I'd carried a knife strapped to my leg when we lived with Grandpapa, I would have felt much braver! Wouldn't you?"

Hope and Faith looked at each other. Faith said, "She's right, twin. It would have made me feel braver."

Grace added, "We probably wouldn't have used it, but at least we could have dreamed of cutting his liver out and feeding it to the dogs!" She said it with such ghoulish relish that Hope and Faith couldn't help but burst out laughing.

The three members of the Reyne family stared at the three Merridew sisters in amazement. Did all London ladies routinely carry weapons? Sebastian wondered whether he should have sought governesses from London instead of the north.

Hope noticed Sebastian's stunned look and explained, "You must think it very odd, but I assure you we are not such bloodthirsty creatures as you probably imagine. We were all born abroad and traveled a great deal, which was often dangerous. Even our mother carried a pistol with her, so we do not think it unladylike. And our grandfather was—"

"Here we all are then!" declared a loud, jolly voice from the doorway. They all jumped at the sound. Lily bustled in carrying a large tray on which rested a cloth-covered basket, plates, cutlery, and cups. A footman followed, carrying a large pot of chocolate and a bundle of long toasting forks.

"Lovely chocolate, steamy hot, so don't gulp it down at once, girls," she said, dumping the tray on the table. "And muffins, all ready for toasting. And there's butter and honey and strawberry jam. Miss Grace, if you could take the forks from James there, you and the other little misses can set to toasting muffins."

They all stood up. Cassie came closer to Sebastian. Regarding him with narrowed eyes, she said slowly, "So you are truly our very own brother, and you really did lose us when we were little?"

Sebastian nodded. The admission still flayed him. "Yes."

"And now you've found us."

"Yes."

"And you want us to be like a family."

"We *are* a family." He almost growled the words. "You don't have a choice, Cassie. You are my sisters, and I am your brother, and I'll never, ever lose you again."

She sniffed, as if it was something she might be prepared to think over. Her next words surprised him. "You talked about me as a baby. What was Dorie like?" she asked, a cautious expression on her face.

It was some sort of test, Hope saw, and he knew it, too.

Sebastian glanced at Dorie, who had turned back to watch him intently. He said, "She was small and sweet and not nearly as noisy as you. She didn't cry very much at all. But Dorie did cry. Good and loud on occasions."

Hope caught the implication. Dorie had a voice in those days.

Cassie nodded, apparently satisfied. She turned away, but Sebastian caught her by the arm and said in a low voice, "We *are* a family, Cassie. And though I haven't done a very good job of taking care of you and Dorie for the first twelve years, it will be different in the future, I promise you."

She gave him a long, thoughtful look, then shrugged in her usual care-for-naught manner and hurried to the tea table to collect her muffin and toasting fork.

The room suddenly took on a party atmosphere as girls scurried to skewer muffins on long forks and crouched in front of the fire to toast them, chattering as if nothing significant had taken place.

Sebastian felt lacerated, exhausted. The telling of the story had raked up all the old grief and guilt he'd tried to suppress for so long.

He watched as Cassie passed Dorie a muffin. She was so protective of her little sister. It was to her credit, of course, but he could not stop wondering about the cause of it. Who or what had Cassie needed to protect Dorie from? When and why did Dorie stop speaking? And had anyone protected Cassie?

Hope Merridew touched him lightly on the arm, interrupting his thoughts. "Don't worry. They need time to take it all in. You have just turned their world upside down.

He shook his head. "I don't think so." He nodded at them. "They are as they were before. I don't think they care at all."

The scent of toasting muffins filled the air.

She shook her head. "Believe me, they care. It's only pride holding them back. And perhaps a little fear."

"Fear?" He frowned. "But I have never, would never—"

She interrupted him, squeezing his arm. "Not that sort of fear. They fear that you are too good to be true. It's very powerful, you know—the thought that someone strong and good, like you, claims them and wants them and will protect them, through thick and thin."

Her eyes were bright with unshed tears. "That story you told, no one could hear it and remain unmoved. They want to believe they are part of a family again, but deep down they are frightened of believing. But those girls *know* what you did for them. They know you were just a boy, only a little older than Cassie is now, and carrying the burdens of the world on your shoulders. No wonder they are so broad and strong." She gave a shaky breath, and her voice broke as she whispered, "Those girls know, as I do, that their brother is a true hero, the likes of which few of us meet in this life."

He made a gesture of repudiation, but she said, "If you want to understand how hard it is for Cassie and Dorie to show they care, just you think about how hard you find it to forgive yourself. Because you still blame yourself, don't you?"

He stared at her, shocked to have his mind read.

In a low, intense voice she said, "You blame yourself for Johnny's death, you blame yourself for losing the girls, you take the blame for all they have gone through, and you are haunted by what they might have experienced." She placed her palm on his chest over his heart and said, "In here, you believe that a lone, desperate fourteen-year-old boy should somehow have managed better."

She paused to let him think about it. And it was true. He did think he should have managed better. But when she put it like that, "a lone, desperate fourteen-year-old boy," well, it sounded different to the way he'd always seen it.

"You are mistaken, Mr. Reyne. That boy was a hero. And he has grown into a fine, strong, heroic man. And those girls will come to love you. They probably already do, secretly. You need to forgive yourself, as I'm sure they have already forgiven you."

Sebastian swallowed and covered her hand with his. His face was working with emotion, but he couldn't control it, and somehow it didn't seem to matter. She understood. Of all people to understand what was in his heart, the feelings he found so hard to explain to his sisters . . . that it should be she. His innocent silken elf . . . a flesh-and-blood woman who could look into hearts and read them.

She said softly, "What you said to Cassie just now about being a family was perfect. It was exactly what they needed to hear."

"You think so?" His voice grated. He could feel her soft warmth pressed lightly against him. He wanted to gather her hard against him.

"Oh yes." Her voice was husky and tender and full of approval. "You claimed them in no uncertain terms. All people, but especially young girls, need to belong, need to feel wanted and loved."

He looked at her doubtfully. That was true . . . for some people. "I'm not sure that's what Cassie and Dorie feel, though."

"They care. They've spent years building up a protective shell of indifference to hide their vulnerable feelings, and they are reluctant to expose them. But those two little girls desperately want to belong. You just keep telling them you want them and love them, and it will all work out, I promise you." She paused, then added in a low voice, "Believe me, Mr. Reyne, no female in the world could resist you loving them."

Sebastian felt as though the breath had been knocked from him. He wanted to wrap his arms around her, wanted to bury himself in her warmth and sweetness, to seek release and oblivion and an end to the relentless loneliness of his life. Too choked up to speak, he covered her hand with his.

Hope gazed deep into his eyes and shivered at what she saw there. Hunger. Possession. Passion.

She shivered, recognizing the source of that hunger, recognizing, too, the instincts that forced him to leash it in, to hide it behind stiffness and stern words. She understood him so much better, having had a glimpse of the boy he'd been. He would think it a weakness, that sort of hunger . . .

Hope knew. She'd hungered all her life. She'd had her sisters to love her, of course—her twin in particular. But there still remained that aching void, deep inside her. To be loved and wanted, just for herself. To find her soul mate.

And he—he'd had no one. The story he'd told had wrenched her heart. If she hadn't already been in love with him, that story would have done it. She ached to hold the lonely young boy he'd been, ached to comfort him, but she could only comfort the man, hold the man, love the man.

She pressed against him, lifting her face.

"Oh no, you've dropped it!" Cassie's exclamation startled them both. Dorie crouched in front of the fire. The others, having already toasted their muffins, were seated around the tea table devouring them, but Dorie's muffin had fallen off its fork into the fire. As they looked, she reached toward the flames to try to retrieve it. Hope and Sebastian leaped forward, as one.

"Don't!"

Faith, Cassie, and Grace were closest to the fire, but Sebastian reached Dorie first. Yet as he stretched his hand to prevent her burning her fingers, she cringed away from him, and he froze. He straightened and said stiffly, "Let the muffin burn, Dorie. It doesn't matter. There are plenty more."

Dorie stared at him with big gray eyes, and he added in a gruff voice, "Your fingers are more important than muffins."

The gruffness and the frozen look on his face ate into Hope. She hurried forward. "Yes, of course there are plenty more muffins. Don't worry about it, Dorie, dear. My muffins always fall off their fork, too, the wretched things."

Cassie made to push in between her sister and Mr. Reyne, but Hope caught her eye and shook her head gently. "Grace and Cassie, finish your muffins before they grow cold." She waited until Cassie sat down again, then picked up the basket of muffins, saying to Dorie, "Your brother will show you how to affix one to the fork so it won't fall off." She passed him the basket of muffins.

He made no move to take it, saying quietly in a voice that broke her heart, "I think Dorie would prefer it if you showed her how to fix the muffin onto the toasting fork, Miss Hope."

At his words, Grace laughed. "Hope is the worst muffin toaster, Mr. Reyne!" Grace told him. "Didn't you hear what she said? Her muffins always fall into the fire."

Hope shrugged and said in a light voice. "Yes, I am shockingly inept." She turned back to Dorie. "So I think it had best be your brother who shows you how to toast a muffin, not me. You are very lucky to have a big brother to show you things. We Merridew girls always wanted a brother. And I think you and Cassie have one of the best."

Dorie considered her words, then solemnly handed the fork to Sebastian. He accepted it gravely and squatted down beside her, showing her how to thread the muffin securely onto the tines of the fork, explaining his moves in a deep, soft rumble. The small girl watched earnestly, and together, man and child toasted the muffin, first one side, then the other. And when it was done, they carried it to the table together, all golden and toasty—the most important muffin in the world.

Hope had no idea why the sight should make her eyes shimmer with tears, but it did.

Dorie slathered the muffin with butter and honey, hesitated a moment, and cut it in half. Then she passed the big half to Sebastian.

Acceptance.

Melted butter and honey dripped all down his immaculate, expensive trousers, but Sebastian Reyne did not turn a hair. He took his dripping half muffin as if she had handed him the Holy Grail.

Dorie, seemingly unaware of the significance of her

gesture, ate hers with relish, carefully licking the honey off her fingers afterward.

After a moment, Sebastian ate his muffin slowly, almost reverently.

And if Hope's eyes were swimming, nobody noticed.

# Chapter Eleven

∞

*And dreams in their development have breath,*
*And tears, and tortures, and the touch of joy.*
LORD BYRON

DROPS OF WATER HUNG FROM THE BRANCHES AND LEAVES, QUIV-
ering in the pale morning light, sparkling like crystals. The
air in the park smelled moist and earthy, clean and fresh, as
if Sebastian were out in the countryside, not in the heart of
London. He inhaled deeply; it was like breathing chilled
nectar. His horse was feeling his oats, and since there was
no one at all about, Sebastian urged it into an easy canter.
Its hooves thudded softly on the rain-dampened ground.

He'd missed this. He liked his regular morning ride.
Apart from the beneficial physical exercise, it was a time
when he could be alone with his thoughts, when his body
could ride hard and disciplined until the blood pounded in
his veins, while his mind soared, unfettered. His best ideas
often came to him at this time.

But lately he'd avoided the dawn ride. He knew the
cause: Miss Hope Merridew. Part of him feared he would
meet her, and part of him longed for it. Duty versus desire . . . Yesterday's incident in the Merridews' upstairs
parlor had shaken his resolve badly.

He'd been convinced that what his sisters needed was routine, order, a systematic approach. Embodied in the person and beliefs of Lady Elinore Whitelaw. And yet haphazard and unstructured acquaintance with the Merridew girls had produced extraordinary results.

Dorie had actually leaned against him in the carriage on the way home. He'd hardly breathed.

And slowly, surely, his little mute sister was putting on weight. He was sure of it. She seemed no longer so frail, as if a puff of wind would sweep her away. Those frequent morning excursions to Green Park with the Merridews had a lot to do with it. Starting the day with good fresh milk and exercise. And kindness.

He frowned. It was some time since the servants had reported the stealing of food. He must check.

A faint breeze stirred the branches, sending down a patter of raindrops from the new spring leaves. He breathed deeply. His spirits rose, and he half closed his eyes and let himself enjoy the harmony of horse and man and earth and air.

"Race you to the big oak on the western border!" He caught a smile, a laugh, a flash of blue before Miss Hope Merridew passed him in a blur. This morning she was in a blue habit, and a hat with a saucy blue plume curling over the brim. At least she was the right way up on the horse for a change.

Sebastian set off in instinctive pursuit. She had the advantage of him at the start, but his horse was bigger, faster, and more powerful. He slowly gained on her. From time to time she glanced back, grinned, and urged her horse to go faster. Damp earth spattered in his face. He bent over his horse's neck and urged it faster, faster. His blood thundered along with the hoofbeats.

Eventually they were riding neck and neck. "Morning, Miss Merridew," he called in a mocking voice. "So sorry to have to overtake you."

She laughed. "Try if you can!"

"Oh, I can. Ungentlemanly, I know, but then—" He bent

even lower over his horse, more like a jockey than a gentleman. "I'm no gentleman!" And he shot past her, drawing up at the oak tree a good fifteen seconds before her.

She arrived, laughing. "Thank you!" she exclaimed, breathlessly. "I detest it when a gentleman lets me win."

He was surprised. "Don't you like winning?"

"Of course. But it's not winning when someone allows you to beat them. It takes all the fun out of it. I'd rather be beaten fair and square in a rattling good race than win by a fit of gentlemanly gallantry!" Her cheeks were flushed, her hat was crooked, her hair was everywhere, she was puffing, and Sebastian had never seen anything so beautiful in his life.

She took off her hat, shook back her hair, and replaced the hat. "A splendid run!"

With an effort, Sebastian dragged his body back under control, forcing himself to say mildly, "Yes. Though I suspect we are not supposed to gallop."

She laughed again. "Ah, but there is nobody about to see."

That reminded him. He looked back the way they had come. Yes, James, the footman-groom, was doggedly following.

She saw the direction of his gaze and gave another gurgle of laughter. "Poor James, he's got the biggest slug in creation again. He mortally offended the stableboy a few weeks ago, and now he's always given the worst mount available." She dimpled and added demurely, "I always seem to get the best."

Sebastian had no trouble believing it.

She took a deep breath. "Doesn't it smell lovely, so fresh and clean after the rain?"

"Yes. Shall we ride back toward your groom?" Sebastian had the vague idea that the groom's presence might save him from doing something he ought to regret.

She shook her head decidedly, making the plume curling over her hat brim dance against her cheek. "No, James will catch up eventually. Let us ride over in that direction, toward the lake. I'd like to see if any more ducklings have hatched. Yesterday we saw three of the sweetest little brown and yellow fuzz balls. If there are more, I thought we might bring your sisters here this morning, instead of Green Park. New-hatched ducklings are such a delight to watch."

Sebastian was unused to such casual kindness. His sisters were—or should be—nothing to her. No relation. He'd told her to her face he was courting Lady Elinore. Gratuitous cruelty he was accustomed to, was equipped to handle. Gratuitous kindness was something new.

They walked their horses in the direction of the pond. The morning sun was well up, warming and stirring the earthy damp fragrances. In the distance the city began to stir. After a time he became aware that they'd been riding in silence. He glanced at her. Her face was serene.

"I'm glad to see you're riding the right way up this time."

She gave him a droll look. "Is that meant to be provocative?"

"No, no," he said hastily. "I'm relieved, that's all. It's devilish difficult to hold a conversation with someone when they're bouncing along upside down on a horse."

She gave him an odd look. "Oh, is that the problem?" She said and then started to giggle. "Forgive me," she gasped. "But your statement struck me as very funny."

He gave her an inquiring look, waiting for her to explain.

She changed the subject. "I am looking forward to visiting the orphan asylum—the Tothill Fields Institution. Lady Elinore invited my sister and me. Did you know?"

"Yes. She told me," he said dampeningly. "Now, would you care to tell me what threw you into the whoops just now?"

With a praiseworthy attempt at a straight face she said, "You're not precisely famed for your conversational skills at the best of times."

Sebastian frowned, puzzled.

Her eyes danced. "I was not upside down when we danced."

She was teasing him! Mocking his taciturnity! No one ever teased him! He rather liked it. He kept his face stern, so she would not realize.

She grinned. "Oh, good. You're not offended."

He abandoned the effort to look severe. "Why did you decide to become a female daredevil, anyway?"

"It was a burning ambition that arose from my first-ever visit to Astley's Amphitheatre, almost two years ago. My brother-in-law took us, and we were all utterly thrilled by the female equestriennes. I instantly wanted to run off and join them."

"What prevented you?"

"Oh, events overtook me. We all had to leave London suddenly. A . . . a family emergency." She was silent for a moment. "But I never lost the impetus to try some of their riding exploits. I'd always loved to ride, you see."

"It shows. You're a splendid rider. But the tricks you perform are extremely dangerous. Why risk your neck?"

"I grew up feeling hedged and bound and enclosed . . ." She shivered. "So I like doing things I'm not supposed to do. It gives me a sense of freedom. And it's not as risky as you might suppose. The extra straps James had attached to my saddle are very ingenious. And there is nothing, *nothing!* like the thrill of success I feel when I pick something up off the ground. I'm not such a Clumsy Clara then!"

"A Clumsy Clara?"

She pulled a self-deprecating face. "In many ordinary things I am shockingly inept."

She had said as much the previous evening. He'd thought it an excuse to get him to help Dorie toast the muffin. "You don't seem the slightest bit clumsy or inept to me."

She gave him a dazzling smile. "Thank you, but I assure you, I am. In everything except riding. Or dancing. I only learned to dance recently, for my grandfather forbade music and dancing. But he was a bruising rider to hounds, so he ensured that we all learned to ride."

"Did you ride to hounds, then?"

She shook her head vigorously. "Heavens, no! Females at the hunt? The world would come to an end! But for some reason, he did insist we ride, and ride well. But it annoyed him to no end that I, being incompetent in all else, seemed born to ride horses. Which naturally inspired me to be better."

"Whatever the cause, you are the best horsewoman I've ever seen," said Sebastian, thinking he sounded like a ton gallant, even though he meant every word.

She laughed unaffectedly. "It's clear you have never been to Astley's. But since riding is my sole accomplishment, I shall accept the compliment with thanks, sir." She sketched a curtsy from horseback.

"Sole accomplishment? You are too modest, I'm sure."

"I assure you it's true. We were not at all well-educated, for my grandfather did not believe in educating females." She wrinkled her nose ruefully. "I do not shine in any of the desirable feminine skills: my watercolors are atrocious, I play no instrument, my handwriting is shocking, and my embroidery is worse." Before he could comment, she changed the subject. "Tell me, do your sisters ride?"

He shook his head. "So far they have refused even to consider the idea, though I suspect Cassie would like to." He added wryly, "Cassie would rather burst than admit she wants anything."

She gave him a teasing look. "Hmm, runs in the family, doesn't it? And Dorie, does she show no interest?"

He was still pondering her first comment as he answered, "No, she is nervous of horses, and I don't intend to force her."

"Of course not. One must be tempted into doing the things one fears, not forced. Would you like me to try to tempt the girls into taking lessons?"

He hesitated, liking the idea, but not wishing to be beholden to her any more than he already was.

She said, "It would be another way you could become close to them. Think of the pleasure of family outings on horseback. But do not decide now; think about it and let me know." She put an end to the conversation by prompting her horse to trot.

There were no new ducklings, or if there were, they had not yet emerged from the nest, so a few moments later she took her leave, explaining she would be late for the visit to Green Park, otherwise. "Adieu, Mr. Reyne." She held out her hand. "Thank you for the splendid race. And I did enjoy our talk, too."

Sebastian leaned across and took her hand.

"The pleasure was all mine." He lifted her gloved hand to his lips and kissed it.

And though it was just a glove and just a hand, he felt it, clear through to the bones.

Sebastian was at his desk writing letters when a cab pulled up outside his house. From it descended Miss Hope and his two sisters. They were early. There was no sign of the rest of the party. Miss Hope had her arm around Dorie, whose face he could not see. She was clinging to Hope. Cassie looked upset. Sebastian shot from the room.

He reached the entrance vestibule just as a footman opened the door for them.

"What's the matter? Dorie? Are you all right?"

Dorie looked up from the shelter of Miss Hope's arms. Her eyes were huge, and her little face was tear-streaked and distressed. She made not a sound.

Sebastian stared helplessly. "Did someone hurt you, sweeting?"

Without warning, Dorie left Miss Hope, hurtled across the room, and flung herself into Sebastian's arms. Wordlessly, moved beyond any speech, he lifted her small, skinny body and wrapped her securely in his arms.

Heart full, he carried her into the sitting room and sat down with her on a plush, comfortable sofa. She shivered uncontrollably, clinging to him like a monkey, clearly terrified. He held her tight, stroking her hair. "Hush, little one, you're safe now. I shan't let anyone hurt you. There,

there . . . You're home . . . safe now, with Cassie and me. And Miss Hope."

He felt Cassie stare at him as he spoke and looked at her across Dorie's head, which was buried against his chest. She hovered, uncertainly, so he beckoned her to him, murmuring to Dorie, "See, Cassie is here, too. We are all here. Cassie and me and Miss Hope. No one shall harm you." He glanced at Miss Hope, who was hovering as uncertainly as Cassie. Her cheeks were wet with tears.

She knew, then, what it meant to him that Dorie had come to him like that. He felt his own face working and buried it in his sister's hair a moment until he had mastered himself. Now was not the time for him to be weak.

"What upset her?" He glanced at Cassie and Miss Hope. "A horse?"

Miss Hope answered, "No, there were no horses nearby. Just people and the cows, and she is not nervous of the cows at all."

"Cassie, do you know what it was?" he asked.

Cassie shrugged, distressfully. Dorie's little protector. He held out a hand to her, and she came, hesitantly. "Come, help me hold Dorie. She needs all her family, Cassie, her sister and her brother."

Stiffly, awkwardly, Cassie moved closer, patting her sister's shivering back helplessly. She blamed herself terribly, he could see, even though she did not know what had frightened Dorie. His poor little little warrior sister. He put his arm around her, too, gathering them both in. She allowed it, a little stiffly at first, and then he felt her relax and put her arms around Dorie and lean fully against him.

He closed his eyes and held them tight. His two sisters finally in his arms the way he'd only dreamed they would be, the way sisters should be. Eleven long, lonely years after the last time he'd held them like this, as babies . . .

And somewhere deep inside him, a gangly, guilt-ridden fifteen-year-old boy began to heal.

• • •

Eventually Dorie calmed, and the two girls slipped out of Sebastian's arms. He rang for a servant and ordered hot chocolate and pastries brought in. The two girls went upstairs with one of the housemaids to wash their faces and hands.

"I don't know what happened," Hope said as soon as they'd left. Her voice was husky with emotion. "We were at Green Park as usual, lining up for milk with everybody else, when suddenly Dorie became upset and fearful. But I have no idea why."

He took a few restless paces toward the fireplace and turned. "Are you sure? Think. There must have been something."

Hope shook her head, feeling helpless. "No, there was nothing out of the usual. Nothing was said, nothing was done. I saw the whole thing. Dorie and Cassie and Grace were standing in line with Lily, our maid, chatting and giggling as girls do, when suddenly Dorie froze, went utterly white, and before I could move, she just bolted—away from Cassie, away from us, just running like a scared little rabbit. I ran after her and caught her, and Cassie came after us, and she was so very frightened and distressed I summoned the nearest cab and brought her home."

He said raggedly, "For which I am more grateful than I can ever say."

She said nothing. There were no words. She had seen his face when Dorie ran to him. And then, when Cassie had come, too.

"And Cassie does not know, and Dorie cannot say." He sighed heavily and clenched his fist. "I wish I knew when and how she became a mute . . . Somewhere in those eleven lost years—"

She put her hand on his arm. "Would Cassie not be able to tell you?"

His big hand came up to enclose hers, and then he froze as if transfixed. "She never has before, but then, she never would so much as touch my hand before. So much has happened in recent days, I've not had time to absorb it all."

He lifted his head; his eyes glittered with hope. "Cassie trusts me a lot more than she used to. Perhaps now she will tell me."

She squeezed his arm reassuringly, and he looked down at her. His grip tightened. "Thank you for bringing my sisters to me," he said raggedly, and it was not the cab ride he was talking about.

The moment stretched endlessly. The hand covering hers seemed to burn to her core. Heat spread in slow, languid waves, lapping at every secret corner of her body. She had forgotten to breathe. She took a long, shaky breath. His eyes darkened, like a pool under moonlight, deep, rippling with emotion. She made a helpless gesture and leaned into him, and with a groan, he drew her into his arms and kissed her.

The kiss was ragged and heartfelt and tasted of gratitude and humility. And of hunger. And of desire. She made a small sound deep in her throat and kissed him back with everything in her.

There were no preliminaries, only his mouth meshing with hers, his tongue tangling hers, his big, hard body crushed against her soft curves. And it was everything she had dreamed of and more.

She was lost in the taste of him. He was intoxicated by the taste of her. He pressed her hard against the wall and covered her with his body, lost in the kiss, the need, the hunger. She pressed herself hard against him, reveling in his strength, his power, and his fierce, compelling, exhilarating desire.

His hands roamed over her body, caressing, cupping, creating trails of shivering sensation. She smoothed her hands over his chest, over his shoulders. How had she ever felt wary of this glorious body? She stroked the strong, tanned column of his throat, explored the delicious abrasion of his jaw, and her fingers buried themselves in the thick, dark, closely cropped hair. And all the time kissing him, kissing his mouth, his jaw, his throat. And he was kissing her as if he would never, could never stop, kissing Hope as if she were life itself.

He touched her breast, and a fiery arch of pleasure speared through her, and she gasped and arched and clutched his hair.

He lifted his head, breathing in jagged gasps, his chest heaving. And pulled back.

"I'm sorry—"

But she was having none of that. She pressed her fingers over his mouth and said, "I'm not sorry. And I never will be." And she tried to tell him with her eyes what she was not yet ready to say, but what her heart and body knew already.

And he gazed into her eyes for a long, long moment and opened his mouth to speak, but there was a knock on the door and they had just seconds to pull themselves together before a servant entered with the hot chocolate and pastries.

The moment was gone. And then the girls clattered in, ready for chocolate and hot, fresh pastries.

"When she was a baby, Dorie had a voice." Sebastian watched Cassie's face as he said it. It was not a question.

They were all seated around the table, Hope, too, even though she'd suggested she should probably leave. He'd given her a look, and Dorie had reached out and taken her hand.

No doubts remained in his mind. Sebastian felt unutterably blessed. For the first time in his life what he wanted and what he ought to do dovetailed perfectly.

"Cassie?"

She nibbled on her sweet, flaky pastry and watched him with a hint of the old wariness.

"Did she ever learn to speak?"

Cassie glanced at Dorie, who returned the look and gave an infinitesimal shrug in response. "Yes," said Cassie.

"Normally?" It had to be asked.

Cassie nodded.

"When did she stop?"

Cassie glanced at her sister again and seemed to read consent in her expression again. "Two years ago. Just after Mam died."

Sebastian sat back, feeling a small trickle of relief. "So she loved Widow Morgan and was distressed because she died. Is that it?"

Cassie said nothing, just drank some of her chocolate. She avoided his eyes.

"Did you both love her?"

Cassie darted a look at her sister, then said, "Mam was all right, she was good to us. She treated us fairly, but we knew we weren't her daughters or anything. She worked us hard, said we owed her."

"Worked you doing what?"

"The inn."

"What inn?"

"The Bull and Boar. Mam ran it. Dorie and me, we did what was needed, made the beds, cleaned, scrubbed, helped with the cooking—whatever." She darted him a glance. "In the last couple of years I helped out in the bar. Not Dorie. She stayed in the back, helping in the kitchen or upstairs."

The inference was clear. Cassie was coming to womanhood, so she'd been put in the bar. Sebastian swallowed. It didn't bear thinking of. She wasn't telling him the whole, he knew. He hoped she would, in her own time. Hoped, too, that he could bear it when she did.

"So if you didn't love Mrs. Morgan like a mother, why did Dorie stop talking after she died?"

Cassie shook her head. "I don't know. She just stopped, that's all."

"The day she died or a few days afterward?"

"The night Mam died. Mam died, and Dorie never spoke another word."

"But why—"

"Look!" Cassie slammed down her cup. "Do you think I

didn't *try*? Do you think I just let my sister stop talking and didn't do anything to find out why? She won't talk to me about it. Won't say a word. Won't even write anything down!" Cassie's face crumpled. "I know I should have been able to help her, but I can't. I tried, I really did."

"I'm sorry, sweeting." He reached across the table and took her hands in his. "I know you tried. I know. You have looked after Dorie beautifully."

Dorie sat frozen, a pastry halfway to her mouth, looking stricken at her sister's outburst. After a moment she carefully set the pastry down on her plate, slipped off her chair, and apologetically put her arms around her big sister.

But she didn't utter a sound or make any attempt to explain. Whatever had caused her silence in the first place seemed destined to remain forever a mystery.

# *Chapter Twelve*

∞

*The miserable have no other medicine but only hope.*
WILLIAM SHAKESPEARE

"MAY I ASK WHY YOU HAVE COME, MR. BEMERTON?" LADY ELInore asked coldly. "It was my understanding that the Misses Merridew were invited, and Mr. Reyne, of course, needs no invitation."

"Lady Elinore." Giles Bemerton bowed gracefully over her reluctantly outstretched hand. "When Bastian here mentioned it, I could not resist. I'm thinking of purchasing an orphan institution myself."

Lady Elinore stared. "You?"

Giles gave a smile, which took in all the ladies and Mr. Reyne and said in a mock-bashful voice, "A gift for a lady." He batted his lashes. "I understand it's all the crack at the moment."

Hope and her twin spluttered with laughter at his mischievous expression. Mr. Reyne cleared his throat significantly. Lady Elinore gave Giles a cold look, then sniffed. "Follow me then," and she led the way into the Tothill Fields Institution for Indigent Girls.

• • •

"And here is the dining hall, where the girls take all their meals. Three nourishing meals a day." The room was large, bare, and very clean, containing two long, scrubbed wooden tables flanked by wooden benches.

Hope heard her sister sigh. Hope knew what she meant. The visit was proving quite depressing. The orphan asylum was rigidly respectable and so very grim and gloomy. Dinnertime was not far off; an acrid well-boiled vegetabley smell wafted from the adjoining kitchen.

Lord Bemerton sniffed. "Cabbage," he pronounced gloomily. "Can't stand cabbage. We're not staying to dine, are we?" His sunny spirits seemed to be fading fast.

"Certainly not," Lady Elinore said.

Two small girls dressed in gray dresses and white aprons, marginally too big for them, clattered about in hard, shiny boots also a little too large for them, setting the tables: a spoon, a bowl, and a beaker of water for each child. A plate containing slices of dry bread sat at the center of each table. Presumably bread and soup were the only items on the menu. Their job done, the girls disappeared into the kitchen. They hadn't uttered a word. Hope had not yet heard one child speak, let alone laugh. It seemed quite unnatural.

Lady Elinore explained, "All of the girls take turns in the kitchen, the scullery, and the laundry. As well as earning their keep, they are trained in habits of cleanliness and good, plain cooking."

The smaller of the girls, a skinny little urchin with dark hair braided in tight pigtails, reemerged from the kitchen carrying two small dishes. On each lay a tiny pat of butter and a dab of reddish jam. She carried them very carefully, as if they were precious or fragile, but the dishes themselves were the same thick and ugly earthenware as the bowls on the table, and the butter was a meager scrape, hardly worth bringing out, in Hope's opinion. With great deliberation, her tongue thrust between a gap in her teeth as she concentrated on the task, she placed one dish exactly halfway down the second table and another beside the bowl three places from the end on the first. Clearly each butter dish was for a particular girl.

Hope was intrigued. There was barely enough butter and jam on each dish for one small slice of bread. Why would only two girls out of so many merit a scrape of butter and a dollop of jam? A reward system?

The small girl turned to leave. "Excuse me," called Hope. "Little girl."

The urchin froze and turned huge, apprehensive eyes on the group of visitors. She glanced nervously at Lady Elinore.

"May I talk to her?" Hope asked Lady Elinore.

"Of course."

Hope approached the child and knelt down beside her. "How do you do?" she said gently, for the child was anxiously bunching her apron in her fists. "My name is Hope. What's yours?"

The child glanced from Hope to Lady Elinore and then back. She bobbed a curtsy. "Please miss, me name's May."

"That's a pretty name. May is one of my favorite months."

The waif nodded fervently. "Mine, too, miss, coz it's me birfday—well, not me real birfday—I dunno when that is. But they give us a month when we first come here, an' all the girls who have that month have a birfday in the middle of it. An' today is the middle day of May."

"Oh! You have birthday celebrations here? How lovely." Hope was delighted. It was the first small human touch she had seen at the institution. "And what happens here on your 'birthday,' May?"

The child jerked her head at the butter dishes. "We get butter an' jam wiv our bread at dinner. And—" She bunched her apron again in her fists, but her eyes were bright with excitement. "We get a present!"

Hope smiled, able to empathize. Her own childhood had been bare of presents, except for small items her sisters had given her and Faith in secret. She still found presents thrilling. "And what do you hope to get this year?"

"A doll."

"And do you think you will get one?"

"I dunno, miss. I hope so. I'd love a little doll." Her eyes were bright with anticipation.

"Were you here last year?"

"Yes, miss."

"What did you get last year?"

The child screwed her face up endearingly. "Wool and a needle to darn my stockings wiv."

"Oh dear." It wasn't much of a present, Hope thought. "And the year before that, were you here?"

May gave a rueful, gap-toothed grin. "Yes, miss, an' I got wool and a needle then, too."

"Oh dear."

"It's what they usually give us, miss. A darning kit."

Hope bit her lip. "And yet this year you're hoping for a doll?

May nodded emphatically. "They say in church if you really want something, you haveta pray for it, and so I've prayed an' prayed for a doll, so maybe . . ." She gave a bright-eyed, optimistic shrug.

Hope smiled warmly. "I hope you get your doll, May."

"Thank you, miss. I 'ope so, too. I've never had a doll. Never had nuffin of me own."

Probably not even a name of her own. Were both butter and jam dishes destined for a child called May? wondered Hope. No wonder she longed for something of her own. A doll was something to love. "How long have you lived here, May?"

"Five years, miss. I come here when I was about four, I think."

Hope couldn't help but smile back. "And yet you keep hoping for a doll?"

The child shrugged. "It don't hurt to dream, miss, does it?"

Hope put her hand on the child's small head. "No, May," she said softly. "It certainly doesn't hurt to dream."

The child ran off to her duties, and Hope returned to the tour, a lump in her throat. She said to Lady Elinore, "The child said today was her birthday. She said there would be a small celebration?"

Lady Elinore nodded. "Yes, we do it on the fifteenth day of every month. All nonsense, of course. Celebrating a birthday is not at all Rational, particularly when you reflect that most of these children were born unwanted. But some of the ladies on the board like it. And it is a reward for good behavior."

"And the children get a present?"

"Yes."

"What will May get?"

"Darning wool and a needle."

"She's been praying for a doll to love."

"Good heavens, why? They always get darning wool and a needle. She knows that. It's a good, useful gift." Lady Elinore nodded in a satisfied manner. "They must darn their stockings anyway, so the expense is justified, and we have found that when they are given their own darning needle, they treat it more carefully. Fewer are bent or broken."

"I see. It is a cost-saving measure."

"Yes." Lady Elinore smiled.

"And she won't get her doll?"

"No. It's not at all practical. Now, shall we move on to the dormitories?"

Hope followed, inwardly frozen. These little girls' lives were so cheerless and grim. Completely devoid of joy.

She thought of little May, with anxious fists and gap-toothed smile, in her tight pigtails and her shiny, too-big boots. And her bright optimism, flourishing in the face of all the grim, gray Rationality.

A doll. Was it so much to ask?

A doll was easily come by—a small hank of rag and a couple of well-placed buttons, and you had a little friend of your own to take to bed and hug, to love and tell your secrets to.

She followed the group silently.

They viewed two dormitories, in each of which were ranged fifteen narrow beds covered with gray woolen counterpanes. Behind each bed was a hook on which hung each girl's Sunday dress. At the end of each bed sat a small chest that contained their other clothes. Lady Elinore showed them the contents of one such chest. Other than the clothes, there were no personal items.

The little ones' dormitory was identical. Not a doll or book or a keepsake in sight. The walls were decorated with texts from the published works of Lady Elinore's late mother,

And everything—everything!—was gray, black, white, or brown. Not a hint of blue or green or pink or yellow or red.

Hope examined it all without saying a word. She kept thinking about little May. The Merridew girls were orphans. If they'd had no one to take them in, they could have ended up in a place like this . . . And this was one of the good places.

They viewed the workroom. Sixteen girls, ranging in age from about eleven to fifteen, sat in rows, silently plying their needles. Their birthday needles, no doubt.

"Girls!" A black-clad woman at the front of the class rapped. "We have guests."

In unison the girls lay down their task, stood, and curtsied to the visitors. Each girl was clad identically in plain gowns of gray serge, with black woolen stockings and thick black boots. Their hair was scraped back from their heads and knotted tightly behind them. Their young faces were pale and solemn.

"Good afternoon, ladies and gentlemen," they chanted, then sat down again and bent diligently over their tasks. The needles barely slowed, though Hope noticed that many of the girls were eyeing her and her sister curiously from under their lashes, taking in every detail of their clothing and appearance. Their heads remained bowed.

Their meek silence depressed her. Faith slipped a hand in hers and squeezed it.

Hope watched the needles flash in and out, in and out. She thought of the hours she'd spent as a child, hemming seams. Her stitches had always to be pulled out for being uneven or crooked.

Faith whispered, "It's nearly as bad as Grandpapa's."

Hope shook her head. It was worse. Grandpapa may have been hate-filled and violent, but her sisters were loving and supportive. These girls seemed to have . . . nothing. No fellowship or camaraderie. No one to care for, no one to love. They were allowed nothing personal, not even a doll. Their bodies were cared for, but not their hearts.

Hope ached for their poor, lonely little hearts.

"It's a treat to watch such happy diligence," Lady Elinore said proudly.

Hope stared at her in incredulity. Didn't she realize?

"Our girls fashion all the garments they are wearing, even down to their knitted stockings. Not, of course, their boots, which are made by a local cobbler. But some of the older girls are being trained as milliners, and they make the hats and bonnets."

Hope looked back at the row of plain gray bonnets hanging on pegs in the hallway. Underneath each peg hung a plain gray coat. All that distinguished one from the other was the size of the garment and the number above each peg.

She wanted to scream, to shatter the silence and order, to run through the bare, echoing rooms, shouting and hooting at the top of her voice. She wanted to knock all the neat, gray, ugly bonnets to the floor and jump on them. She wanted to drag all the girls outside and run with them to the park, to skip and sing and play.

"Each girl is trained to be as independent as possible, so they leave here equipped to earn a living," Mr. Reyne added. "As soon as they are old enough, they are apprenticed to a trade."

"Yes, as milliners, seamstresses, cooks, housemaids, servants of all sorts, naturally. It is unlikely any of them will marry, of course," Lady Elinore added in a whisper. "Not with their backgrounds."

Hope could not even look at Faith. If she did, she would not be able to contain herself.

"And where do the children play?" she asked.

"Play? Oh, you mean take exercise. Out here." Lady Elinore conducted them to the small cobbled yard.

They stepped out into the air. High stone walls on all sides. A square glimpse of sky above. Not a shred of green, nor anything to break the grim grayness.

"They walk out here twice daily. Regular exercise is necessary for their health, of course."

"Here?" exclaimed her sister. Faith was clearly as horrified as she.

"I meant play, not simply exercise," Hope said. "Do they not have free time in which to play and be children? I saw no toys or personal items in the dormitories—not even in the little ones'."

Lady Elinore stared, as if she did not understand the question. "What would they want with toys? They are orphans. Their lives will be hard. They must prepare for that."

There was a long silence. Hope clenched her fists and told herself that Lady Elinore meant well, she did. She was a kind person. She did not know what she was doing to these children.

Mr. Reyne, picking up on the tension between them, explained. "Most children in the world do not have the luxury of play, as the children of the rich do. Most children must work for their daily bread. It is that or starve."

Hope could not believe he was defending this policy. She opened her mouth to give him a piece of her mind, stared at the harsh, grim line of his mouth, and remembered how he had been pulled out of his life of privilege and flung into a factory, working for his daily bread. And his gutter-bruised fruit and vegetables. The thought silenced her.

He said forcefully, "Most orphans would consider the life these girls have as luxurious. I know of institutions where all the inmates, children as young as five or six, must work twelve-hour days and longer in a factory. Some from five in the morning till eight at night. The children are whipped to keep them awake. Sleepy children cause mill accidents. Accidents mean the loss of income for everyone, while small bodies are cleared from machinery."

Hope shuddered at the image his words produced. He was right, she knew. She thought of his little brother, Johnny.

He continued in a low, hard voice, "In time, the work cripples them. Young bones are not strong enough to stand up to the strain of standing in one place day in and day out. Their bones bend, and their young spines twist. I have visited an institution that contains a hundred young boys on crutches or carts, crippled by their working youth." He hesitated, then went on, determined to make her understand. "Girls fare worse. I know of one man who keeps a hundred young female orphans to use in his factory. He has a reputation as a rake. From time to time a young girl will simply disappear. No one asks questions." He paused to let his words sink in, then added, "If Lady Elinore is proud of this institution, she has good reason."

It was a clear reprimand. And Hope knew she deserved it. He knew what he was talking about. He'd experienced it himself. Hope glanced at Mr. Bemerton. His eyes were somber.

Sebastian Reyne had suffered as a child, worked in a manufactory. His body bore scars, the legacy of a childhood that had been far from easy. His crooked nose was a testament to the knocks he'd taken. His very bearing, always alert, always expecting trouble, showed he'd had to fight to survive. She thought of his poor fingers, crushed in vain, trying to save his little brother from a horrible death.

Of course he saw no lack in the way these girls lived.

They were fed, they were clothed, they were housed. They were clean, and they had work. In his eyes, they needed nothing else. He thought them lucky, well off, and perhaps in the greater scheme of things, they were.

But no wonder his eyes were so stark, so lonely.

She ached for him, for the happiness he was snatched from as a child, for his bleak and joyless outlook on life. She ached for Lady Elinore and her Rational existence, and she ached for each and every girl in the institution.

Because although he was right, he was also wrong, so wrong. They were all wrong. Except for little May.

The child had said it all: *"It don't hurt to dream, miss, does it?"*

She said, "So, you would teach a child to expect nothing but hard times? I disagree. Children have a right to expect some joy in life. We all do—each and every one of us, no matter who we are; child, adult, rich or poor, orphan or not." She took a deep breath and announced, "And to that purpose, I am inviting them all to take tea with my sisters and me next week."

There was a flurry of concern at her words.

"You can't!" Lady Elinore gasped. "It will disrupt their routine."

"Only for a few hours. I'm sure they will be all the better for a change of pace."

"Excellent idea, Miss Hope," Mr. Bemerton said. "Dreary things, routines. Made to be broken, if you ask me."

At his words, all Lady Elinore's uncertainty vanished. She gave him a quelling look and said severely, "No, I'm sorry, Miss Merridew, it's not possible. There are too many girls. Besides, they wouldn't know how to behave in a lady's drawing room."

"I don't agree. You have obviously done a beautiful job in training them, Lady Elinore, but it is not an exercise in etiquette. All I ask is that they enjoy themselves. Have fun."

"Won't know how to behave? Unnervingly correct, if you ask me," Mr. Bemerton offered. "Be a relief to see them crack."

Hope and her sister beamed at him.

Lady Elinore sniffed audibly. "Nobody asked your opinion, Mr. Bemerton."

He grinned unrepentantly. "Oh, that's all right. I'm not shy."

Lady Elinore bristled, and Hope hurriedly said, "There are not too many girls. I own, twenty-eight is a large number, but my great-uncle's house can accommodate them, I'm certain. We shall hire carriages to convey them there and back."

"Reyne and I can organize the transport," offered Mr. Bemerton. "Eh, Bas?" He glanced at Mr. Reyne, who didn't look at all pleased with the turn of events.

Hope was delighted at Mr. Bemerton's unexpected offer. "Thank you, Mr. Bemerton, you are most kind."

She took Lady Elinore's hand. "Please say yes, Lady Elinore. It will give my sisters and me such pleasure to entertain your girls."

Lady Elinore looked to Mr. Reyne in appeal. He came to her rescue. "These are not the sort of girls you and your sisters ought to be associating with," he said stiffly in an undertone. "They are not fit for your company."

"I don't agree!" Hope said. "They are clean and well behaved—better behaved than I am, I know. And my sisters and I are orphans, too." *As are you,* her look reminded him. "I don't care about their past; it's a very small piece of their future we are talking about. Please, Mr. Reyne, let them come," she said softly. "If they were your sisters, would you not want them to enjoy a small, occasional treat?"

He stiffened, his face a frozen mask for a few seconds. "They are not my sisters!"

"No, but if they were—"

"But they're not!" he said vehemently. "The very idea of my sisters in a place such as this is ridiculous."

He turned to Lady Elinore. "It is your decision, Lady Elinore; it is you who designed the program the girls follow."

"Actually, my mother planned it as a model institution. I simply follow in her footsteps, continuing her work. What do you think?"

He made an impatient gesture. "To be frank, I don't care one way or the other whether the orphans take tea or not. I shall be bound by your decision."

Hope pounced. "So, if Lady Elinore agrees, you would help arrange the transport?"

"Why not?"

"And bring your sisters?"

His mouth tightened. "No. I would not permit my sisters to attend such an event."

"Why ever not?" Hope demanded. "They would enjoy it, I am sure. Our sister Grace will be there."

He shrugged indifferently. "You must do as you see fit, as must I. My sisters will not be associating with any orphans from this institution.

"I cannot believe your attitude!" Hope exclaimed.

He gave a her a level look. "I cannot help that."

It was clear from the set look on his face that he would not budge from his position. Hope stared at him, wondering what had made him poker up like that. She had caught Lady Elinore's hints that some of these girls had lived less-than-respectable lives before they came to the institution, but in Hope's view, they were simply children in need. And everyone deserved a fresh start. She, for one, would not hold their background against them.

Her twin's gentle voice interrupted her thoughts. "Please let them come, Lady Elinore. A small outing cannot hurt, surely. An hour or two out of their normal routine."

Hope turned away from the grim-faced man in front of her, slipped an arm around her twin's waist, and squeezed it affectionately.

Lady Elinore chewed her lip uncertainly. "I am not sure it is a wise thing. It may overturn everything we are attempting to instill in these girls. Unsettle them. The institution is run on my late mother's *Principles of Rationality*.

There is no Rational purpose in mindless play or frivolous entertainment. They are occupied for every moment of the day. It is what gives their lives direction." Her voice gained in confidence as she uttered the familiar, well-worn phrases.

*She probably grew up on this sort of stuff,* Hope thought. Lady Elinore's mother might be dead, but she still ruled her life.

"And what gives their lives meaning?" Hope asked.

There was a long pause. Lady Elinore gave her a blank look. Doubt slowly crept into her expression. "Their routine," she said on an uncertain note.

"And what do they dream of?"

"Nothing, I hope. Dreaming is a waste of time."

"That's a terrible thing to say!"

Lady Elinore blinked at the vehemence in Hope's voice.

"And what joy do they have in life?"

Lady Elinore frowned. "Joy? There is satisfaction in doing a job well, and in behaving correct—"

"I am not talking of satisfaction! Children thrive on joy—we all do!"

"Extreme passions are to be avoided. The girls are better off without them."

Hope stared at her, flabbergasted. "If children are brought up to believe there is no joy in the world, to expect only hard times and grim endurance, then what is there to live *for*?"

Lady Elinore seemed honestly confused by the question.

Hope said passionately, "You say dreaming is a waste of time, but you could not be more wrong! Dreams are as necessary as food! Dreams and hopes are what give us the strength and courage to endure the hard times. Will the girls not work with a better will this week, knowing that there is a treat in store for them at the end of it?"

Lady Elinore said absently, "Yes, rewards for good behavior are Rational." Her mind was not on Rational rewards though, for she added in a troubled voice, "But you are mistaken about . . . about dreams, I'm sure. Mother used to say that dreams were nonsense, just rubbish left over from the day's events. She said even dogs dreamed and that people were hardly on the same level as dogs."

"Your mother was wrong," Faith said with absolute certainty. "Dreams are important. They give us the strength to try to change our lives for the better."

Hope smiled at her sister. Nobody who had been raised under Grandpapa's bleak regime could undervalue the power of dreams.

Hope was hesitant to criticize Lady Elinore's mother, knowing Lady Elinore had based her whole existence on her mother's dreary principles. But it needed to be said. And not only to Lady Elinore.

She looked at the man who expected nothing of life but harsh reality and said softly, "Dreams can bring us out of the darkness."

"Dreams make us weak and sap the fortitude with which a woman must approach life," Lady Elinore said as if parroting a lesson.

Hope shook her head. "Not so! Dreams are the source of fortitude. In the bitterest winter, dreams give us the promise of summer and the strength to endure. Dreams show us the path. They give us purpose."

Lady Elinore pronounced in a thready voice, "Dreams are meaningless rubbish."

"No! Dreams can give our lives meaning."

"Mother said people who indulge in dreams will amount to nothing. Or go mad."

"Then your mother was wrong!" Hope declared passionately. "If we deny our dreams, we deny ourselves, the very heart of our selves."

There was a short, fraught silence, then Lady Elinore burst into tears.

For a moment, everyone was too shocked to move. Mr. Bemerton leaped to the fore. "You are overwrought, Lady Elinore. Onset of the headache, no doubt. My mother was plagued with them. You need to go home, lie down, burn a few pastilles. I shall escort you home immediately. Mr. Reyne will take care of your guests. He is owner of this institution, after all."

He hustled the sobbing Lady Elinore out of the orphanage before anyone could collect their wits. Hope looked at her sister in remorse. "I did not mean to distress her so." She turned to Mr. Reyne. "I promise you I did not mean her to take my words personally. I will go after her, explain . . ."

He shook his head slowly, still staring after Mr. Bemerton, a frown darkening his brow. "No. Giles will look after her. He is right; I am responsible now for this institution. What would you like to see next?"

Hope shivered. "I have seen all I want, thank you! But I am worried about Lady Elinore. I didn't mean to upset—"

He interrupted. "So you would take back your words then?"

She regarded him a moment and shook her head. "No. I believe in them wholly."

Faith stepped forward and took her hand. "As do I. If we hadn't dreamed, we would never have found the courage to escape from our grandfather and would still be dwelling in utter misery." She turned to Hope. "Don't be too upset, dearest. You weren't being nasty. I think you inadvertently touched on a tender spot."

Hope thought about that. "You mean . . ."

"Does not Lady Elinore have the look of an inveterate dreamer?"

Hope considered the idea. "And with that horrid mother of hers doing her best to crush the dreaming out of her . . ."

"No wonder she was upset. She's convinced her mother was infallible."

Hope glanced back at the exercise yard. She thought of grim, gray dresses and improving tales and little girls who dreamed of dolls and got darning needles instead. "Her mother has a lot to answer for." She turned to Mr. Reyne. "I am sorry for upsetting Lady Elinore, but I hold by my views. And I am determined to bring some cheer into these girls' lives, Mr. Reyne, so be warned." And not just into the lives of orphan girls, she resolved. Why did so many people think to have fun was a sin?

He had remained silent throughout their discussion. He considered them both thoughtfully. "I don't suppose an outing with tea and cakes can do much harm."

She took his hand. "Oh, thank you, Mr. Reyne. Of course it will do no harm, and it will do us all a great deal of good, not just the girls. It makes me happy just to think of it."

He held her hand tightly for a moment and then released it abruptly. "I shall inform Lady Elinore this afternoon. I shall send a note around as soon as I get home."

"Yes, so will I, to apologize," said Hope. "And Faith and I shall call on her in the morning. And I hope you will bring your sisters to the tea."

His face hardened. "I shall not. I will not have them associating with the girls of this institution! I said it, and I meant it."


Giles procured a hackney cab and helped Lady Elinore into it. She was still sobbing, though trying to hide it from him, holding her face averted from him and scrubbing at her eyes with a small square of linen. It was quite inadequate for the job. The tears kept flowing, but she fought them valiantly.

Giles endured it for a moment and then said gruffly, "Oh, for God's sake, here, let me." He moved beside her, took the crumpled, damp handkerchief from her hand, and stuffed it in his pocket. Then he pulled out his own handkerchief, put an arm around her, and proceeded to mop her cheeks gently.

She stiffened at his touch and said through hiccups, "I-I'm s-sorry . . . I . . . do not . . . kn-know . . . what is wrong . . . w-with—"

"Hush," Giles said firmly. "You may cry as much or as little as you wish, but do not apologize for it. You are entitled to your emotions."

She was so surprised she blinked at him through the tears, jerky sobs rocking her thin frame at irregular intervals.

He pulled her tighter against his shoulder.

"Oh but—" She tried to pull away.

"Now stop that. There is nothing personal or improper in this," he said mock severely. "You are a lady in distress. Being a gentleman, I can do no less than offer the proverbial shoulder to cry on. I would do the same for any lady, so think nothing more of it."

"Oh." She stopped trying to pull away and lay against his shoulder like a small, stiff piece of wood.

Giles found her awkwardness oddly endearing. He moved back in the seat a little, unbalancing her enough so that she ended up half lying against him. She stayed rigid for a moment or two, but gradually her body relaxed—in increments. Every now and then she would catch herself relaxing and stiffen up for a moment, then the rhythmic rocking of the moving cab, the light pressure of Giles's arm, and her own exhaustion would conspire to make her soften against him.

They trotted along in companionable silence for ten minutes or more, Giles lazing back against the seat and Lady Elinore half lying against him, his arm gently but firmly supporting her, but as the cab reached Leicester Square, she seemed to recall herself. With a start, she thrust herself away from Giles and skittered along the seat until she was a good two feet away from him.

She said in a voice husky with embarrassment, "Th-thank you, Mr. Bemerton. I believe I have recovered from my bout of—"

"The vapors."

She sat up straighter. "I was not *vaporish*! Merely overcome for a moment."

Giles shrugged provocatively. "Whatever you wish to call it."

"It was *not* the vapors. My mother despised vaporish women. No true lady succumbs in public to *any* strong emotion."

"Oh, it wasn't so public. Just you and me. Our little secret." He smiled lazily and leaned back against the leather squabs of the cab, watching her. She raised her nose high, pretending to be unaware of his regard. The more he lounged and watched, the straighter she sat. She twitched her dress straight, her bonnet straight, and her mouth compressed in a straight little line of disapproval.

By the time they'd reached Piccadilly, she'd regained her composure completely. The only sign of her tearful outbreak was her slightly reddened nose and eyes and the damp square of linen in his pocket.

"Tell me about your mother," he said.

She looked at him suspiciously. "What do you want to know?"

"When did she die?"

"Last February. But it was a very slow death."

"Do you miss her?"

"Of course! We were very close."

"In what way?"

"In all ways. My mother depended on me for everything," she said proudly. "I answered all her mail, and she received a great deal, for she was quite well-known, and I copied out all her papers for the printer, for my hand is clear and neat. I ran our house also, for Mother's mind was on too lofty a plane, and she was impatient of mundane details. She used to call me her good right hand in all things."

"Her dogsbody, in fact."

"Not at all! I resent that remark. You have no idea." She shifted another few inches away from him, looked out of the window, and said crossly, "This cab is very slow."

"And since she died, how has your life changed?"

She thought about it a moment. "Not very much. I live the life she designed for us and have continued her work as best I can."

He said gently, "Were there no dreams of your own you wished to pursue?"

"Oh no," she said quietly. "My life with Mother was busy and fulfilling."

He raised his eyebrows at that but said only, "Fulfilling? I see. I did not think you used to attend assemblies when your mother was alive."

She flushed. "No." She compressed her lips in a clear signal that she would say no more.

"Some would say it is rather late to join the marriage mart. Most of the young ladies making their coming-out are a dozen years younger." It was ungentlemanly of him to mention her age, but he could think of no way else to prod her out of her shell.

She flushed darker, struggling with herself a moment, not wanting to explain to him but not wishing him to jump to the wrong conclusions. She said starkly, "My late father made a will, in which he leaves me a fortune, to come to me after I have been married three years. My mother left most of her money tied up in her various important works." She gave a short, embarrassed twist of her shoulders. "So I have no choice but to seek a husband."

Giles was silent a moment, thinking about a mother who cared more about her self-aggrandizing crackpot enterprises than the security of the daughter who had devoted her life to her.

"Do you have an aversion to marriage?"

Her brow wrinkled. "Not precisely. In any case, needs must."

He said bluntly, "I would not wish my friend Mr. Reyne to take a wife who holds him in secret aversion. You are aware, I suppose, he is courting you."

She hesitated, twisting her reticule in her hands. "He has said nothing, but I am aware of the directions of his attentions, yes. And I do not hold him in aversion. He is a decent enough man."

"Yes, he is. He will make you a fine, strong, lusty husband."

She stared at him, appalled.

He continued suavely, "And no doubt you will find comfort in any children you may have."

Her jaw dropped. "Children!" There was a short silence, then she said in a shaken voice, "I must admit I hadn't thought of children. I thought I was too—" She broke off, flustered.

Giles said it for her. "You are not too old for *anything*, Elinore."

She flushed, instantly pokered up, and said crisply, "I did not give you permission to use my given name, sir. And I think this conversation has become quite improper. See, we are coming to Berkeley Square. My home is but a few steps away. We shall finish the journey in silence, if you please!"

Giles lolled against the worn leather squabs, well pleased with his morning's work.

# Chapter Thirteen

∞

*What are young women made of?*
*Ribbons and laces, and sweet pretty faces.*
NURSERY RHYME

"I FELT SO DREADFUL, AUNT GUSSIE. I HAD NO NOTION MY words would upset Lady Elinore so much."

The twins and Mrs. Jenner had come to tea at Lady Augusta's and were sitting in her front parlor, discussing the recent visit. Mrs. Jenner, offended that she hadn't been invited to the Tothill Institution—even thought she'd earlier declared she couldn't abide poor people—was sulking in a well-bred fashion. The others ignored her.

"Pshaw! No need to rebuke yourself. Dreams are important. Your sister is right, you inadvertently touched on a nerve, that's all." Lady Augusta's eyes narrowed. "You say young Bemerton hustled her off home? I must say, that surprises me."

Faith explained, "The rest of us were too shocked to move."

Mrs. Jenner said waspishly, "And Mr. Bemerton is, after all, a gentleman born and knows how to treat a lady. Unlike others we could name."

Hope said hotly, "What do you mean by that? Mr.

Reyne is perfectly gentlemanly! Mr. Bemerton just got in first, that's all."

Faith laid a calming hand on her knee. "Dearest, do you know why Mr. Reyne was so admant about his sisters not coming to the tea party?"

Hope shook her head. "No. He is very protective of those girls—perhaps a little overprotective."

Mrs. Jenner said, "I don't understand why a man who is supposed to be courting Lady Elinore allowed another man to see her home, particularly when she was distressed."

Lady Augusta snorted. "If she'd had any sense, Lady Elinore would have fainted, and then that lovely big Mr. Reyne would be forced to catch her and carry her out. No idea, that gel."

Hope was very glad of Lady Elinore's lack of idea. If lovely big Mr. Reyne was to catch and carry anyone, he would carry Hope Merridew! She said firmly, "Mr. Reyne, as owner of the institution, had a duty as host to remain with his guests."

Lady Augusta considered the notion and wrinkled her nose. "Possibly that was it. Did he do his duty as host then, the lad with the divine shoulders?" She gave Hope a wicked look and added, "Lovely hard thighs, too. I like a man with powerful thighs."

"Aunt Gussie, *please*!" Hope blushed at Lady Gussie's embarrassing descriptions of Mr. Reyne. Accurate, but embarrassing.

"Well I can't help noticing, now that men wear those nice tight—"

Faith interrupted hurriedly, "Mr. Reyne stayed for a short time and then escorted us home."

Lady Augusta winked at Hope, picked up a cream-filled chocolate meringue, and looked at it thoughtfully. "I pity Lady Elinore. Agatha Pilton always was a peculiar gel!"

"Agatha Pilton? Who is Agatha Pilton?" Hope asked, puzzled.

Lady Gussie took a large bite and after she had finished chewing said, "Lady Elinore's mother. Was a Pilton before she wed. She married Billy Whitelaw, the Earl of Ennismore—an Irish title—and made a complete mess of it. Got hysterical when she found out that Billy had a mistress—well, what did she expect? Not as if it was a love match. All the world knew poor Billy was on the lookout for an heiress. Didn't have two sixpences to rub together, but oh! He was a handsome devil! Agatha Pilton was a good-looking gel, but no personality to speak of. She must have known she was married for her fortune. That's how things were arranged in those days. It's how it was with my first marriage. You just have to make the best of things." She shook her head and ate the rest of the meringue.

"What did Lady Ennismore do?"

Lady Gussie made a disgusted noise, swallowed a mouthful of sherry, and said, "Made huge public fusses. She stood outside the mistress's house and made the most appallingly vulgar scene. Followed Billy to his club and made another one. Stood under the bow window of White's and just screeched! Shocking!" Her hand hovered over the plate of cakes indecisively. "In the end, she refused to allow him into the house. Started to dress like a fright. Took up a career as a living embarrassment. Billy went off to Ireland or India or somewhere and died in some bizarre accident. Typical of Billy." She selected a lemon curd cake. "Last I heard, Agatha was running with a coven of bluestockings—that was round about the time when I was leaving for Argentina."

Hope poured herself and her twin another cup of tea. "How very fascinating. Lady Ennismore published a book called *The Principles of Rationality for Enlightened Ladies,* you know."

"No, I didn't know. It sounds perfectly frightful!" declared Lady Gussie with an elegant shudder. "Sounds exactly like the sort of thing an enlightened lady should avoid!"

"Lady Elinore was reared according to those principles."

"Well, that goes to show what rubbish the book must be.

Poor gel looks appalling, dresses atrociously, and acts as if she's never had any fun in her life. I bet she's never even been kissed!" Lady Gussie nibbled delicately on the lemon curd cake, then sighed. "What a waste of a life. If I had the dressing of that gel, I'm sure I could make her into something passable at the very least. But all that gray!" She shuddered. "No one should go through life clad in gray."

"I do so agree," said Faith fervently. "Our grandfather used to dress us all in gray homespun, and it was horrid."

Lady Gussie looked appalled. "I knew that man was insane, but to dress you beautiful young things in gray homespun! It's criminal, that's what it is! Criminal!"

Hope stared at Lady Gussie and sat up straight. "Aunt Gussie," she said slowly. "You're absolutely right!"

"Of course I'm right." Lady Gussie finished the curd cake and dusted sugar off her fingers fastidiously. "What about, in particular?"

Faith stared at her sister. "You've had an idea."

Hope grinned and nodded.

"About Lady Elinore?"

"No, about the orphan girls." She sat forward excitedly on her chair. "We shall not simply have those girls to tea. It shall be a little more exciting than just tea and cakes. I am determined to bring some real joy into their lives! I do hope Lady Elinore won't mind it very much—I don't want to upset her any more than I already have. I felt dreadful when she burst into tears like that, because I do like her, even if she does have odd ideas."

"Yes, me, too," Faith agreed.

"Agatha Pilton should have been strangled," muttered Lady Gussie. "Teaching a daughter to want to look like a fright! A crime against nature!"

Faith nodded. "Yes, her ideas about life must be horrid! Imagine saying dreams are only rubbish fit for dogs!"

The old lady snorted. "Indeed! Lady Elinore is fortunate her mother died. Pity it didn't happen when she was a child, instead of when she was thirty."

Hope laid an affectionate hand on Lady Gussie's dimpled arm. "Dear Lady Gussie. Poor Elinore would have been so much happier if you'd been her mother."

Lady Augusta nodded thoughtfully. "Yes, she would. Still, it's never too late for anything. Agatha's gel might make something of herself yet."

Faith said, "I'm dying to know, twin. What do you mean to *do*?"

Hope explained her plan. When she finished, she sat back and looked at her sister and Lady Augusta. "So, will you help me? You know I'm useless at that sort of thing, but with help . . ."

"Help you? Of course we will!" her twin exclaimed. "It's a delightful plan! Count me in. And Grace will want to help, too, I'm sure."

They both turned to Lady Augusta for her verdict.

Lady Gussie beamed at Hope. "I'll help you, Miss Hoyden. Indeed I will." She downed her third glass of sherry and chuckled. "I adore a plot. And you know, I'd like to know a bit more about this orphan asylum, too. Poor motherless little souls. D'ye mind if I get Maudie and some of her cronies on board? She'd love this." She gave a sudden crack of laughter and added, "Maudie despised Agatha Pilton. Now, Hope, my dear, what are you going to wear to Lady Thorn's gypsy ball?"

Hope blinked at the sudden change of subject but answered, "To be honest, Aunt Gussie, I haven't the slightest notion. I hadn't given it any thought. What do Hungarian gypsies wear? Does anyone know?"

"Fleas, I'll be bound." said Lady Augusta sardonically, "But there I'll draw the line! Faith, my dear gel, you spend a deal of time talking to that pretty Count Rimavska. Do you have any thoughts on the matter?"

Faith looked a little self-conscious. As well she should, thought Hope, considering the amount of time she'd spent with the count lately!

"Masks, of course, in any style you want. And for the dress, I think lots of bright colors, Aunt Gussie. Plenty of red and black and white, and ruffles and flounces and embroidery. The men will wear boots and——"

"Boots, at a ball!" Aunt Gussie exclaimed in horror.

"Yes, and either baggy gathered trousers or tight black ones."

"No guesses as to what the count will wear," muttered Hope waspishly.

"Yes, he does like to wear his trousers snug, does he not?" Lady Augusta chuckled. "Mind you, dear, he does have the figure for it, unlike many other men of our acquaintance, poor dears—and I say, when a man has the figure for it, he may wear his pants as tight as may be; I for one shall never complain!"

Everyone laughed. "Aunt Gussie you're outrageous!"

"Oh, pish tush! What else are eyes for? Now, what else will they wear, Faith?"

"The men's shirts should be white, full and gathered at the sleeve and a brightly embroidered vest. And he will wear a head scarf—"

"A head scarf? A *head scarf*?"

Both twins giggled at her appalled tone.

"Yes, or a black hat."

"No man in London will wear a head scarf!" declared Lady Augusta firmly. "Well, that's the men outfitted, but what shall we wear? Faith, what are you wearing?"

Faith said, "I did ask Fel—Count Rimavska, and he helped me to come up with a number of different ideas. I have brought my sketchbook with me, as it happens." She took a small sketch pad from her reticule.

The ladies pored over the sketches, exclaiming over each in pleasure and excitement.

"Very pretty, Faith."

Faith said, "You are welcome to take any of these you like."

"Oh, what a sweet gel you are! I might have this one— only in a different color—purple, I think."

Hope met Faith's eye then, and they twinkled at each other. Aunt Gussie did love the color purple.

Lady Augusta sat back in her chair. "What fun! With this gypsy ball and the plot for the orphan gels in the meantime, it's going to be a busy time for us all! Ring that bell, will you, dear, and tell Shoebridge to bring me another drink. After all this talk of dresses, I'm parched!"

"It's no use, Bas, you won't get in; it's a female-only affair," Giles lounged in the driver's seat of his chaise, his collar turned up and his curly brimmed beaver hat crammed low over his eyes.

Sebastian had just pulled up in front of Sir Oswald Merridew's house in Providence Court, ten gray-clad, nervous girls squashed into his barouche, the last load of orphans.

"Females only?"

Giles nodded as he descended from his carriage and walked toward the barouche. "Secret female matters, apparently. We males are only valued for our driving skills." He shrugged. "Greetings, ladies!" He bowed extravagantly to the girls as he threw open the barouche doors and let down the steps. "You have arrived at your destination."

It was exactly the right approach, Sebastian saw. The nervous girls giggled shyly as they descended and filed into the house like obedient mice.

"Lady Elinore not coming then?" Giles asked.

Sebastian shook his head. "No. She's had to accept the outing, but she doesn't approve of it. She'll meet the girls afterward." He made to follow them into the house.

Giles detained him. "I told you, it's females only." He shrugged. "Of course, we were invited to take refreshment with Sir Oswald, but to be perfectly frank, Bas, you couldn't drag me into that house today if you tried."

"Why?" Sebastian frowned.

Giles glanced up at the blank windows of the house in a hunted manner and confided, "The Merridews have enlisted a gaggle of dowagers—Lady Augusta, Lady Gosforth, and a dozen or so of their cronies—and I use the word advisedly. Terrifying collection of crones. They treat me like a scrubby schoolboy! Me! And d'you know what? I *feel* like a scrubby schoolboy the minute any one of them claps a beady eye on me! I might once have been a *small* schoolboy, possibly even a trifle on the *flimsy* side, but I was never in my life *scrubby*!"

He gave the house a baleful glance and pulled his hat lower over his eyes. "And today, there's a pack of 'em in there!" He shuddered. "So I'm away to the safety of my club. They want us back for transportation duty in two hours, I'm informed. Are you coming?"

Sebastian was. Not having known them since birth, the dowagers held no terrors for him, but the thought of a house full of forty or more females and himself and Sir Oswald the only males . . . The club was infinitely appealing.

Two hours later they returned to Providence Court. They were admitted by the ancient butler, who showed them into the library. "Miss Merridew says to tell you gentlemen that they are running a trifle late. If you would wait here . . ." He gestured to the comfortable seats. "Miss has ordered refreshments for you." As he spoke, the door opened again, and a footman entered the room carrying a tray on which a plate of sandwiches, several slices of pie, a plum cake, and some biscuits had been set out. Another footman followed with wine and ale.

Sebastian eyed the supplies. "Clearly we are in for a long wait."

Giles took a sandwich and glanced warily at the door. "As long as that door stays closed and hordes of dowagers aren't released." He paused and cocked his ear upward. "Seems to be a lot of noise for a tea party. You don't think they've cracked open a few bottles, do you?"

"For girls not fifteen years old? I hardly think so." Sebastian listened, his brow furrowed. "It does sound quite noisy, though."

They had made good inroads into the sandwiches and ale when the front doorbell jangled a peremptory demand.

A moment later, a female voice was raised with some insistence. Giles cocked his head. "That's Lady Elinore's voice. Er, I think." He rose and stepped out into the hall. Sebastian followed.

Lady Elinore was addressing the butler in high dudgeon. "It was agreed that the girls would be returned some forty-five minutes ago, and they have not returned! They must be returned, immediately."

Giles sauntered forward. "Afternoon, Lady Elinore. Delightful to see you. What an outfit you're wearing! What color would you call it—gray, perhaps? Amazing. Makes you look quite—er. And that bonnet, truly appalli—er, apparel for the Rational. Your milliner is a brave creature! Or did you get it in a job lot with those girls upstairs? Charmed." He picked up her clenched fist, kissed it with great gallantry, then started with assumed surprise. "Gray gloves by George! What a devilishly clever notion. Contrast, that's the job!"

She snatched back her hand crossly and said to Sebastian, "Those girls are supposed to be at their lessons by now." She tipped her head on one side. "Listen to that racket! One would think I'd come to Bedlam instead of a gentleman's residence!" She turned to the butler, "Be so good as to inform Miss Merridew that Lady Elinore Whitelaw is here to collect the orphans. Immediately."

The butler wheezed off.

"Like a sandwich, Lady Elinore? Glass of ale? Slice of pie?"

"Hush, Giles," said Sebastian, perceiving that Lady Elinore was seriously discomposed. "There is no need to worry, Lady Elinore. The girls are perfectly safe."

She gave a sniff. "Miss Merridew promised they would be back nearly an hour ago, and they are not. It is of the utmost importance that those girls live smooth, uneventful lives. Only then can we retrieve them from their past!"

"A little tea, an outing, a few cakes," Sebastian said in a soothing voice. "What can it hurt?"

As he spoke a bell tinkled above them. Miss Hope Merridew stood on the landing, looking down into the hallway. "Lady and gentlemen," she announced gaily, "I give you the young ladies of the Tothill Fields Institution for Indigent Girls." She turned and said, "Go along, girls."

The girls came downstairs, two by two, in a long, neat line, the same way they had entered the house nearly three hours before. But there all resemblance ended. The older girls came first.

Lady Elinore gasped.

"Oh, I say," murmured Giles.

Sebastian blinked. They were not the same girls. Pinched nervous faces now glowed with excitement and pride. Their tight buns of scraped-back hair had disappeared, and ringlets and curls had sprung forth, bearing ribbons or silk flowers or fashionable hair ornaments.

The girls were still clad in the gray dresses they'd arrived in, Sebastian realized, but there was no resemblance to the shapeless dull garments of before. These gowns fitted their young owners better, and each was individually decorated with braid or colored ruffles, lace trim or knots of ribbons, and new, contrasting buttons. In some dresses, panels of colored material had been inserted; in others, the collar and cuffs had been covered with a bright hue and a colored ruffle applied to the hem. Each dress was now unique to its wearer and almost bore the look of a fashionable garment.

Each girl walked with shy pride, like a young rose unfurling her petals.

The girls floated down the stairs as if walking on air, holding their skirts carefully in one hand and their bonnet in the other. Their movements were accompanied by a faint swishing sound that Sebastian could not identify. He frowned, trying to work it out.

"Silk petticoats," Giles murmured. "If I'm not mistaken, each one of them is wearing a silk petticoat that they didn't arrive with. Nothing like silk underclothes to make a female feel feminine! Have to take my hat off to Miss Merridew—it's a miracle. Never seen such a transformation. Gray mice into—"

"Birds of paradise!" snapped Lady Elinore. "After all we've done to save them from this!"

"What balderdash," Giles retorted. "Save them from what? A bit of braid and a feather or two?"

"It is much more than braid and feathers, it is—"

"Both of you be quiet!" said Sebastian in a voice that brooked no argument. "If there is any difference of opinion here, it will be dealt with in private and not in front of these children!"

The older girls reached the hallway and gathered in a circle, tying their bonnets on carefully over their new hairstyles, awaiting the younger ones. Hope tinkled her bell again, and down they scampered, a dozen little girls, aged six to ten, descending the stairs a little more excitedly, a little less gracefully, their newly curled ringlets bouncing with exuberance. Their dresses had also been refurbished and brightened with pretty braid and ribbons, and their bonnets also sported daisies and roses and satin ribbons, but it was apparent that the clothing was not the highlight of the day for this group.

Each little girl clasped something precious to her chest; Sebastian could not see clearly what. He caught a glimpse of wool, a gleam of satin, a froth of lace. The last little girl came clattering down the steps, still in her too-big boots. It was the child Hope had talked to in the dining room that time, May, the child whose so-called birthday it had been.

Today her angular little face was incandescent with joy. She hugged something to her skinny little body possessively. Then she saw Lady Elinore. Her sharp little face lit with fierce delight. "Look, m'lady. Look what I got!" she shouted.

And Sebastian saw what she was was carrying, what each of the little ones carried with such joy and such care: a doll.

He glanced up at the landing. Miss Hope Merridew was watching the little ones, smiling. Even from here he could see how her eyes shimmered with tears.

Sebastian swallowed convulsively.

The little ones rushed over to the older girls to show them their dolls. To Giles's consternation, they were followed down the stairs by a group of middle-aged and elderly ladies, who fell upon Giles in glee.

"Giles, dear boy, how is your mother? Have you seen our handiwork? Don't these little gels look pretty now?"

"Good gad, if it isn't little Giles Bemerton! My how you've grown! Last time I saw you, you were covered in spots, poor little fellow!" An elegant raddled old lady reached up and pinched his cheek.

"Giles, you young rascal. I didn't know you were in on this. Splendid results. Have to say, didn't think it could be done. Took us all afternoon—don't know when I've enjoyed myself more! Tell me, how is your dear mother?"

Giles bowed and attempted to smile and respond with some semblance of grace. It was difficult to remain a sophisticated man of the world when your cheek was being pinched by old ladies.

Sebastian, preserving a wooden countenance as best he could, thought the stag-at-bay expression suited his friend beautifully.

Lady Augusta interrupted the festival-of-Giles. "Maudie, you remember Agatha Pilton? This is her daughter, Lady Elinore Whitelaw."

Instantly the gaggle of old ladies surrounded Lady Elinore and began to pelt her with questions. From what they were saying, the old ladies had developed a new passion in life: orphans.

Giles cravenly abandoned Lady Elinore to her fate. He wriggled past the knot of dowagers and said to Sebastian in a low voice, "Come on, Bas. Let's get these children home before the storm breaks."

Sebastian glanced at the clear bright sky.

"Not that sort of storm, cloth-head!" Giles jerked his chin. "Lady Elinore. She might be currently buried under a landslide of dowagers, but you saw her face! She's not going to take this lying down. She's going to have to have it out with Miss Merridew. So let's get the audience out of the way."

Sebastian nodded and catching sight of James the footman in the hallway, beckoned him over. In minutes Sir Oswald's carriage was at the front gate, and James was loading it with orphans. Giles and Sebastian's vehicles followed. Giles would have driven his, but Sebastian detained him.

"Sorry, Bas, have an urgent appointment, with my . . . hatter."

"Coward."

"Absolutely." Giles agreed.

Sebastian pleasantly maintained his grip on his friend's arm until Giles said, "Oh, very well. My groom shall take them."

Moments later the ladies' carriages started to arrive, and one by one they took their leave, thanking Miss Hope Merridew for the splendid afternoon's fun, Sir Oswald for the refreshments, exhorting Giles to be a good boy and not worry his poor mother so much, and ordering Agatha Pilton's child to come and visit them soon! A hush fell in the hallway as the last of them left.

"The calm before the storm," whispered Giles. Lady Elinore's face was pale except for two bright pink spots in her cheeks. Her lips were compressed. Her eyes snapped with anger.

Lady Augusta, perfectly well aware of the tension in the room, declared, "Oswald, I'm exhausted, take me upstairs and give me something to drink!"

"This is what comes of maudlin' your insides with tea, Gussie. I shall order you a nice herbal draft—"

Lady Augusta snorted. "I don't want herbs, Oswald! They're very well in their place, but right now I need brandy!"

They went off, Great Uncle Oswald expostulating about the evils of brandy and the virtues of herbal tinctures and Lady Augusta scoffing and demanding good French cognac. Grace and Faith retreated to the nursery to tidy up. Sebastian, Lady Elinore, Giles, and Hope were left in the hallway. Sebastian ushered them into the library.

Lady Elinore glared at Hope. "I suppose you are proud of what you have done!"

"Yes, actually. I am." Hope said. "Didn't you see how happy those children were?"

"That is not the point."

"That is exactly the point. What harm can a few hours of happiness and a few bits and bobs do?"

"A great deal!"

"A great deal of good, I think."

"I allowed this outing against my better judgment, and I see now how right I was. Those girls will never settle back down to their routine."

"Good," said Hope.

"How dare you just waltz in, with your frivolous tonnish ways, thinking you know what is best for girls like these?"

"I was once a girl very much like them."

Lady Elinore scoffed. "Very much like them, my foot! You may be closer to them in age than I, but you've led a completely sheltered life! What would you know about the sort of hardship and abuse my girls have suffered?"

Hope wanted, oh so much, to give Lady Elinore a sharp set-down, but she was very aware of Mr. Reyne standing by, a troubled frown in his face. He looked so uncomfortable by the rising atmosphere of feminine hostility between herself and Lady Elinore that Hope forced herself to keep a check on her temper. She responded calmly, "My life has not been so sheltered as you think."

A voice from the door interrupted her. "Hardship and abuse? My sister knows all about it! Our grandfather used to beat her mercilessly. He did his best to crush her spirit." Faith came forward and grabbed her sister's hand and held it up. "You may have noticed—"

"No, Faith," Hope tried to pull her hand away. "This is not about me."

"Yes, it is. It's why you did what you did today." Faith turned to the others and explained, "My sister and I are mirror twins: where I have a mole on my left shoulder, hers is on the right shoulder. Where I am right-handed, she is left-handed."

Lady Elinore sniffed. "So?"

"My grandfather believed Hope to be evil, because she used her left hand by preference. He claimed her left hand was a tool of the Devil. And so she spent most of her childhood with that hand tied behind her. Not gently." Faith grabbed Hope's hand.

Hope tried to pull away. It was a part of her life she wanted to forget, but Faith held tight. She brandished Hope's left wrist. "Tied with ropes by my grandfather so tightly that they rubbed her flesh raw. From the time she was a little girl, newly orphaned at the age of seven, until the day we escaped, two years ago. So do not *dare* say she knows nothing of hardship!"

There was a long, embarrassed silence. Hope uncomfortably pulled her hand away. She said quietly, "I am sorry, Lady Elinore, if what I did distressed you."

Lady Elinore said in a stiff voice, "I am sorry for what you endured as a child. Nevertheless, your actions were ill thought out and reckless and have severely undermined the entire basis of this institution and all our good work with these girls."

Hope raised her brows. "How so? A few bits to furbish up their clothes? A doll for the little ones?"

Lady Elinore snorted in a genteel fashion. "There is nothing Rational in a few bits of material with a face painted or embroidered on!"

Hope interrupted. "It is not about Rationality but about heart. It is about a child, who has no one in all the world, finding comfort in the lonely darkness of the night by hugging a doll."

"It is just a bit of rag! They can as well hug the blanket they sleep in."

Hope stared at her incredulously. "You've never had a doll, have you, Lady Elinore?"

Lady Elinore looked uneasy. "Of course not! Sentimental nonsense! Playing with dolls is nothing but a foolish waste of time."

Hope shook her head. "A doll is so much more than a bit of material and a few buttons. A doll becomes a person, a friend, a sister, a confidante. A doll is something of your own—completely private and solely yours, someone to love and hug and tell your dreams and fears to."

Lady Elinore looked skeptical. "What's the point?"

"Comfort. Love. Reassurance," said Hope softly. "Have you never lain in your bed, awake in the middle of the night, perhaps with the rain falling and the wind whistling? Feeling lost and unloved and alone . . ."

Lady Elinore looked so uncomfortable Hope said quickly, "I don't mean you, specifically. We all have moments like that, children, too. The middle of the night can be the loneliest time. I remember a time when I was a child when I thought that life could get no more miserable, that not a soul in the world loved us or cared about us . . ."

There was a hushed silence in the room, as everyone there remembered . . .

Giles Bemerton, sent off to school at the age of seven, small, alone, and vulnerable, tortured by the older boys . . .

Lady Elinore, who felt closest to her mother at the British Museum . . .

Sebastian Reyne, a young boy shouldering a man's task, trying so desperately to keep a family together, failing, and losing everything in the process . . .

For several moments, nobody spoke. Lady Elinore took a small starched square of white linen from her reticule and blew into it. "Very well," she said. "I accept your argument in favor of the dolls. But as for what you did to their clothing! You have no idea of the dangerous tendencies you have stirred up!"

At her words, much of Hope's sympathy for Lady Elinore began to dissolve. Her temper rose. "Dangerous tendencies? I had not realized a few trimmings and some buttons could have such a dramatic effect."

Lady Elinore's chin took on a stubborn jut. She threw up her hands. "The effect was obvious! Did you not *see*?"

Hope gave Lady Elinore a narrow look. "I saw a group of happy young girls who look a vast deal prettier than they did yesterday. What did you see?"

"Girls garbed with the purpose of attracting male attention! Girls on the verge of corruption!"

"Rubbish!"

"You may scoff, but even Mr. Bemerton noticed it."

Giles held up his hands defensively. "Leave me out of this."

"But you did!" Lady Elinore insisted. "You saw how they went in looking like . . . like—what was it you said?"

"Like quiet little mice," he offered.

"Yes, and they came out looking like birds of paradise."

"No!" Giles stood up. "You said that, Elinore. Not I."

She looked shocked at his contradicting her. "But it was true!"

"It was *not* true! How can you say such a thing?" Hope began. "They are merely—"

Lady Elinore turned on her. "What you don't realize is that many of these girls were rescued from a life of depravity! From houses of ill fame!"

At this, Sebastian intervened. "Lady Elinore, I do not think it is proper for us to sully Miss Merridew's ears with tales of depravity—"

"Sully my ears!" exclaimed Hope in sudden fury. "What complete and utter nonsense! If some of these poor children have managed to survive the depravity inflicted on them by others, then I can certainly endure hearing about it!"

Sebastian looked at her in shock.

Hope stormed on, "And if they have suffered from the evil in the world, they are victims, yes?"

"Y-yes," Lady Elinore agreed.

"Then why do you treat them as if they are naturally wicked?"

"What do you mean? I don't. They must be reformed, of course and their tendencies to immorality eradicated—"

"*Reformed?*" Hope exploded. "*Tendencies to immorality?* I have heard this kind of rubbish all my life from my grandfather—only he says all females are born sinful! Those girls are but *children* who had *no choice* in what they did! If you are robbed, do you need reforming?"

Lady Elinore looked confused.

Hope didn't wait for a response. "No, of course not. And these children were robbed of their childhood and their innocence. They understand fear and hate and evil and hardship. What they need to learn about is love and hope and pride and how to be happy in life." Her voice softened. "Their clothes don't make them potential birds of paradise—they are just young girls feeling natural excitement over a few pretty things. Don't you remember what it's like to get a pretty new dress—" She broke off, looking at Lady Elinore's gray, shapeless gown. "No, I suppose not."

Lady Elinore's mouth quivered.

Hope came forward and took her hand. Her voice softened. "Please don't be upset. I know you mean well. But you are following your mother's precepts so blindly. And they are so harsh and joyless."

"My mother was a great woman." Lady Elinore said shakily.

"But why would she wish females to take no joy in wearing pretty things? Why deny a lonely child the comfort of a doll?"

"A great many people admired my mother's ideas."

"Perhaps," said Hope gently, "but she does not seem to have been very happy. And has her Rational approach brought you such happiness?"

Lady Elinore's face quivered. "One's duty is more important than one's personal happiness." It had all the earmarks of a quote from her mother.

Hope squeezed her hands. "Perhaps, but if duty and joy

can be combined, why deny personal happiness when it is possible?"

Lady Elinore's brow furrowed. She made no response.

There was a long silence in the room. Finally, Lady Elinore said in a shaken voice, "I see. Thank you for explaining your point of view. I . . . I shall leave now." She stood and looked around helplessly, a little blindly.

Sebastian and Giles were both standing.

"Bas?" Giles queried.

Sebastian didn't move. He was staring fixedly at Hope, then as his friend jogged him with his elbow, he started and said in a vague manner, "Yes, yes, to be sure."

Giles opened the door. "Lady Elinore."

"Th-thank you, Mr. Bemerton." Quietly, with great dignity, Lady Elinore took her leave. Sebastian and the others followed her into the hall in silence.

A footman was sent to summon a hackney cab, and the moment it arrived, Mr. Bemerton helped Lady Elinore into it. He glanced at Sebastian, who was lost in thought, his expression blank. Giles rolled his eyes, leaped nimbly into the hackney cab, and gave the order for the jarvey to get the cab moving.

As the carriage moved off, Giles said quietly, "Do you need a handkerchief, Elinore?"

But Lady Elinore didn't respond. She was staring vacantly ahead, a deep pucker between her brows.

# Chapter Fourteen

∽

*May I ask whether these pleasing attentions proceed from the impulse*
*of the moment or are the result of previous study?*
JANE AUSTEN

"IF ONLY SHE WOULD REALIZE THERE IS SCIENTIFIC REASONING
behind my mother's theories of clothing!" Lady Elinore
was rapidly recovering from her distress and had begun to
work herself into a self-righteous temper. "Wearing such
bright colors brings out the excessive passions in men. We
have a duty to protect our girls from that!"

Giles stared at her. "You can't possibly believe such
nonsense!"

The cab drew up in front of Lady Elinore's house. "It's
not nonsense! It's quite true. My mother conducted investigations into the matter. Masculine passions are stimulated
by colors."

He stepped from the carriage and turned to help her
down the steps. "And that is why you wear those dreadful
gray rags?"

She gave him a haughty look but accepted his hand.
"My clothes are not rags. They are made of the finest ma-
terials: silk, velvet, merino."

"All of them gray and all cut to have about as much shape as a merino sheep."

She flounced up the steps to her house, opened the front door with a key, then turned and said indignantly, "My clothes are warm and effective, and they answer the Rational purpose for clothing."

He followed her inside with a narrow, sleepy-lidded look. "Which is to disguise any female shape you have and avoid inflaming masculine passions."

She sniffed, not liking to confirm such a bald statement, and tried to struggle out of her coat. He stepped forward and smoothly drew it from her shoulders. He held it up. "Where does it go?"

"Here. I'll take it." She opened a door and hung the coat on a hook. She stepped back out of the closet looking self-conscious. She smoothed down her gray dress.

Giles looked at the shapeless garment, the hair scraped back and hidden under an ugly gray cap, and then he looked at the woman beneath. "You have no idea, do you?"

She raised her brows and gave him a look of disdain. "About what?"

"About this." He flung open the closet door, pushed her into it, and followed her in, closing the door behind him. Darkness wrapped around them.

She hit out at him with her fists. "How dare you!"

He caught her hands in his and held them. It was pitch black. "You're not afraid of the dark, are you?"

"Of course not!"

His voice sounded deeper than usual as he said, "I'm not going to hurt you. You know that, Elinore." He waited.

"I-I never gave you leave to use my first name!"

"You know I'm a rake, Elinore. Rakes don't wait for leave. We take"—he stepped closer, until his body lightly touched hers—"liberties."

She gave a little gasp and tried to step back, but the cupboard was small. She pressed back among the coats. "Wh-what do you think you are doing?"

Her hands were trembling in his. He soothed them with

his thumb, stroking gently and rhythmically. She tried to pull her hands free, in vain.

"It is an experiment in color."

"What?"

"I'm testing your mother's theory. About color. Seeing if my unruly masculine passions can be quelled by a lack of color. Having been exposed to all those female bodies outside, clad in a positive riot of colors, I am in need of a calming experience. Which is why I sought you out." His thumbs never ceased their caress of her soft skin.

She said not a word. After a moment he added, "It might take a few minutes to achieve the calm I need, but you shall not begrudge that, I know. In the name of . . . science."

Silence. He could hear her breathing and the flutter of the pulse under his fingers quickened.

"So, what shall we talk about while the experiment runs its course? Oh, I know—you are aware, I suppose that my friend Sebastian Reyne is courting you?"

She hesitated. "Yes."

"Are you aware that he doesn't love you?"

There was an interminable wait before she said, "Yes. I don't mind."

His grip tightened. He wanted to shake her but forced himself to say mildly, "You should. Every woman deserves to be loved." He waited a moment, but she didn't respond, so he asked, "Do you love him?"

"No." She added in a small, desperate voice, "Love is not Rational."

"No, thank God, it isn't!" He waited, but she said nothing. "So . . . you don't mind that Sebastian's only reasons for marrying you would be what he conceives of as his duty to his sisters?"

"Duty is a solid foundation for most endeavors. I admire his devotion to duty. It is a Rational quality."

"Is it now? And I bet you are just stuffed full of Rational qualities, aren't you?"

"I try to be."

"I bet you've never had an undutiful moment in your life, have you?"

"Not that I can remember. As I said, I admire an adherence to duty." Her voice was cool, quite composed, but still, there was a faint tremble.

"Sebastian is another one who has sacrificed his entire life to duty."

"Then we should suit, shouldn't we?"

"I doubt it. Duty is a damned poor bedmate!"

She stiffened. "Must you be vulgar?"

"Yes, I'm a rake, remember? We're vulgar fellows. And we believe duty is a poor substitute for love."

"Duty endures. Love does not."

"Maybe. I am not convinced of that. Rather unrakely of me, I know." He shifted his grip on her hands, so that they were pressed against his chest. "And you have forgotten the glory of love. Ahh, the glory . . . Even if love does not endure, it is worth it, for just a few moments of glory," he said softly.

"Indeed." As an attempt to be arctic, it failed miserably. She sounded uncertain, almost wistful. She rallied, "Something so ephemeral would make a poor foundation for a lifetime endeavor."

"You've never been in love, have you, Elinore?"

"Certainly not!"

He smiled at her tone. "No, love is not at all rational, and you only do Rational things, don't you?"

"Of course!"

"For that matter, it is not particularly Rational for you to be in this cozy dark cupboard with me, is it?"

There was a small pause, then her voice quavered out of the darkness. "I believe you were wishing to test my mother's theory about colors."

"Do you?"

The silence thickened. Giles bent his head lower and murmured against her ear, "You know, of course, that I've never done a dutiful thing in my life."

"You ought to be ashamed to admit such a thing."

"And we've established that I have a . . . shall we say, a devilish reputation with the ladies."

"Shall we say plain wicked and be done with it?" she said tartly.

He laughed softly. "Very well, wicked, though not, I hope, plain . . . So here we have an interesting combination; a lady who has never done a wicked thing in her life, and a gentlem—well, all right, a rake who has never done a dutiful thing in his."

"You could still redeem yourself."

"I could, couldn't I? Redemption and duty are such interesting concepts. Their definition depends entirely on where one stands to begin with." She moved restlessly, brushing her body inadvertently against his. She froze.

He said softly into the darkness, "So, Elinore, you think I ought to be more dutiful?"

"Y-yes, I do."

"Then I think that it is my duty, as a friend, to prevent my good friend Sebastian Reyne from making a disastrous mistake."

She said in a thready voice, "And that mistake would be?"

"Marrying you."

She began in a stiff, hurt little voice, "I know I am not the usual sort of woman men want to marry, but—"

"There is no usual sort. I also think it's my duty to teach you that there is more to life than being Rational." He slid his hands down her arms and wrapped one arm around her waist. With the other he wrapped his hand around the nape of her neck and drew her against him.

She started struggling. "I've had enough of this! Let me out immediately! The experiment is over!"

"Oh, but my uncontrollable masculine passions have been aroused now," he said. "See?" He drew her hand down to the front of his body. He felt her jump and freeze.

"Wh-what is that?"

"Hard evidence of uncontrollable masculine passion." He let his words sink in and wondered whether she'd realized she hadn't moved her hand away. It was pressed, ever so lightly, against his erection. Her fingers tentatively moved in exploration. Giles closed his eyes and tried not to groan, feeling the whisper-soft flutter of curious feminine fingers through the fabric of his trousers.

"Oh, it's y—!" She bit off the word with a gasp.

He managed to say with a semblance of control, "Yes, it's what you think it is. So what are you going to do about that, Elinore?"

Her hand flew up and came to hover back near his chest. "N-nothing! D-don't you dare," she quavered. "I warn you, I-I am armed!" He could feel her breath as she spoke.

"Yes, and dangerous. So use your hatpin," said Giles. He waited a long moment, but no hatpin was forthcoming. Lady Elinore waited, breathless, vibrating with tension and expectation, like a small harp in the darkness. He lowered his mouth to hers.

"Love?" Sebastian halted his pacing at the question. "I don't know if I love Miss Merridew or not." He tossed the idea around in his mind a moment. "I'm not sure I have it in me to love anyone."

"You think not?" Giles raised a skeptical brow. "You love your sisters."

Sebastian stopped, thought for a moment, and then waved the suggestion aside. "That's different. Family is different. They are children, and I owe them my protection and my care."

"So why not pay someone to protect and care for them?" Giles shrugged. "It would solve all your problems."

"It would not!" Sebastian snapped. "Besides, I need to see to their care and safety myself. They need to grow up knowing that someone cares for them—not because they are paid to, not because they are forced to, but because they want to, because they are family. They need to know how much they and their happiness matters."

"And that you would die for them if necessary?" Giles asked softly.

Sebastian shrugged, uncomfortable with such statements. "Whatever is necessary for their safety and happiness." And yes, even unto death.

"That, my dear fellow, is love."

"That's not what I feel for Miss Merridew then." Although that wasn't quite true. He did feel a powerful urge to protect her and care for her and make her happy. And he would die to protect her, too.

He also felt an equally powerful urge to take her to bed and make love to her until neither of them could move. Just the thought of it made him begin to harden with desire. "Oh, damn it all! I don't know what to do, Giles. I've never felt this way before."

Giles chuckled softly. "Welcome to the human race, my friend."

Sebastian groaned. "It's what she said the other day. 'If duty and joy can be combined, why deny personal happiness when it is possible?' I can't get it out of my head. Because there's no denying, she would be good for the girls."

Giles waited, but he said nothing more, so Giles said it for him. "And she'd be good for you, Bas."

He groaned and put his head in his hands. "I know. I've never wanted anyone more in my life. But I'm as good as bound to Lady Elinore."

Giles shrugged. He poured brandy into two glasses and said in a thoughtful voice, "You haven't actually made Lady Elinore an offer, have you?"

Sebastian flung himself into a chair. "No, but having courted her so obviously, I'm honor bound to do so." He groaned and ran his hands through his hair. "You begged me to display a little finesse, some subtlety, to go more slowly! Why the hell didn't you clout me over the head with a brick, knock some sense into me?"

His friend looked pained. "A brick, my dear Bas? I would never use anything so crude!"

Sebastian took no notice. "A woman like that—you said yourself she was at her last prayers. And now I've raised her hopes. Made a spectacle of her."

Giles raised a brow. "In what way a spectacle?"

"I'm aware of the tales. Pushy cit of murky background pursuing aristocratic older lady heiress. But to give her her due, she never once looked down on me or treated me as her social inferior. I can't in all conscience abandon her now to pursue an acknowledged society beauty like Miss Merridew. Lady Elinore would become the laughingstock of the ton."

"That's possible." Giles passed him the glass of brandy.

"I wouldn't wish that on any woman." Sebastian took the glass mechanically. "Besides, I like Lady Elinore. She might be dull and bookish and drab, but her heart is in the right place. She really does care about those destitute girls."

"She does indeed," Giles agreed. "Bored me for hours about it the other evening."

"What did happen after you escorted her home?" Sebastian asked curiously. "Thank you for that, by the way. My mind was elsewhere." Ringing with Miss Merridew's words and the possibilities they'd opened up.

"Hmm? Oh we discussed Rationality and her mother's scientific theories." He grinned. "A fascinating discussion it was, too."

"The mother was a crank, if you ask me,"Sebastian said. "The daughter isn't as bad, but—"

"She's nothing like her mother!" Giles objected. "Lady Elinore has had much to bear and deserves a great deal more respect than most people accord her."

Sebastian regarded him gloomily. "You're right. I suppose my duty is clear." He drained the glass in one fiery gulp. "I've never shirked a duty in my life."

"No. Very uncomfortable I've found it, too." Giles leaned over and refilled Sebastian's glass. "Remind me, which duty are we talking about?"

"To marry her, of course!"

"Lady Elinore? You just said yourself you don't love her. Is that fair to her? To either of you?"

"I told you, I know nothing of love. But if I married her, I swear I would be a good husband. I would treat her well and be faithful, at least, which is more than can be said of many men of the ton."

"You didn't love Thea, either," Giles reasoned. "And though you were a good husband by your lights, and faithful, I had the strong impression that neither of you were happy."

Sebastian shifted uncomfortably in his chair. "That was different. I was young and foolish then, and I didn't understand. I thought Thea wanted me, but . . .'Twas her father proposed the match, after all. It was about the future of the mill." He shrugged. "Thea wanted more than I could give."

He'd given Thea everything he knew how to give: his body, his loyalty, his care, and protection. He'd worked hard to build the business, to provide her with everything she wanted. It hadn't been enough.

"Exactly. And when you married Thea you weren't in love with someone else." Giles swirled the brandy in his glass, held it up to the candle, and stared meditatively at the amber liquid. "Do you honestly think you and Lady Elinore could be happy in a marriage of convenience? That woman is crying out to be—er, *hrumph, cough!*"

Sebastian stared. "What did you say?"

Giles finished his sudden coughing fit, swilled down the last of his brandy, and explained. "She is crying out to be strangled! You have to admit, a woman who works so hard at repressing her femininity and her tender feelings is a woman who would be pretty damned difficult to live with. Believe me, Bastian, Lady Elinore will be no tame, undemanding wife. Your whole life will be Rationalized most horribly." There was a short pause, then he added carelessly, "She seems a lonely little creature, too. Needy. Vulnerable. What if she, like Thea, demanded more of you than you could give?"

"Oh, God! I don't think I could stand it again." Sebastian groaned and sank his head into his hands.

Giles set down his glass and sat up. "Then that's settled. You cannot marry Lady Elinore, and since you have promised nothing, you owe her nothing. But you are right; it would not be kind to drop her like a pile of old washing. Even if her clothes resemble one. You have raised her hopes. You must let her down gently. And I, your oldest friend and wise in the ways of women, shall help you."

"You?" Sebastian said doubtfully.

"I," affirmed Giles with assurance. "And we shall begin with the opera. You made an arrangement to take her, I believe. I shall accompany you, make a party of it—the virtue twins, Lady Elinore, you, and I. I should, of course, invite my friend Bertie Glossington to make up the numbers, but he's a frivolous fellow, Bertie, and would no doubt offend the ladies by ogling the opera dancers."

Sebastian knew a red herring when he saw one, and Bertie Glossington was undoubtedly a red herring.

"Why on earth would you want an opera party made up of myself and Lady Elinore and yourself and the Merridew twins? It sounds like a recipe for disaster to me. If I am to see less of Lady Elinore, then—"

"You cannot cry off an invitation you've already made, and besides, Lady Elinore loves opera, and you don't want to disappoint her. No, you must go. And so must Miss Hope. Trust me, Bastion. It is all to do with strategy. We must bring the two ladies together more frequently, encourage them to become friends—females pal up with each other at any opportunity. Lord knows she could use a few hints from the Merridew sisters about fashion and graciousness to the opposite sex." He snorted reflectively.

"So?" prompted Sebastian, jolting his friend out of his reverie.

"So we plan outings together, you and the little gray ghost, myself and Miss Merridew. And then, gradually, you shall be seen to transfer your attentions from one lady to the other."

"Leaving Lady Elinore looking and feeling the fool?" said Sebastian bluntly. "I don't like that at all."

"Ah, but that's because you have not perceived the brilliance of my cunning plan," Giles informed him. "I shall, in the meantime, begin to pay more attention to Lady Elinore, thus distracting her from you."

Sebastian snorted. "Oh, yes. She would consider herself vastly better off when two men come to drop her like a pile of old washing, instead of only one."

"No," Giles said in a patient tone. "With two such dashing blades as ourselves seeking out her company " He eyed his friend critically and amended his statement. "Well, with one dashing blade and your good, plain, sturdy self seeking out her company, Lady Elinore will begin to acquire a certain cachet. Having attracted first you—immensely rich, if something of a bear—and then me—a known connoisseur of female charms—she is bound to garner the attention of the ton. Others will decide she must be more interesting than she at first seems and seek her out."

"And if they don't?"

"Trust me, dear boy, they will. I know it may strike you as a touch immodest, but where a Bemerton leads, others will follow."

"Sounds daft to me, I can't see any of the ton beaux in hot pursuit of a dowdy little gray bluestocking. Besides, there's an enormous hole in this plan of yours: Lady Elinore doesn't even like you."

Giles looked affronted. "Doesn't like me? Me? What nonsense! Of course she likes me. Everybody likes me!"

Sebastian grinned. "Ah yes, but she's a woman who goes her own way, Lady Elinore. I seem to recall she once danced with you—you! And according to your own account, made it abundantly clear she found you repugnant! And later she didn't even recognize you—you!"

Giles waved a hand. "Pah! She recognized me. She was just indulging in female stratagems."

"Didn't look like it to me. She doesn't seem the type to use female stratagems. Not very Rational."

Giles snorted and said darkly, "Believe me, Bas, all females use female stratagems. From three-year-old girl children to hundred-year-old nuns, mark my words."

"Snubbed you again, several times that I know of," Sebastian reminded him. "Didn't seem too happy with your comments at the orphan institution the other day. Practically snapped your nose off at least three times."

"Nonsense! It would take more than that little creature to damage the Bemerton Nose," Giles said with a grin, rubbing the nose in question.

"Nose, self-consequence, both enormous," murmured Sebastian.

Giles declared loftily. "You may scoff, but jealousy is the sign of a small, mean spirit, Reyne. Bemertons prevail—it's the family motto. You may be without rival in business affairs, but I am a nonpareil in affairs of the heart, and I—I understand women."

Sebastian arched his eyebrows. "Famous last words."

"Bah! Doubting Thomas! Now, you go off and try to make Miss Merridew fall for your dubious charms. Leave Lady Elinore to me!"

"Don't worry, Mr. Reyne. We are not late," Lady Elinore assured him as she came down the stairs in a gray velvet cloak. "Nobody goes to the opera on time."

Why? It was foolish in his view, since the hire of a box for the evening was not cheap. Why pay to go to something and not watch all of it? He did not understand the ton.

"In fact, we shall be unfashionably early." She pulled on a pair of long gray gloves. "But I approve of that, because I hate missing the beginning of a story, don't you?"

Sebastian nodded, feeling marginally more cheerful. If opera was a story as well as singing, it might not be so bad.

In the carriage Lady Elinore said, "Dear Mother did not approve of the opera. She considered the excessive passions inherent in the art form vulgar. And they are, of course, but I find the music quite spiritually uplifting. And Cosi is a delight. Do you find it so, Mr. Reyne?"

Having no idea who Cosi was, Sebastian decided to make a clean breast of it. "I'm afraid I know almost nothing about opera, Lady Elinore. This will be my first experience."

The confession proved an error in judgment. His ignorance apparently thrilled her. She spent the entire carriage ride describing the history of the art form—what she unnervingly called a brief sketch.

When they arrived at their box, the pit was in relative darkness, the limelights across the stage were blazing, and the curtain rose just as they seated themselves.

Sebastian looked around him with interest. He'd attended plays in Manchester theaters, but nothing so elaborate or fine as this. A number of other boxes were set around the walls of the theater, most of them empty.

The orchestra struck up a tune, and the singers began to sing. He liked the music, but it was hard to pick up the words.

He glanced at Lady Elinore. She seemed totally absorbed. There was a faint smile on her face.

Sebastian leaned forward and stared at the figures striding about onstage. They sang and sang, and no matter how hard he concentrated, he couldn't work out what the devil they were singing about and what the story was supposed to be. There were two women and two men. He thought they might be lovers. And then there was this other fellow . . .

He sneaked another sideways look at Lady Elinore. She was swaying and inclining her head along with the music, apparently completely caught up in it.

Eventually he gave it up and entertained himself observing the other theatergoers. Some of the other boxes were slowly filling up. He saw several persons he recognized from various balls and routs he'd attended. Lord and Lady Thorn entered a box directly opposite, with a party of friends. He spied Count Rimavska among them, a glossy black fur cloak lined with red silk flung carelessly around his shoulders.

Few of the people slowly filling the boxes took notice of

the stage. They waved to friends, scanned the crowds with their opera glasses, and talked and laughed in quite audible tones. The ladies were dressed very finely, and most sat at the very front of their box so that their gowns and jewels and coiffures could be admired.

Lady Elinore also sat at the very front, but it was so she could see all that was happening onstage, not because anyone would be admiring her shapeless, gray silk dress, her lack of jewels, and her scraped-back hair. Sebastian rather admired her stubborn adherence to her principles. There was something very classy in her refusal to bow to society's dictates, he decided. He admired strength of mind.

On the other hand, strength of mind could also be stubborn rigidity. Where did one end and the other begin? he pondered.

"Here you are." Giles poked his head around the door of the box. "You must have got here devilish early." He spoke in a normal voice.

"Shush," hissed Lady Elinore.

Giles grinned and withdrew his head. "After you, ladies."

"How do you do, Mr. Reyne," whispered Miss Faith Merridew. "Have we missed the start?" She hurried to the front of the box, seated herself one seat along from Lady Elinore, leaving an empty seat between them, and glued her gaze to the stage.

"Mr. Reyne." The chaperone stepped in, offered him two limp, disdainful fingers to shake, and went to collect Miss Faith's sky-blue cloak, which she'd tossed onto a seat. She hung it and her own on some hooks at the back of the box. She looked as sour as ever.

Sebastian swallowed. He knew who would follow.

Miss Merridew entered, wrapped enticingly in a ruched cloak of wine-colored velvet. The rich, dark color enhanced her golden loveliness, framing her like a jewel. She gave him a dazzling smile and murmured, "Good evening, Mr. Reyne."

Sebastian managed to say in a gruff voice, "May I take your cloak, Miss Merridew?"

She inclined her head, turned, and shrugged slowly, allowing the sumptuous dark crimson material to slide off her smooth, bare shoulders into his waiting hands.

Sebastian swallowed, his mouth suddenly dry.

Her dress was green silk, with wine-red lace panels and satin insets. High-waisted and low-cut, it clung to her slender curves lovingly.

Her skin was silken soft, creamy against the rich green color of her gown. Golden, silky curls clustered high around her head, leaving her soft nape exposed, vulnerable and enticing. If he just bent his head a little, he could kiss her just there. The faint scent of her perfume teased his senses. He longed to press his mouth to that sweet curve, to bury his face in that faint, creamy hollow, to taste her skin and know her . . .

He swallowed again.

"Oh, do take care! You're crushing that cloak, and it's new!" The chaperone's voice grated into his consciousness. She twitched the cloak from his nerveless grasp and pushed past him to hang it up.

Giles gave him a wicked grin over Miss Merridew's alabaster shoulder. "Knew you'd enjoy the opera, Bas." He strolled to the front of the box and peered out into the audience. "How's it going? Many arrived yet? Anyone interesting here?"

"Shush," hissed Lady Elinore again. "Some of us come here for the music!" She barely turned her head as she said it. She'd nodded briefly at the others as they entered the box, but had made it clear that she would not talk until the intermission. Miss Faith seemed to approve of this.

Giles winked at Sebastian and said in a perfectly normal voice, "I think the lady is inviting us to sit down and enjoy the show, Bastian, so by all means, let us find a seat. Where would you like to sit, Miss Merridew? Mrs. Jenner?"

Lady Elinore turned and glared at him. "Mr. Bemerton!" she hissed crossly.

"Evening, Lady Elinore. My word, that color suits you. You should wear it more often," said Sebastian's irrepressible friend. As her glare intensified, he added in a soothing voice, "Yes, yes, we'll find a seat. Never fret, dear lady. There's plenty of room for everyone."

Lady Elinore turned back to the stage with a sniff and what in a less serious lady might even be called a flounce.

The chaperone, Mrs. Jenner, took the seat next to Miss Faith. She gave Sebastian a repellent look, indicated the empty seat between Faith and Lady Elinore, and said, "Hope, dear" in a compelling voice. Clearly Miss Hope was to sit as far away from Sebastian as possible.

Hope gave Sebastian a faintly comical look of regret and was about to step forward and sit where she was bidden when Giles said, "By George! There's my old friend Bertie Glossington! Hey, Bertie! Bertie!" He stepped right up to the balcony and leaned over it, waving a handkerchief, then paused and said, "Nope, not Glossington at all. Pity."

"Mr. Bemerton!" snapped Lady Elinore. "Will you sit down and be quiet!"

"Delighted to oblige you, ma'am," said Giles and plonked himself down in the vacant chair beside Lady Elinore, then added in a hoarse, loud whisper. "Shame about Glossington. You would have liked him, Lady Elinore. A delightful chap, Bertie. Barrel o'laughs."

Lady Elinore sniffed and glued her eyes firmly to the stage, her chin jutting militantly in a manner that boded ill for the next interruption. Giles sat back, grinning. He turned and winked at Sebastian.

Sebastian might have laughed at his impudence, had he not been so distracted. He took his place in the only vacant seat left—the one beside Miss Hope Merridew.

He could smell her perfume. It filled his senses. He was unprepared. He had no idea of what to do. He couldn't think of a thing to say.

Her shoulders were silken smooth and creamy in the light reflected from the stage. Her dress of green silk clung to her in vales and shadows of emerald.

Make conversation? How could any man possibly do such a thing with Miss Hope so near? He couldn't concentrate on a thing. Not the music, not the incomprehensible plot, not even Mrs. Jenner's attempts to change places with Hope, which Hope refused, citing Lady Elinore's further disturbance as her reason.

Her gown was cut low over her breasts, cupping them tenderly. He could hardly take his eyes off her. He was turning into a rake. She was a guest in his opera box. He was the host for the evening. He should not even notice her breasts, let alone imagine his own hands cupping them, his own mouth . . .

Sebastian closed his eyes. Removing temptation from sight.

A mistake. In the darkness he could hear her breathing softly beside him. How he could hear such a tiny, intimate thing with all the racket of the opera was a mystery, but he heard her every breath, felt the small movements of her body as she moved her limbs or altered her position in her seat. The delicate feminine scent of her wreathed about his brain, and in the intimacy of the darkness his imagination ran riot . . .

He opened his eyes and sat up straight. *Concentrate on the opera*, he told himself. *Look at the people in the audience. Stare at that irritating blasted Hungarian. Anything except think about Miss Hope Merridew!*

She turned her head and smiled at him, a smile of warm intimacy in the shadows.

The effect was instantaneous. The very thing he'd been fighting for the last few minutes happened. He tried not to groan. He was sitting beside Miss Hope Merridew, in public, almost fully aroused. He hoped the dim lighting would disguise his condition. He wished he hadn't hung up his greatcoat.

He stared out across the cavern of the auditorium, willing his problem away with all the self-discipline at his command.

There was not a lot. It was as if, having given himself permission to court Hope Merridew, his body had decided the courting was done and the honeymoon begun.

But he had to be seen to gradually transfer his attentions from Lady Elinore to Miss Hope. Gradually, he told his body fiercely, did not mean carrying her out of the opera and galloping off with her into the night. His body ignored him.

# *Chapter Fifteen*

∞

*And in the lowest deep a lower deep still threatening to devour me opens wide.*

JOHN MILTON

MR. REYNE DIDN'T SEEM TO BE TAKING MUCH NOTICE OF THE opera, Hope thought. He sat beside her, stiff and uncomfortable, radiating waves of tension.

It occurred to her that a man who'd spent most of his life in factories would know very little about opera. She and her sisters had never even heard music performed until they came to London, but with Faith as a twin, even a tone-deaf person would soon learn practically everything there was to know about opera, and Hope was far from tone deaf. Maybe Mr. Reyne had no one to explain it to him.

She leaned across and, in deference to Lady Elinore's peculiarity in wanting silence, whispered in his ear, "Did anyone tell you the story?"

He jumped about a foot. "Story? Oh, the opera. No."

"Well then . . ." She leaned toward him, her hand on his shoulder for balance, and began to whisper the story in his ear.

• • •

"In *Italian!*" he exclaimed.

"Shush!" hissed Lady Elinore and Faith in unison.

He fell silent but stared at Hope in amazement and not a little indignation. "Italian!" he muttered. "No wonder I couldn't understand a word!"

She giggled at his expression. "Did nobody warn you?"

He shook his head. And then suddenly it occurred to them both that their faces were just inches apart, and they froze. He stared into her eyes. Mesmerized, she stared back.

She did not know how long they sat, gazing into each other's eyes and breathing each other's breath while glorious music soared all around them, but it seemed to her that somehow, something very important was said, without a word being uttered.

The curtain came down to a storm of applause, and they both jumped. "Is it over?" Mr. Reyne asked.

"Bastian, you know very well there is an interval between the acts. Interval is the best part of the opera," explained Mr. Bemerton. "It's a time when—if we are allowed to *talk*"—he darted a glance at Lady Elinore, who lifted her nose in response—"we all visit each other's boxes, admire each other's finery, drink and eat and gather and spread as much gossip as possible. That is what most people come to the opera for." He glanced provocatively at Lady Elinore.

"Look," she exclaimed, oblivious, "is that not Count Rimavska, the famous violinist? He seems to be waving at our box."

Hope glanced across, and sure enough, there he was, garbed in some dramatic outfit in red and gold and fur. He was waving at their box, all right—directly at her twin, Faith. She glanced sideways. Faith was blushing.

"He always looks frightfully romantic, doesn't he?" Lady Elinore commented thoughtfully.

"Romantic?" Mr. Bemerton stared at her.

Lady Elinore's pale cheeks tinged with faint color. "In the poetical sense," she said with dignity. "Besides, he has prodigious musical talent, which any rational person would admire."

Mr. Bemerton glowered at the count. "With any luck he'll fall out of the box and break his neck."

"That would be a tragedy, for the world would lose a great talent," said Lady Elinore with composure.

Mr. Bemerton made a rude noise.

She looked down her nose at him rather as someone would regard an impertinent insect. Her color was heightened.

Mr. Reyne stood up, frowning. "I ordered refreshments to be brought at the interval, and they have not arrived. I shall investigate."

"I'll accompany you. I need some fresh air," declared Mr. Bemerton with a frown at Lady Elinore and Faith. "I am feeling nauseous."

Hope barely noticed their leaving. Faith waved shyly back at the count, her face glowing with animation. "He wants me to go over and join them in their box. May I, Mrs. Jenner?"

"I don't see why not, my dear. Lady Thorn is there, so there can be no objection. And I see my friend Lucille in the next box. Hope, you will accompany us."

*And not remain here to talk to Mr. Reyne,* Hope added silently. She smiled sweetly. "Thank you, but no."

Her chaperone was annoyed. "Then be so good as to remain at all times with Lady Elinore. I shall be observing you the whole time from Lucille's box."

She paused at the exit, glanced at Mr. Reyne's empty chair, and added, "And when I return, you and I shall trade seats for the remainder of the performance." They filed out, leaving Hope and Lady Elinore alone.

They hadn't spoken a word to each other since the day of the orphan tea. Hope had twice called on her, but Elinore was not in. Hope had sent around a note but had received no response. She glanced sideways. Lady Elinore stared out over the auditorium, apparently entranced with the sights. Hope wasn't fooled for a moment.

She wanted somehow to bridge the gulf between them, but no words came to mind. They had little in common: Lady Elinore was a highly educated woman with strict and lofty principles, who worked tirelessly for the good of others. Hope was minimally educated, hopelessly clumsy at most things of refinement, and her guiding principle was a selfish quest for personal happiness.

Hope knew her words that day had somehow hurt the older woman. She hadn't realized until too late how vulnerable Lady Elinore was. She'd seemed so certain of herself and the rightness of her mother's theories.

Worse, Hope coveted Lady Elinore's beau. She'd been more than half in love with Mr. Sebastian Reyne for some time, and since they'd kissed . . .

The silence in the box thinned to an unbearable tension. Hope broke first. "Lady Elinore, I know I offended you deeply, and I regret it sincerely. Please accept my apologies. I should not have spoken so disrespectfully of your late mother."

Lady Elinore didn't move a muscle. Just as Hope was wondering whether she'd heard her or not, she said inconsequentially, "Mother did not approve of music. She used to say that while it was useful for soothing the savage breast, it also inflamed the passions therein. She decided it was better to avoid music at all costs."

Hope gave her a sympathetic look. "Our grandfather thought music was sinful. We never heard music at all until we came to London, except for Faith's little wooden flute, which she played in secret against all his dictates. The servants were even forbidden to whistle."

They both fell silent again, only this time it was not awkward.

Lady Elinore sighed. "I've tried to live up to every one of Mother's dictates—she was an extraordinary woman, you know, with marvelously Rational ideas—but music is the one thing I cannot seem to eschew."

"I do not see why you should have to eschew anything," said Hope. "Your mother made those decisions for herself.

Surely you should have the same freedom. I certainly intend to make my own choices at every opportunity."

"Do you?" Lady Elinore looked thoughtful.

"Yes indeed. In fact, when we were sixteen and immured at our grandfather's, I vowed that I would one day be free, and that nobody would ever . . . bind me . . . imprison . . . me again."

Lady Elinore looked fascinated, so Hope continued. "I promised myself that if—no, *when* I escaped from his control, I would enjoy the rest of my life to the fullest. I vowed I would turn down no opportunity for joy, however small." She hesitated self-consciously, aware that she was on thin ice. But this quiet, plain, odd woman had moved her in unexpected ways, and Hope so wanted her to understand.

"There was little joy of any kind at Grandpapa's, you see. He was a hate-filled, bitter old man. Evil, in fact."

"My mother was not evil," said Lady Elinore quickly.

Hope was embarrassed. "No, of course not. I never meant—"

"No, I know you didn't. But you're right all the same. You were right in what you said the other day. I have thought much on it since. Mother was bitter, and there was little joy in our lives. My father treated her . . . us very badly, I gather. Before he died."

"I'm sorry."

"I never knew him. They lived separately, and he died when I was a small child. Which was a fortunate thing, for he was somewhat of a spendthrift, and had he not died, he may have spent his entire fortune instead of only half of it."

"I see."

"I am to inherit it . . . eventually," said Lady Elinore sadly. "It is somewhat of a trial."

Hope raised her brows. "My sisters and I are heiresses, too, but I think it's lovely. I would so much rather be rich than poor. Why do you find your fortune a trial?"

There was a long silence. Then Lady Elinore nodded across the balustrade. "Your sister has entered Lady Thorn's box."

"I know." She'd seen the count leap to his feet and bow dramatically over Faith's hand, kissing it with extravagant gestures. Could her twin really be falling in love with this man?

"I wouldn't have minded meeting the count in person," admitted Lady Elinore. "I tried to at Lady Thorn's soiree, but the press of other ladies was too great. I wanted to tell him how much I admire his playing. It is utterly brilliant, you know."

Her words gave Hope an idea. She stood and gathered her shawl. "Come on then. Let's go to Lady Thorn's box. You shall meet the count, and I shall protect my sister from his blandishments."

"But you were told to stay here."

Hope dimpled. "Not quite. I was told to stay with you."

Lady Elinore looked doubtful. "The gentlemen were fetching us refreshments. They will wonder where we are."

Hope shrugged and said in a rallying tone. "It is one of Lady Augusta's maxims that it is good for gentlemen to wonder. We are not ornaments to be placed in a box and left waiting. We are independent ladies. We have an opportunity to please ourselves, a small opportunity for joy, Lady Elinore. Shall we take it or let it slip by us?"

Lady Elinore looked torn.

Hope said, "Of course, I completely understand if you prefer to stay here and bandy words with Mr. Bemerton—"

Lady Elinore jumped to her feet. "Absolutely not!" she gasped. "I abominate the man. He has no proper feelings whatsoever!" She snatched up her shawl and reticule. "Shall we?"

But when Hope opened the door to the corridor, she collided with James, the footman. "Sorry, Miss Hope," he said. "Orders from Mrs. Jenner not to let any visitors in unless she or Mr. Bemerton are present—him being your escort tonight. And Mr. Bemerton isn't back yet."

"Excellent, James, but we are going out, not coming in. So stand aside, if you please."

James hesitated.

"Ja-ames," said Hope in a tone he'd known all his life.

James rolled his eyes. "Miss Hope, you know very well she wishes you to stay here."

Hope smiled sweetly. "If wishes were horses, James . . . Besides, you cannot imprison Lady Elinore, and she wishes to leave the box, and Mrs. Jenner instructed me to stay with Lady Elinore. And I wouldn't dream of disobeying." She swept airily past him. "Take good care of the box, won't you? Our things are still in it."

James shook his head. "One of these days, miss . . ."

But Hope and Lady Elinore were gone, hurrying toward the place where the corridor widened and people had gathered to chat. The din of shouted conversation and scent of overheated, overperfumed humanity was most unpleasant.

Seeing the crowd, Lady Elinore hesitated, clutching her shawl and reticule nervously. "It is a terrible crush. Are you sure we should proceed? I don't think . . ."

"Do you want to meet the count or return tamely to our box?"

Lady Elinore thought for a moment, then nodded. "Yes. Yes, I do. Very well. Let us proceed, Miss Merridew."

Hope grinned. "I think you ought to call me Hope, now that we're partners in crime."

Lady Elinore flushed. "Thank you. I should be honored," she said in an intense voice.

Hope, observing her gratitude, abruptly realized that Lady Elinore was unused to friendship of the kind that she and her sisters took for granted. She looked at the small, thin older woman with the ugly gray clothes and the scraped-back hair and found herself putting an arm around her and saying, "I think we should become friends, Lady Elinore, yes?"

Lady Elinore stared at her a moment and then, to Hope's embarrassment, her eyes flooded with tears. "Oh! Yes, please." She squeezed Hope's arm affectionately.

Hope resolved then and there to do something about Lady Elinore. She wasn't sure what, but it would be something. If a simple offer of friendship with a girl ten years younger than herself could bring her close to tears, Lady Elinore obviously had far too little friendship in her life.

"Come along." Hope took her hand. "Let us get you introduced to this musician—oops!" Over the heads of the people in the crowd, she spotted Mr. Reyne heading back their way. He hadn't seen them yet. She hesitated, trying to decide whether to enlist his escort or avoid him.

A narrow door lay to her left, marked Private. Hope knew what it was; a staircase for servants and others to bypass the more public areas. A gentleman had once tried to coax her into one, hoping to steal a kiss, no doubt. She'd refused. She hated dark, narrow stairways. She didn't much like the gentleman, either.

"Lost, are you, my li'l beauty, where are you goin' in such a hurry?" An elegantly dressed young blood, obviously the worse for drink, reached casually out and grabbed Hope's forearm.

"Let go of me!" She tried to tug it away. Several of the man's friends crowded around, commenting and laughing. Clearly they had all been drinking for some time.

"Unhand me, sirrah!" she said in freezing accents.

The men roared with laughter. "A hoity-toity beauty!" said one. They all seemed to find that hilarious. "Hoity-toity beauty! A hoity-toity beauty!" they chanted.

She threw a harried glance over her captor's shoulder. Mr. Reyne was getting closer. His face was pure granite. He'd seen. He was ploughing steadily through the crowds, still some twenty or thirty yards away.

"Let *go*!" She stamped on the man's instep hard, and he cursed and released her, to the loud mockery of his friends. Hope stepped quickly away from them before she could be grabbed again and found herself with her back to the door marked Private. If they took these back stairs, she would prevent a scene, for she had no doubt once Mr. Reyne arrived, there would be more than words between him and the drunken young men.

"In here," she said to Lady Elinore, who had been ignored by the young bloods. "We can bypass the crowds and go back up to this level when we reach the other side of the auditorium." She thrust Lady Elinore before her into the shadowy space, followed her in, and closed the door.

Instant darkness.

It closed in on Hope, confining, suffocating. She tried to take a deep breath, but her chest was tight, as if some great weight were pressing on her. "Hurry," she croaked and pushed Lady Elinore. "Where are the stairs? Got to get out."

"I cannot see anything," Lady Elinore complained. "Ouch! Oh dear." She laughed. "It is not a staircase after all. It is just a large cupboard. There are brooms . . . and a bucket."

"Oh God!" Hope turned and scrabbled for the handle of the door. She had to get out. She had to. She couldn't see. Her mouth dried.

There was no handle. Hope scrabbled for it desperately, then started hammering on the door. The darkness closed in on her, thick, oppressive, obliterating everything. She would die here. She clutched at her throat, suddenly finding it hard to breathe. She was going to be sick any minute.

From a long way away, she heard Lady Elinore say, "Miss Hope. Is there something wrong? Can't you open the door?"

Hope choked, unable to muster enough breath to talk. It was all she could do to keep breathing, rapid, shallow breaths.

She scrabbled at the door. She was going to pass out. She felt Lady Elinore's arms go around her. "Miss Hope. Are you ill? Can I help?"

The arms were confining, imprisoning. Hope thrust them away, fighting for breath. Her heart was beating rapidly, palpitating. Feebly she hammered. *Faith!*

She was going to faint at any minute. Her chest was so tight, so tight. Not enough air. *Faith! Twin!*

Suddenly there was light. Blessed light. And air. And

him. Not Faith. Him. She could not see his face, her eyes were blurry, they didn't work anymore. But she heard his voice, from far, far away, deep, strong, worried.

"Good God, Miss Hope. What happened?"

She tried to stagger toward him, to climb out of the black panic, but her knees gave way. She found herself scooped up by strong arms, held against a strong, broad chest.

*Safe, safe, she was safe.*

"She's near to swooning. Do you have any smelling salts, Lady Elinore?"

"No, I'm sorry. A woman of Rationality never faints. My mother used to say that fainting in ladies is usually induced by hunger and tight lacing, neither of which are Rational behaviors."

He swore.

Hope could hear his heart beating, strong and sure. Her own heart was fluttering madly, *like a fish, a landed fish, flopping and gasping for air in the fisherman's arms.*

"Perhaps she has contracted a fever. Her skin is drenched, and she is shaking. My late mother used to say—"

"I don't think it's a fever. Why were you in the cupboard?"

"We thought it was a private stairway down to the next level, and by the time we realized it wasn't, the door was closed, and then we discovered that the handle had fallen off so we could not get out."

"And that was when this happened to her?"

"Yes, I suppose it was."

"Then she's not ill. I have seen this before. I know what to do."

"Is it hysterics? My late mother used to recommend a sharp slap—"

"No one shall slap her!" His voice was harsh, peremptory. Hope flinched at the sound. The voice softened to a deep rumble in her ear, "There now, Miss Hope." A big, calloused hand gently smoothed her hair back. "No one shall harm you. You are safe now with me. 'Tis but a passing fright. You shall recover directly, as soon as I get you to the air." The tenderness in the deep growl shivered all through her, soothing, calming.

The voice changed again. Crisp command. "Giles, escort Lady Elinore back to the box, and fetch Miss Merridew's warm cloak. She is frozen. Send that footman to inform her sister what has happened. I daresay Miss Faith has seen her like this before and will know what to do. You there, conduct me to the roof of this establishment by the quickest route. There is a guinea in it for you. You, usher, see if there is a doctor in the theater. I think I know what is the matter, but if I'm wrong, we'll need a physician. Waiter, fetch me some brandy—your finest—and some water, and bring them instantly to the roof. A guinea in it for each of you. More if you're faster. Now hop to it!"

Hope felt herself moving along the corridor. She closed her eyes against the faces. She could not feel her hands or feet. *Cold. So cold.* She struggled feebly, the world spinning.

The arms tightened, and a deep voice rumbled in her ear. "Hush now, sweet, I have you safe, now. Do not fear. No one shall harm you."

"C-cold."

"I know," he murmured soothingly. "Your cloak is coming, but in the meantime, I'll warm you. Here." He pulled his coat open.

Confused, she tried to stare into his face. Still blurry. A large hand pressed her face against his chest, against the fine linen shirt. "Closer. Let my body warm you." The big hand urged her gently against his chest. Warmth radiated from him. She pressed her shivering body against it.

"That's the way. You'll feel better soon."

She lay against his chest panting, soaking in the warmth and the soothing rhythm of his hand along her spine.

"Now, I want you to try to slow your breathing. It will help, I think. Breathe in. Slowly," he instructed. "Now out . . . slowly. That's it. Good. Now keep breathing just like that. I am taking you outside, into the air."

The air. She could breathe there. The fear that she was dying receded a little.

She breathed against his shirt as he strode along, taking her to the air. She did not suffocate. Her frantic heartbeat slowed. With each breath she inhaled him, scent of man, starched linen, sandalwood soap. The panic subsided a little. The spinning slowed.

He turned sideways as they came to some stairs.

*Helpless. Not helpless.* "Can walk," she muttered. "Put me down. Can walk."

He hesitated for a moment, and she pushed at his chest. Gently he set her on her feet. She took a step, and her knees buckled. The dizziness swept over her.

"I think not," he growled gently.

Again she was swept into his arms, held secure. She clutched his shirt and buried her face in his chest. The smell of him was familiar. Beloved. *Safe. Strong. Protected.*

"Breathe in . . . now out. That's my girl. It's passing now, see? And in a moment you'll be outside in the air, yourself again."

*Safe.* She relaxed against his chest and let him take her out into the air.

Lady Elinore's forehead puckered worriedly. "I think I should be with her."

"Bastian has it all in hand," Giles said. "There's nothing more to do. He has brandy, and her sister and chaperone have been informed, and when I passed him her cloak, he said she was recovering rapidly."

She glanced at the door at the top of the stairs. "But she—she's alone out there on the roof with Mr. Reyne."

"Exactly. It's what she needs. Privacy in which to recover."

She considered his words, then relaxed. "Yes, it would

be most uncomfortable to have people staring." She straightened, "In that case, I shall return to my seat."

He reached out a hand and detained her. "Not so fast, Elinore."

She stiffened and glared at his hand. "Unhand me, sir!"

He grinned but said in a mild voice, "Miss Merridew has need of you yet. You need to stay, for the sake of propriety."

She glanced at the door to the rooftop. "But you said—"

"If after her recovery she returns with you, me, and Bastian, no one will turn a hair, but if she returns alone, with Bastian . . ."

"Oh."

"Exactly. Now, come and sit down. I suspect we will have quite a wait." Giles dusted the stairs with a handkerchief and gestured for her to sit down. "Plenty of room for two."

She eyed the narrow space, then said frostily, "Thank you, I shall stand."

He shrugged and sat down. She stood like a little stick. After a few moments he said softly, "Elinore."

She whirled on him crossly. "I have not given you permission—oof!"

Giles pulled her down onto his lap. She struggled a moment, then sat still and rigid. "Mr. Bemerton, this is most improper!" she hissed.

"Yes. Fun though. Remember the closet? That was fun, too, wasn't it, Elinore?" There was a long pause, then he asked, "Why didn't you use your hatpin?"

She looked away and bit her lip.

"You could use it on me now if you wanted to."

In a tremulous voice she said, "Mr. Bemerton, why are you doing this? You can't possibly desire me. So why do you make fun of me in this way?"

"Elinore, I am not making fun of you, believe me." Giles tipped her gently back into his arms and kissed her very softly on her trembling lips. "And you have no idea of what is possible and what isn't." He kissed her again, less softly.

She made a little sound deep in her throat. Her hand wavered, moved toward her bodice, then trembled and came to rest on the back of his neck, then slid up to bury itself in his thick, golden hair.

# Chapter Sixteen

∞

*Above the smoke and stir of this dim spot, which men call earth.*
JOHN MILTON

HOPE STOOD LOOKING OUT OVER LONDON, silhouetted against the gentle lemon moon and the gaslights reflecting from the streets below. Sebastian took the luscious folds of ruched velvet and wrapped her in it. She seemed to sag beneath its weight, yet it was not so heavy.

She turned, her face pale and resolute in the gaslight, and faced him. He was prepared for reaction to set in, for tears. She surprised him.

"I must apologize," she said in a composed voice in which only a hint of quaver remained. She looked unutterably beautiful and quite desolate.

Sebastian swallowed. "For what?"

She raised a brow and said with a faint edge of bitter sarcasm, "To be afraid of being locked inside a cupboard? A simple, ordinary, harmless cupboard. Without even any spiders in it?" She said it as if repeating a lesson learned by heart. There was an odd cadence, not her own, as if she was unconsciously imitating someone. There was a degree of self-loathing there that shocked him.

He poured brandy into a glass and handed it to her. "Sometimes our fears overcome us, no matter how hard we try. There is nothing to be ashamed of. Now drink that. It will restore you a little."

She held the glass in limp fingers and stared at him. "A cupboard! What sort of pathetic creature is frightened by a mere cupboard?" She closed her eyes in brief self disgust. "And I was not even alone in it. What must Lady Elinore think of me?"

"It's not her business to think anything!" Sebastian growled. "You are not to be upset by anything of the sort, do you hear me? Now drink that brandy."

She stared at him a moment, then the bitter look faded from her eyes. She smiled ruefully. "I suppose you will order her not to think poorly of me."

"No." Sebastian shook his head. Barking at her like an overseer on the factory floor! No wonder she thought he might try to order a lady what to think. "Lady Elinore has a kind heart. She will understand."

"She does have a kind heart. But who can understand fear of a cupboard?" she said so sadly he wanted to snatch her into his arms again. She turned away from him, setting her untouched glass down on the balustrade and looked out over the streetscape below them. Sebastian felt helpless. He wanted to hold her tight, to force her to receive comfort. He hated that look of shame and misery in her eyes. He didn't know what to do.

Her cloak slipped off one shoulder. He stepped forward and wrapped it more securely around her. His arms stayed around her waist, supporting her. He could feel the faint shivers that still occasionally rocked her, and he drew her back against him, offering his warmth and strength. She leaned against his chest, staring miserably out across the London rooftops. Her hair was disordered and slightly damp. He drew in the scent of her with each breath. She seemed completely desolate.

He said the first words that came into his mind. "I knew a man once, in the mill. Reuben Davy. A big, brawny fellow he was. Could lift anything. I thought he was the strongest man in the world. I was just a lad, myself. He was a fighter, too, county champion."

She gave no sign she was listening. The breeze ruffled her curls. Below them they could hear a barrow man trundling his wares home, a carriage going past, the horses' hooves clip-clopping on the cobbles.

"One thing Reuben wouldn't do: go down into the cellar. Not for anything or anyone. Some of the other men thought it was funny, a big strong fellow like Reuben, afraid of the dark. They tricked him one day. Threw a bag over his head, locked him down there in the cellar. For a joke."

There was a long silence. She didn't move a muscle. Far away, a lone seabird circled down near the river, its cry mournful and bleak.

"When they found him, Reuben was weeping like a babe, gasping for breath, in a grip of a panic so deep it took him hours to come out of it. They had to carry him out of the cellar, all sixteen stone of him."

She stood as still as a statue, staring blankly out over the darkened city. A barge glided silently along the river, sending dark ripples in its wake.

"He told me much later that when he was only seven years old, he'd started off working in the mines. He never minded the dark then. He worked there for years. One day toward the end of the shift, the tunnel came down around them. It was five days before they dug him out. All the other men and boys down there were dead, including his father and two of his brothers. He lay there for days, under the earth, dead men all around him, waiting to die. He was twelve years old—the same age I was when he told me the story. Reuben never went down another mine again. Couldn't. Never went into a dark cellar or a small, dark cupboard either."

A wagon rumbled noisily past in the street below. Somewhere a dog barked. Sebastian placed a hand on her shoulder.

"He beat those men to a pulp, afterward. A man to demand respect, Reuben Davy. No matter that he couldn't abide closed, dark spaces. We all have things we cannot abide."

He felt the tension sigh out of her. Slowly, slowly she turned, and he released her. Her eyes were swimming, liquid; her face was working with emotion. "Thank you," she whispered.

He wanted to haul her into his arms and kiss all the distress away. He picked up her brandy glass and held it to her lips. "Drink. It will burn a little, but you will feel better afterward."

She gave him a shimmering, unfathomable look and then leaned closer. He could smell the faint scent that was uniquely hers. His mouth was dry as she put her lips to the glass he held. He'd never held a glass for a woman to drink from before. It was strangely intimate.

He cupped his other hand around the nape of her neck and tilted the glass. Her lips closed around the glass, and she took the golden liquid into her mouth. Her eyes locked with his, she swallowed, shuddering as the liquor burned its way down her throat. She gasped as the cognac reached her stomach and shuddered again, extravagantly. She threw her head back, savoring the heat of the brandy, her eyes closed, her cheeks wet, her mouth glistening with brandy in the moonlight.

When she opened her eyes again, she said simply, "My grandfather used to lock me in the small cupboard under the stairs." She gave a jerky sob. "I cannot bear to be confined, and he knew it."

He nodded. He'd thought it would be something like that.

"Never again, I promise you. Never again," he whispered and smoothed her hair. His fingers looked big and crooked and ugly against her delicate beauty. "Now, another mouthful."

She licked her lips and pursed them around the glass again. He ought not to watch so hungrily, but he could not force his eyes to look away. He was already rock hard with wanting her.

She swallowed and shuddered again under his hand as the spirits hit her. Her eyes were huge in the moonlight, her lips moist and pale and slightly parted.

He stroked the place he'd been staring at earlier, the soft, delicate groove of her nape. Soft wind stirred her silver-gilt tendrils against his fingers. His finger moved in slow rhythms, savoring the velvet, silky texture. She shivered.

"Cold?" he asked.

She shook her head. Her cheeks were tear-silvered in the moonlight, her eyelashes damp and spiky. She lifted her face to him, and he possessed her mouth in one swift movement.

She was all heat and softness and brandy and woman, and she kissed him back with a clumsy honesty that shot straight to his heart. And loins.

He tasted tears and need and desire. And innocence. And exhaustion. He pulled back, fighting for control, cupping her nape, smoothing her hair, breathing deeply as he forced his body into submission. She was worn out by her recent emotional storm, and he should be protecting and caring for her, not keeping her out here to face his uncontrollable lust on the roof of the opera among discarded bits and pieces in the cold moonlight. What was he thinking of—taking her up against the stone facade?

He wasn't thinking at all, that was the trouble.

He stroked her hair again, and she shivered again. She must be cold. He held her close and reversed their positions, angling them so that he leaned back and she could lean against him—or pull back. She didn't pull back. She leaned into him more fully, soft breasts, soft thighs pressed lightly against his racked, tensed body.

The chill of the cold stone balustrade seeped into his back, a necessary cooling, he thought grimly. Her eyes were in shadow now. Her softness pressed against him. He was fully aroused.

Hope tried to read his grim expression. The cognac burned deep in her stomach and throat. His eyes were shuttered, shadowy depths of hidden thoughts. In moonlight his mouth was fully lit in all its sculptured perfection. Carved masculine beauty.

Why didn't he kiss her again? Didn't he know she wanted, needed him to kiss her now, more than ever? He'd claimed her; now she wanted the possession. And she needed to hold him, kiss him, love him, to drive out some of those dark, lonely shadows from his eyes. He'd taken her out of the darkness into the moonlight. She wanted to do the same for him. Because he was the one, the man of shadows and moonlight she'd dreamed about and waited for all her life.

In the cold, lonely bleakness of the night he'd come to her then . . . and now.

He'd held her, one arm wrapped around her waist, and turned, drawing her away from the cold stone wall behind her toward his heat. His strength and his heat. Powerful, life-affirming heat. His other hand cupped the back of her head, gently, as for a newborn babe. One finger stroked her nape, slow, rhythmic strokes . . . sending secret shivers of pleasure down her spine.

So gentle. He was so big and powerful and tough-looking . . . and so gentle.

"Kiss me again." she whispered. "I need you, Sebastian."

He froze, and she poised on the brink of who knew what for a long, long moment. And then he lowered his head and took her mouth.

Heat. Hunger. Possession in one soul-scorching touch. His kiss rocked her to her depths. Fierce, implacable need, hunger like she'd never felt, instantly leashed and controlled.

She knew about hunger, knew about need. She kissed him back with everything in her, holding nothing back, showing him what she could not say in words.

He drew back, breathing heavily. She could not see his eyes but felt them devouring her. She lifted her face to him, hoping he would read in her eyes the message there. His mouth tightened, then he bent forward and kissed her gently, reverently, as if she might break, as if he needed to ration himself.

He feathered kisses along her jawline, smoothing away the last dampness of her tears, kissing first one wet eyelid, then the other, with ravishing delicacy. Beneath the careful tenderness she could feel his hunger, simmering, severely leashed. His big, powerful body was braced, hard and wanting, yet he held her lightly, just enough to support her while he lavished her with silken angel kisses. Angel kisses that sent quivers of sensation rippling through her body, like brandy in her blood. Burning, soothing, exciting . . .

She ran her hands along his arms. Beneath the superfine cloth of his jacket, each powerful muscle was rigid with the effort, racked with controlled desire.

It was just like the waltzes, she realized, the reason he was so stiff and awkward with her. He was holding back, like a stallion, champing at the bit. He wanted to do more than just dance with her. He wanted more than feather kisses across her eyelids.

She wanted more as well.

Any remnants of doubt she had about giving herself to such a big, powerful man dissolved with the realization. Never in her life would she have believed any man could be so tender, so gentle, let alone such a hard-seeming, tough, controlled man.

She felt safe. In his arms, for the first time since her parents died, she felt safe. Wholly cared for, wholly protected, wholly desired. She had longed for this all her life, yearned for it. And now she wanted to fly, fly in his arms.

Below them they heard the faint strains of music. Another act had begun. His eyes were dark shadows, his voice was thick and strained as he said, "We should return. Do you feel ready to go inside now?"

"No," she whispered. "I want to stay here with you. I want to be yours." She pressed against him, savoring his strength and heat. She slipped her hands up the strong, warm column of his neck and ran her fingers through his cropped, dark hair, pulling his head down to her level. Her mouth found his, and she kissed him with all her heart, blindly, feverishly.

For a few seconds he let her kiss him, let her explore him almost passively, and then, with a great, racking shudder, he took control, planting his mouth deeply over hers, possessing, searching, cradling her head, angling his mouth to taste her deeply, intimately. She reveled in the intimacy, the powerful sense of connection. The heat spread in waves.

His taste, the insistent demands of his tongue and hands, set her body thrumming to an unfamiliar rhythm. She could not think, only react. She wanted to climb him like a tree, get somehow closer. She clung, returning kiss for kiss, her awareness spiraling out of control until she could barely think, only react.

His hands roamed up and down her body, leaving hot trails of pleasure in their wake. He brushed his knuckles across the tips of her breasts, and she was dimly aware of arching her back and making some sort of sound. He groaned and caressed her breasts again and again, and she rubbed herself against him like a cat.

He hesitated. "May I?"

She frowned in confusion, not knowing what he meant and not truly caring. She rubbed herself against him. "More."

He kissed her hard, then fumbled for the drawstring of her dress, loosening it, then drawing it down over her shoulders in the moonlight. She felt the chill, the whisper of the night breeze on her naked breasts, and felt suddenly self-conscious and unsure of herself—until she saw his eyes. Worship took on a new meaning. She watched as his big hands moved to cup each pale breast, and she felt suddenly as if she was close to tears.

"You wore a dress with yellow ruffles once," he said. "And I looked at those yellow ruffles, at the way they cupped your breasts, and I wished my hands could be those yellow ruffles."

His eyes were dark and intent. "I dreamed of it often afterward. But I never thought my dream would come true."

"I always knew my dream would," she whispered and pressed her hands over his.

"So beautiful." He bent his head and kissed each breast lightly, reverently, moving his mouth softly back and forth in waves of silken pleasure. She watched his dark head bent over her in the silvered light, unbearably moved. And then his beautiful hard, gentle mouth closed over one damp, aroused nipple, and she arched as if lightning had flashed though her body.

He looked up, and his look burned through her with the same heat, and he returned to lavish his attentions on her breasts until she was arching and burning and shuddering.

"Sebastian," she heard herself mutter. "Sebastian."

She felt the cold night air on her legs and was warmed by his big hand smoothing up them, over her silk stockings, caressing the flesh where the garter was tied. Her legs were trembling, and at his touch they sagged beneath her.

His arm tightened as he supported her, half leaning against him, half lying on him. His eyes burned into her, filled with the sort of hunger and desire she hadn't even known to dream of. Desire for her. Hunger for her . . .

His big, rough-skinned hands moved higher, circling and stroking until they cupped her so intimately she stiffened for a moment, as self-awareness asserted itself briefly, then flickered out as his fingers caressed her lightly, and sensation swamped her.

His fingers were long and strong and seemed to know exactly what to do, and she quivered and pressed against them, pushing rhythmically, frantically wanting more, more, more.

His mouth returned to hers, hard, hot, demanding. Half biting, thrusting, demanding, taking. No gentle angel kisses now but pure, passionate glory, blazing glory that demanded, even as it gave. He drove her, carried them both, to the brink; insistent, feverish, burning. Like being carried on a wave, out of control. Flying? Yes, and yet much earthier.

She clung to him as she felt herself spiraling, shuddering—

*Rrrraoull!* The scream shattered the night. Unearthly. Like a soul lost in hell. *Rrrraoull!* Then a crash.

She clutched him, dazed, still partially in the grip of the waves of sensation. "What is it?"

His head was flung back, his eyes closed, and he held her hard against him for a second, before he slowly, reluctantly released her. When he opened his eyes, he looked devastated. He swallowed convulsively and said, "I'm sorry. I should not—" He tugged her bodice up around her shoulders, tying the drawstring ribbons with shaking fingers. A grimace almost of pain crossed his face, and he said in a heavy voice, "I took advantage of your emotional state. I'm sorry. I should not have done such—" He looked mortified.

She stared at him, not quite knowing what to say, unable to fathom what had just happened. One moment she had been on the verge of something . . . momentous, and the next she was plunged back to reality, standing cold and shivering as if someone had thrown cold water over her. He finished tying the ribbons and tucked the ends neatly inside her neckline, his fingers—the fingers that had brought her to a state of mindless rapture—now barely skimming her skin.

*Rrrraoull!* An unearthly wail of torment. She shivered. "What *is* that noise?"

He sighed, heavily. "Cats."

"Cats?" She was incredulous. "It sounds to me like children lost and terrified and hurting."

He looked a bit embarrassed. "Well, it's not children. It's cats. On the rooftop."

She frowned, doubting his story. "Are you sure it's not children?"

"Positive."

"I've never heard any cat make a noise like that. If it is cats, then someone must be torturing them. I'm fond of cats."

He gave her a shuttered look. "No one is torturing them."

"But they sound like they are in pain."

He muttered something she could not quite catch. Something to do with knowing the feeling.

"I beg your pardon?"

"They're not. In pain. They're perfectly all right. Now, I think it's time we returned to the others. They will be wondering what has become of us." He started to lead her toward the door.

*Rrrraourraouulll!*

She stopped, worried. "How do you know those cats are all right? They sound in the most frightful pain."

He closed his eyes briefly, sighed, and with a grim, mortified look on his face, ground out, "That's what cats sound like when they're copulating."

*Copulating?* She clapped a hand over her mouth in surprise. And then she thought about it. And realized why he was so very embarrassed. If they hadn't been interrupted by copulating cats . . .

He looked so grim and forbidding she could not say it. She allowed him to wrap her securely in her ruched velvet cloak and escort her to the door, his hand resting lightly in the small of her back, burning effortlessly through the layers of her clothes there like a brand.

*Mrrrrraouwwwll!*

A small sound escaped her.

He stopped instantly. "Are—are you all right?" He bent over her, trying to see her expression in the shadows. "I'm sorry. I know I shouldn't have done what I did. I-I lost my head, got carried—"

*Rrrraaaoull!*

"Damned cats!" he exploded.

"My thought exactly," she murmured and giggled again.

He stared incredulously. "You—you're laughing?"

"I know, I shouldn't, I know . . . but you must admit, it's funny. There we were . . . and there they were . . . and—"

*Mmmrrrrraoull!*

She giggled again, falling against him in her mirth. "Their timing was appalling, but—"

Seeing the look on his face, she sobered. She reached up and took his face in her hands. "Oh, please don't look like that. I regret not a moment of what happened. Tonight was magic. Thank you for rescuing me from my own personal hell." She kissed him softly on the mouth. "And thank you for starting me on the journey toward my own personal heaven. We didn't quite get there tonight, but we shall . . . shan't we? Sebastian?"

He stared at her wordlessly, his face somber and austere, a tiny muscle in his jaw working. He said nothing; he just pulled her into a hard embrace and held her there a long, long moment.

"Do you mean that?" he said gruffly.

"I do." And it was a vow.

At her softly spoken words he hugged her hard again, burying his face in her hair. Then he turned her face up and gave her a deep, ravishing kiss, looked her in the eyes, and said simply, "I will make it right. I promise you."

They found Giles and Lady Elinore sitting at the bottom of the stairs, side by side in silence. Lady Elinore jumped up. "How do you feel, Miss Hope? I am so distressed that you—"

Hope embraced her. "Thank you, but I am perfectly well now, Elinore. It was kind of you to wait, and in such an uncomfortable spot."

"Yes, what are you two doing here?" Sebastian asked. Lady Elinore looked distinctly flustered.

"Minding your reputation," Giles responded. "Mrs. Jenner and Miss Faith were all set to come storming out to see to Miss Hope, but I explained that Lady Elinore and I would remain with you at all times. Miss Faith persuaded the chaperone to return to the box."

"Excellent," Hope said. "Faith knows I cannot bear it when Mrs. Jenner fusses." She gave a swift, self-conscious glance at Sebastian and added, "Not that there was anything improper in our trip to the roof." She felt her color rising.

Giles arched a brow at Sebastian but said only, "Of course not. None of my business, anyway."

Lady Elinore looked uncomfortable. "It will be noticed. It has been five and twenty minutes at least. We have missed most of the second act."

"I am so sorry, Lady Elinore. I know how much you enjoy the opera—"

"Oh that's all right," interrupted Giles casually. "Lady Elinore and I have been getting to know each other, have we not, Lady Elinore?"

Lady Elinore flushed bright red. She said to Hope, "I was worried about you."

Hope squeezed her hand. "Thank you. It—it is a foolish weakness of mine, that's all, that I cannot bear being confined in a small, dark space."

"Nothing foolish about it," Sebastian growled behind her.

His words warmed her. As did his hand resting on the small of her back all the way back to their seats.


"What does it feel like, twin?" Faith said in a wistful voice as they were preparing for bed that evening.

Hope turned quickly. Surely her twin couldn't have felt *that*—what she'd felt in Mr. Reyne's arms on the rooftop. "What?"

But Faith was folding her chemise and not looking for telltale blushes. "When you're in love." She looked up. "You are in love with Mr. Reyne, aren't you?"

Hope hesitated.

"I know you let him kiss you. I could tell when you entered the box." She sighed. "Oh, Hope, you were lit up like a candle from within, so beautiful, so happy. And to look like that after one of your attacks . . ." She smiled tremulously. "It must be love. Just like Mama promised."

Hope nodded, and feeling suddenly teary, hugged her twin convulsively. "Yes," she whispered. "I do love him." She'd never said the words aloud before and hugged her twin again. "Oh, Faith, I *love* him." She'd never felt with anyone what she felt about him.

"The real thing?"

Hope nodded. "The real thing."

"And he's the one in the dream?"

"I don't know, and I don't care. The dream doesn't matter anymore. I love *him*."

Faith's jaw dropped. "How can you say the dream doesn't matter? It must. It must be true." She looked quite distressed.

Hope shook her head. She would never forget the magical sensation of waltzing in the moonlight in the arms of her dream man, but her big, gruff, darling Sebastian would never waltz like that, as if two could move as one. She smiled tenderly. "No, the dream was just a dream. But my Sebastian is real. Wonderfully real, and our love is true."

"But I thought . . . if the dream—" Faith broke off. "He's told you then? Said the words?"

Hope shook her head. "Not yet. But he will."

Faith looked thoughtful. "I think I might be in love, too. I think Count Rimavska might be the one, Hope."

Hope did not know what to say. Faith was dazzled, that she knew, but love . . . "Are you sure, twin?"

Faith gave her a half-rueful, half-excited look, then nodded. "I don't know. I suspect so. He . . . he fascinates me. When I am with him . . . I feel . . . enthralled. On the brink of something terrifying, like a huge chasm and yet, I cannot help wishing to throw myself into it."

Hope understood then. She had faced the same chasm herself with Mr. Reyne. And in his arms had thrown herself into it, happily, joyfully. *Sebastian*. She hugged his name to herself.

Faith looked at her mistily and heaved a gusty sigh as she climbed into bed. "Isn't it wonderful? All these years we've dreamed of finally falling in love, and now, at long last, it's happened. Both of us, at once."

Hope smiled back. "At least yours is rich and titled. Lord knows what Great Uncle Oswald will say when I tell him I want to marry my Sebastian."

Faith giggled. I know exactly what he'll say." She said in a gruff voice, "Shockin'! To waste a diamond like you on a cit, when there are dukes goin' beggin'! Shockin'!"

# *Chapter Seventeen*

*The cause is hidden. The effect is visible to all.*

Ovid

Sebastian called on Lady Elinore first thing next morning. He was not looking forward to the interview. He had not treated her well. He hoped she would not become angry or distressed, but he owed her honesty, he'd decided.

She opened the door herself, ushered him into the small sitting room, and offered him a cup of tea. When he accepted, she went off to make it herself. Again he was made aware of her straitened circumstances. Outrageous for a woman of her standing to be forced to take a husband, merely to inherit what should be hers by right. Neither parent had done right by Lady Elinore.

Sebastian felt even guiltier. He had not done right by her, either. But he was resolved. He would not compound his error by prolonging the misunderstanding.

The moment she reentered the room, he said, "Lady Elinore, I'm sorry if this distresses you, but—"

She stopped him with a hand on his sleeve. "There is no need, Mr. Reyne. I know what you are going to say. You are in love with Miss Hope Merridew, are you not?"

Sebastian nodded.

"I'm very glad," she said simply. "We might have made a convenient match of it . . . and a few weeks ago, convenience was all I expected."

Sebastian raised a brow. The interview had taken an unexpectedly personal turn. "And now you don't?"

"No," she said quietly. "Now I want more, much more."

He kissed her hand. "I'm glad, Lady Elinore. You deserve more. Shall we remain friends, do you think?"

"Oh yes, please. We are bound to keep meeting." She said, adding with a faint flush, "I have become friends with Hope, you see. And I am also seeing quite a lot of Lady Augusta Montigua del Fuego. Lady Augusta has decided to join the board of the Tothill Fields Institution."

"Lady Augusta?" Sebastian was amazed. He couldn't imagine any odder pairing than the flamboyant, earthy Lady Augusta and this repressed little spinster, but Lady Elinore was full of surprises.

"She is very kind, you know, and very fond of children. She has plans for a number of them already. She's an extraordinary woman, with a great deal of energy." She dropped her head, a little embarrassed, and added, "She has taken me under her wing, as well."

"Good heavens."

"She never had a child, you see," said Lady Elinore softly. She meant the children at the institute but, Sebastian thought, as he looked down at the small, lonely figure, Lady Elinore had never really had a mother, either.

Later, as he was heading home, it occurred to him that there was something different about Lady Elinore. He frowned, perplexed. Something about how she looked. Then he shook his head. What did he know? There was only one female who interested him: Miss Hope Merridew.

"I can't see any ducklings," complained Cassie.

"A few days ago I saw three," Sebastian said. "Try around the bend there. Any ducklings, Dorie?"

She shook her head and went farther along, peering among the reeds excitedly. Cassie, too, went right to the edge, searching.

"I'd prefer it if you didn't join the ducks today, Cassie," he said in a mild attempt at a joke. She pulled a face at him, unoffended, and Sebastian reflected how much had changed in a short time. Cassie was a different person from the hostile, angry girl he'd found only a few months ago. He was not sure whether or not she'd given up carrying her knife, but he wasn't going to ask and make an issue of it. She would leave off the knife when she felt safe.

Dorie had not made such clear progress. She still secretly pocketed bread from the dinner table. And she remained nervous and clingy, particularly if they were out in public, among strangers. At least she also clung to him and Hope now, and not just Cassie. A child should not have to feel responsible for the well-being of another child. Cassie mightn't acknowledge it, but she was visibly happier for being able to share the responsibility of Dorie.

Sebastian smiled as he watched Dorie search. She looked a little like a duckling herself in that yellow dress. The family of ducklings was a few yards away, and Dorie would discover them any minute. He'd received a note from Hope this morning, telling him that she and her sisters intended to ride in the park this morning. If he wished to begin interesting his sisters in taking riding lessons, the opportunity would be there. So he'd taken it.

The thought of family outings on horseback did appeal, not the least at the thought of the wife who would be riding beside him. Besides, most gentlewomen rode, and he didn't want his sisters to be exceptions.

Hope would tempt them, he knew. She could tempt anyone to do anything.

The thought struck him like a blow to the chest yet again. He was going to marry Hope Merridew. He could hardly believe it.

He hadn't asked her yet, he would need to speak to her and her great-uncle. But after the night at the opera he knew: no other woman would do. He had never been a man for dreaming. Plans, yes. Plans dealt with actions and things of substance; those he had lived his life by. But dreams . . .

He would never have dared to dream of Hope Merridew.

He suddenly realized that Dorie was waving excitedly. "Have you found them?" he called.

She nodded vigorously, then placed a finger to her lips, telling him and Cassie to be quiet. They both hurried up, and sure enough, there was the mother duck with seven fluffy brown and yellow fuzz balls paddling importantly after her.

They fed the mother, and Dorie crumbled tiny duckling-sized crumbs, which she threw in the water for the little ones. Her sharp little face was lit with tender excitement. She needed a pet, Sebastian suddenly realized. Dorie had an instinct for looking after small things. It would do her good to have something of her own to care for.

He suddenly remembered the horses and consulted his pocket watch surreptitiously. Eleven o'clock, Hope's note had said. It was almost that now.

"Have we run out of bread?"

Dorie nodded.

"Then it is time to return."

The light died from her eyes, and he found himself explaining, "The mother duck will get nervous if we show too much interest in her babies." He had no idea how mother ducks thought, but it worked. She and Cassie left the edge of the pond and came obediently back to his side. Again he marveled at the change in them.

As they walked, Sebastian raised the notion of getting a pet. As he'd thought, both girls were excited by the idea. "We've never had a pet," Cassie confided. "Dorie tames mice all the time."

"Does she now?" He raised his brows. That would explain the sudden rise in the mouse population, not to mention the bread she hid in her pocket. He felt suddenly happier.

Dorie glared at her sister, and Cassie said hurriedly,

"And we found some sweet little kittens once, only Albert drowned them."

"Albert?" Sebastian asked casually. He valued these snippets of information about their previous life. Slowly he was piecing them together. One day, he hoped, he would know.

"Mam's younger brother. He was a horrid beast," said Cassie shortly, as if regretting she'd mentioned him.

"You haven't mentioned him before."

"No. He only came to live with us after her older brother died. Just before Mam died."

Dorie slipped a hand into Sebastian's and clutched it hard. They were coming to an area of the park where more people were gathered. He smiled reassuringly down at her.

"Oh, look, there are the Merridews!" Cassie exclaimed suddenly. "On horseback! All three of them and James, too."

Sebastian followed the direction of her gaze and felt a powerful surge of possessiveness. There she was, his own beloved, in her blue velvet habit, a saucy hat perched on her curls. She saw him and smiled a dazzling smile, and he felt his heart lurch, still barely able to believe that this wonderful, glorious woman actually wanted him—plain Sebastian Reyne.

The four riders trotted to meet them.

"Grace rides well, doesn't she?" Sebastian commented.

"Hmm," Cassie agreed thoughtfully.

He kept a straight face. Grace and Cassie were excellent friends, but a faint thread of competitiveness ran through their friendship. "Yes, she looks splendid up there, mastering her horse so effortlessly. Not that it matters, for, as you said, you don't wish to ride stupid horses."

She sent him a quick, displeased sidelong glance.

The Merridews arrived, and they exchanged greetings. Hope immediately said, "Cassie, tell me what you think of Grace's new habit. I think it very fetching, don't you? But Grace is cross because she wanted velvet." He immediately perceived her tactics. Cassie had a hidden but growing passion for clothes.

Faith said, clearly repeating an old argument, "Grace is too young for velvet."

Sebastian added his mite. "I can see it is the finest wool."

"Yes and the frogging is extremely dashing. Green suits her, doesn't it? What color is your habit, Cassie?" Hope asked innocently.

"I don't have a habit."

"Don't you?" Grace said in surprise. "Then what do you wear to ride?"

Cassie said nothing.

Sebastian said, "Cassie doesn't have a habit, because—" Cassie sent him a desperate look of appeal. "Because it's not yet finished. What color was it to be, Cassie? Dark red? With gold braid?"

"Yes," Cassie sent him a grateful look. She glanced shyly up at Hope and admitted, "I've never ridden a horse before."

"Would you like to sit up here with me a moment?" Hope offered. "Your brother can lift you up."

Cassie looked a bit taken aback, but when Sebastian put his hands around her waist, she made no demur. He lifted her into Miss Hope's lap. It was a bit of a squeeze, with the sidesaddle, and Cassie looked very nervous. "Let us walk a little way," said Hope, and before Cassie could object, the horse moved off.

She sat, tense and nervous, as Miss Hope bent over her, explaining what was what. Grace walked her horse beside them, chatting animatedly, her presence a wonderfully stiffening factor in Cassie's determination not to show fear.

"Do you want to come up, too, Dorie?" Miss Faith asked.

Dorie shook her head.

"There's a boy with a basket of puppies over near the fountain," Miss Faith said. "Would you like to see them?"

Dorie looked at Sebastian and nodded.

"Come along then. Excuse us, Miss Merridew." He took her hand and made for where a small crowd of children and adults had gathered around the boy with a basket of squirming black-and-white pups. Dorie held back initially, but as soon as she saw the puppies, she forgot her fears and crowded eagerly forward.

The pups were about six or seven weeks old, a motley breed. The boy was selling them for a few shillings. Dorie was entranced. She watched the puppies with bright eyes, utterly absorbed in their antics as they clambered over each other, rolling and biting and wrestling.

"Sebastian, look at me," he heard and turned to where Cassie was riding past the crowd, sitting up in front of Hope, as proud as punch. "I'm riding," she called excitedly.

He grinned and nodded back.

"What are you looking at?" she called.

"Puppies."

"Oh! Oh! Can I see? Can I get down now, Miss Hope, please?"

"I'll get you," Sebastian called. He glanced at Dorie, still entranced with the pups. "I'm just going to lift your sister down," he told her. Dorie gave no sign she heard, so Sebastian left her and went to lift Cassie down.

"Oh, it was wonderful," Cassie exclaimed as he lifted her out of Hope's arms. "I can't wait to start my lessons. Where is Dorie?"

"I couldn't drag her away from the puppies. She's choosing one now."

"I must see." She started off.

Sebastian snagged her by the arm. "Say thank you to Miss Hope first."

"Sorry. Thank you, Miss Hope. Good day to you." Cassie bobbed a hurried curtsy and ran off.

Sebastian rolled his eyes. "I thought I was in for a puppy. Now I fear there shall be two at least!"

Hope laughed. "It is a wonderful idea."

He took her hand and looked up at her. "You are the wonderful one." He said softly, "I haven't been able to get the thought of last night out of my mind. It was—"

Cassie came running back and thumped him furiously on the arm. "I thought you said Dorie was with the puppies!"

Sebastian frowned. "She is." Cassie still had some manners to learn.

"No, she's not! She's nowhere to be seen," Cassie said accusingly. "You were supposed to be looking after her!"

Sebastian glanced back at the group around the pups. "Are you sure, Cassie? She was there only a moment ago."

"She's not there now."

"Oh God." He looked around worriedly, knowing how easily Dorie became frightened. "Hope, can you see her anywhere?"

From her higher vantage on horseback, Hope anxiously scanned the park. "There!" she exclaimed. "Someone's got her!" and she urged her horse after them.

Sebastian followed on foot, running as if the Devil were after him. In the distance he could see a man running, a small figure in a yellow dress slung over his shoulder. She was struggling. The sight gave him extra speed.

How the devil had the villain snatched a child from among a crowd of people? And why? And why Dorie? Sebastian raced onward, slowly but surely closing the gap between himself and the kidnapper.

Hope, on horseback, gained on the man swiftly, yelling like an Amazon at him. The man sped up. Hope galloped past him, and he swerved. She turned her horse and came back at him. He dodged and changed direction, but as he did, he slipped and dropped Dorie. She scrambled away and started running off as fast as she could, running like a terrified rabbit, in no particular direction, just away. The park gates were not far away. If in her panic, she ran out into the streets, pursuit would be much more difficult.

"Dorie, Dorie, to me, to me!" Sebastian shouted, but she didn't hear him.

Her abductor started after her, shouting, "Come back 'ere you little rat, or I'll kill you! And your sister, see if I don't." The man pulled a knife and continued his pursuit, repeating his threats.

Her sister? He knew she had a sister?

Dorie faltered. Sebastian's heart almost stopped when

he saw her hesitate. If the abductor got hold of her now, he'd use her as a hostage. Or kill her outright. He'd hang for kidnapping as easily as murder.

"Keep running, Dorie," Sebastian yelled. "I'll stop him."

She heard him this time and started running again, but her hesitation had allowed her pursuer to gain on her. He was three or four yards behind her and gaining fast when Hope came thundering along from behind. As she closed on the child and her pursuer, she yelled, "Dorie, hold out your hand, I'm going to pick you up."

To Sebastian's horror, Hope was hanging off her horse in the way she'd done when performing her outlandish tricks. He had no time to tell her to stop, he was almost upon the man himself. Under his horrified gaze, Hope Merridew came galloping down on his frail little sister, bent over, and scooped her up, just as the man's knife slashed out at her, once, twice.

Hope teetered for a minute—Dorie was much heavier than a twig—then righted herself and continued on. Holding Dorie to her chest, she let out a yell of triumph. "Got her, Sebastian!" Dorie clung to her like a terrified monkey, arms and legs wrapped tightly around Hope. She watched from over Hope's shoulder, her little face as white as a ghost, but when she saw Sebastian, she gave a little flip of her hand, as if to say, *I'm all right*.

A shout came from the left. The park attendants had been alerted and were coming in hot pursuit.

The man glanced around fearfully and fled.

Sebastian followed, driven now by rage instead of fear for his sister and Hope. He swiftly closed on him and brought him down in a leaping tackle. They both rolled on the ground.

The man scrambled to his feet, swearing horribly and brandishing his knife. He gave a rotten-toothed snarl, "Come on, me fine toff, let's see the color of yer blood!" He feinted with the knife, a vicious-looking blade. He was desperate. If he was caught, he would hang. He had a knife, and he had nothing to lose. He closed in on Sebastian, clearly intending to wound him and make a getaway.

But Sebastian had learned gutter fighting the hard way, in the backstreets of a factory town. He swayed back just enough to dodge the slashing knife, then followed it instantly through with a kick to the man's side. The man staggered, off balance, and Sebastian leaped in and smashed a punch in his face. He grabbed the knife hand, twisted it, and slammed his fist down hard on the man's wrist. The knife dropped from his hand, and Sebastian kicked it away. Half a dozen punches, and the man was on the ground, gasping. He was bleeding from the nose and mouth.

Sebastian stood over him a moment, gasping for breath, but the man didn't move.

"You got him! Hurrah!" yelled Hope, clearly delighted with the outcome and showing no signs of ladylike distress. Her horse danced around restlessly, affected by her excitement.

"Dorie?" he asked.

Dorie nodded. She hadn't quite relaxed her death grip on Hope's neck, but she seemed perfectly happy to remain on the horse. No doubt it had something to do with the alternative. He glanced at the man on the ground, who gave no sign of life. The park keepers were a few hundred yards away. They would take the fellow into custody.

Sebastian walked toward Hope and his sister. He'd seen that knife flash as Dorie had been lifted to safety by his mad, brave, daredevil lady, and it had seemed to him— though he had been running—that the the blade caught in something. "I saw that fellow slash at—"

"Sebastian!" The thin reedy scream was like nothing he'd ever heard. "Behind you!"

He whirled. The man grabbed the discarded knife and tried to plunge it into Sebastian, but the warning had come in time, and the knife glanced off his sleeve. Sebastian threw a mighty punch. The man's head snapped back, and he collapsed, insensible, just as the park keepers arrived with Cassie, who had fetched them, followed shortly afterward by Faith and Grace Merridew and James on horseback. A small crowd of onlookers was growing, too. His sisters needed to be out of this as soon as possible.

The keepers had seen the villain's last attempt with the knife and, taking no chances, they bound him hand and foot while he was still unconscious, before making arrangements to take him off to prison. Sebastian gave them his card and promised to call on the nearest magistrate at his earliest convenience. But first, he stressed, he needed to get his ladies home.

"Didn't you hear—" Hope began excitedly.

Sebastian gave her a quick look and shook his head in a silent message. "We shall return home first," he said. "Then we can talk. Hand Dorie down to me, please."

Dorie came willingly, clinging to his chest the way she'd clung to Hope. She was trembling and buried her face in his neck. He hugged her to him and stroked her hair. "You were very brave, little one, but it's all over now. You're safe. He can't harm you ever again."

He glanced at Cassie, who was staring at the unconscious man. "It was very clever of you to fetch the keepers, Cassie," he said. "Thank you. Both my sisters are very brave."

She looked gratified but uneasy. She opened her mouth as if to speak, then thought better of it.

"Tell us what his name is, Cassie," Sebastian said quietly.

She jumped guiltily and bit her lip.

Sebastian gave her a nod of reassurance. "It's all right. Just tell them. It's Mam's brother, isn't it?"

"How did you know?" she blurted.

"You forget I knew her. The family resemblance is unmistakable."

She nodded. "Yes, it's Albert. Albert Watts. But what did he want Dorie for? He hated us. He never wanted either of us around. He was the one who brought us to London to be sol—"

"Not here!" Sebastian cut her off sharply. He swallowed and forced himself to say in a milder voice, "Sorry, but we'll talk of these matters in more private surroundings." Her words had confirmed his worst suspicions. He stared at the unconscious man and briefly wished it had been a killing blow. He wanted to stride forward now and grind the man's head under his heel. It took several moments to harness his rage and get it under control.

"Gentlemen," he addressed the keepers. "I shall leave this piece of filth, whose name is Albert Watts, in your capable hands. He is an out-and-out villain. I think you will find he is wanted for other crimes by Bow Street. I shall follow you there when I have taken my sisters home." He passed them a gold coin each. "Thank you for your prompt assistance."

One of the keepers shook his head. "Did it all yourself, sir—you and the lady!" He gave Hope an admiring look. "Never seen anything to equal it, miss, not at Astley's nor nowhere else. Wonderful, you were, picking up the little miss like that from that great big 'orse."

Hope blushed prettily.

The keeper waxed enthusiastically on, "And as for you, sir, well, I hope you don't think I'm takin' liberties when I say as you ought to be in the ring, sir, with a left hook like that. Marvelous it was, sir, marvelous. Gentleman Jackson couldn't do it better, sir!"

Sebastian inclined his head as best he could with Dorie in his arms. He had no intention of letting her go. He thought most of the pieces of the jigsaw puzzle had fallen into place now; he only needed his sisters to fill in the blanks. "Thank you, gentlemen, but I think I'd like to get my little sister home now. She's had a nasty fright." He glanced at Cassie. "They both have."

"Shall I fetch you a hackney, sir?" his admirer asked.

"That would be excellent," responded Sebastian, and the keepers bustled off, taking the trussed Watts and curious onlookers with them.

"We shall leave you then," Hope began.

"No. Come with me—with us. Please." He sent her an intense look and said in a low voice. "I need you, Hope." In his arms Dorie stirred, and with a pleading look, held out a hand to Hope.

It was all she needed. Her eyes shimmered, and she said, "Of course. Faith, Grace, you don't mind, do you?" They shook their heads. "And James shall take my horse back for me." She lifted a booted foot over the saddle and jumped lightly down.

Handing her reins to James, she came to Sebastian and put her arms around Dorie and him, gathering in Cassie with her other arm. "Safe now," she said. "Let's go home."

# Chapter Eighteen

*Silence propagates itself, and the longer talk has been suspended,*
*the more difficult it is . . .*
SAMUEL JOHNSON

"Now Dorie, I think you need to tell us what all that business at the park was about," said Sebastian. They were seated in the snug back parlor at Sebastian's home. A fire blazed in the hearth despite the mild spring weather. The girls were drinking hot chocolate with biscuits while Hope and Sebastian drank coffee laced with brandy.

Cassie's head came up sharply. *"Dorie?"* She looked bewildered.

Hope nodded. "So you did hear her before."

"Oh yes, I heard her. It was the sweetest sound I'd ever heard—as well as saving my life," Sebastian replied. He said to Cassie, "You sister spoke, Cassie. She warned me of Albert Watts's second attack and saved my life." He touched Dorie's cheek gently.

She gave him a quick, uncertain smile, looked at her sister sheepishly, and gave her an apologetic grimace. "Sorry, Cass."

Cassie's jaw dropped. "You can talk! That's wonderful, Dore." She gave her a hug.

Sebastian asked, "How did he snatch you? I mean, with all those people there . . ."

"He didn't snatch me," said Dorie. Her voice was small and thready with nerves, but she was speaking perfectly normally.

Her lower lip quivered, but he had to ask. He needed to know. "You mean you went with him?"

She bit her lip and nodded.

"Why? You knew I was only a few feet away."

"H-he had his knife. He was behind me when I was looking at the puppies. He pricked me with his knife," she whispered. "And he said in my ear that if I didn't come with him quietlike, he'd knife me then and there." She shivered, and Sebastian tightened his arm around her.

Hope said, "It was very brave of you, Dorie. And it was the right thing to do."

Dorie stared at her and looked at Sebastian for confirmation.

"Yes, it gave us a chance to rescue you."

Cassie said, "But why would he want Dorie to go off with him?"

Sebastian prompted her, "You knew something about Albert, didn't you, Dorie? Something that Cassie didn't."

She nodded.

"You can talk now," he said softly. "He's locked up safe in prison, and he's never coming out again. I'll see to that. He can't hurt you now. It's all right to speak."

"He killed our Mam," she whispered.

He put his arm around her. "Did you see him do it?"

Her face quivered, and she nodded. "Mam was sick, up in her bed. I was upstairs, too. I saw Uncle Albert sneak up the stairs, all quiet." She looked at Cassie. "You were downstairs, working. He picked up a pillow. I thought he was going to make her more comfortable—but he put it on her face and held it down. Hard."

Hope put a hand over her mouth in horror.

Dorie went on in a thin, flat voice, "She kicked and struggled . . . but he held it down on her face, pushing and pushing . . . And then she went quiet." She gave a jerky sob. "I was scared. I didn't move or make a sound. He put the pillow back under her head. That's when he found me. I had a cup of tea in my hand, and it rattled."

"What happened then?"

She was silent a moment, then said shakily, "I tried to run away, but he hit me. He knocked me down the stairs."

"I remember," Cassie interrupted. She explained to the others. "I heard something smash and came running. The teapot and cup. It was a really loud crash."

"Louder than Mam dying." Dorie gave another choked sob, and both Cassie and Sebastian put an arm around her.

Cassie said wonderingly. "You hurt your head. It bled and bled. There was blood everywhere, and you had to go to bed for a couple of days." She opened her mouth in surprise and said slowly, "And when you woke up again, you couldn't talk. Uncle Albert said the fall had turned you simple." She looked at Sebastian. "I didn't even remember that until now. Why didn't I remember?"

Hope touched her arm. "Your mam died. That probably overshadowed everything else."

"But you're not simple, Dorie, so—"

"Uncle Albert told me if I said a word, he'd kill me, and Cassie, too." She looked at Sebastian and Cassie and said, "So I didn't." She shivered. "I never said a word."

Sebastian held her tightly, his eyes closed in mixed anguish and relief. To think that all this time she'd taken the bastard's words so literally and simply not spoken again.

"I think he killed Uncle Eddie, too."

"Uncle Eddie?" Sebastian said.

"Mam's other brother. He was the oldest. He owned the inn." Cassie explained. "After he died, the inn went to Mam, and after she died—"

"Uncle Albert got it," Dorie completed the sentence.

Now Sebastian truly understood why the girls had rejected him so roundly at the beginning. Their matter-of-fact use of the word "uncle" for these strangers, one of whom was a murderer, had instantly become abhorrent to him.

"You stayed at the inn for how long, after Mrs. Morgan died?"

"A while," Cassie explained. "More than a year. But Albert was no good with money—not like Mam or Uncle Eddie. That's why he kept us on. He didn't like us, but I'm good with figures and money and stuff, and Dorie is good in the kitchen. We kept the inn going for him." She added wryly, "That's when I started carrying my knife."

Two little girls, slaving away to survive and keep a business going for a murdering swine! A child of twelve running an inn and having to carry a knife to protect herself! Sebastian tamped down on his deep rage and managed to say, "Aren't my sisters marvelous, Miss Merridew? To be able to handle such a difficult situation so bravely and competently—and so young!"

She smiled mistily. "I think all the Reynes are special in that way."

There was a lump in his throat, and he could not talk.

Cassie continued, "We left the inn when Albert came in one day and said he'd lost all his money. He had to sell everything, even the inn." She shrugged, "So he did. That's when—" Dorie nudged her, and Cassie broke off. There was a long, private, silent exchange between the two children, then Cassie looked down, as if ashamed and mumbled. "You might not want to hear where we went next. The lady at the Tot told us we weren't to tell a soul."

*Oh God, no.* Sebastian thought. He didn't want to know. He'd pushed aside the knowledge ever since Morton Black had broken it to him where the girls had been found. He didn't want to hear where his sisters went next. He couldn't bear to hear their childish lips telling him that. He stood, almost knocking the chair over in his haste. "You're right, Cassie. You've told us quite enough. We'll—"

"I'd like to hear it," said Hope quietly.

"They're tired. They need to—"

"They haven't finished their story," she said softly, firmly.

"*No!* You don't know what you're asking!" Sebastian

said in a low, desperate voice. He stared at her, trying to convey a silent, urgent message. *No more. The girls have said enough.*

She gave him a long, clear look. "May I speak to you alone?"

"Very well." He led her from the room, into his office. "You don't know what you are asking. They know. I know. It is enough."

"I can see it must be very bad, but have they actually told you what happened?"

He shook his head and said bleakly, "They don't need to. I know all about it. My agent, Morton Black, made a very full report when he found them. For some reason he thought, given the circumstances, I might not want them back, after . . . After."

She smiled then. "He does not know you well, my love, does he?"

He hugged her then, hard, the anguish in his heart showing. "You can guess what—"

She pulled back and took his hands in hers. "Sebastian, you must let them tell us. Everything. No matter how ugly, or painful, or horrifying. Those children need to get it all out in the open. Then they can heal."

He pondered her words, his face twisted with grief. He shook his head. "I cannot," he said brokenly and collapsed in a chair. He put his head in his hands and said in a jagged voice, "I cannot . . . *bear* to hear it. It does no good to rake up the pain of the past. Best to leave it lying."

She put her arms around his bent head and pressed it to her breast. "No, my love. If you do, it will only fester inside you and in them, and your guilt and their shame will grow. And a gulf will remain between you and your sisters that will never be breached. You must hear them out, love, for all your sakes."

"You cannot know what it's like, knowing *I* am responsible for what happened—me! It was *my fault*!" He groaned.

She sighed. "Yes, just as it was Cassie's fault when Dorie was kidnapped."

He looked up, horrified. "No! It wasn't Cassie's—"

She shook him. "You were the same age as Cassie when your sisters were lost, Sebastian!"

He was silent.

She caressed his hair. "You need to forgive yourself, my love. Everyone else has."

"Perhaps," he said slowly. "But I cannot stand to listen to the *details*. They are my *sisters*. *Children!*"

She caressed his face and kissed him on the top of his bent head. "Then, my darling, stay here. I will listen for you. For those girls need to tell it all, and someone needs to listen." She kissed him again. "Stay here, love. I'll fetch you when it is over."

She had taken six paces toward the door when a heavy voice behind her spoke. "No. I will come."

He stood. "You are stronger than I gave you credit for." He gave her a shaky smile. "What was it you said at the orphan asylum? 'If these children can survive the depravity inflicted on them by others, then I can certainly endure hearing about it!' " He took her hand, and they returned to the sitting room, where the girls awaited them, their faces anxious.

"Tell us everything, Cassie. Miss Hope has convinced me we all need to get it all out in the open. And whatever you tell us here will make no difference, Cassie. You and Dorie are my sisters, and I love you. Nothing that has happened can ever change that, nothing."

Hope came out of her seat and knelt in front of the settee. She took Cassie's and Dorie's hands in hers and said with warm intensity, "And I have come to love you both like sisters, and whatever you tell me here will go no further, I promise you."

He stared at her. What had he ever done to deserve this miracle of a woman? He came and knelt beside her. She took his hand, and they sat back and waited. Cassie glanced at Dorie and hesitated.

"Albert didn't just sell the inn," said Dorie in a clear little voice. "He sold us, too."

It was like a kick to his chest. He'd known for months, but hearing it in raw, bald words like that hurt more than he would have believed.

Cassie said, "He brought us down to London on the stage. He told us he was getting us a job, since we were such good workers."

"But he sold us to a lady who owned a brothel."

Dorie's matter-of-fact tone horrified him. Few twelve-year-old girls would even know what a brothel was. Sebastian braced himself to hear the rest. He'd long suspected it, after all. The moment he'd found that many of the girls from the Tothill Fields Institution had come from child brothels, he'd known. And the knowledge had eaten away at him.

He set his jaw and waited. If they could bear it to happen, he could bear to listen. He held Hope's hand tighter. His love, his lifeline.

Cassie explained, "We tried to run away, but Auntie Sadie—that was what the lady said to call her—had brought two men with her, and they grabbed us and hung on to us."

Dorie said, "They took us to the brothel and gave us each a bath. That's when they found Cassie's knife and took it off her. She got it back later. And then they made us put on these awful dresses, and then they locked us in a room. It was really high up. In the attic, right under the roof." She tilted her head, remembering, and said reflectively, "The roof sloped down like this, with a little window set into it. You could see out over the rooftops of the city." She grimaced. "I didn't look much. I'm scared of being too high up. But it was nice to see the sky."

Sebastian ran a shaking hand over his face. Hope put her arm around him and squeezed. With his other hand, he held her even tighter.

Dorie continued, "But Cassie likes being up high. That's when she got the idea." She grinned at her sister and hunched her shoulders in excitement.

Sebastian waited tensely. "What idea?"

Cassie said, "There was a trunk at the foot of the bed. Dorie's good at squashing into small places, so I told her to hide in there. We threw the things in it out of the window."

"I fitted perfectly," said Dorie proudly.

"And I climbed out of the little window," said Cassie. "It was a really steep roof, and slippery because it was slate, but in bare feet it was all right." She grinned at Sebastian. "You know me and roofs."

He tried to muster a smile, but failed.

"I climbed to the top bit, where you can sit with your leg on either side."

"The roof ridge," Sebastian said numbly.

"Yes, that bit. It was very high up, and I could see right into the street from there." She smiled at each of them.

"What happened next?" Hope asked.

"I waited until some people came past, and then I started chucking slates down into the street. They smashed really well, made such a loud noise. And everyone was looking up, so I yelled out as loud as I could that my sister and I had been stolen away and were being sold in a brothel and could someone please help us because we didn't want to be sold in a brothel."

Hope gasped at such bold audacity. Sebastian stared, dumbstruck.

"And I yelled and screamed and chucked slates into the street. And then Aunt Sadie stuck her head out of the window and screamed at me to 'come inside, you naughty girl' and she tried to tell the people I was her niece and playing a trick on her—"

"But Cassie yelled back that she wasn't anybody's niece, and that this horrible woman is a horrible brothel keeper, and we didn't want to be here! I could hear her, even from the trunk!"

"And I yelled that we'd been stolen from our home, and I just kept flinging slates and yelling and flinging slates until I ran out of slates, and by then people had come from everywhere, and they knocked down Aunt Sadie's door and came bursting into the attic room, and some men took Aunt Sadie away to the magistrates, and then they told me to come in off the roof, and so I did!" Cassie ended triumphantly.

"And then I got out of the trunk, and everyone was amazed!"

Sebastian regarded his sisters with stupefaction. "You *are* amazing!" he said shakily, and gathered them in a huge, exuberant hug.

*They hadn't been forced into child prostitution!* His little sisters hadn't been raped and violated, after all. He gulped in huge thankful breaths of air and hugged them tightly to him. The worst hadn't happened. He'd thought Cassie's knife and Dorie's timidity and silence were a result of their hideous brothel experiences. The thought had tortured him for months.

They'd escaped! Rescued themselves from a horrible fate through sheer, bloody brilliance and bravery!

He couldn't speak. His eyes were wet with tears. He blinked the tears back and hugged his sisters again, sending up a silent prayer of thanks for their ingenuity and their bravery and their blessed, blessed escape.

"And then what happened?" Hope asked, a short time later. Somehow they'd all come to be sitting on the floor in front of the fire. Cassie and Dorie were between Sebastian and Hope.

Cassie answered; she was still in the habit of speaking for both of them. "They took us to the magistrate, and he asked us all about it, and I told him what happened, and he said Aunt Sadie would go to prison. But they didn't know where Albert was anymore, so they couldn't punish him."

"And when he found out we didn't have any family, he sent us to the Tot."

"The Tot?" Hope queried.

"The Tothill Fields Institution for Indigent Girls," explained Cassie. "We were there for—I don't know—about two months."

"It's where I found them," explained Sebastian. "Or more accurately, where Morton Black found them, acting on my instructions."

"Oh!" exclaimed Hope. "So that's why you—"

"Purchased it? Yes," said Sebastian, giving her a meaningful look. He'd cut her off deliberately. He knew what she'd been going to say, but he didn't want his sisters to know why he'd kept them from the tea party, not wanting them to meet up with their erstwhile fellow Tot girls. He had no intention of them ever being recognized as former inmates.

He added, "Lady Elinore doesn't know they were there. They were listed as Carrie and Doreen Morgan, not Cassandra and Eudora Reyne. They never met her. Lady Elinore's mother was dying, and she didn't come to the institution at all during that time."

As the words came out of his mouth, it occurred to Sebastian to wonder about Lady Elinore. Once she found out, would she have treated his sisters as fallen girls, in need of rehabilitation?

He looked across at Hope Merridew, who sat on the floor hugging his sisters and lavishing them with unquestioning love, and he sent up another heartfelt prayer of thankfulness.

After a time, Hope said, "Well, I don't know about you girls, but I think a celebration is in order."

"Celebration?" Cassie asked.

Hope said briskly, "Decidedly! We have a number of things to celebrate! First we must celebrate Dorie's escape and the capture of the evil Albert Watts." She counted them off on her fingers as she spoke. "And the return of Dorie's voice, and we must celebrate your brilliant escape from horrid Aunt Sadie, and also, we had another first today."

They all looked at her.

She winked merrily and said, "Both you and Dorie had your first ride on horseback today, and both of you did marvelously well. So I think we need to all go to Astley's Amphitheater this afternoon and watch one of the spectacular shows. And you will see the brilliant lady equestriennes there who inspired me when I first came to London."

She caught Sebastian's eye and added with a mischievous twinkle, "Not, of course, that you will wish to emulate them. But they are tremendous fun to watch, and if one thing is clear to me, it's that none of us had enough fun when we were children, so it is our duty to make up for it now."

She stood up, a lissome, graceful movement that made Sebastian's mouth dry with longing, and said, "Now, I shall return home to change and fetch my sisters, and you will wish to change also. And then at two o'clock, you shall come and collect us in your carriage, and we shall go to Astley's. And after that, perhaps your brother will buy us all ices at Gunter's? What say you?"

"Yes please!" both girls exclaimed in excitement, as if all thoughts of past terrors were forgotten. Sebastian belatedly realized her intention. She'd returned them to childhood and innocence again. He'd wanted to wrap them in cotton wool and comfort them. He'd thought maybe they should take a nap to recover from their ordeal. She offered them a fun outing, a treat, and the opportunity to accept the past and move on.

His lovely miracle woman. It was no accident she was named Hope. She was his Hope, now and for the future.

The girls raced out to change and get ready, and Sebastian and Hope were left alone in the room.

"I thought it was going to be so much worse," he said raggedly. "I thought—"

She reached up and cupped his cheek. "I know. So did I."

"They're extraordinary, aren't they, my sisters?

"I haven't yet thanked you for saving Dorie," he said softly. "Come here." He pulled her against him and kissed her tenderly and long. "You didn't just save Dorie. You saved all of us. Me especially. Have I told you I love you, Miss Hope Merridew?"

She smiled mistily. "Mmm, if I saved you, it's for purely selfish reasons. I love you, too, Sebastian Reyne. So very, very much!" She smiled at him with such a look of blazing love, he kissed her again. And again.

"Do you have to go home and change?" he muttered against her throat. "I think you look beautiful as you are."

She pulled away and regarded him through half-closed eyes. "Yes," she said softly. She walked to the door. And closed it. And turned the lock. She faced him with a secret little smile.

"We have half an hour."

Her habit was blue velvet, but when Sebastian unbuttoned the jacket, he saw she wore only a thin silk shirt. He could see the flesh beneath it, the soft pink nipples that rose as he watched. He laid her gently back on the chaise longue.

She saw the gray of his eyes darken and his jaw lock with tension. And stubbornness. Half an hour was not enough, she decided. He was going to be noble.

He kissed her, deeply, the intensely masculine taste of him filling her mouth, swamping her senses, sending her blood thrumming through her veins with a dizzying, hectic demand. She kissed him back, clutching at the powerful shoulders that had once intimidated her.

His strength was at her service. And she wanted it, wanted it with an intensity that almost frightened her. She pushed his coat open and fumbled at the buttons of his shirt. Heat radiated from him, and she could not get enough of him. His chest was solid and hard and exquisitely different from hers. She scratched his skin lightly with her nails, and he groaned deep in his throat and shuddered under her hand. "My tiger," she whispered.

He made a harsh sound and reached for her, and she felt a surge of deep, feminine pride in his hunger. For her. For clumsy, bad Hope Merridew. He cupped her silk-covered breasts, moving his thumbs over the hardening nipples, silk and flesh sliding back and forth in delicious friction.

She threw her head back and arched as heat arrowed into her. "Oh that feels so . . ."

His mouth closed hotly around one silk-clad nipple, and she stiffened and made a great juddering movement, almost screaming with the intense pleasure-pain of it. She clutched him.

"Little tigress," he growled. "Do you like that?"

"Mmm," she clutched his head mindlessly and pulled it back down, and he took her other nipple in his mouth and sucked, hot and demanding through the thin, silken shirt.

Her limbs thrashed restlessly under him. She could feel his hard, erect member thrusting against her skirt. She wanted no barrier between his flesh and hers. She started to unbutton her shirt, tugging on the tiny mother-of-pearl buttons.

His big hand stopped her. "No."

"Why not? I want to feel you——"

"Not here, not now. When I take you, my impatient little love, it will not be some hasty coupling on a hard chaise longue. It will be slow, and in a bed. I want to make it perfect for you." He paused and said, "I want you for my wife, Hope Merridew. Will you wed me?"

She thought her face would split. Half smiling the biggest smile she'd ever smiled in her life, half weeping— and why she should weep when he was everything she'd ever wanted was a mystery to her. She took his jaw in her hands and kissed him all over, ecstatic, clumsy, moist kisses. "Oh yes, Sebastian. I will wed you, with pride and with pleasure." She paused and then added meaningfully, "Much pleasure. Now, please."

He threw back his head and laughed. "Very well then, my impatient little tigress, here is your pleasure." And he slipped his hand under her skirt. She gasped as she felt his hand close over her most intimate part the same moment his mouth enclosed her nipple. His hand and mouth started to move, and she was lost in waves of intense, impossible, glorious sensation.

Afterward, she thought she might have screamed. She could not be sure. She lay bonelessly on the chaise longue, staring up into the gray, gray eyes of her man.

After a long time, she was able to speak. "Oh, my," she whispered. "Whatever was that?"

He grinned. "What you asked for."

She shivered sensually. "Oh. I didn't know one could ask for that."

He kissed her and said, "When we are married, you can ask for it as often as you want."

"Oh, my." She thought about it. "I think Aunt Gussie gets it, and she's not married. Even cats get it on the rooftops."

He laughed, an abandoned, joyous sound, and began to do up the buttons of her habit. "No, my beautiful baggage. You will have to wait."

She looked thoughtful. "Did it happen to you, too?"

"No," he said shortly.

"But it can?"

"Yes, it can. When we're married. Now, enough talking, my love. My sisters will be down any minute."

Hope looked at the clock. To her amazement the half hour was up. It wasn't nearly long enough. And then she thought of his words and smiled. *When we're married.* She was going to marry Sebastian Reyne.

After the visit to Astley's, while Hope and her sisters took his sisters to Gunter's, Sebastian called on the magistrate at Bow Street, to present all the information he had on the villain, Albert Watts. He was determined to spare Dorie the ordeal of having to give evidence in court, if at all possible.

"No need, as it happens," the magistrate said. "Watts was found dead in prison an hour ago. Throat slit from ear to ear. I gather we put the fellow in with some of his enemies, and from what I gather, he had plenty." The magistrate shrugged. "Bad for discipline, of course, but it's saved the hangman a job. We had enough on Albert Watts to hang him several times over."

# Chapter Nineteen

~∞~

*She is a woman, therefore may be wooed;*
*She is a woman, therefore may be won.*
WILLIAM SHAKESPEARE

"AT LEAST I HAVE ENTERED INTO THE SPIRIT OF THE EVENING.
Whereas you——" Giles looked Sebastian up and down dis-
paragingly. "You are not even in costume!"

Sebastian shrugged. "It is a masked ball. I am masked."

"It is a masked *Hungarian gypsy* ball!"

"I am the plain sort of Hungarian gypsy. Not all of us
can be dashing," Sebastian said soothingly. His lips
twitched as he added, "Besides, you look dashing enough
for both of us. The head scarf and the gold earrings are utterly fetching!" And he ducked back, grinning, out of range
of Giles's fist.

"I suppose I look ridiculous," Giles said gloomily.

"You do," agreed Sebastian, "but then so does everyone
else. No self-respecting gypsy would be seen dead in these
costumes, Hungarian or otherwise!"

"It doesn't matter—it's all for fun!" Giles explained in
long-suffering accents.

"Oh, fun is it? Well, off you go then, have fun. Find

Lady Elinore and go and bring her into fashion. She at least will not be hard to spot in this colorful crowd—just look for a small gray blob."

Giles sighed. "Yes, where she finds such garments is beyond me. Presumably somewhere in London there is a deranged dressmaker who perpetuates atrocities for a price. Or perhaps they are produced by her orphan waifs—I don't know." He frowned. "It's quite late. What if she doesn't come?"

"Why wouldn't she come?"

Giles said darkly, "Who knows how that woman thinks? I offered to escort her here—with the strategy in mind, of course—but she refused! The woman refused! *Me!* One would have thought that a woman who'd never had a male escort would jump at the opportunity, but . . ." He made a frustrated gesture.

"Well, don't fret. Hope's not here yet, so there's plenty of time. Why don't you go off and enjoy yourself, Giles? Plenty of beauties here tonight. I don't know whether it's the masks or what, but several ladies have made a number of extremely improper advances to me, so—"

"I don't believe it!" Giles exclaimed in outraged accents.

"They did, I promise you. One lady even suggested—"

"I don't mean that. I mean—look!"

"At what?" Sebastian turned his head to follow Giles's gaze. The staircase divided into two arms, which embraced the ballroom. Hope and her twin, with Count Rimavska and Sir Oswald, were descending the right arm of the staircase, while Lady Augusta, unmistakable in a low-cut purple dress with orange and green feathers, and two other ladies descended on the left.

Sebastian straightened at the sight of his love. "Oh, good, she's arrived."

"Good! *Good,* you say? It's utterly outrageous!" Giles sounded enraged. He was staring at the left-hand staircase.

Sebastian followed his friend's gaze and shrugged. Lady Augusta's gowns were frequently outrageous, but

Giles could fuss all he wanted; Sebastian wasn't interested in anyone except Hope.

His chest tightened and his mouth dried as he gazed at her. She was a vision in amber, cream, and gold. Her gown was silk, in dozens of shades of amber and, as she moved, her dress flowed around her as if honey dripped down her body. The small bodice of the gown was dark amber velvet with a deep, triangular, almost transparent lace inset in the center. The bodice was laced tightly and provocatively with gold braid in a faint nod to gypsy or peasant style, and the whole was cut low against the creamy skin of her bosom.

She looked utterly ravishing. Delectable. Utterly edible.

Giles exploded, "That dress is an affront to decency! What the devil has got into her? She was forced into this, mark my words!"

His vehemence jolted Sebastian out of his rapt contemplation, but Giles was still staring at the left-hand staircase, not at Hope. "Who are you talking about? Lady Augusta?"

"Oh, don't be ridiculous!" Giles snapped.

Sebastian looked again; it took a lot to shock his rakish friend. "I can't see anything that would horrify anyone but a genuine Hungarian gypsy. Who was forced? Talk sense, man!"

"Lady Elinore, dammit! I'll soon put a stop to it!"

"Lady Elinore? Where? I can't see her anywhere."

Giles took no notice. Muttering furiously, he cleaved his way through the aristocratic crowd and strode up to the small group of ladies just reaching the foot of the left-hand staircase. Sebastian cast a quick look at Hope and followed him, fearing trouble.

"Elinore, what the *devil* are you doing?"

Sebastian blinked. Had Giles been secretly imbibing? His friend loomed, glowering, over a masked lady who could not possibly be Lady Elinore Whitelaw. Admittedly, she was small and waifishly slender, but there all resemblance ended.

This lady was dressed in a brilliant scarlet gown slashed

low across a dainty bosom. It was saved from indecency—just—by a teasing ruffle of black lace. Her head was a mass of short, soft, dark curls, not a scraped-back bun, and she wore a rakish headband of scarlet feathers, black lace, and glittering diamantés. A dozen gold bangles glittered on each slender, naked arm, and a black velvet band studded with diamantés encircled her elegant throat.

There was no way in the world this dashing little creature could be Lady Elinore. Sebastian nudged his friend, but Giles seemed oblivious.

"Well? Who is responsible for this?" Giles glared at Lady Augusta.

"Good evening, Giles," Lady Augusta said, deliberately obtuse. "Responsible for what? The ball? Lady Thorn, of course. In honor of Count Rimavska. What a pretty gypsy lad you make, Giles, I declare! Those pompoms are divine."

Giles's color rose, but he did not deign to respond to the older lady's comments. "Elinore!" he growled.

The small lady said not a word, just stared at him with a haughty expression.

"Giles, come away," Sebastian began, and put a hand on his friend's shoulder. "This is not—"

Giles shrugged off his grasp furiously. "Elinore, who has done this to you?"

Finally, the lady spoke, "I do not believe we know each other, sir. Have the goodness to let us pass, if you please."

"Don't be ridiculous—" Giles began.

The lady produced an ebony fan and poked him in the chest with it. "Out. Of. My. Way. If. You. Please." She punctuated each word with a poke of the fan.

Dumbfounded, Giles fell back a step, and the little scarlet lady swept imperiously past him, nose in the air. Lady Augusta followed, pausing to pinch Giles on the cheek and say, "If you're verrry good, my bonny gypsy lad, I might introduce you to my pretty little friend." She chuckled evilly and sailed away.

"That woman is a witch!" Giles muttered, rubbing his cheek angrily.

"Well, it's your own fault," Sebastian declared. "It wasn't Lady Elinore, and I don't understand why you pushed it so far. What maggot got into your brain?"

"Maggot? Are you blind? It was Elinore, all right. Half naked and in scarlet, of all things!" Giles stared after her and said in a hoarse, desperate voice, "Oh God, Bastian, what have I done? She's cut all her hair off and is wearing a dress more suited to an opera dancer than a lady. In *scarlet!*"

Sebastian couldn't quite believe that the lady in red was Lady Elinore, but Giles's complete lack of doubt was quite convincing. He looked distraught.

"If she is Lady Elinore, I'd have thought you'd rejoice to see her in colors, Giles. And looking so very fashionable."

His friend groaned. "But not in *scarlet!* Oh, what have I done, what have I done?" he said remorsefully.

Sebastian frowned. "What *have* you done, Giles?"

Giles closed his eyes in momentary anguish. "Seduced her in a cupboard! And again on the stairs at the opera house."

*"What?"*

"Not entirely. Not all the way. She's still a virgin. Sort of." He groaned again. "Although she obviously doesn't believe so. Look at her, Bastian! She's dressed herself as a fallen woman! And it's my fault! I've trampled over every one of her principles, ground her morals into the dust, ignored her boundaries. I thought because she didn't pull her hatpin on me, she liked what we were doing. I was sure she did!

"With her upbringing, she probably believes what we did makes her a scarlet woman, almost a prostitute." Giles ran his hands distractedly though his hair, dislodging his gypsy head scarf. "I've destroyed her!"

Sebastian thought about it. The small, elegant woman in scarlet and black didn't look at all like a woman overcome with shame and self-loathing. In fact, she seemed to be enjoying herself. And that dress was not a last-minute acquisition. He looked at his friend, and his lips twitched.

Giles's anguished expression of guilt sat ill on his ludicrous gypsy costume.

"If that's what you think, you'll have to make it right."

Giles gave him an anxious look. "How can I make it right? That's the question."

Sebastian shrugged. "There is a time-honored method of righting the wrongs of the flesh."

Giles looked blank.

Sebastian rolled his eyes at his friend's thickheadedness. "You said yourself she needed to be married."

*"Marriage! To Lady Elinore Whitelaw? Me?"*

Sebastian wasn't sure whether Giles was appalled, stunned, or simply disbelieving. He spread his hands in a conciliatory gesture. "It's only one time-honored solution to this sort of problem. There are others. You must sort out the mess in whatever way you choose. It's your problem, Giles."

He glanced across the room to where Hope had just been joined by Lady Augusta, the chaperone, and the mysterious lady in red. "My immediate need is to engage Miss Merridew for the supper dance." He patted Giles on the cheek in mocking imitation of Lady Augusta. "Come on, bonny gypsy lad, and see if you can get a dance with Lady Augusta's new little friend."

Giles gave a warning snarl but followed him meekly across the dance floor.

A gaggle of gypsified gentlemen clustered around Hope and her sister like bees in search of honey. When Sebastian looked at the way the tightly laced velvet bodice cupped Hope's creamy bosom, he felt distinctly, blatantly primitive. They could cluster around Miss Faith all they wanted, but Hope was his!

Sebastian cut a determined swathe through the crowd, Giles in his wake. The small, scarlet lady tossed her head haughtily as they approached and hurried away. Giles veered off after her, and then Sebastian was standing in front of Hope, and he forgot all about anyone else.

"Miss Merridew." Sebastian bowed over her hand, resisting the urge to bring it to his lips. He scanned her face intently. A faint blush stole over her features as she lifted her eyes to his. He stared down at her a long moment, wishing they were alone again. He needed to kiss her. Again. And again. Their eyes met, clung, kissed. It was not enough. They swayed toward each other.

Sir Oswald Merridew cleared his throat ostentatiously, and Sebastian recalled his surroundings. Somehow he managed to greet Sir Oswald, Lady Augusta, Hope's twin sister, the count, and the chaperone, who glared daggers at him. Bilious again, poor woman.

"Mr. Reyne!" the chaperone snapped.

"Yes, madam?" He inclined his head politely at her, wishing he could remember her name.

"Your hand?"

"Eh?" Sebastian was confused. He hadn't asked the chaperone to dance. The woman was puffing visibly with disapproval, Sir Oswald was scowling at him, Lady Augusta and Miss Faith were grinning openly, and Miss Merridew was blushing rosily and trying not to smile. Around him he could feel aristocratic gypsies seething and muttering.

"Your hand, sirrah!" The chaperone glared pointedly at his left hand.

What was the matter? He'd remembered to put on his gloves. He glanced down. "Ah!" He hurriedly dropped Miss Merridew's hand, which had somehow remained encased in his and come to be placed against his heart. "Sorry." He had no memory of doing it.

Miss Hope's blushed intensified. Her eyes glowed up at him. A tiny dimple quivered to the left of her lips. He stared, fascinated.

"You wanted to ask Miss Merridew something?" prompted Lady Augusta, with a less-than-discreet nudge in the ribs and a broad wink. Sebastian's scattered wits began to function again.

"Ah, yes. Miss Merridew, I've come to beg the honor of dancing the supper dance with you."

"The supper dance? Yes, of course." She took out her dance card and said as she wrote on it, "I will put you down for the supper dance . . . and . . ." She gave him a bewitching smile. "And also for the last waltz, Mr. Reyne."

*The last waltz!* It was as if someone had punched him in the stomach. For a moment he couldn't breathe. Had he heard her aright? *She had put him down for the last waltz!*

The chaperone made an odd hissing sound between her teeth. Sir Oswald Merridew snorted with surprise. A mutter rippled through the masculine crowd surrounding them. She *never* put *anyone's* name down for the last waltz.

Sebastian bowed over her hand and slowly, deliberately, pressed his mouth to the inside of her wrist the pulse point. "I shall count the moments," he said gruffly.

He turned to Sir Oswald. "May I have a private word, sir?"

Sir Oswald's eyes narrowed. "Very well, young Reyne. Come this way."


"You'd better make her happy, young man!"

"It will be my life's work," Sebastian said simply. Sir Oswald had given them his blessing without a murmur. Sebastian could hardly believe it.

The old man gave a grunt. "Had you investigated, Reyne. Dark horse, ain't you?"

Sebastian raised his brows. "In what way?"

"I have more than a few fingers in trade myself, though it's not well-known. You've done well." He gave Sebastian a shrewd look. "It's widely believed you married the boss's daughter for her fortune."

"Is it?" Sebastian feigned interest in a painting. He would not justify himself to anyone. What was done was done.

"Tale for the tabbies, though, ain't it? Boot on the other foot, I discovered. Her father did the courtin'. Wanted you for your clever fingers and your head for business, didn't he?"

Sebastian deliberately flexed his hand, exposing the damaged fingers.

Sir Oswald made a dismissive gesture. "Don't mean it literally. They say you have a genius for machinery. Made so many adjustments and improvements in his manufactories that he nearly doubled his production. Fellow was frightened he'd lose you to another employer. Married you to his daughter to keep you. Visions of foundin' a dynasty."

Sebastian didn't deny it. It was pretty much the truth. What Sir Oswald had left out were Sebastian's own feelings in the matter. He'd been twenty-three, and though he didn't love Thea, he'd had hopes of rebuilding his family.

It hadn't worked out that way.

Sir Oswald interrupted his thoughts. "From what I heard, she wasn't an easy woman."

Sebastian said nothing.

"Demandin'. Spoilt. Shrewish."

Sebastian shrugged.

The old man nodded, satisfied. "They said that, too."

Sebastian frowned. "Said what?"

"That you were a model husband. Faithful. Patient. And never said a word against her."

Sebastian returned to his perusal of the painting. Such talk made him uncomfortable.

"How did she die?"

Sebastian swallowed. He still found it hard to talk of. "She miscarried a month or so after her father died. She was found dead in a pool of blood."

Sir Oswald nodded, "Hence the lurid tales. But I checked with the doctor. It wasn't her first miscarriage, was it?"

Sebastian's brows rose. "You're very thorough."

Sir Oswald looked smug.

Sebastian sighed. "No, it wasn't the first time she'd miscarried. I didn't want her to risk any more, but her father was obsessed with heirs." He clenched his fist.

"What I don't understand is why the devil you didn't scotch the gossip when it started. You weren't even there when it happened. You were out west, seein' to one of the mines."

Sebastian shrugged. "People believe what they want to."

The old man snorted. "We'll see about that!"

Sebastian rose to leave, but Sir Oswald's next words stopped him cold. "I traced your family connections."

He turned back furiously. "Dammit, Sir Oswald, you had no right! My family connections are my own business!"

"Not when half the ton thinks you're a bastard, it don't! Why the devil did ye let that tale stick?"

Sebastian gave him a flat look.

"Hah! Pride, is it? Well let me tell you, young Reyne." Sir Oswald wagged a severe finger at him. "Pride won't butter onions!"

Sebastian blinked. "I never thought it would."

"No indeed!" The old gentleman looked pleased with himself. "Second cousin to the Earl of Reyne. Now why keep that hidden?"

"He's no family of mine!" Sebastian muttered, annoyed with himself for revealing his anger.

"They don't recognize you?"

"*I* don't recognize *them*!" He scowled, realizing he was going to have to explain. "The Earl of Reyne abandoned my mother, my brother, and my two baby sisters when they were in desperate need. I'll have no part of the house of Reyne!"

The thick white eyebrows rose. "Weren't you abandoned, too?"

Sebastian made a dismissive gesture. "I survived."

"And your mother and brother didn't. I see." He added after a moment, "Your sisters survived."

"No thanks to the blasted Earl of Reyne, devil take

him!" Sebastian moderated his tone. "In truth, the girls almost did not survive! You have no idea of how close to tragedy they skated. So no! I do not recognize the Earl of Reyne!"

The old man nodded, a compassionate look in his eyes. "I understand." He paused for a moment and said diffidently, "The new earl is your own age or younger. The old one died without issue. This earl could not have been part of what happened."

Sebastian shrugged indifferently. He didn't care one way or the other about the new earl. He hoped the old earl—the one his mother had written to and he himself had written to countless times—was rotting in hell.

Sir Oswald said, "Would you object if I sent out some feelers in that direction?"

Sebastian said impatiently, "What the devil is it to you?"

"Hope will make me a great-great-uncle one day soon." He sniffed. "Child ought to have no stain on its background. Better its father is second cousin to the Earl of Reyne than a cit with no background."

He paused, letting his words sink in. He steepled his fingers and added casually, "Better for those sisters of yours, too, come to think of it. Improve their chances of a good marriage. Little Dorie now, when she grows up, she'll be a beauty. Right background, and she could snare a duke!" His eyes gleamed with bright ambition. "Wrong background, and . . ." He shook his head and gave a mournful sigh. And watched Sebastian from under his bushy white brows.

Sebastian knew very well the old man was trying to manipulate him, but he also knew he was right, dammit! "Very well! Do what you like—but I won't go cap in hand to them!"

Sir Oswald looked horrified. "I beg you won't take a cap anywhere at all, dear boy! Most unfashionable, caps—apart from the bedchamber. Very lower orders, if you know what I mean. In any case, it's more likely the Reynes will come courtin' you."

Sebastian made a rude noise. "In a pig's eye they will!"

The old man wagged a reproving finger at him. "Aha! Fine old family—yes. Lovely old house, too, and plenty of land. And all encumbered to the hilt!" He grinned. "You're the only Reyne with any money, m'boy. Take my word for it, they'll welcome you with open arms!"

Sebastian snorted.

Sir Oswald said in a coaxing voice, "If young Cassie had her coming-out ball at Reyne House, would make a big splash. You'd have to fund it, o' course. Cost you a pretty penny, but it'd be an investment in the girl's future."

Sebastian thought about it. He'd originally sought a wife among the members of the ton so his sisters could take their rightful place in society, the place to which their birth entitled them. In the face of that, his pride didn't matter.

Besides, he'd moved a long way past the hurt and bitter man he used to be. The new earl was not responsible for the actions of the old earl. He thought of Hope, his beautiful dreamer, his new beginning, and nodded to Sir Oswald. "Very well, sir. Do what you will."

"Splendid! Excellent! Now, your own wedding—St. George's, Hanover Square, I trust?"

Sebastian shrugged. "Whatever Hope wants. I don't mind."

Sir Oswald rubbed his hands in satisfaction. "Good, good. St. George's it is, then. Most fashionable church in England. Only possible choice."

"Aunt Gussie has taken Lady Elinore under her wing," Hope explained as she twirled around Mr. Reyne in the supper dance.

He made an interested sound, so she continued, "I'm not surprised you didn't recognize her, but Mr. Bemerton is wrong if he thinks someone is making her do something she does not wish to do." She chuckled. "I thought he would strangle poor Mr. Hathaway when Lady Elinore decided she preferred to dance with him instead of Mr. Bemerton. And I'm sure Mr. Hathaway isn't the dreadful rake Mr. Bemerton claimed he was."

He made another indeterminate noise. Hope decided he was concentrating on the dance steps. Lady Thorn had daringly introduced a new Hungarian dance, calling it the Rimavska Galop. Luckily, it was quite simple and very exciting—a little like a fast waltz, in pairs in a circle around the floor. Glissade . . . chasse . . . then alternate.

"Aunt Gussie can be quite forceful, but I believe Lady Elinore is just as stubborn. Their, er, initial debates were positively explosive, but the results are extraordinary, are they not?"

He twirled her—glissade . . . chasse . . . alternate— watching her with tender, hungry eyes. That particular way he looked at her never failed to thrill her.

He said in a soft growl, "I don't care if Lady Elinore is dressed as a gray ghost or Lady Godiva. The night is young, the music is playing, and I have you in my arms. Not wholly the way I want . . . I'd prefer you all to myself." He looked at her with that dark and potent hunger that started her trembling, deep inside.

Desire.

Hope instantly forgot all about Lady Elinore and Aunt Gussie. She stared back, her mouth dry. Distracted, she stumbled, but he caught her smoothly and swept her on in the dance. He was so deliciously strong. She recalled the feeling of being carried in his arms . . . And the sensation of his mouth caressing her flesh . . .

She scanned the ballroom and checked the whereabouts of her chaperone, her twin, and her great-uncle. All were concentrating on the new dance. "We could slip out into the garden for a few moments," she suggested. "No one will notice. Everyone is watching their steps."

He led her to the farthest corner of the garden, out of reach of the bright lozenges of light that spilled from the French windows of the ballroom onto the terrace, away from the burning brands in their specially fitted sconces.

He circled a bed of roses, their rich fragrance filling the

air. The music receded into the distance. The garden was still and silent, clean and moist and fragrant from a recent shower. The air was warm and filled with perfume, the night velvety dark. There was no moon. A whisper of breeze stirred the leaves of the birches that lined the garden's high stone walls.

His arms tightened around her, and she shivered in them, though she was not cold. His lips were devastatingly gentle, teasing, persuading, arousing. She clung to him, wanting more, seeking more.

His body pressed against hers, and she felt herself rubbing against him, reveling in his strength and his heat and his power, feeling her own heat and power reach to complement his.

"More," she whispered. "More." She pushed her body against him, wanting a closer connection, reaching for him blindly, blissfully, feeling the hard thrust of his arousal, yet not knowing how to complete the action she craved.

He kissed her deeply then, long, drugging kisses, passionate and intense and focused on her, just on her. She tasted his male hunger and his need. Female hunger and need came bubbling up to meet it, and heat rose between them like a fever.

The scents of the night rose all around them, and eventually Sebastian pulled back, breathing hard. "We must stop," he ground out. "Or else . . ."

"Why?" she panted, feeling shaky, incomplete.

He released her and stood leaning against a stone urn overflowing with mint and lemon verbena. The scent of the crushed leaves was sharp and clean. He breathed in deep, unsteady breaths. "If we do not stop, I will end up taking you here, in the garden, and that I will not do. Not where anyone can stumble across us."

She bit her lip as it occurred to her that on the chaise longue that time, she'd screamed. If that happened here . . .

He caressed her face tenderly and said in a rough, soft voice. "There will be another time, another place, my love. And when we are married, we will not have to stop."

She reached out a hand to him. "Promise?"

He nodded slowly. "I promise."

The final waltz was about to begin. Every gentleman had heard of the extraordinary rumor that Hope Merridew had signed that fellow for the last waltz—the third one she'd granted him, too! But not every gentleman accepted it. As Sebastian strode up to take Hope's hand and lead her out onto the floor, three men stepped forward, blocking his way.

"Look here, Reyne. Where you come from it might be all right to make a lady the object of persistent attentions, but in the polite world we do things differently."

Sebastian's brows rose. "Indeed?"

The three gentlemen pressed forward threateningly and were joined by several more. "Yes, indeed. Miss Merridew chooses a different partner for the last waltz every night. It is something of a tradition."

"Indeed?"

"Yes, so why not try at least to imitate the gentleman you ape and leave the girl alone!"

Sebastian said in a voice of soft menace, "I ape no one. And Miss Merridew has, of her own free will granted the last waltz to me, for tonight and every other night in the future."

There was a hiss of outrage at his words.

Sebastian smiled. "Miss Merridew has done me the honor of agreeing to be my wife." He paused to let the words sink in, then added, "And Sir Oswald has, this very night, approved the match. And now, if you'll excuse me, gentlemen, my betrothed is waiting, and where I come from, a gentleman does not keep a lady waiting."

In deep shock, the solid bank of men parted to let him through.

The final waltz drew slowly, reluctantly to a close. Sebastian stood with Hope in his arms, not wanting to release her.

Her eyes were dreamy, half-closed, her body still swaying to the silent echoes of the music. "I wish it could go on forever," she murmured. "Will you dance me home, beloved?"

His arm tightened involuntarily. He wanted to pull her close.

"Anywhere you want, love. To the ends of the earth and back, if you wish."

A moment later the sound of a violin playing drifted in from the garden.

"The count," said Hope. "And I remember now, Lady Thorn said the evening is to end with a fireworks display! Come along—let us find a good vantage spot. I adore fireworks."

People crowded out onto the terrace, drawn by the haunting, beautiful music of the lone gypsy fiddler. The count stood partially in the shadows, only his silhouette and the outline of his violin visible in the flickering flames of fiery brands placed nearby. The violin soared and sobbed in a strange lament that pulled at the heartstrings.

No wonder Faith could not resist him, thought Hope, watching. He was the very embodiment of the romantic hero they'd imagined in their girlhood. And his music was irresistible.

She felt the hard, strong arm of the big man at her side tighten around her waist, and leaned into him, dizzy with love. No imaginary hero could live up to her Sebastian.

The music reached a long, quavering crescendo and suddenly died. In the sudden hush, there was the sound of a loud slap, followed by a muffled masculine exclamation. "I am not in the least ruined!" exclaimed an unseen female crossly. A genteel ripple of amused speculation passed through the crowd.

Sebastian choked. "If I'm not mistaken that was—"

Hope giggled. "It was, I'm sure."

Hope pressed against Sebastian. "It's a magical evening, isn't it? Look."

Sebastian followed her gaze. Her twin, Faith, stood pressed against a pillar, her eyes glued to the gypsy fiddler, her face dreamy, entranced. Then, as the last note of the fiddle music died on the evening air, a shower of stars filled the sky. The fireworks display had started.

The glittering silver and gold sparks lit up the night in a series of brief, brilliant displays. The crowd watched each new burst to the accompaniment of oohs and aahs.

Hope and Sebastian watched, enchanted. Or at least Hope watched the fireworks, enchanted, and Sebastian watched her face, which was enchanting. He'd seen fireworks before and enjoyed them, but he'd never seen them with her. Her capacity for pleasure and enjoyment was contagious. He absorbed it like a starving man.

Under the pretext of finding a better vantage point, he drew her farther along the terrace and found a place where, in the brief lulls between rockets or showers of colored sparks, he could steal a kiss or two. Most faces were turned skyward, but as he bent to kiss Hope, something caught Sebastian's eye.

He murmured in Hope's ear. "It must be catching. Look over there." He pointed to where a slender, golden-haired gypsy lad stood locked in a passionate embrace with a small, dark-haired lady dressed enticingly in scarlet.

"I'm so glad," Hope said. "Now we can be completely happy." She twined her arms around his neck and began to shower him with kisses. "This is the most heavenly night. I think love must be in the air."

Actually, there was a lot of smoke from the fireworks in the air, but Sebastian didn't care. He had Hope in his arms, and that was all that mattered.

# Chapter Twenty

∞

*For love, all love of other sights controls,*
*And makes one little room, an everywhere.*
JOHN DONNE

THE NEXT AFTERNOON SEBASTIAN RECEIVED AN URGENT SUMmons from Hope.

"My sister Charity has begun her labor," Hope explained the moment he arrived. "We leave today for Carradice Abbey."

"But I thought—"

"Yes, but my sister Prudence is increasing herself, and carriage movement makes her vilely unwell, so Charity and her husband, Edward, came to Carradice Abbey several months ago to await the birth. Prudence has to be with her, you see."

"I see." His chest tightened. She was about to be snatched from him, now, when he'd just found her. "When shall I see—"

She grabbed his hands. "Come with us. Bring the girls. Gideon and Prudence won't mind. They'll love them." She blinked a tear away. "I want you with me, Sebastian. Charity is the first of us to give birth, and I haven't seen her in an age." She bit her lip, gazing up into his face.

She was frightened for her sister, he realized. Women died all the time having babies. He thought of Thea, dying alone.

"If you want me, of course I'll come," he said simply.

Within an hour, a line of carriages was ready to set out. To Sebastian's surprise, Lady Augusta was one of the party. "Wouldn't miss it for the world, dear boy!" she exclaimed. "I'm about to become a great-aunt. Didn't you know these girls' sisters are married to my nephews?"

They made excellent time and stopped in Leicester for the night. The inn was small and snug and clean, and their party filled it completely.

The plump and motherly wife of the landlord whisked all the ladies upstairs, where hot water for washing awaited them. She fed them on chicken soup, fresh rolls, and a hearty meat pie, followed by apple tart and cream. Within an hour of their late arrival, everyone was tucked up in bed.

Sebastian could not sleep without first checking on his sisters. He peeped in at the door. They were snuggled up in a big bed with Grace, fast asleep, like kittens. Lily, the maidservant, slept on a truckle bed in the corner.

He would have liked to check on Hope, too, but she was sharing a room with her twin. The landlady saw him hesitating outside her door. She said firmly, "The ladies will all be sound asleep by now, so you look to your own bed, sir."

Sebastian went. But despite his weariness, sleep did not come easily. Rain started pattering on his windowpane.

"Are you asleep?" It was Hope, dressed only in a flannel nightgown, her cheeks flushed and her golden curls tumbled about her face. Her nightgown was voluminous and buttoned to the chin, yet he'd never seen anything more appealing. She looked so clean and fresh and lovely and yet rumpled and sensual at the same time. Like a deliciously wrapped package.

He sat up, then recalling he was naked, pulled the covers up. "What is the matter?" She shouldn't be here.

"I can't sleep," she said and padded across to the bed. "I want to stay with you."

He hesitated and said weakly, "You shouldn't."

"You're right." She climbed up onto the high bed in her nightgown and bare feet and knelt there, looking woebegone and impossibly beautiful.

"I hate the middle of the night when I can't sleep. I need you to hold me, Sebastian." Her lower lip wobbled. It was so unlike his brave little elf, he could not bear it. He held out his arms, and she fell into them.

He was instantly aroused.

She nestled against his naked chest and rubbed her hand over the faint sprinkling of masculine hair. "This is nice."

Battling with fierce desire, he forced himself to put her gently away from him and pulled the sheet up to cover his nakedness. She'd called him noble, earlier. Nobility did not involve taking her virginity in a small country inn while her great-uncle and the rest of the family slept a few yards away.

She shivered, and he bent and pulled bedclothes up around her, insulating him further from her softness and warmth.

She frowned. "But I want to get into bed with you."

"You can't," he said shortly. "I have no nightshirt."

"Really?" Her eyes widened, and she looked at his naked shoulders with feminine appreciation. She reached out and stroked them, then kneaded them like a cat, very lightly with her nails.

His arousal intensified. As did his determination to treat her as a virtuous innocent should be treated. He would hold her chastely if it killed him. Even if he was harder than he'd ever been in his life. It would not kill him. He hoped.

She slipped out of the cocoon of blankets he'd made for her, and instead of relieving his agony, he felt immediately bereft. She climbed across his legs and sat on his thighs, her nightgown riding up on slender limbs, and his breath disappeared in a whoosh.

"I'm not a child, Sebastian."

He groaned. "I'm well aware of that."

She snuggled her bottom down over his thighs, and he groaned again. She gave a secret little feminine smile. She wiggled again, then leaned forward and began to stroke his shoulders. Across his shoulders and down his chest and arms, stroking and squeezing. His muscles flexed of their own accord.

"To think I used to be nervous of these," she murmured. "Lovely."

She circled his nipples, around and around, grazing them oh so lightly with her nails. "Are you being noble again, Sebastian?" she asked softly.

"I'm trying my damnedest to be," he ground out.

"But we're going to be married, aren't we?"

He tried not to think about what her innocent touch was doing to him. "You know we are."

She leaned back, smiling the smile of Eve. "Then why must we wait? I want you, Sebastian." Her hand moved lower. "Don't you want me?"

"You know damn well I do!" he growled.

"When I was at the opera house that time, you showed me a whole new world, and I don't mean the view of London." She leaned forward and nibbled on a flat, masculine nipple. "Fascinating," she breathed. "Like me, only not like me . . . and I don't mean in yellow ruffles."

The images her words created in his mind brought an agonized groan to his lips.

"That night, at the opera, you showed me what pleasure a man—the right man—could give a woman." She leaned forward and cupped his face in her hands. "And on that day when Dorie talked, on the chaise longue in your drawing room afterward, you gave me a taste of your heat and your strength. And you gave me glorious oblivion. I want that now, and more." She looked a little shy, then said, "I want to be loved, fully loved. Right here, right now, in this big, high bed, with the rain on the windows outside and my sister laboring with child. I want to shut it all out and be alone, here with my lovely, strong, protective Sebastian."

Her words brought a lump to his throat. Before he could say a word, she added, "Do you know, you have the most magnificent shoulders. They make me weak just to look at them." Her eyes glowed softly as she added, "So will you please love me now?" Would he please love her now?

As if she were the one racked with desperate need, not he. A violent shudder passed through him, and he swallowed, leashing his fierce desire to his lady's service. His innocent lady. Tonight would be all for her.

He let the sheets pool around his waist and hungrily watched the fascination flare in her eyes as she examined him with shy, feminine curiosity. He placed his hands on her hips and slid her slowly toward him. The movement pulled her nightgown higher, sliding up her long, slender limbs until it bunched across her hips, just covering the shadowed mystery beneath.

It would be the work of a moment to rip away the covers and sheathe himself in her. His whole body throbbed with the need to complete the act. She was already aroused; Sebastian could smell the heady female scent of her. His woman. His mate. His love.

For a long moment he didn't move. Then he cupped her face and gently guided her mouth to his. She leaned forward, her hands on the shoulders she'd called magnificent, and kissed him softly.

His mouth and tongue teased her lips apart, and he deepened the kiss gradually with insistent rhythmic strokes that had her clutching at him with frantic hands, wanting more.

She clutched and stroked and rubbed at his shoulders. She thrust her fingers through his short-cropped hair, holding him tightly, her eyes closed tight as she threw herself into the kiss.

His tongue tangled with hers, dueled and stroked, and he cupped her breast through the thick flannel, savoring the weight, feeling the nipple rise and harden in response to his touch. She made small, soft sounds of pleasure as her fingers gripped his shoulders and her legs gripped his hips. He gently scratched the nipple's tip through the flannel, and her hips made jerky little movements in response. Each tiny quiver resonated right through his body.

She broke the kiss and jerked back, staring down at his hand as it cupped her breast. As she watched, he stroked the nipple again, back and forth in the same rhythm as his tongue had made, and even as her eyes widened in surprise, she arched her back, pushing her breast into his hand more as her hips convulsed and she made a sound deep in her throat.

She flung her head back and almost purred with pleasure as he used both his hands to pleasure her through the flannel.

Then, abruptly, she caught his big hands in hers and stopped him. She stared at his chest. "Does the same thing work for you?" she said in a husky voice.

He shrugged, feigning ignorance. She purred, "Then let us investigate, shall we?" She placed both soft palms on his chest and stroked him with blatant approval. "So nice and hard."

He instantly cupped her breasts. "So nice and soft."

She laughed and batted his hands away. "Stop it. I want to concentrate, and I cannot when you touch me like that." She rubbed her hands across the planes of his chest in circular movements, narrowing in slowly on the nipples. He watched her, loving the earnest look of concentration on her lovely face. Finally she brushed her fingers across them and pinched them gently, and he arched as a fiery bolt ran from her questing fingers straight to his groin.

"Aha." She touched his small nipple and squeezed it experimentally. He arched again. She frowned thoughtfully, then looked from his naked chest to her own expanse of flannel. Was she remembering the last time, when he'd freed her breasts and taken her nipple in his mouth?

"On the opera roof you said you had envied my dress with the yellow ruffles, that you wished your hands could replace the ruffles. And on the chaise longue, you, um, suckled me through the silk shirt. Am I supposed to remove this thing?" She blushed the moment the words were out of her mouth. "I mean, I don't—"

He stopped her words with a kiss. "No," he said. "You are not supposed to take that thing off."

The blush faded. "Oh." It was a mix of relief and disappointment.

He said softly, "I am."

"Ohh." The blush returned. She sat there and waited.

Twenty small polished mother-of-pearl buttons, from just beneath her chin to a point almost at her waist.

One button, two. The slender column of her throat was revealed. He kissed it, tasting the delicate scent of her skin.

The third and fourth and fifth buttons showed the hollow between her collarbones. He leaned forward and dipped his tongue into it.

By the seventh and eighth buttons his mouth was dry and his breath was coming faster. He looked at her. She gazed back and licked her lips slowly. His heart thundered.

By the tenth button, the creamy valley between her breasts was visible, and he bent forward and pressed his face between them, tasting, licking her silken, warm skin. She clutched at his head, running her fingers through his hair and kissing him.

By the fifteenth button, both breasts were free, rosy nipples thrusting for his attention, and his hands were shaking. He fumbled the last three buttons and gave up at that point. His breath came in ragged bursts, and she was panting, too, as if they'd both run in a race.

He reached for the hem where it bunched at her hips and slowly, slowly began to lift.

"Ohh." She moaned at the slight friction against her aroused skin.

He lifted it over her hips. This was his woman. Over her waist. It caught on her breasts, lifting them. He tugged, and like a child, she lifted her arms for him to pull the nightgown off her completely. Only she was no child. She was wholly, supremely woman.

He cast the garment aside and drank in the sight of her nakedness. He had seen a copy once of a famous Italian painting, a golden-haired beauty standing in a huge scallop shell. Venus, the girl in the painting was called: a shy, pensive creature, Madonna-like in her purity.

But the Italian beauty was not more beautiful or more sensual than his own dear Venus sitting shyly, proudly astride him, one hand delicately covering the vee of gold curls, the other hovering uncertainly.

She glowed with life, with warmth, with love. For him. For plain Sebastian Reyne. He could hardly believe it. This glorious, loving creature was going to be his wife, his love for all time. He would never be alone again.

He caught her hand, kissed it, and laid it against his heart. "My own precious Venus."

"Venus was a pagan goddess, was she not?"

"Yes. The goddess of love," he affirmed. Would she be insulted by the comparison?

She gave him a brilliant smile. "I'm not sure I know how to be a pagan love goddess, but I would dearly love to learn," she said. "Show me how."

And before he could respond, she lifted herself off him and tugged at the sheet covering him. "Ohh," she said on a long note of discovery. She touched him lightly. "This is what I could feel pushing against me before, isn't it? It's so warm and—"

"Mmmph!" he managed to say though gritted teeth. He caught her questing hand in his. "Not. Yet."

"Oh."

"If you do much more of that, it will all be over."

She frowned. "But—"

"I want us to take our time so that your first time will be very special."

"It will be special. It is already special." She regarded him thoughtfully and started stroking him. "I think you're trying to be noble again."

Sebastian blinked. He'd just stripped her naked. Where was the nobility in that?

She scratched him lightly on the chest, circling his nipples, and he shuddered and arched helplessly under her. "And I'll have you know, Sebastian Reyne, that if I'm to be your pagan love goddess, I don't want you to play the noble martyr." She bent down and sucked his nipple, then bit it gently.

His body bucked under her.

She sat back, a look of deep, feminine satisfaction on her face. "It's very sweet of you, and I love you for it, but truly, you don't need to hold back, being careful. I have waited quite long enough. I told you, I want you to take me." She scratched delicately along the length of his rigid member and said softly, "I want to feel possessed, in a . . . a ravishing burst of passion."

"A ravishing burst of passion, I see," he repeated, using every ounce of self-control he had.

She squeezed him gently. "I want the hungry, passionate man who nearly seduced me on the roof of the opera house. The man whose hands were shaking with desire as he caressed me on the chaise longue. You denied yourself both times. This time I don't want you to hold back. I don't want you to stop. I want you to feel that glory, too, with me."

His eyes blazed with some powerful emotion. Exultation perhaps. Triumph. Passion.

"Very well, my goddess. Your wish is my command."

He gave a great heave and flipped her over on her back. He plunged his tongue into her mouth and ravished it with fierce need, and Hope felt what she had felt the first time he looked at her and had craved ever since.

His soul-scorching hunger. For her. For Hope Merridew. It warmed and completed her as nothing else could. It transformed a clumsy girl to . . . to a magnificent, beloved man's love goddess.

She kissed him back as hard as she could, losing herself in his scorching, spiraling passion, following his lead blindly, joyously. His hands were everywhere, stroking, squeezing, caressing, arousing. She ran her hands over him, reveling in his heat, his strength, and his desire.

He kissed her down her jaw, down her neck, kissed the hollow at its base, and then moved to her breasts. The slightly roughened male skin rubbing against hers created a delicious friction, and then he took one nipple in his mouth and sucked, and she almost screamed. Not pleasure, not pain; something powerfully, addictively *other.*

He sucked and caressed in hot, rhythmic waves, and she shuddered and rode the waves in glorious abandon, wholly in his power. His hand slid between her legs and stroked her there.

She was dimly aware of herself thrashing and bucking, of his mouth burning, sucking, and his hands stroking, and her body was on fire and suddenly . . . conflagration.

He paused a moment, and she hung, suspended, out of time, out of place, and then he covered her body wholly with his and entered her with one long thrust.

She gasped and clutched him in sudden panic.

He said raggedly, "It's all right, love. The worst is over."

*The worst?* It wasn't bad, what she felt. It was just . . . different. Stretched as if to bursting point. Impaled, but not in pain. Invaded, but not by an enemy. And connected, gloriously, intimately connected.

*Over?* "I don't want it to be over." She wrapped her arms and legs around him, blindly savoring the connection, refusing to let him leave her.

He began to stroke her again, and she felt her body shudder and clench around him. He stroked again, and her hips thrust upward. And then he began to move inside her, in powerful, rhythmic thrusts, driving her with him, upward, elsewhere, over the edge.

Until she shattered again in his arms, into sublime oblivion.


"Are you all right, love?"

Hope blinked and stretched. She noticed with a sense of amazement that rain was still pattering against the leaded windowpanes, that water continued to gurgle down the gutters.

How could everything be the same when she felt so different?

"My love?" His voice was deep. Anxious.

She turned in his arms and stared at him. Her man. Her

beloved. He looked troubled. Gently he stroked her cheek with his thumbs. She was amazed to see they came away wet. Had she wept, then? She didn't remember.

"How do you feel?" The question seemed momentous.

Hope thought about her answer, trying to think of the perfect way to tell him how she felt. It was so special, she wanted to get it right, make him see.

"When I was a little girl," she began slowly, "I watched a snake split its skin. I feel like that snake now."

"Oh God!" he exclaimed.

He bent to kiss her, but she held him back with her hand, cupping and stroking his jaw in loving reassurance. "No, wait, let me finish. I want to explain."

He swallowed, looking unhappy.

"The snake was a dull mottled gray, and when it split its skin slowly, it looked painful, but I don't think it was. It rubbed and rubbed against some rocks and then, suddenly, the skin started to split."

He groaned, and she pressed her fingers over his mouth, saying, "Wait! The snake pushed itself between two rocks and wriggled and suddenly it just glided out, leaving its old dull gray skin behind. And, oh, Sebastian, the new snake was so fresh and beautiful, the colors on its skin were so bright and brilliant." She looked at him and felt her vision blur with tears. "I feel like that snake, all new and different and beautiful. And you made me feel this way."

Her words moved him, so that he was obliged to bury his face in her hair, lest he shed unmanly tears. Finally he was able to say, "But you are beautiful. An acknowledged belle of the ton."

"Oh that!" She shook her head. "No matter what other people think of my looks, I have never *felt* beautiful. I have a twin who looks just like me. My sister Charity is much more beautiful than either of us, and Grace, I think, shall outshine us all one day. Prudence, the eldest of us, is the most wonderful person in the world, and yet the ton thought her plain." She smiled. "But Prudence's husband,

Gideon, thinks her utterly beautiful and is honestly bewildered when others do not see it."

She gave him a luminous look and stroked his cheek. "You do that to me. I have always felt like the clumsy, inadequate sister, the one who can never do things properly, never get things right. I am the hoyden, the one who breaks the rules, who acts before she thinks and gets everyone into trouble. I am frightened of the dark, of being shut in. I am argumentative, impatient—"

He hushed her with a kiss. "You are beautiful, inside and out. If people call you a hoyden it is an endearment, not a criticism." He kissed her again. "You are generous and loving, and you bring joy wherever you go. You heal old hurts and open others to the joy in life you feel." He took her face in his hands and said quietly, "And tonight you have made me the proudest and happiest man in the world."

Her face crumpled, and she hugged him convulsively and mumbled into his neck, "I love you, Sebastian Reyne."

"And I love you, my beloved silken elf."

"Silken elf?" she queried.

"When I first saw you dancing, I thought you were a silken elf," he explained. "You are so light and dainty on your feet."

She gave a delicate yawn and snuggled her head on his chest. "I like it," she murmured sleepily. "I can be a silken elf or a pagan love goddess."

"Or a bold hoyden," he added. "I love every gorgeous aspect of you." He punctuated each word with a kiss.

She drifted off to sleep in his arms, smiling. The wind howled in the eaves, rain pelted the windowpanes, and Sebastian lay in the high bed of the small inn, feeling happier and more at home than he'd ever felt in his life.

At dawn, she awoke and they made love again before she tiptoed down the passage and returned to her bed.

Late the following afternoon, the line of carriages turned in at a pair of stone-mounted iron gates. Carradice Abbey stood in a parkland of rolling hills. An imposing three-story building, it was somewhat in the classical style, though with the odd baroque feature, and a terrace all around the rooftop.

Sebastian made a note of that rooftop terrace. It might be a nice private place to take Hope. For the view, of course.

A flight of perhaps twenty broad stone steps rose to an imposing entrance flanked by four Grecian columns. As the coaches drew up, a tall, dark-haired gentleman came running lightly down the steps.

*"Gideeeonnnn!"* came a shriek from the second carriage, and before the carriage had even stopped, young Grace flung open the door and leaped out. She ran pell-mell across the raked gravel driveway and flung herself at him.

He received her flying body on his chest and staggered back, laughing, as she planted kisses on his cheeks. "Greetings, young Limb, I've missed you, too."

Hope squeezed Sebastian's arm and explained. "That's my brother-in-law, Lord Carradice—Prudence's husband. Grace adores him. You would never believe Grace was once a timid, gloomy child, would you?"

Grace hugged Lord Carradice, hanging off his neck, and he hugged her back, saying, "Gently, Limb. Delighted as I am to see you, I have aged since I last saw you last."

"Oh, pooh!" said Grace.

"Such an elegant expression, Limb—or should I call you Aunt Limb now?"

Grace stopped dead. "Aunt Limb? You mean—?"

Hope and Faith flew up the steps and grabbed Gideon's arm. "Is it true? The baby is born? And Charity? How is she? What is the baby? Boy or girl? Is it healthy? When was it born? How is Charity?"

Lord Carradice put Grace down, kissed Faith and Hope on both cheeks, and said, "All is well, my dears, I shall answer all your questions, only be calm. Everything is splendid. In any case, here comes Aunt Gussie, who will hurl twice as many questions at me twice as fast. Aunt Gussie!"

To Sebastian's amazement, Lord Carradice picked up Lady Augusta in a bear hug and twirled her around in a circle as if she were as light as a feather. She shrieked quite as loudly as Grace and slapped and kissed her nephew happily. "Gideon, you dreadful boy, stop that at once! You say Charity is well and the babe delivered safely? What did—"

"Stop!" He held up his hand dramatically. Into the brief, surprised silence he said rapidly, "Charity is perfectly well, though tired. The baby is a girl, born two days ago. She is small, red-faced, and between you and me, a little ugly, but neither Edward nor Charity, nor even my Prudence, can see it, so please do not mention it as they all get unreasonably testy when the subject is raised. Edward is quite besotted, so do not expect any sensible conversation from him at all. The baby is strong and healthy and yells the house down at regular intervals. They've called her Aurora—perfectly accurate, too—she is a roarer. Ouch!" He turned and stared in mock indignation at the small, very round lady who had descended the steps unnoticed and biffed him lightly across the head. He added severely, "And what did I say about you going anywhere near any stairs alone?"

She ignored him and came toward the Merridew girls with tears shining in her eyes. The oldest sister, Prudence. All four sisters and Lady Augusta hugged, kissed, and shed a few more tears.

Gideon watched with a proud smile on his face. As he pulled out a handkerchief, he noticed Sebastian. He gave him a measured look, then held out his hand. "How do you do? I am Carradice, by the way."

Sebastian introduced himself and shook hands. He nodded at Hope, "She's been very anxious."

"Yes, they are all very close. My wife misses them, too. Ah, here is Edward, the proud papa!"

A man of medium height came down the steps, his round face wreathed with smiles. Lady Augusta surged forward, exclaiming, "Edward, my dear boy, congratulations!"

"Thank you, Aunt Gussie! You look wonderful. Gideon's

told you the news, I gather. Isn't it splendid? Charity is asleep now, but she will be so happy to see you all."

Edward greeted each person carefully, then turned to where Sebastian and his sisters stood. He held out his hand to Sebastian, but his smile embraced the girls as well. "How do you do? I don't think we've met, have we?"

"Oh heavens! My manners," Hope exclaimed. She rapidly performed all the introductions.

"Come inside, everyone," Prudence said. "Tea will be ready in twenty minutes."

She started toward the steps, when her husband said, "No stairs, remember?" and swept her into his arms. Ignoring her halfhearted protests, he carried her up the steps, then set her on her feet as if she were made of spun glass. Everyone else trooped into the house after them, talking and laughing and hugging.

Dorie and Cassie hung back a little, watching shyly. "They're a real family, aren't they?" Cassie said in wonder.

"So are we," said Sebastian firmly and crooked his elbows. Arm in arm the small Reyne family marched up the steps into Carradice Abbey.


"Hope, love, you look positively radiant." Prudence and Faith sat on the bed in Hope's bedchamber, watching her unpack. Hope had just picked up her flannel nightgown. She hugged it to her chest. "Oh, Prue, I'm so happy. Do you like him?"

Prue nodded. "He's very quiet, but he watches you the same way Edward watches Charity."

"And the way Gideon watches you, Prue. It's lovely." Faith said.

"You must tell Mama and Papa the news," said Prue. "Gideon brought The Cairn here. We'll visit it tomorrow."

"The Cairn? Mama and Papa's cairn?" It was a pile of loose stones the sisters had built when they were children, newly orphaned and missing their mother and father terribly. Mama and Papa were buried in the warm, sun-kissed earth of Italy. The Cairn was built with the cold stones of Grandpapa's Northumberland property. They'd told it all their secrets, and for years it was their sole place of comfort.

Prue nodded, her eyes shining. "Yes, knowing none of us would ever want to return to Dereham, my darling husband had every stone brought here. He even found one of Grace's baby teeth in it and brought that, too." She stood up. "Now, come along, let us go downstairs. Tea must be ready by now, and I am ravenous."

They were just finishing tea when a maidservant knocked on the door. "Your Grace, you asked me to tell you when Her Grace woke."

"Ah." Edward beamed. "Charity is awake. Come on, everyone, up you come. You will want to see her and our beautiful Aurora."

Lady Gussie, Hope, Faith, and Grace hurried upstairs at once. Edward looked at Cassie and Dorie. "Would you like to come and see the baby, too? I understand your brother is going to marry Hope, which will make you the baby's aunts-by-marriage."

Cassie and Dorie looked wide-eyed at Sebastian for confirmation. He nodded, realizing he should have told them of his marriage plans earlier. It had all been such a rush. He started to explain, but they cut him off.

"Oh, we knew you were going to marry Miss Hope," Cassie said, "but we didn't realize that we would get other new relatives. If Hope is our sister-in-law, then would Grace be like a sister?"

"And you mean we are to be aunts? Of a real baby?" gasped Dorie in wonder.

He nodded, a little amused by their priorities.

Edward held out his hands to them. "Then come and see your new baby niece." With no hesitation, each girl took his hand and excitedly began to climb the stairs.

Another step, Sebastian thought gratefully. His sisters were learning to trust.

Edward paused halfway up and looked back. "You, too, Reyne. We need the whole family with us."

Sebastian nodded and followed in silence. He couldn't talk. There was a lump in his throat. It hadn't occurred to him that he'd get new relatives either. He was part of *the whole family*.

Charity sat up in bed, a golden, glowing woman. In her arms she held a small bundle. First Hope held Baby Aurora, looking, to Sebastian's eyes, like the most beautiful of Madonnas. Then Faith took her. Grace cuddled her next, making happy little cooing noises. Lady Augusta took Aurora in her arms with great care. Great Uncle Oswald patted her on the shoulder, peering into the bundle, grinning, and making fatuous avuncular noises. Lady Augusta handed the baby to Gideon five minutes later, saying gruffly that the dratted child had made her eyelash-black run. The whole room watched as Gideon turned instantly to mush, making goo-goo noises and claiming she'd smiled at him. The baby made no objection to any of it.

"Would you like to hold her?"

The duchess had spoken to Dorie. Cassie had hung back, but Dorie had been pressed silently, inconspicuously up against the corner of the bed, watching the bundle avidly.

Dorie blinked and nodded.

The duchess patted the bed beside her. "Come up here with me—Dorie, isn't it?"

Dorie nodded again and scrambled up on the bed.

Charity smiled. "Grace has written lots of letters to us about you and Cassie. Welcome to the family." She placed the baby in Dorie's arms. "Aurora, this is your Aunt Dorie."

Dorie looked at the baby, then looked at Sebastian. "*Aunt Dorie*," she whispered, then bent and kissed the baby carefully.

Sebastian took one look at Dorie's face and walked to the window. He stared blindly out. His throat was working. He felt Hope slide into his arms and held her gratefully.

• • •

The next morning, Prudence invited Sebastian, Hope, and the girls to accompany her to the gamekeeper's cottage. "Anslow and his wife are expecting us. I expect Mrs. Anslow will have made her famous plum cake."

"But why?" Hope asked.

Prudence grinned. "It's a surprise." She winked at Sebastian.

He nodded. Gideon had told him about the surprise already.

The gamekeeper's cottage stood on the edge of a leafy coppice, looking out over rolling hills. The front garden was filled with flowers.

Mrs. Anslow answered the door and ushered them proudly into her front room. "I'll fetch Anslow and tea," she said.

A tall, grizzled man in leathers joined them a minute later. He was followed by Mrs. Anslow, carrying a tea tray, and behind her came . . .

*"May!"* Hope exclaimed, blinking in surprise. "It is you, isn't it?"

The small skinny urchin gave her a huge gap-toothed grin and said excitedly. "Yes, miss, it's me. I live here now, wiv the Anslows!"

Mrs. Anslow put an arm around her and gave her a hug. "And a dear, sweet child she is." Little May's face shone with happiness. She ran over to the tea table and started to set out cups.

"We never did have any of our own, Anslow and me, so when m'lady asked me, well, I thought it wouldn't do no harm. Anslow wasn't so sure about taking in an orphan child from London . . ."

The tall man said gruffly. "Aye, but it's all worked out. She's a grand little lass, our May. Now, would anyone here be interested in seeing my pups?"

"Pups?" Dorie squeaked. She looked at Sebastian who grinned.

Anslow jerked his head, "In the shed, out back. Come on, May, let's show the girls." He led the way, May skipping along beside him, holding his hand with such pride of ownership it brought tears to Hope's eyes. Dorie and Cassie, not to be outdone, grabbed Sebastian's hands and followed.

Mrs Anslow said, "That's surprised you, didn't it, miss? M'lady fixed it up. She knew I was lonely, with no chick nor child to call my own."

Hope stared at Prudence. "You arranged it? But how?"

Prudence grinned happily. "You wrote to me, remember, and told me about that poor little child, praying for a doll to love . . . and I thought of the Anslows, praying for a child. Then Aunt Gussie wrote that she was now on the board of the Institution. So I told her about the Anslows and she sent us May."

"Aye," agreed Mrs Anslow. "And we couldn't be happier."

Everyone was gathered downstairs, more or less in the crimson saloon. It was a warm evening, and the French windows were open. A soft, scented breeze stirred the curtains.

Cassie and Grace were on the terrace playing with their new pups. Yaps and youthful laughter floated in through the windows in gusts.

Charity had come downstairs with Baby Aurora. She and Edward sat quietly on the sofa, smiling and murmuring. Edward held the sleeping baby in his arms, the very picture of a proud, doting papa.

Dorie sat in an armchair nearby, looking equally doting. She had a small bundle cradled in her arms. Big brown eyes stared up at Dorie's face, a fat little honey-colored snout poked out of the bundle, then lunged suddenly and licked her nose. Dorie giggled and cuddled her puppy, Honey, tighter.

Sebastian's chest grew tight with emotion. It was going to be all right. More than all right. It was going to be . . . bloody wonderful.

Prudence and Gideon strolled on the terrace, arm in

arm, talking quietly. Lady Augusta and Sir Oswald were playing cards with the twins.

Sebastian looked around the room. He had more than he ever dreamed would be possible, and the thought suddenly frightened him. What if his life slipped out of his control? It had before. Things could go wrong. People could disappear. Families could be dissolved on a whim of fate. Plans could come to naught . . . if they were not carried out immediately.

He marched over to Hope and put his hands on her shoulders. "Let's get married soon."

Sir Oswald looked up from his cards. "It cannot be for several months at least. One cannot rush an affair at a fashionable London church like St. George's."

"And Hope must buy her bride clothes," added Lady Augusta.

Hope leaned back against Sebastian, kissed the hand that gripped her shoulder, and gave him a reassuring smile. "When are you christening Aurora?" she asked Charity.

Edward answered, "In three weeks. I arranged it this morning."

Hope said to Sebastian, "Then let us be married the following day. Friends and family members who come for the christening can stay on for the wedding, and we won't have to worry about booking any silly old fashionable churches, for Gideon has a charming little church right here on the estate—St. Giles's. And besides," she added softly, with a glance at Prudence, "Mama and Papa's Cairn is right next to the church. It's like they will be with us."

Sebastian bent and kissed her. She'd told him about The Cairn. "Perfect."

Great Uncle Oswald watched the sudden hum of activity as wedding plans were instantly hatched and exclaimed in disgust, "Will no member of this dratted family *ever* get married in St. George's, Hanover Square?"

Into the silence that followed, Lady Augusta drawled, "Well, Oswald . . . I'll do it, if you want."

Another silence fell, more intense. Expectant.

"You mean—Gussie! After all these years, you're acceptin' me at last? You really will marry me?"

She nodded, looking suddenly girlish. "Yes, Oswald, I'll marry you."

He leaped up, grabbed her hands, kissed them both, then kissed her on the mouth. He said to the room in general, in a dazed tone, "I must have asked her a hundred times!" He swung back and demanded, "In St. George's, Hanover Square?"

She raised an incredulous brow, as if the question were entirely redundant. "Naturally! I wouldn't dream of having it anywhere else. If I'm going to be married for the third time, I want a huge, splashy wedding with all the works! I am *not* the retiring type."

Great Uncle Oswald said fervently, "No, you're not. Thank God!"

# Epilogue

∞

*If music be the food of love, play on.*
WILLIAM SHAKESPEARE

FROM CARRADICE ABBEY, ST. GILES'S CHURCH WAS A SHORT BUT charming walk along a narrow, winding pathway flanked by tall trees. A sixteenth-century church, the floor was of large stone flags worn smooth by many generations. It was built of local stone, partially lined inside with oak paneling, and plastered around the chancel. Over the years it had been endowed with several lovely stained glass windows, which on this glorious June day filled the church with a mass of color. Set into the walls were engraved plaques and memorials, and there were several brasses depicting medieval knights and ladies.

Inside, the church was filled with flowers: pink and white clematis, wild purple orchids, lilies, tall canes of creamy, fragrant philadelphus, spikes of lavender, and masses of roses. Roses in every shade and size. Tightly furled buds and lush, fully opened blooms. Their scent filled the church.

The same flowers covered a small stone cairn outside the church. The Merridew girls had laid them there the day before, taking the newest member of the family with them: the newly christened Aurora, carried by her godmother, Dorie.

The oak pews were packed with people, quietly talking. The organ played softly. Late arrivals were still quietly trailing in.

In the front pew sat Prudence and Gideon, Edward and Charity. Giles's mother sat on the other side. Behind her sat Lady Gosforth and a group of her friends. The rest was a host of people Sebastian didn't know.

Prudence nudged her husband. Sebastian and Giles had spent the last ten minutes pacing, their eyes darting every few seconds to the door. It was hard to tell which man was more nervous—Giles or Sebastian. Now they'd stopped pacing and, in low voices, were apparently arguing. "I wonder what they're saying?" she whispered.

"But she has no bosoms!" Sebastian said. "You can't marry a woman with no bosoms!"

"What? Oh," Giles groaned, remembering the old conversation. "Lady Elinore has bosoms, all right . . . tiny, exquisite bosoms . . . to which I am utterly, completely addicted. I am beside myself with lust, Bastion. Me!"

Sebastian's lips twitched at his tone of despair.

Giles continued, "Do you know, I even long—nay, I *yearn* for her to return to wearing her seventeen acres of gray cloth!"

"What difference would that make?"

Giles sighed again. "None. I lusted after her long before she took to going about half-naked and in colors! But at least when she was smothered in gray draperies, she was my own special secret. Now . . ."

"You're jealous of other men looking at her?" Sebastian was incredulous. "You?"

"Pathetic, isn't it? I have no willpower, no control, not even any dignity when it comes to that woman. I am besotted—a soppy, sentimental heap! How did I come to this sorry state?

Sebastian smiled. "I believe it's called falling in love."

"I thought love was a game." Giles said heavily.

"And I thought it a lie told to children, but we were both wrong, weren't we?"

"Yes." Giles pulled out a fob watch and glared at it. "I think my watch has stopped."

"No, it hasn't."

"Are they late?"

"No, or only a minute. We got here early, remember." They stared at the oak doors of the church, but there was no movement, no sign of a bride. After a moment Sebastian said, "So Lady Elinore has permanently abandoned her gray draperies?"

"Mmm. She has discovered they don't work, you see." There was a trace of smugness in his tone.

"I see . . . Are you sure about this decision? She is older than you by ten years at least." Sebastian was determined Giles would eat every last word.

"Only six." Giles gave him a satyr's grin. "But what I lack in years, I make up for in experience."

"I heard she was as plain as a pikestaff."

Giles made a disgusted gesture. "Did I truly say that? I was a blind fool! Her looks are not in the common way, but once she stopped doing her hair in that hideous scrape . . ." He sank his head into his hands. "She's the sweetest little beauty, Bastian."

Sebastian was enjoying himself enormously. "But you danced with her once. She found you repugnant! *You!*"

Giles glanced complacently down at his well-formed person. "She has changed her mind," he purred.

Sebastian shook his head in mock sorrow. "And I thought her a woman of discrimination."

"She is. She didn't want you. She wanted me. Shows immensely superior taste, if you ask me."

"Pooh!" Sebastian waved his hand dismissively. "As I

recall, her only passion is for good works. Orphans and charitable causes. Are you a charitable cause then?"

"Far from it!" Giles wagged a finger in reprimand and said smugly, "You have forgotten her fascination for matters scientific."

Sebastian was surprised by this unexpected turn. "I know of it. But what have *you* to do with matters scientific?"

Giles explained in a dulcet tone, "Lady Elinore is planning to spend the next twenty years or so investigating some of her mother's theories in greater depth. And I am to be her sole assistant."

Sebastian could think of at least a dozen of Lady Ennismore's crackpot theories, none of which was worth more than a cursory glance, let alone twenty years of solid investigation. "You must be joking. What theories?"

Giles looked like the cat that had swallowed the canary and followed it off with a jug of cream. "Those concerning the excitement of uncontrollable masculine passions."

Sebastian choked.

"I am to be her sole subject," Giles explained modestly. "It will be an exhausting task, I know, but there is a strong streak of nobility in all the Bemertons, and we *always* rise to the occasion. Besides, you know I've always been devoted to . . . science."

The oak doors opened, and both men's minds were immediately wiped blank. The organ music swelled, and Sebastian and Giles swallowed, threw out their chests, and took their places by the altar.

Four bridesmaids, achingly lovely in their fresh, bright youthfulness, stepped solemnly down the aisle. First Dorie and Cassie, then Grace, then Faith.

Hope entered, a vision in creamy silk and lace, on her great-uncle's arm, and Sebastian's eyes blurred, and he could see no one else, only the woman he adored floating toward him. His beautiful, loving Hope. His Hope, eternally.

Lady Augusta followed, and on her arm was a small, slender woman, Lady Elinore Whitelaw, also dressed in lace. And Giles's eyes blurred, and he could see no one else, only the woman he loved coming to him. At last.

The organ music came to a final crescendo, the magnificently robed minister stepped forward, and the weddings commenced.

The wedding of Sebastian Reyne and Hope Merridew.

And of Giles Bemerton and Lady Elinore Whitelaw.


And afterward there was laughter and tears and much kissing and embracing.

And in the evening there was feasting and music and dancing.

Hope and Sebastian stood kissing on the terrace. The night was warm, the moon was full, and they planned to slip away to make love for the first time as man and wife. As they tiptoed away, the band inside struck up a waltz.

"Dance with me, my husband." Hope held up her arms. "It's the last waltz, and you know I never dance it with anyone but you."

Sebastian made no reply. He'd said very little all day. He doubted that he could. His heart was too full for mere words.

She'd brought him out of the shadows of his past, into her unique, special light. The light of love.

He wrapped himself around his Hope, kissing her deeply. As they kissed, their bodies moved slowly to the music. They danced slowly, sensually, pressed together so closely there was no space at all between their bodies, breast to chest, thigh to thigh. Two people dancing as one, a living part of the music, in the warm night air, bathed in moonlight.

And it was perfect.

Award-winning author **Anne Gracie** spent her childhood and youth on the move. The gypsy life taught her that humor and love are universal languages and that favorite books can take you home, wherever you are. In addition to writing, Anne teaches adult literacy, flings balls for her dog, enjoys her tangled garden, and keeps bees.

Visit her website at www.annegracie.com.

# *The Perfect Rake*

by
## Anne Gracie

To escape her brutal grandfather,
Prudence stages a plan involving a phony
engagement—and the man she approaches is
so taken with Pru that he willingly
joins in her game.

0-425-20395-6

**"For fabulous Regency flavor, witty and
addictive, you can't go past Anne Gracie."
—Stephanie Laurens**

Available wherever books are sold or at
penguin.com

# *BERKLEY SENSATION*
## COMING IN DECEMBER 2005

### *Dead Reckoning*
### by Linda Castillo
Linda Castillo is "at the top of her game" (*All About Romance*) with this romantic thriller about a D.A. with a dark secret and a shadowy past.

0-425-20720-X

### *Undead and Unappreciated*
### by MaryJanice Davidson
In this *New York Times* bestseller, vampire Queen Betsy Taylor comes face to face with her destined nemesis—who is also her long-lost sister.

0-425-20722-6

### *Taste of Temptation*
### by Amelia Grey
Chaos ensues when a notorious rake and a darling of the ton are sent unwillingly to the altar.

0-425-20721-8

### *The Lady Killer*
### by Samantha Saxon
The smash follow-up to *The Lady Lies* set in the tumultuous era of the Napoleonic Wars.

0-425-20732-3

### *Strange Attractions*
### by Emma Holly
A hot novel of one woman's sensual education in the hands of a reclusive professor.

0-425-20503-7

Available wherever books are sold or at penguin.com

Cupid can be such a little troublemaker...

# A Little Mischief

### by

## Amelia Grey

An earl is at his wit's end when his sister joins Miss Winslowe's Wallflower Society—and winds up accused of killing London's most eligible bachelor.

0-425-19277-6

Also available:

## A Dash of Scandal
0-515-13401-5

Available wherever books are sold or at penguin.com